REACH FOR INFINITY

Edited by

Jonathan Strahan

Also Edited by **Jonathan Strahan**

Best Short Novels
(2004 through 2007)

Fantasy:
The Very Best of 2005

Science Fiction:
The Very Best of 2005

The Best Science Fiction and
Fantasy of the Year:
Volumes 1 - 8

Eclipse: New Science Fiction
and Fantasy (Volumes 1-4)

The Starry Rift:
Tales of New Tomorrows

Life on Mars:
Tales of New Frontiers

Under My Hat:
Tales from the Cauldron

Godlike Machines

Engineering Infinity

Edge of Infinity

Fearsome Journeys

With Lou Anders
Swords and Dark Magic: The
New Sword and Sorcery

With Charles N. Brown
The Locus Awards: Thirty
Years of the Best in Fantasy
and Science Fiction

With Jeremy G. Byrne
The Year's Best Australian
Science Fiction and Fantasy:
Volume 1

The Year's Best Australian
Science Fiction and Fantasy:
Volume 2

Eidolon 1

With Jack Dann
Legends of Australian
Fantasy

With Gardner Dozois
The New Space Opera
The New Space Opera 2

With Karen Haber
Science Fiction: Best of 2003
Science Fiction: Best of 2004
Fantasy: Best of 2004

With Marianne S. Jablon
Wings of Fire

REACH FOR INFINITY

EDITED BY **JONATHAN STRAHAN**

Including stories by
PAT CADIGAN
ALIETTE DE BODARD
GREG EGAN
KATHLEEN ANN GOONAN
ELLEN KLAGES
KAREN LORD
KEN MACLEOD
IAN MCDONALD
LINDA NAGATA
HANNU RAJANIEMI
ALASTAIR REYNOLDS
ADAM ROBERTS
KARL SCHROEDER
PETER WATTS

SOLARIS

First published 2014 by Solaris
an imprint of Rebellion Publishing Ltd,
Riverside House, Osney Mead,
Oxford, OX2 0ES, UK

www.solarisbooks.com

ISBN: 978 1 78108 202 7

Printed in Denmark

For my dear friend Ellen Klages.

ACKNOWLEDGEMENTS

THIS PAST YEAR has been a challenging one, but I have loved working on this book and would like to thank my Solaris editor Jonathan Oliver, Ben Smith, and the whole team at Rebellion for all of their kindness, help, and consideration over the past year. Also for the absolutely kick-arse cover by Adam Tredowski, which totally nails the book. I would also like to thank all of the book's contributors for letting me publish their wonderful stories. As always, I'd like to thank my agent, the ever wonderful Howard Morhaim and his new assistant Kim-Mei Kirtland.

And, finally, an extra special thanks to my wife Marianne and to my two daughters, Jessica and Sophie, for their love and support.

CONTENTS

Introduction,   11
Jonathan Strahan

Break My Fall,   15
Greg Egan

The Dust Queen,   41
Aliette de Bodard

The Fifth Dragon,   65
Ian McDonald

Kheldyu,   89
Karl Schroeder

Report Concerning the Presence of Seahorses   127
on Mars,
Pat Cadigan

Hiraeth: A Tragedy in Four Acts,   155
Karen Lord

Amicae Aeternum,   169
Ellen Klages

Trademark Bugs: A Legal History,   179
Adam Roberts

Attitude,   201
Linda Nagata

Invisible Planets,   227
Hannu Rajaniemi

Wilder Still, the Stars,   239
Kathleen Ann Goonan

'The Entire Immense Superstructure':   281
An Installation,
Ken MacLeod

In Babelsberg,   297
Alastair Reynolds

Hotshot,   315
Peter Watts

INTRODUCTION

SOMETIMES YOU ONLY discover what you were attempting in retrospect, when you realize that something which could have been tight, focused and coherent is actually much better served by being open, loose and diverse. So it is with this thing that I have come to think of as the 'Infinity Project'.

The Infinity Project started six years ago with the simple idea of assembling a collection of new hard science fiction stories. Hard SF has always sat at the heart of the science fiction field, and putting together a collection of stories that summarized something of what net's up, play by the rules, hard SF – the sort of SF that emphasizes scientific detail or technical detail, and where the story itself turns on a point of scientific speculation – looked like in the early 21st century seemed like a fine idea.

The stories that went into that book, *Engineering Infinity*, were a diverse bunch ranging from pathological stories of runaway cyborg zombies to a foray into the minds of attack military artificial intelligences discovering their own ethics. That diversity, that lack of an attempt to force an editorial perspective on hard SF was the book's strength, and highlighted to me that there was more to do.

Not long after publication of *Engineering Infinity* I began work on a new book, one that seemed to be a response to the far future hard SF of that book, one that retained that focus on the underlying principles of hard SF but opened itself up to more of the romance of science fiction too. At the time it seemed to me, as I wrote in the introduction to the book that became *Edge of Infinity*, that we had lost faith in the possibility that humanity might go to the stars, and that there might be a place for a book that gathered together stories of an achievable future, one where we had taken our first steps off our home world and into space, but hadn't yet left our solar system.

The stories in *Edge of Infinity* held to that vision telling of everything from mannered societies existing deep in a far future Mercury and people who modified their bodies to better live in interplanetary space, to how people carved out lives on and in between the planets of our solar home, everywhere from within the corona of the sun to the distant, coldest reaches of the edge of interplanetary space.

Edge of Infinity was well received by readers and as time passed my mind began to return to it, and to its predecessor. Did they tell the whole tale? Were there more stories to tell? I began to think of a book that would tell a different kind of story, the story of how humanity might actually climb out of its own gravity well, if it could, and begin to make its way out onto the broader stage that could be seen in *Edge of Infinity*.

From the very earliest stages, though, that vision began to change and evolve, to shift in my hands and become something else. Where I had seen originally a book of stories that would happen in a clearly defined time, although not within a singular or thematic setting, it soon became clear that what I was essaying instead was a look into a state of mind, into a point in the evolution of a thought more than anything else. *Reach for Infinity*, the book you're now holding, became a collection of stories about striving, reaching for that next elusive state in the development of each world created by the writers who took part.

Many of the stories take place on Earth in the next hundred years, looking at points in time where people, or a person, look to make a critical difference and push forward towards something greater. Some of them take snapshots from places – deep within the future colonies of Mars or perched in the chromosphere of the sun – where humanity as a whole is pushing its boundaries and stretching its limits in order to achieve more. All of them are about, one way or another, reaching for infinity from within and without.

And that brings me back to the Infinity Project. Where *Reach for Infinity* tells of our striving to leave Earth, *Edge of Infinity* of how we live in the Solar System, and *Engineering Infinity* takes us out beyond the Solar System to the stars, the Infinity Project itself encompasses more than that, or I think is becoming more than that. By presenting a diverse range of science fiction stories centered on our collective future and how we might live in it, it has evolved into an attempt to map how science fiction can address tomorrow, how we can respond to science itself, and how we might be able to retain an element of romance and optimism, without sacrificing the kind of realistic assessment our collective future needs from science fiction in the 21st century.

I hope you enjoy the fourteen stories that make up *Reach for Infinity* as much as I have. And yet, another book has already formed in my mind's eye, the next step for the Project. I look forward to it and to meeting you again within those pages, but for now prepare to sit back and enjoy some of the best science fiction that our field has to offer. In the introduction to *Edge of Infinity* I wrote, "For all that some individual stories may be darker or lighter in tone, it's a love letter to our home, to our future and to science fiction. It won't be the last." I now know it's only the beginning!

Jonathan Strahan
Perth, Western Australia
February 2014

BREAK MY FALL

Greg Egan

THE FIFTEENTH STEPPING Stone came into view behind the *Baza*, pairs of spokes glinting as they caught the sun. At this distance nothing else was visible, but Heng had no trouble picturing the Stone's topography from these flickering splinters of light. Each turning spoke whose anchor point lay in the asteroid's day side was partly hidden behind the rock as it crossed the angle where it offered its mirror flash, while its opposite number rising up from the night side lay partly in shadow. A perfect sphere would have taken equal bites out of the two lines, but the Stone revealed its misshapen peanut form in the dark gap's cycle of shifts and asymmetries.

Heng glanced away from the window towards Darpana, two couches from his own in the square of nine bunks. Most children enjoyed a fairground ride, but this roller-coaster was relentless, and her vitals log showed that she still hadn't slept in the twenty-four hours since boarding. With one elbow propping her head up from the couch against the elastic tug of her harness, Darpana did not look tired, let alone distressed. But if she didn't nod off soon Heng would have to talk to her grandmother about giving her a sedative.

The Stone's rocky core was visible now, its outline mutating as it spun, like a pallid grey half-moon reflected in a trembling puddle. The asteroid was approaching at an absurdly slow rate by astronomical standards, outpacing them by a mere fifty metres a second; they might have been back on Earth, hurtling along a railway line – albeit in some surreal ghost train ride where a turnstile wrapped around a giant boulder threatened to block their way. But as the boulder drew closer and the *Baza* passed between the two layers of cables that stretched out from the rock, any sense of a horizontal passage skirting the obstacle vanished. They were swerving around it, but they were swerving *upwards*.

Darpana's gleeful cry was barely audible, but to Heng it sounded subdued more out of consideration for her fellow passengers than from any lack of energy or enthusiasm. As their weight shot up from nothing towards a gee and a half he could see her grimace with delight, as if the visceral thrill that had gripped her the first time remained as intense as ever. The portions of the cables nearest to them were travelling backwards with the asteroid's spin, putting them almost at rest with respect to the *Baza*, and the eddy currents induced in them by the ship's magnets served as a brake, quickly dragging the relative velocity down to zero. Within seconds the *Baza* was firmly locked to the cables at two points, swinging along with them but still free to pivot around its centre of mass and stay true to its original alignment. While the stars beyond the window remained serene and motionless against the frame of the cabin's interior, the nine bunks turned like roasting spits, swivelling to remain horizontal under the shifting centrifugal gravity. The view that had lain to Heng's left was dropping below him; the whole ship, and the whole cosmos beyond, seemed to be rotating around the fixed axis of his spine.

In ten seconds they'd completed half a circle, and the stars were rising on his right. He tensed himself for the fall of release, but the navigator opted for another full turn as it worked to refine their course, ensuring that the next encounter would be as perfectly aligned as this one. As Heng gazed up at the stars they were replaced by a blur of rock, sunlit for a moment then fading to black and slipping away.

When the stars rose for a second time the navigator finally broke its grip on the cables, and Heng's surroundings stopped tumbling. The Stone came into view on his right, retreating, the stars behind it unchanged.

The *Baza* had performed a U-turn around the Stone, but with respect to the Earth, rather than reversing its motion it had just gained an extra hundred metres a second. Over the next hour the Stone would give a similar boost to every ship in the convoy – and then it would be free to spend a couple of years harvesting sunlight, replenishing its spin and tweaking its orbit until it was back in position to reprise its role for another group of travellers. It had taken three decades to nudge this rock and its companions out of the Amor group and into their tailored orbits, but the foresight of the pioneers who'd begun the process had paid off for the generation that followed. The *Baza* was not so much a spacecraft in its own right as a life support capsule being tossed from Stone to Stone, but this choreographed relay race would deliver it to Mars in just four and a half months.

Rohini addressed her granddaughter calmly. "You should sleep now, darling, if you can."

"But it's exciting!" Darpana protested.

"It is," Rohini agreed. "But we have thirty more days just like this ahead of us, and if you make yourself sick you won't enjoy them at all."

Darpana was silent, but then she seemed to accept the argument. "I'll try to sleep before the next one."

"Good girl." Rohini relaxed back onto her couch.

Darpana looked past her and caught Heng's gaze. He smiled, then let his eyelids grow heavy, hoping the action would be as contagious as a yawn but less obviously manipulative. By the time he thought it might be safe to check whether he'd had any success, he'd fallen into a warm half-sleep himself, ready to wake in an instant if the *Baza* required it but unwilling to surface for anything less.

* * *

IT ONLY TOOK a small change to the sun-side window's tint to brighten the cabin and bring on a notional dawn. Heng rose before any of the passengers to use the toilet, sponge his body and change his clothes. When the *Baza* finally reached the hundredth Stepping Stone and they climbed aboard for the middle stage of the journey it would feel as if they'd gone from a shanty boat to a luxury ocean liner, but until then these few minutes each day would be the pinnacle of privacy.

As he swung out of the ablutions room he was hit by the glorious aroma of someone's breakfast sizzling in the microwave. Only Iqbal and Noor were in the kitchen nook, but the other passengers were stirring, woken by the smell.

"Do you feel like sharing?" Heng inquired. The couple's meal looked like some kind of spiced omelette rotating in its sealed bag under the lights, and though Heng had dozens of cherished recipes of his own, the sensory appeal of this visible, olfactible reality was far stronger than any remembered culinary delight.

"Of course." Iqbal turned towards the couches, swivelling on his hand-hold. "Anyone else?"

There was a deafening chorus of requests, and Iqbal waved the count up from two to nine. Heng was pleased; so far as he knew there was no acrimony between any of the families travelling on the convoy, but the smallest sign that they weren't going to turn cliquey on him was welcome. Company policy was to allow no more than three related people on the same ship – to ensure that a single ruptured hull could take only a limited toll from each family – but the resulting assortment of travelling companions had made his last outward journey an ordeal, as he'd struggled to keep the members of two rival clans from goading each other into violence. Whether Mars itself would prove big enough for both of them was, mercifully, not his problem.

Everyone managed to get through breakfast before the klaxons warned that Stone nineteen was on its way. Heng looked on solicitously as Rohini helped Darpana into her harness, but they didn't need his assistance; they'd both been rated as 'diligent' by their trainer in the course back in Shanghai. Dozens of children had made the trip over the years, and Heng had flown in convoys with a few of them, but he'd never had anyone so young on his own ship.

The log showed that Darpana had slept deeply, and as they tumbled around the first Stone of the new day she whooped with unabashed pleasure. Once they were weightless again Heng climbed free and set about the first round of system inspections, starting with the laundry press and moving through all the water-recycling components. It was tedious work, and this early in the trip it was hard not to assume complacently that nothing could yet have grown clogged, infested or leaky, but he had his cans improvise some rousing percussive music, invigorating but not catchy enough to be distracting, and he managed to get through the tasks without a single nagging beep from the overseer.

When he was done, Heng cast his gaze around the cabin, reassuring himself that everything was in order. Akhila was using the spring set, grunting softly as she forced her legs straight against the machine's tug, then fighting just as hard to bend them again. Heng's exercise of choice was running – in the middle stage, when he had the freedom of the Stone's corridors – but the *Baza*'s zero-gee treadmill was a poor substitute, and in a space as small as this it just left him feeling more hemmed in. The drugs that lied to his muscle fibres and osteocytes, assuring them that they were still bearing their usual loads, seemed to be enough to keep him from any drastic decline in his weightless months.

Everyone else remained on their couches. Iqbal and Noor were facing each other, smiling slightly, conversing privately or sharing an overlay. Rohini had her eyes closed, but Heng had no reason to snoop on her vitals to check if she'd dozed off or was merely engrossed in some study or entertainment. Punita, Aabid and Chandrakant were all clearly in that state, staring attentively into the middle distance. Only Darpana was looking out the window.

She saw Heng's reflection in the glass and turned towards him. "Are we in front of the *Tragopan*, or behind now? I've lost track."

"In front."

"My cousin said he'd aim his laser pointer out the window."

Heng doubted that she'd be able to spot it, but if hunting for a faint red speck against the stars helped her pass the time he wasn't going to disillusion her.

Darpana had another question for him. "Why do the orbits for the Stepping Stones stick out so much?"

"Ah." Heng summoned an overlay of the asteroids' trajectories. Darpana joined the view, and gestured at the largest of the ellipses traced out on the illusory pane between them. "We only want to get from Earth to Mars!" she said. "So why do half the orbits go further?"

"What do you think would be more sensible?" he challenged her.

Darpana replied boldly, "Just start with Earth's orbit and make it bigger, step by step, until you've reached Mars."

"Show me," Heng suggested. He cleared the Stones from the pane, leaving only the two planets.

Darpana drew a sequence of a dozen concentric circles, bridging the gap in equal increments. "If I draw hundreds it will be hard to see what's going on," she explained.

"No, that's fine, I get the idea." Heng waited to see if she'd spot any problems for herself, then he pointed out gently, "None of these orbits cross each other, do they?"

"No." Darpana didn't understand the complaint. "Why

should they? The Stepping Stones don't need to meet up! If the orbits are close enough, they could still throw the ships to each other."

"So the Stepping Stones have one kind of orbit – these circles – but the ships move between them on different kinds of orbits?"

Darpana hesitated. "Yes."

"How different?"

Darpana sketched a short line from one circle to another. "That's the kind of path we should take. Straight out to the next Stone – like throwing a ball up to your friend on a balcony. Then she throws it to someone on the balcony above... and on it goes, all the way to the roof."

Heng could see the appeal of this metaphor, but the reality wasn't much harder to grasp. "One small problem," he said, "is that you'd need a phenomenal velocity to go straight up like that. Remember, these Stones are in orbit, so your first one will be moving sideways at about thirty kilometres a second."

"Right." Darpana took his point and erased her original line, replacing it with a curve that spiralled around at a modest pitch on its way out from the sun. "How's that? The Stone above is moving sideways too, so it still ought to be able to catch the ship."

"How far apart are these orbits?" Heng asked.

"I'm not sure," Darpana confessed. "How far can a Stone throw us?"

"If you throw something at fifty metres a second from the Earth's orbit, it will travel a quarter of a million kilometres outwards before it starts falling back towards the sun."

"That's plenty!" Darpana replied. "A few hundred steps like that would get you to Mars."

"The catch," Heng said, "is that each step would take about three months." Darpana's spiral had an implausibly steep ascent; he sketched in an elliptical arc that hewed closer to

21

the initial circle, wrapping a quarter of the way around the sun before reaching aphelion. "Of course you could always space your Stones closer than this and catch the ship while it's still moving outwards... but so long as *the Stones themselves* aren't moving outwards, the ships can't build up speed in that direction. They'll be forced to cross the whole gap between the orbits at fifty metres a second, or less."

Darpana gazed at her concentric circles: an endless set of speed bumps if you tried to cut across them. "So the trip would take decades this way?"

"Yes." Heng brought back the real Stones' orbits. "We want to head out as fast as we can – which in the middle stage is so fast that if we kept it up we'd overshoot Mars completely. The Stones need to move on similar orbits to us, so some of them do need to overshoot Mars. You can't just take Earth's orbit and enlarge it step by step; you need to squeeze it, making it longer and skinnier so it carries you away from the sun."

"I think I understand now." Darpana smiled. "I'll try explaining it to Lomash, and if I can make him believe me then I'll know I've got the hang of it."

Heng closed the overlay and left her to commune with the *Tragopan*, her lips moving silently. It was a shame that her cousin couldn't have been on the same ship, but the two could still chat endlessly and compare their different views of this leg of the voyage. Heng couldn't understand how the girl's parents could have left her behind in the first place, but they'd all be reunited soon enough. The ever-growing warrens of Cydonia Station would be a rich playground for an imaginative child, and if in adulthood she wanted to return to Earth's wider horizons there'd be nothing stopping her.

His overseer buzzed a reminder: it was time to start checking the air scrubbers.

* * *

"THE WEATHER'S TURNING," Liana announced grimly. "There's still a chance that you'll be able to ride it out to the mid-stage, but you'd better start getting the passengers accustomed to the possibility of taking shelter early."

Heng stared at the delicate yellow lacework of coronal loops beside her on the overlay. Before they'd set out, the models had promised them a quiet journey – with just enough solar activity to limit the incursion of cosmic rays. A healthy solar wind repelled a fair proportion of the high-velocity particles from interstellar sources, and the trade-off was usually worth it, with the sun's own slower protons not too hard to block. But a coronal mass ejection could form shockwaves that accelerated the normally tolerable wind up to energies that would penetrate the ships' hulls. If that happened, only metres of solid rock could protect them.

"What's the worst case?" Le asked. His worried face faded into view beside Liana's as he spoke.

"Two days' warning," she replied. "The models aren't perfect, but they've never failed to spot an impending CME once it was that close."

Heng listened as the other captains questioned her, seeking reassurances that she could not provide. Nobody's life was in danger; the next Stepping Stone would never be more than twenty hours away. But if the travellers were forced to accept the nearest sanctuary, they'd have no hope of reaching their scheduled mid-stage ride. At best they'd face a massively expensive extraction mission – a fully powered ship launched from Mars orbit, if the families could afford it. If not, all the company itself could offer them was two years or more hunkering down in their shelter, until enough Stones could be brought into position to allow them to resume their journey, or to form an off-ramp taking them back to Earth.

When the conference ended, Heng was left staring at the grid of couches in front of him. There weren't enough cubic metres of air in the *Baza* to dissipate the stench of his sweat. "I have an announcement," he said, more loudly than he'd intended, but no one showed any sign of having heard him. He gestured to shut off their overlays and cans, and the passengers shifted in surprise on their bunks.

Heng explained the forecast, and the possibilities ahead. "The one sure thing is that we won't be taken by surprise," he stressed. "The conditions on the sun are being monitored in real time by a dozen satellites, and the models can predict these mass ejections very reliably, days in advance. Whatever's coming our way, we'll know about it in plenty of time."

Chandrakant was indignant. "In time for what? To imprison ourselves! Why didn't your astronomers see this coming before we left?"

"I'm very sorry," Heng said. He doubted that it would help to start debating the reasons why the long-range forecasts couldn't be perfect. "We still have a chance of reaching the mid-stage, but we need to be ready either way."

"What kind of facilities do the other Stones have?" Punita asked anxiously. "What kind of food, what kind of space for us?"

"The interiors are all identical," Heng assured her. "And they're all stocked with supplies..." He almost said "to last for decades" but thought better of it. "For as long as we could possibly need."

"But this is nothing for you," Chandrakant declared bitterly. "Where else would you be? It's just life as normal."

His brother Aabid muttered something to him in Gujarati; Heng only knew Hindi but the tone sounded reproving. Aabid addressed Heng in English. "This is nobody's fault. Every traveller faces these risks."

"It's a shock," Heng said. "But what can we do?"

"We'll make the best of it," Rohini replied firmly. "Hope for a reprieve, and make the best of what comes."

Heng finally dared to glance towards Darpana. She was ten years old; two years cooped up inside an asteroid would feel like a lifetime to her.

"Would the whole convoy end up together?" she asked. "Or would it be some of us in one Stone, some in another?"

Heng said, "There's a good chance we'd all be together." If the warning came as early as expected they wouldn't have to settle for the very next Stone on their itinerary, regardless of whether or not the rest of the convoy had already left it behind.

"That's all right then," Darpana ruled amiably. "On Mars we'd be underground most of the time anyway." She gripped the sides of her couch and turned her body around to face the window.

Heng watched the other passengers dialling down their angst. If this child wasn't going to shed a tear or throw a tantrum, it would be shameful for them to make a greater fuss themselves.

"DO YOU HAVE a big family?" Akhila asked Heng as she moved a piece across the backgammon board overlaid between them.

"Just my parents," he replied. "I can't afford to marry yet. Maybe after a couple more trips."

Akhila looked surprised. Perhaps she'd overestimated the portion of her fare that was ending up in his pocket. "And then you'll settle back on Earth?"

"Yes. I'm not the pioneering type."

"Ha!" She gestured at their spartan surroundings.

"This is a job," Heng replied. "I don't mind a few small hardships for myself, so long as there's an end in sight."

"In twenty years Cydonia will be more liveable than Shanghai," Akhila boasted, rather implausibly.

"You can send me a postcard when it happens." He hesitated. "So what's the attraction for you? Elbow room, or ideology?"

She laughed softly. "Both. Humanity needs a permanent

settlement away from Earth, and though some people want to postpone that until our descendants are bitstreams with much lower shipping costs, I don't think we should pass up the chance we have right now."

"But you'll have no relatives on Mars?"

"No, thank goodness." Akhila smiled. "I come from a family of infuriating meddlers, who delight in being up to their elbows in each other's business. I love them all, but it's exhausting. On Mars, I'll finally have a chance to breathe."

Heng's cans chimed with an incoming call. "Please excuse me." He turned to face the wall.

Liana appeared in front of him, and she wasted no time on pleasantries. "There's a CME coming," she said. "We expect the protons to hit you in about fifty-three hours."

"Is it worth waiting for a later Stone?" Xun asked. "In terms of the eventual reconfiguration?" Heng was impressed by her calm demeanour; he could feel his own jaw locked tight, his own thoughts still trapped in a bitter wail of resentment. *Could they shorten their time in exile by a judicious choice of Stone, right now?*

"No, there's nothing to be gained by a delay," Liana replied. "We're advising you all to dock with seventeen forty."

That was the very next Stone they'd encounter, scheduled to catch up with the convoy's hindmost ship in about four hours. But the *Baza* was currently leading the pack, and as ever the first would be last.

When Heng made the announcement most of the passengers seemed resigned to their fate. "Is there anything special we need to do to prepare?" Punita asked.

"Everyone needs to be suited in advance," he said. "I know it's awkward doing that weightless, but it's even harder at a gee and a half."

Heng looked to Darpana. She was dutifully trying to appear solemn, but he could tell that she was excited by the news.

They were fleeing for their lives from a surge of radiation – but the race was fixed squarely in their favour, and it would soon reunite her with her beloved cousin. With all the thrill of the chase but no real danger, why shouldn't she revel in it?

He struggled to quell his own anger and disappointment, to be grateful for the prospect of safety and put the rest of their problems aside. He'd even ended up with a reasonably harmonious group of inmates to share his sentence in the rock; if this had happened on his last run it might have led to civil war.

Noor said, "My parents went around the world twice on their honeymoon, but it looks like I'll be setting a new family record."

Xun's ship, the *Monal*, was the first to dock with their heavenly Alcatraz. Harnessed to his bunk, Heng watched an overlay of telemetry from the ship as it locked onto the whirling cables and then applied its ion thrusters to end its tumbling relative to the rock. Before the cradle had been winched down from the asteroid to start bringing the passengers inside, the *Lapwing* had joined the *Monal* on the opposite spoke.

Heng was always nervous when he was approaching a crowded Stone, even if the satisfaction of having reached the mid-stage usually took the edge off it. The navigators had had plenty of time to determine the best spoke for each ship and tweak their precise moments of arrival accordingly, but there was no denying that the safety margins shrank each time another obstacle lodged itself between the cables.

The *Snipe* docked smoothly, followed by the *Curlew*. As Heng watched a schematic of the Stone spinning towards the *Tragopan* he found himself extrapolating the motion in his mind's eye, picturing the inevitable meshing of ship and reserved parking space. The *Baza*'s fit would be no tighter, with neighbours sixty degrees away on either side. In twenty minutes all the stress would be over; in twenty more he'd be sitting around a table joking with his colleagues about their long internment and the challenges of remote sex with distant partners as the light-speed lag grew longer.

The schematic began blinking, and a list of mismatches between the docking plan and real-time sensor readings began scrolling across the margin. Le's voice came over the link. "We're not holding! The magnets have – no, the magnets are holding. The cable's come free, and there's rock with it. *We've torn off a piece of the asteroid.*"

Heng switched to a radar image of the *Tragopan* falling away from Alcatraz, a four-hundred-metre length of cable twirling lopsidedly around it. He couldn't tell if the cable had swiped the *Curlew* on its way into the void, but Doppler annotations on the image warned that all the remaining spokes were now swaying dangerously, pendulums set quivering by this seismic disruption.

Shen spoke from the *Curlew*. "We're all right here. Swinging like a chandelier, but nothing's broken. Xun?"

"The Stone's maintaining pressure," she replied. "One airlock is gone, but the bulkheads have sealed the breach. Le, what's your status?"

"Shutting down the magnets," Le replied tersely. Though both ship and cable were in free fall, the combined system had been rotating; severing the link would fling them apart, with no guarantee of a clean separation. Heng stared at the radar for a few tense seconds as Le fired his ion thrusters and managed to manoeuvre the *Tragopan* out of harm's way.

Heng's attention snapped back to his own problems. The pair of cables that the *Baza* had been meant to grab were oscillating back and forth, and though the radar could track this motion and the navigator could model its gradual damping, the uncertainties were so great that if the ship tried to dock now there was no guarantee of completing the process safely. Heng absorbed the numbers and then issued the command himself before the navigator intervened and made the decision for him.

"Abort docking," he subvocalised.

He waited for confirmation that they were steering clear of Alcatraz, then he banished the overlay and pulled himself out of his harness. "We've had a change of plan," he announced. "We'll be docking at the next Stone instead." The passengers had trained for this scenario in Shanghai, so they all knew exactly what it would entail.

"Why?" Darpana demanded. "You said we'd be with everyone else!"

"The cables have developed a problem." Heng saw a flag in his peripheral vision; Darpana was requesting a passenger-to-passenger link with the *Tragopan*. He refused it. "We have two hours, so you can de-suit for a bit if you want to."

Rohini was looking worried, but she turned to her granddaughter. "Will you help me get out of this suit so I can wash? I want to feel fresh before I'm stuck in it again for who knows how long."

Once Rohini and Darpana were in the ablutions room, Iqbal approached Heng. "What happened, exactly?"

"The *Tragopan* broke its mooring."

"Was anyone hurt?"

"No."

"So how do they get back to the Stone?" Akhila asked.

"They still have their ion thrusters." Heng couldn't meet her gaze.

"But that will take forever," she said.

"It will take days," Heng replied. "They'll get back, but it's going to take days."

HENG TRIED TO push the fate of the *Tragopan* out of his mind and focus on his own responsibilities. The passengers had been assigned partners to check each other's suits, but he followed up with checks of his own. The suits were meant to be able to monitor their own integrity, but then, so were the Stones, and if the smallest leak could be perilous in a normal disembarkation, the harsher version they were about to attempt could turn any flaw into a fatality.

As they took their places in the bunks, he could see the grief in Rohini's posture and the confusion and resentment in Darpana's. Rohini had told Heng that she'd explain everything to her granddaughter once they were out of the *Baza*; until then, the other passengers were doing their best to conceal their own distress.

Heng caught sight of the fallback Stone, approaching at three times the usual speed. It was like being strapped to a bullet that had been aimed at the edge of a throwing star. The *Baza* was on a trajectory that would pass between the cables almost at their tips, so there was no margin for error: if they were half a metre further from their target than intended, the magnets would get no purchase and they'd pass on by, as doomed as the *Tragopan*. He watched an overlay of the navigator iteratively refining its model of the encounter as better radar measurements came in, and the ghostly blue error cone around the trajectory grew ever narrower. But the error that would kill them would be invisible: an undetected crack deep in the machinery that would announce itself only at the instant it became impossible to rectify.

The Stone's core shot out of view from the window beside the bunks, and the sun-side window on the adjoining wall was too heavily tinted to reveal anything meaningful. Heng held his breath and desperately willed his body to be crushed.

The four and a half gees slammed him down instantly: as the magnets grazed the cables' extremities they'd had no chance to ease the ship smoothly up to the full centrifugal weight. The *Tragopan* had torn free at a third of this load; what right did he have to expect the *Baza* to hold?

But it did.

Heng lay pinned to his couch, his ribs burning with the effort of each breath, the cabin turning around him. Gradually the ion thrusters killed the spin; the room stopped moving, and there was a satisfying thud as the docking magnets gripped the cables at two more points, doubling the strength of the *Baza*'s hold.

There was nothing to do now but wait for the Stone to invite them in. Heng's status overlay showed the cradle inching its way down from the rock towards the ship. Strange bright points streaked across his vision, but he couldn't tell if it was his contacts or his retinas that were hallucinating fireworks under the strain. He wondered what kind of light show they'd see on the *Tragopan*, when solar protons boosted by the CME shock wave crashed through their vitreous humour and into their brains.

Heng felt his suit puff out around his forearms, the air it contained no longer opposed by the cabin's pressure. The *Baza*'s hatch slid open, admitting a silver light reflected from the rock above that cycled between full-moon brightness and pitch black three times a minute. According to the overlay, the cradle was almost in place. Heng was half tempted to send Darpana up first, to spare the girl any more time under the punishing gravity, but the protocols were clear: if anything was amiss up on the asteroid it couldn't be a passenger dealing with it, let alone a child. The captain had to be the first to leave the ship, however unchivalrous that seemed.

A chime sounded in his cans, and he focused on the flashing message in his overlay. The cradle was touching the *Baza*'s hull, but it was misaligned by a few centimetres, stopping it from passing through the hatch. The fucking thing had an air jet to deal with that kind of problem; what did the Stone expect him to do? Not even Akhila could have climbed up and helped the cradle through the entrance. Heng squinted at the image his contacts were painting until the final line of text became clear. The air jet had been tried but it wasn't working; either the nozzle was blocked or a control wire had been severed.

"Navigator," he subvocalised. "Compute the thrust to reposition us ten centimetres along the y axis." They were hanging from the asteroid like a dead weight on a string, but they ought to be able to shift the equilibrium.

The force required was within the thrusters' capacity. Heng had it build up as slowly as he could bear, giving time for the cables to dissipate energy so he wouldn't set the *Baza* swinging.

After ten minutes, the cradle dropped down into the cabin and the winch positioned it next to Heng's bunk. His harness disconnected from the couch beneath him; the cradle locked onto it at the side and slid him over into the suspended sling.

He rode up in airless silence, unable to turn his gaze to the side to look across at the stars. All he could see was the rock straight above him, cycling through its ten-second days and nights: a lighthouse, a prison, a safe port for all the loneliness and grief to come.

"Will you talk to her?" Rohini pleaded. "She trusts you."

"Trusts me?" Heng was confused. "She can't believe you'd lie about something like this." He could hear Darpana's wailing, rising and falling like a song.

"Not deliberately," Rohini replied. "But you're the expert. If you explain to her why there's nothing we can do, she'll believe you. When I tell her the same, she just screams that I don't know what I'm talking about."

Heng gathered his courage and strode down the corridor. The child had brought joy and innocence to the *Baza*, but now it was his duty to help her understand her cousin's fate.

He knocked on the door of Darpana's cabin. She stopped her keening and he heard her spring up off the bed. When she slid the door open she did not look surprised; Rohini must have promised to send him to talk to her.

"Why aren't we rescuing them?" she demanded. "Why aren't we going after them?"

"If we met up with them, how would that help?" Heng asked gently. "Our thrusters are no stronger than theirs."

Darpana stared at him contemptuously. "We don't just have our thrusters!" she replied. "We have this whole Stone! We can throw the *Baza* in any direction at a hundred and fifty metres per second!"

"Yes," Heng agreed. "So we could reach the *Tragopan* quickly, but what good is that if we can't match its speed? And if we did match its speed, we'd all be in the same boat."

Darpana said, "We don't match speed with the Stones, do we?"

Heng rubbed his eyes; he was still giddy from all the changes in weight. "We do, though: we match speed with the cables." She knew that perfectly well, but he couldn't blame her for saying or thinking anything as she sought some miraculous reprieve. Heng had met Lomash briefly before the convoy set out from orbit, but now he tried to wipe the boy's smiling face from his mind. Le would haunt him; that was hard enough.

"So we take some cable with us!" Darpana retorted. "And spin it as fast as we have to!"

Heng stood with his arm resting on the door frame, squinting to try to see past the defects swimming through his eyeballs. *Taking cable with them* would have sounded like nonsense a day ago, conjuring up an image of him packing a reel of it in the cabin and then trying to deploy it as the rendezvous approached. But the *Tragopan* had certainly *taken cable with it* when it ripped a whole double strand loose from Alcatraz.

If they could find a safer way to mimic that feat, could they turn the *Baza* itself into a kind of impromptu Stepping Stone? The ship wouldn't need to be crewed; it would merely have to cross paths with the *Tragopan*, carrying enough speed and spin for the *Tragopan* to effect the necessary U-turn and get back to

Alcatraz. One of the four docked ships could be sent between the Stones to replace the *Baza*.

"Let me think," he told Darpana. He turned and walked away.

Heng contacted Liana first, privately. He did not want to give Le and the others false hope if the scheme proved impossible from the start.

"You don't have the tools to slice through nanotube cables," Liana declared bluntly.

"Are you certain?" Heng wished he'd queried the inventory first, but if the company didn't want him to have the means to hack a spoke off the Stone, the computer would have lied to him anyway. "If this isn't the emergency that justifies some serious vandalism, what is?"

"It's not about damaging property," Liana replied. "Your responsibility is to your own passengers. If you breach the integrity of your living space, you'll just kill nine more people."

"You're right." Heng cut the link; he was wasting his time with her. The legal position would be crystal clear: the company could not endorse his plan, let alone facilitate it. And he had no right to endanger the *Baza*'s passengers without their consent.

Heng gathered everyone in the conference room, Darpana included, and explained precisely what he wanted to do.

"We don't have much time to make a decision," he said. "If this goes wrong, it might damage the Stone badly enough to kill us. Or we might spring a leak and lose pressure, so we'd have to live in suits until we can make repairs."

"Or we might get away with it unharmed," Punita suggested.

"We might," Heng agreed. Alcatraz had survived its own amputation. "But don't ask me for the odds."

He passed a sheet of paper around the table, with two columns to record the votes. Everyone would have the power of veto; he couldn't let a mere majority coerce anyone into risking their life.

As Chandrakant accepted the ballot he looked up at Heng with an expression of pure loathing. Heng shifted his gaze and stared at the far wall; he'd done nothing deliberately to alienate the man, but it was too late now to try to placate him.

Iqbal touched Heng's shoulder; the paper had only taken thirty seconds to come full circle. Heng accepted it and unfolded all the creases that people had made to hide their votes from the next recipient.

There were nine marks in the YES column.

HENG ORGANISED THE passengers into work teams, fetching trolley-loads of rubble from a cul-de-sac that the tunnelling machines hadn't fully cleaned out. Each courier weighed their contribution on a set of bathroom scales, and Darpana had the job of double-checking the readings and the running total.

The company had had the Stone's automation disable the motorised winch for the cradle, so Heng and Akhila took turns operating it by hand. A purely mechanical regulator prevented it from unwinding uncontrollably, even as the weight it was bearing quadrupled, and Heng had offset the rope so that the combined centrifugal and Coriolis forces saw it drop squarely into the hatch below. The real effort went into hauling the empty cradle up again.

Safety regulations precluded any interference in the airlock's function, and it opened and closed its doors at the push of a button as always. As they delivered each load through the *Baza*'s hatch – spilling it by sheer force of impact, since the cradle was playing dumb – Heng waited for the mounting tension in the cables to fracture the stone around him and send him tumbling out into the vacuum. Suitless for the sake of efficiency, at least he'd have a mercifully quick death.

He had decided to postpone the call to Le until the launch was a *fait accompli*; he knew that if they spoke any sooner his friend would feel compelled to beg the *Baza* team not to take this risk. But in purely pragmatic terms an early warning would make no difference; the *Tragopan*'s navigator couldn't start plotting a rendezvous before the *Baza* had actually commenced its flight and its precise trajectory was known.

Akhila said, "The cradle's stuck. The load's not coming off."

Heng joined her at the winch. They strained together against the handle, and abruptly the drum began to move again.

When they'd wound up all four hundred metres of rope, Heng sprinted down the steps and opened the airlock. The cradle had been torn right off; there was nothing left but frayed strands of polymer.

They didn't have time to try to secure a more robust platform to the rope; they'd have to go ahead with exactly as much rock as they'd delivered.

Akhila caught up with him and took stock of the situation. "I'll go down and finish things off," she said.

"No. I need you up here, to haul me back."

Akhila shook her head. "People can work the winch two at a time, even three at a time. If we lose you, we wouldn't last a month in this place."

Heng's skin prickled with shame. He'd seen her vitals log from the docking. There was no doubt that her heart was stronger than his, and her cerebral blood flow would be less compromised by the punishing weight at the rope's end.

"I can't let you do it," he said.

"I'm terrified enough as it is," she replied. "Don't make it any harder."

Heng's shame deepened, but the source had shifted. What mattered to him more: emerging from this disaster with his pride intact, or giving the survivors the best chance he could? He was not indispensable, but he couldn't deny that his absence would make their long exile more dangerous.

"All right," he said.

* * *

HENG SAT IN the conference room, looking through Akhila's eyes while Iqbal, Chandrakant and Aabid fought her growing weight. The winch's regulator alone would have kept her from falling freely, but her arrival at the *Baza* would have been fatally abrupt if no other force had slowed her descent.

Akhila was staring straight down from her improvised sling. As the sky reeled past behind the ship's silhouette, her helmet's face plate sent the same rainbow sliver of refracted colours flickering across her vision before it tinted in response to the sunlight, three times a minute. The company had disabled the utility robots that could have done the job in her place, ensuring that if this folly led to deaths they could not be treated as accomplices.

"Are you all right?" Heng asked.

"I'm glad I haven't eaten for a while," she replied.

"If you want to close your eyes until you reach the *Baza*–"

"No, I want to see where I'm going. If I close my eyes I'll feel like I'm being lowered down a well."

As her weight approached three gees, Heng saw the sky shudder: the rope had slipped a few centimetres, then been caught. He brought up an inset of all the winch operators' vitals. Iqbal's heart rate had risen dangerously high, and his breathing was laboured.

"Punita? You need to relieve Iqbal." Heng spoke on an open channel to everyone, in the hope of precluding any arguments. Iqbal did not dispute the call.

When the *Baza* filled the view Akhila's helmet lamp came on, its steady beam drowning out the rise and fall of asteroid-light. Heng gazed down through the hatch. He could see the rubble piled up below, and a hint of white that must have been the broken cradle.

As Akhila drew level with the hatch, Heng called "Stop!" to the winch team. Her orientation had looked perfect as she'd approached, so if her right arm was still resting at the edge of the sling, the lever that would close the hatch ought to be well within her reach.

"Akhila?"

"I'm ready," she subvocalised, wasting no breath on speech. "Are you clowns ready to get me clear?"

Chandrakant replied, "Absolutely."

Heng called out the cues they'd agreed on. "One. Two. *Lever*. Three. Four. *Raise*."

His viewpoint jerked upwards as the door slid shut, centimetres below Akhila's face. "Well done." He could feel his own heart thumping now.

The welding laser tucked under Akhila's left arm couldn't burn through the nanotube cable, but it could certainly raise its temperature. She managed to turn her head to face the cable, switch the laser on at its lowest power, and then nudge the beam back and forth until a small red spot could be seen shimmering on the cable four metres away.

With the Stone's computing resources out of bounds, Heng had modelled everything on Darpana's wristwatch. He raised the device from the table beside him and counted down to the moment when the predicted time lag to release would see the *Baza* move off on a course that the *Tragopan* could intercept. "Three. Two. One."

The laser spot became dazzling for a moment, then Akhila's faceplate darkened to tame it. Heng glanced down at the wristwatch and it streamed an animation to his contacts, showing the modelled temperature profile of the cable and the attached magnets. The magnets could function well above room temperature, so they had no special cooling system, but their superconductor's transition temperature was not hard to reach. As a patch of the false colour image shifted from blue to green, Akhila's bright target vanished and Heng heard a high-pitched whine from the rock around him.

The *Baza* had lost its grip on one half of the spoke to which it had docked – but the two pieces formed a continuous length of cable, looped through a U-shaped tunnel in the Stone. Unbalanced, and bearing more weight than it had ever been intended to hold, the cable was unthreading, the unburdened end rushing up towards the rock while the *Baza* dragged the other end farther away, increasing its centrifugal weight even more.

The noise of the cable scraping through the rock stopped abruptly. The *Baza* would be falling free now, with luck still attached to the cable. The timing looked good: within half a second of the model's prediction. The trajectory would lie within the *Tragopan*'s reach. Le and his passengers would have a second chance of reaching shelter.

Heng called out triumphantly, "We did it!" Exuberant cheers came back from the winch team, from Iqbal and Noor, from Rohini and Darpana. Akhila was silent, but she'd be saving her breath for the celebrations when she returned.

Heng looked through her eyes again as he prepared his words of thanks. He saw the stars – and then he saw the Stone, its spokes glinting in the sunlight as it receded into the distance.

THE DUST QUEEN

Aliette de Bodard

QUYNH HA HAD expected the Dust Queen to be…tall and large, filling the room with her presence. But the woman sitting before her was old and frail – breathing, it was clear, only with the help of the bots clinging to her throat; her skin as pale and translucent as the best jades; the skin of her hands bearing the peculiar tightness of too many rejuv treatments.

It was hard to believe that a gesture of hers would send bots dancing; that on her command they would bank and dip and turn over the red soil of Mars, mould the clouds of dust they raised into the ephemeral figures from Quynh Ha's childhood – the boy Cuoi and his banyan, the strategist Khong Minh and his crane-feather fan. It was hard to imagine them whirling and rearing, tracing words in the flowing writing of calligraphy masters, poems like the ones hung at compartment doorways for New Year's Eve – all the wonder and the magic that filled Fire Watch Orbital once a year; that made life bearable in a world of airsuits, processed food and long watches of a planet they could not set foot on.

When she saw Quynh Ha, the Queen, Bao Lan, looked puzzled for a split second; and then her eyes narrowed, focusing on Quynh Ha with an intensity that made her shudder. "Child. You must be wondering why you're here."

Her voice was low and pleasant, with a bare trace of an Earth accent. Quynh Ha had heard it, on broadcasts after performances, commenting on the choices Bao Lan had made, elegant, cultured and refined, a scholar in an age which barely had use for them anymore. She'd never thought, from the broadcasts, that it would be so slight; and yet it had no trouble filling the room.

The Dust Queen. She was in the presence of the Dust Queen herself. She lowed her eyes as was proper; but it was hard not to scream, not to smile, not to explain to Bao Lan all that she meant to the orbital, to Quynh Ha. "Grandmother."

"I picked you because you're the best rewirer we have on Fire Watch." Bao Lan's voice was calm, thoughtful; considering a problem she couldn't solve.

"I'm not–" Quynh Ha opened her mouth to protest, and then closed it again. She wasn't a proper master, no, not like out there on the asteroids, where everyone was rewired and all companies had their rewirers; where deaders like Peter Cauley came from, having done it to themselves so many times they looked at the world with eyes like a fish on a monger's display. Out there emotions were a hindrance, for who needed to think of a husband left behind when clinging to the outside of a craft, piloting repair bots with hairbreadth's precision? On Fire Watch it was just the dregs of the profession, those who hadn't quite made the companies' cut to go further out; or people who hoped for a quick fortune and set exorbitant fees.

"I'm just an apothecary," Quynh Ha said at last. She did rewirings, sometimes, because they were a complement to the drugs Second Aunt sold; but that was hardly the core of her business. "I don't do that many rewirings."

That was it. She shouldn't have admitted it; she'd had her one chance to help Bao Lan, to speak to her, and that stupid honesty had doomed her, yet again. She braced herself for a dismissal – which didn't come.

"More than that, I should think," Bao Lan said. "I can afford the best, child. If I picked you, there is a reason."

Quynh Ha bit her lip before she could ask why. No doubt she'd know, in due time. Or perhaps she never would. It wouldn't matter one bit. "How may I help you then, Grandmother?"

There was a sound from Bao Lan: laughter or anger or both. "I picked you because you're known for your delicateness; and because you're Viet, like me, so you will understand what it is that I want. It's a simple enough thing, child.

"I want to go home, and you're the one who'll help me do it."

GOING INTO SOMEONE'S brain is almost like being in space: that curious sensation of hanging, weightless, like floating in water without the water; of hanging in darkness with the stars around her like hairpin wounds in the fabric of the heavens.

Here, of course, there are no stars; but the wounds are memories – a dizzying array of them, every one of them so close she could touch them – and yet to reach out, to catch them all, would drive her insane under the weight of information and emotions that aren't hers.

She does reach out, all the same – because it's what she's here for, because it's the reason Bao Lan picked her out of the multitude – and the images come in, fast and hard, crammed so hard together that they're almost inseparable.

A family on a cyclo, father and mother and two children, weaving their way through the traffic of an overcrowded city; a New Year's Eve dinner, plates strewn over a red table cloth, wrapped rice cakes, candied coconut and lotus seeds; a quiet day out at the graveyard, burning paper money and paper houses for the ancestors' souls...

And the other, darker ones: an old woman on a roof in the midst of a flood, raising a fist at some officials in a boat; children creeping out in the kitchen one morning, and looking down at the unfamiliar sensation of wetness, to see the widening spread of water on the floor; the smell of rain as they sit under tarpaulin in a foreign city, waiting to be assigned a new compartment...

And all the memories, the good, the bad, the heartbreaking – they're all sealed under glass, tinted the colour of old, obsolete photographs – she reaches out to them, and rebounds as if she'd hit a wall, everything preserved in that unbreakable stasis, where nothing matters, where nothing hurts...

SHE CAME TO with a start; to see Bao Lan looking at her, with that same weary expression she'd seen, time and time again, on her own grandmother's face; and she knew. "You want to go home," Quynh Ha said, feeling as though she were speaking through cotton. Everything felt out of sync, as it always did when she went under – unbearably sharp and cutting, every noise a wound, every object blindingly illuminated. "To a place that would mean something to you."

They'd raised the Mekong Delta again, with seawalls and embankments and sluices, rebuilding its cities from the ground up. Sixth Aunt had gone back there, to help with that effort; and Mother and Grandmother had both started to save money for a return holiday, though none of that news, none of those unfamiliar images relayed by the comms system really seemed to lift the cloud of sadness that hung over the family.

So Bao Lan could, physically, go home; but that wouldn't be what she wanted. Nothing would have emotional heft: the streets and the scents and the canals would have no particular associations; and she would walk in the city where she'd grown up, feeling a stranger to her own childhood.

Unless one could fix her.

Bao Lan nodded. "I had myself rewired, in the early days of the resettlement. It was... easier to go that way."

Easier, perhaps; avoiding all the loaded conversations between Grandmother and Mother at Tomb Sweeping festivals; when they sat at a table and spoke of graves in a cemetery that the sea had since long swallowed; of ancestors, bewildered and lost without the care of their descendants – as if ancestors couldn't be with them, regardless of where their graves were.

"Can you do it?" Bao Lan asked; and for a moment, her old, anxious face was the same as Grandmother's.

Quynh Ha said, carefully, "Theoretically, yes. I don't know how much you know about rewiring–"

"Imagine that I know nothing," Bao Lan said.

Quynh Ha doubted that. Bao Lan, who made a point on researching obscure epics for her dust cloud performances so she could get the costume details on the characters right, would not have left anything to chance; but she went on, regardless. "It's a good scrub, I'll grant them that. Worth good money at the time, I imagine."

"My first pay as a cyclo driver in Ho Chi Minh City," Bao Lan said, with a bare smile, a tightening of lips over yellowed teeth. "That was in the days before my entire life changed. I'm glad to know it wasn't all wasted."

Quynh Ha allowed herself a smile she didn't feel. It had been a good scrub, a thorough rewiring; and she wasn't altogether sure she could undo what had been done. "Rewiring is... like deadening. You can't completely suppress the emotions involved, or the person will go mad. There'll be one, or several cracks somewhere; tiny remnants of the original emotions. All I have to do is find one and amplify it – I can't give you the original back, but it will be something much like it."

It would be like a zither melody to a full orchestra: a single voice, and with none of the body and complexity of the real memories, the ones that had hurt so much. But, because it was the mind's own emotions, the brain would take them, and compensate, creating something that would, in the end, be quite close to whatever had been there before – to the love and the loss and the pain that made up home in Bao Lan's mind. The tricky part, however, would be finding a crack: a rewiring that thorough wouldn't have left large ones.

"Then that will satisfy me, yes," Bao Lan said. "We haven't discussed the matter of payment, but rest assured I will make it worth your time. If you agree, I'll call your place of work and tell them I need you."

The image of Second Aunt picking up the comms – of her face when she realised she was speaking to the Dust Queen – flashed across Quynh Ha's mind, and was gone just as swiftly. "There won't any problem. I'm sure they'll understand–" Quynh Ha had to swallow, to sort out the words in her mind. Bao Lan. The Dust Queen needed her. Trusted her. That was worth a talk with Second Aunt, many times over. "I'll sort it out, Grandmother."

"Good. Let me know when you can start." Her voice was that of an Empress to a supplicant; and Quynh Ha nodded.

"I'm honoured by your trust." She was honoured, but she was also scared stiff, as if she were dancing tightrope outside Fire Watch with no tether. To think that she was the one in charge of something that mattered this much to Bao Lan – to the heroine of her childhood – it was almost too much on her shoulders.

Almost.

But she'd do it, because how many times in her life would she have an opportunity like this?

THERE WAS A woman, waiting for her outside the Dust Queen's quarters. She was sitting in one of the high chairs, apparently engrossed in Fire Watch's entertainment system; but she rose when Quynh Ha walked through the door.

"Miss Quynh Ha? My name is Le Anh Tuyet. I'm Bao Lan's daughter. "

She was perhaps forty, fifty years old; though like Bao Lan she bore the hallmarks of numerous rejuv treatments. Her face was eerily reminiscent of her mother's, reminding Quynh Ha of the broadcasts of her youth. Her clothes had an odd, almost old-fashioned cut seen nowhere on Fire Watch; and the sheen of Earth silk, grown on mulberry trees and sunlight. "You're an Earthsider?" The words were torn out of Quynh Ha before she could think. "I'm sorry."

"That's quite all right." Tuyet smiled. "I lived here a while, but yes, I emigrated back to Earth twenty years ago."

"I see," Quynh Ha said; and wondered how much lay hidden behind that simple sentence. "You haven't told me what I can do for you."

Tuyet shook her head. "It's what you can do for Mother, younger aunt." She'd slipped, effortless, into the Vietnam vernacular, with its myriad set of pronouns.

"She's already asked–"

"I know," Tuyet said. "I came to accompany her home, to Thoi Binh." Her gaze, for a moment, was distant.

Quynh Ha's curiosity got the better of her. "Did you take part in the land reclamation?"

"In Thoi Binh, yes." Tuyet shrugged. "Mostly boring stuff, and we couldn't salvage everything. Districts Ten and Fifteen are still underwater, I'm afraid."

"It must be very different from here," Quynh Ha said before she could stop herself.

"It's home," Tuyet said, and shook her head. "Apologies. We all have homes, of course; but Thoi Binh is where I was born. You must have relatives–"

"Of course," Quynh Ha said, and bit her lip, thinking of her own grandmother. If she'd rewired herself, would she be more like Bao Lan? It wasn't fair, of course; Grandmother's wandering thoughts might as well be old age, and she'd been sharp enough when Quynh Ha was young: had established the family restaurant on Fire Watch, had paid for the schooling of her numerous grandchildren out of the money she'd saved. But lately... "Never mind that. I'll go plan the rewiring."

"You have much experience."

Quynh Ha was not about to be caught a second time; and she could hear the scepticism in Tuyet's voice. "You don't have rewiring, on Earth?"

Tuyet shrugged. "No, we do. It's just–"

Oh. Like the older generation; the ones who'd been too old at the inception of rewiring; and therefore distrusting it. "Rewiring is only dangerous if you keep doing the same rewiring all the time," Quynh Ha said. "Like the deaders? You must have seen them on the shows. That's because they keep doing it to themselves – dozens of times a day, it's more an addiction than anything, really. Otherwise, it's like anything; a tool that has its uses. I've done it for customers; and I've done it on myself." She rewired herself periodically when making complex preparations: it was useful to be able to ignore fear and the previous memories of failure so she could focus on getting the drug proportions right.

"I see," Tuyet said. Quynh Ha could tell some of her confidence had got through. "I guess it's what Mother wants, and I won't argue with her. Not this time." Her voice was bleak.

Quynh Ha said nothing; it was obviously not her place to pry. At length Tuyet sighed. "Ah well. It's what you do, on Fire Watch, and if it makes her happy..."

Quynh Ha bowed her head. "Thank you. I'll set to work immediately."

"Great. Do you have everything you need to work?"

Quynh Ha shrugged. "I can do a lot of things from the dispensary." She had remote access to a simulacrum of Bao Lan's memories; enough to find the best places for her rewiring and test her results; though of course anything in a rewiring was unpredictable enough that only live testing would help.

"Good," Tuyet said, and handed her a piece of paper with a private handle. "Do let me know if I can do anything for you. Mother and I–" she grimaced "– have had our differences in the past, but they're over now. We both want her home, no matter the cost."

ALL REWIRINGS HAVE cracks; points of weaknesses, where the protective fabric has been deliberately torn; where the emotions keep seeping in. If she can find one memory that feels different from the other ones – where the glass has fissured, where the colours have bled – then she'll have all she needs to unlock the Mekong Delta again.

What she finds, rifling through Bao Lan's brain, is not that, but something else entirely.

She finds the other memories: the ones associated with Fire Watch, with her role as the Dust Queen, the official entertainer for New Year's Eve: years and years of dust cloud dances all packed together like grains of sand. The Committee that rules over Fire Watch wants something to allay the frustration of Fire Watchers, forced to watch over the terraformation of a planet they're not allowed to set foot on for fear of a cross-planet contamination that would disturb the entire, delicate process mapped out a generation ago. They have decided to hold a celebration on the planet; something that will remind people that one day, when the cyanobacteria and the bots have done their jobs, humans will breathe the air of Mars.

The earlier memories are of technology in its infancy: of frustrated scientists in labs; of bots that die on the surface of Mars, choked up on dust; of implants that short circuit, almost taking out a portion of Bao Lan's brain with them. The lead scientist, Zhu Chiling, comes to hospital to apologise, and almost gives up; but Bao Lan shakes her head, and tells her she's willing to try again – and they do, and she feels the pride and the wonder when it finally works – when Bao Lan sits in the chair of the broadcasting room and makes bots crawl on the surface of Mars for the very first time.

She's with Bao Lan when they inaugurate the seventh cyanobacteria greenhouse; when everyone on Fire Watch gathers to see Bao Lan's bots weave images of villages and houses, with tiny figures running in the street, cutting the strings of kites for good fortune. And she sees every performance after that, establishing a ritual that becomes an anchor for the inhabitants of Fire Watch, a promise renewed year after year.

There's one in particular that Quynh Ha remembers; a New Year's Eve that has no special meaning – another worship of the ancestors, another meal with the family. But, nevertheless, she remembers crowding with the cousins around the huge screen in Mother's compartment; sitting, rapt, as bots dance below, retelling the story of Cuoi and his banyan tree. In the clouds of dust Cuoi meets the tiger; plants the seed of the magical banyan; and is finally whisked to the moon, clinging to the tree's roots as it rises.

And she understood, then; that they're all like Cuoi; that they rose into the Heavens and made their home there; that the banyan's roots, drawn in the dust by the bots, now cover the surface of Mars. That all of this is Bao Lan's message, Bao Lan's hope: one day their children's children will leave their footprints in the dust and bring their own legends to life on the red soil.

But Bao Lan's home, like Mother's, like Grandmother's, isn't Fire Watch, isn't Mars: it's the land they left in the resettlement, the land that was once submerged under the sea. With difficulty, Quynh Ha tears herself from the feasts, from the beautiful dances of the bots; and goes back to the other memories, the sepia-tinted ones that she finds no purchase on.

She rifles through car rides; through afternoons by the sea at Vung Tau; expeditions to the metropolis in Can Tho. Everything is quaint and old and outmoded – no implants, no bots, just clunky machines and a network that still requires dozens of antennas to function properly. But it's Bao Lan's childhood – this small corner of Viet Nam, those gardens with pomegranate and papaya trees; those boats weaving their way on the muddy expanses of the Mekong; the smell of monsoon rain and fried dough, a promise of a meal of rolled rice cakes and dipping sauce that will be an explosion of flavour in the mouth, salty and acid and sweet all at the same time, a perfect taste that will never again be reproduced, no matter how many cakes she orders.

Quynh Ha realises, then, that she finally has the memory she was looking for. It's small and insignificant, a brief moment of a child running on a bridge clogged with cyclos, and then stopping by a food vendor's cart, but it's alive and vibrant in a way none of the others are. This is her crack; this is the emotion she was looking for. And it's also oddly familiar, in a way she can't place. It can't be shared experience, for she's never been to Can Tho, never been to Earth even, and those wide streets interspersed with trees mean nothing to her. She sets her extrapolations algorithms on it, watching as the fragile network of emotions gains body and heft with each pass – grows like crystals in caves, becoming a complex, fragile assembly of ten thousand details.

She sets up the graft, though she expects only minor issues; and logs out to await the result in the morning.

WHEN SHE GETS to the compartment early in the morning, there is an error message waiting for her in the console.

For a moment, Quynh Ha freezes. There is no reason this should fail, especially not at the simulacrum stage. The hardest part had been finding a crack, but normally everything from there on should have been smooth – like a sleek craft set on ice, gathering momentum and sliding straight to its destination. Why?

She throws a glance at the shop's entrance. At this early hour, the customers aren't there yet, though old Miss Hanh should be there any moment to pick up her medication. Quynh Ha wraps the drugs in a piece of paper, and leaves them in evidence with a message for Miss Hanh: since the drugs are tailored to a client's biology, it is unlikely anyone will steal them. Then she turns on her implants, and dives back into the simulacrum.

THE MEMORIES ARE still there, sepia tinted and under glass, and as inaccessible as ever. There are shards of her algorithms clinging to their edges – broken bits of crystal, jagged edges that made her shudder when she brushes too close, singeing herself on their heightened intensity. But nothing seems to have grown; her graft has been summarily rejected, something alien and unacceptable.

Was the memory wrong? If it didn't belong to Bao Lan, but to the original rewirer? Sometimes things get confused when rewiring; but no, the emotions associated with it were too strong. She's seen them ten thousand times: in Grandmother's gaze when she sits with her friends playing; in the catch of Mother's voice when she speaks of her childhood; in Second Aunt's careful, fragile movements; in the weight of the air at every Tomb Sweeping festival, where the presence of the ancestors is as thick as incense smoke.

There is no reason for that failure then; it makes no sense...

She zooms in on one of the shards, staring at the details – fear and longing and happiness; and a hint of rainy skies, of heavy air. The emotions are real, or as real as Bao Lan allows them to be – the graft is what she's done a dozen times for a dozen customers, surely it shouldn't be such a difficulty?

Still... still, she stares at the shard; and remembers that feeling of familiarity when the extrapolation was being built; remembers dismissing it as of no matter. Her mistake. Every little detail matters.

The shard feels solid and transparent at the same time – the original feelings she got from the crack; the raw pain of losing home mingled with what home means – the joys and the sorrows and the dreams that made up Bao Lan's life in the Delta – the sound of cyclos on the bridge, the patter of the street vendor peddling her fried dough; the sense of vastness opening up all around her, childhood stretching like a vast, endless plain with so many adventures left – and yet already, at the fringes, is the smell and shadow of the rising sea; the inescapable knowledge that all of this is a suspended moment of grace; a fragile dream in a place doomed to vanish.

And she sees it, then. She sees why it hasn't worked; why it can never work.

"I FOUND A crack," Quynh Ha told Bao Lan.

The Dust Queen was sitting in her broadcast chair again, staring at one of the screens in front of her. Tuyet was in one of the smaller chairs, reading a printed book; an oddity on Fire Watch, where nothing was printed much anymore. She reminded Quynh Ha of Second Aunt and her brocade dresses; youthful face, but mannerisms from another generation.

On the screen was a scene from a familiar tale, rendered as in shadow theatre: a man kneeling before the Buddha, watching a hundred stems of bamboo come together to make the hundred-knot bamboo that will win him his sweetheart's hand in marriage. As Quynh Ha watched, Bao Lan made a gesture with one hand; and the scene gradually faded; and then rearranged itself, emphasising the kneeling posture of the man and the larger-than-life size of the Buddha. Then it broke apart; became the dance of bots on a simulated Mars – clouds that slowly built up the apparition of the Buddha; the surprise of the man, who attempted to throw himself backwards; the gathering of the hundred bamboo stems in the forest, so well rendered one could see the sweat on the dust-man's brow; could hear the sound of bamboo falling on the ground of the forest.

Quynh Ha found herself holding her breath, so hard it hurt.

Bao Lan made a dismissive gesture. "It's not yet ready." She pinched her lips; and made another gesture. The scene dissolved; played itself out again; the Buddha slightly larger; the man slightly smaller – and, when he went into the forest, it wasn't sweat that was falling from his brow, but tears – his fear, his anguish at the thought he might never return in time, never marry his bride...

"Better." Bao Lan shook her head. "But not quite there, I think. Sorry for making you wait, child."

"I don't mind," Quynh Ha said. Her heart still hung suspended in her chest. "Is this how you do your performances?"

"Sometimes, yes." The Dust Queen had an oddly nostalgic look in her face. "There wasn't this, in the old days: it was all gut instinct, but this helps."

"I know," Quynh Ha said, and bit her tongue.

"You've seen the memories." Bao Lan nodded.

"I didn't know you'd based it on shadow theatre."

Bao Lan shrugged. "It seemed as good an inspiration as any. I had... good memories of shadow theatre, when I was a child. There was this itinerant Hoa performer, back in Thoi Binh..." She smiled. "But never mind, we're not here for this old woman to babble on. You said you'd found a crack."

Quynh Ha would have listened to her all day; but she knew that wasn't what Bao Lan was expecting. "Yes," she said.

"And you're here to finish your work, I take it."

Quynh Ha took a deep breath. "I can't." From the corner of her eye, she saw Tuyet set aside her book, and turn her head to her, with a gaze sharp enough to pierce metal.

"I don't understand," Tuyet said. "Surely, once you've found your crack, everything else should be easy?"

It was what she'd told Bao Lan; and there was, indeed, no reason to suppose it would go otherwise. Except...

"I've extrapolated it, as I said. And I could rewire you right now, but it wouldn't take. It's not just a crack. It's everywhere."

"Everywhere?" Bao Lan shook her head. "I don't think so. When I think of my childhood, all that comes up is empty memories. Images that mean nothing. Sounds and tastes that are a stranger's."

"It's not–" Quynh Ha paused, struggling for words that seemed to have escaped her. It had seemed so clear, staring at the pattern yesterday; but that had been yesterday; and today she was in the presence of Bao Lan again, and as tongue-tied as a child. "Your crack is your art. The thing that makes your dust clouds sing, that gives them meaning, emotion, depth: it's that tiny little remnant of what it meant to lose your home."

Bao Lan opened her mouth to speak – Quynh Ha barely noticed, as she went on through her memorised speech. "You're the Dust Queen. That's who you've been, for decades. I've seen the memories. Your entire life revolves around your art." There had been memories of Tuyet in the simulacrum, but Quynh Ha had steered clear of them. They were none of her business, and she'd felt ashamed enough spying on Bao Lan's performances. Nevertheless, she'd seen enough: a lonely childhood, with a mother that had little time for her child; but who had still resented Tuyet for leaving Fire Watch – abandoning Bao Lan for the lifelong work of raising the Delta from the sea.

There was silence, in the wake of her words. Surely she'd gone too far, had been too frank, too honest? "I see," Bao Lan said at last. "And it won't take–"

"Because you won't let it," Quynh Ha said.

"What makes you so sure?"

Quynh Ha spread her hands. "The simulacrum–"

"Is a simulation." Bao Lan's voice was quiet, but forceful. Behind her, the little shadow play was still going on; the man abasing himself before the Buddha; the hundred-knot bamboo rebuilding itself, time and time again. "You can't know what will happen in real life."

"No," Quynh Ha said.

"You've known cases of divergence," Bao Lan said, softly. "Cases where the simulacrum didn't follow the patient."

"Not this way!"

Bao Lan said, softly, quietly, "I'm told there are ways and means, to make a graft take. Forcefully, if need be."

Demons take her. Of course she'd do her research; and of course she'd find out all about the more shady practises of rewiring. "We don't do this," Quynh Ha said. "Not on Fire Watch." Out there in the asteroids, perhaps – who knew what the companies got up to, when their profits were on the line? But here on the orbital, where the only thing at stake was watching Mars grow? No. "And even if we did, it would be an even more difficult procedure." To make a graft take when it didn't cling, you had to add anchors everywhere; to tie hundreds of knots in the nerve fabric, to implant emotion after emotion in such a way that they never came loose, and yet didn't damage the brain... "Hours of work, and the slightest deviation could make everything fail."

"Ah. But I did say I'd picked you out for your delicate touch, didn't I?"

She – she – "You knew," Quynh Ha said, sucking in a burning breath. "You knew all along."

"No," Bao Lan said. "But I suspected that it might come to this, yes; and I gave a long thought to what I would do, if that were the case. I knew I would ask you to go ahead."

"But I can't–" She struggled for breath and words. "Having a stable simulation is the basis of rewiring. I can't just let anything loose in your brain!"

"That would seem to be the definition of rewiring," Bao Lan said, with a tight smile. "At least as far as I'm concerned. I'm not a fool, child. All things come with their cost. I admit I didn't expect the price to be so high, but–"

"Not like that," Quynh Ha said. "Even if I make it take, you might wake up a vegetable. You might not wake up at all. You might be completely different."

"I'll be different in any case, no?"

"Yes, but–"

Bao Lan lifted a hand; and that same sense of presence filled the room; that same reminder that she was the Dust Queen, with decades of commanding the attention of Fire Watch. "I'm old, child, old enough to be your grandmother, as you and I well know. I've done my duty to Fire Watch. Now it's time for me to think of my ancestors; and to honour their graves. Tuyet is right; it's time for me to return home." She smiled a little; and in that moment the mask cracked, and the expression of vague longing on her face was the same as Grandmother's.

"The dust clouds–" Quynh Ha started, but Bao Lan shook her head.

"The dust clouds are only a thing." A brief expression of pain crossed her face, then; and was as swiftly gone. "Pieces of art I loved, yes; but if you cling too much to what you love, they destroy you in the end. I won't lie and say I won't miss them; but I can live without them."

She couldn't. She was the Dust Queen. She was–

No more dust clouds. No more performances; and worse than that, Bao Lan turning her back on them, on what they meant to Fire Watch – going home to die in obscurity, forgetting all that passion that had gone into making them; dismissing them as not important, as something that could be erased from her – no different, after all, from Mother, from Grandmother...

For a moment Quynh Ha stood frozen where she stood; and then the truth was torn out of her. "I – I can't help you. I just can't. I'm sorry." The Dust Queen stared at her, expressionless for a second; and then a look of mild disappointment gradually took over, as if Quynh Ha were six again, standing in the kitchen unit of the family compartment in a puddle of water and sugar she'd spilled on the floor – and a sense of growing, unbearable shame, unbearable fear that seemed to squeeze her heart into burning shards – and before she knew it, she was up and running out of the room, and a long way into the corridors of the orbital before she could catch her breath again.

It was Tuyet who found her, later; sitting moodily at the counter of the dispensary, staring into her console as if it could yield some unfathomable truth. Second Aunt had left her some noodle soup; and the aroma of star anise and beef marrow filled the shop, strong enough to overpower even the smells of drug compounds.

"I thought I'd find you here."

"I can't do it," Quynh Ha said. "I'm sorry I ran out, but there's just no way I can do it."

"Can't, or won't?" Tuyet asked, with disturbing perspicacity. "It's her wish. Why would you deny her that?"

As though a customer with excess asked her to remove cucumber seeds from a drug preparation: would she do it, if they assured her they'd weighed the effect of the harm on their own bodies? "She'll change," Quynh Ha said. "She might even regret it."

"Perhaps. But she's given enough thought to the consequences, hasn't she? In the end, it's what she wants, now."

"What would you do?"

Tuyet shrugged. "She's my mother. Of course I would do as she asks. 'Do no harm' only applies to doctors."

And she was only an apothecary. Quynh Ha smiled, bleakly. Shouldn't the customer's well-being take precedence over everything else? "She'll never be the same."

"Of course she won't. It's a rewiring that she wants to live with. You know how I feel about rewiring. It's hardly innocuous."

"She won't do any dust art, ever again," Quynh Ha said, finally; and knew that this was the truth, the rock bottom of her existence; her own crack around which everything was built. There were other artists, other people working in dust clouds; but none of them were Bao Lan.

Tuyet's face was carefully blank. "We all have our homes. We all have our childhood treasures. I've had my share of disagreement with Mother; but this is her choice, and I won't take it away from her."

And Quynh Ha would. "I – I can't do it. I told her the truth: it's a delicate procedure." She took in a deep breath – it hurt, to admit even that. "I can give you the name of someone else–"

"She trusted you."

"I know," Quynh Ha said; reliving, again and again, her conversation with Bao Lan; that awful moment when she'd frozen, and some incoherent mush had taken over her brain. "She'll learn to live without that trust. It will be easy." Depressingly so; after all, what need had the Dust Queen for broken tools? She'd go back to working in the dispensary for Second Aunt; burying that shame, that moment of failure deep into herself. Part of wisdom, Second Aunt always said, was knowing when you were outmatched, and this was the case – she knew what ought to be done, but couldn't even bring herself to contemplate the possibility of it.

Tuyet didn't speak for a moment. "I can take that name," she said at last. "I can bring them to Mother and have them perform the procedure–"

"Then do it!"

"Just answer me one question first, younger aunt: what will it do to you, if I do this?"

"I don't understand–"

Tuyet's smile was bitter. "I know all about regrets, younger aunt. Can you look me in the eye and tell me yours won't eat you up? That you had your chance to help the Dust Queen, and passed up on it?"

"I–" She was right; Quynh Ha knew it. "You asked if I couldn't, or if I wouldn't? The answer is that I... I can't knowingly remove Bao Lan's art from her – it would hurt me too much. She's right: it requires delicacy, and absolute control.

That's... not something I can provide." Not now; not ever – it was her childhood, her dreams, and how could she ever wreck them?

"As you wish." Tuyet's voice was stiff, carefully controlled. Disapproval, again. Well, she was no longer six years old, and Tuyet wasn't Mother or Second Aunt, not someone whose mere glance would induce burning shame. She would simply turn aside, and finish her soup; and go back to Second Aunt; and feel no regrets, none at all, over failing the Dust Queen in her moment of need.

No regrets...

Quynh Ha looked at the other's emotionless face, and heard her own voice again, stating the obvious. Absolute control. Delicacy. She was completely right: she couldn't provide it. Not in her current state.

But there was always a way to change one's current state.

Carefully, she laid her chopsticks on the side of the bowl, over the sodden remnants of cold noodles and wilted coriander. "Give me a minute," she said, "and I'll be with you."

Going into someone's brain is almost like being in space: that curious sensation of hanging, weightless, like floating in water without the water; of hanging in darkness with the stars around her like hairpin wounds in the fabric of the heavens.

Here, of course, there are no stars; but the wounds are memories – a dizzying array of them, every one of them so close she could touch them – and yet to reach out, to catch them all, would drive her insane under the weight of information and emotions that aren't hers.

She does reach out, all the same – because it's what she's here for, because it's the only thing she can decently do – and takes the images one by one, delicately threading her assemblage into their very fabric – adding longing and hurt and joy to memories of a cyclo weaving its way through the traffic of an overcrowded city; to images of plates strewn on red table cloth, of wrapped rice cakes, candied coconut and lotus seeds; to tombs in a graveyard, with paper money and paper houses burning in a copper dish; to an old woman on a roof in the midst of a flood, raising a fist at some officials in a boat...

And, as she does so, she sees the other memories – the ones of Cuoi and his banyan, of Khong Minh and his fan; of bots dancing in the dust, weaving images of villages and houses, with tiny figures running in the street, cutting the strings of kites for good fortune – she sees them shrivel a little, become a little smaller, a little more distant, like feelings of affection for acquaintances one sees once a year. She sees them wither and die, and knows that this is the end; that there will be no more Dust Queen, no more of her heartrending performances to tell them who they are.

It would have made her cry, once; would have stopped her in her tracks as she weaves through memory after memory, spreading the crack to every single image of the Mekong Delta. There's one performance in particular that she would have been unable to see without wrecking everything: a New Year's Eve with no special meaning; another worship of the ancestors, another meal with the family – save that this was the New Year's Eve when she understood at last – the New Year's Eve where she took Bao Lan's message into herself, when she knew with absolute certainty that the banyan's roots now were in the planet itself; that her children's children would leave their own footprints in the red dust, and bring to life their own legends on the red soil.

But all those memories of performances, the good, the bad, the heartbreaking – they're all sealed under glass, tinted the colour of old, obsolete photographs – preserved under glass in that temporary stasis, where nothing matters, where nothing hurts.

It doesn't have to be temporary, of course – she could make it last forever, but she's not Bao Lan, and she won't live with her childhood memories cut off. Bao Lan did what she had to, to survive – and, in the end, so will she. She will keep the performances, and remember the way they showed: forward, into a future where Mars belongs to her descendants; and further on, perhaps – when humanity is spread among the stars, like so many grains of rice in fallow fields.

SHE SAW THEM off at the spaceport, afterwards.

"We've got you something else," Bao Lan said – handing her a velvet box, which contained a piece of translucent jade the colour of the pandan leaves in Bao Lan's memories. "In addition to your payment. I know it's not much, but this is with my gratitude." She held herself hunched now, with the same familiar hurt in her eyes all the time; the same look Quynh Ha knew all too well from Mother, from Grandmother. The Dust Queen – that tall, imperious figure that had brought attention to a room by simply lifting her hand – was no more.

Quynh Ha took the jade: it was engraved, with a simple design of a man in a banyan tree. She felt queasy, as though she would weep; though it might simply have been part of the after effects of undoing her rewiring. What was it Tuyet had said? Hardly innocuous. Perhaps that was the truth of all rewirings. "Thank you. Have a safe journey home, both of you."

"We probably won't see each other again," Tuyet said. "But I hope you live a long life, with the ancestors' blessings on your health and children."

Quynh Ha nodded, accepting the traditional parting. "Thank you for believing in me," she said.

Tuyet smiled. "You were Mother's choice; and she's seldom wrong."

And then they were gone; leaving her alone once more. She

came to stand before the screens, watching their shuttle depart from Fire Watch – the ion drives lighting up in the darkness, before they were altogether gone on their months-long journey back to Earth – and the huge image of Mars appeared once more on the screen, with a few dots denoting the cyanobacteria greenhouses.

No more dust clouds.

She raised the jade to the light, until the image of Cuoi in the banyan was superimposed on the red planet; and thought of Bao Lan, hunched and subdued and entirely unlike who she had been.

"Safe journeys," she whispered; and wondered if she'd ever be able to forgive herself, for sending the Dust Queen home.

THE FIFTH DRAGON

Ian McDonald

THE SCAN WAS routine. Every moon worker has one every four lunes. Achi was called, she went into the scanner. The machine passed magnetic fields through her body and when she came out the medic said, you have four weeks left.

WE MET ON the Vorontsov Trans-Orbital cycler but didn't have sex. We talked instead about names.

"Corta. That's not a Brazilian name," Achi said. I didn't know her well enough then, eight hours out from transfer orbit, to be my truculent self and insist that any name can be a Brazilian name, that we are a true rainbow nation. So I told her that my name had rolled through many peoples and languages like a bottle in a breaker until it was cast up sand-scoured and clouded on the beaches of Barra. And now I was taking it on again, up to the moon.

Achi Debasso. Another name rolled by the tide of history. London born, London raised, M.I.T. educated but she never forgot – had never been let forget – that she was Syrian. Syriac. That one letter was a universe of difference. Her family had fled the civil war, she had been born in exile. Now she was headed into a deeper exile.

I didn't mean to be in the centrifuge pod with Achi. There was a guy; he'd looked and I looked back and nodded *yes, I will, yes* even as the OTV made its distancing burn from the cycler. I took it. I'm no prude. I've got the New Year Barra beach bangles. I'm up for a party and more, and everyone's heard about (here they move in close and mouth the words) *freefall sex*. I wanted to try it with this guy. And I couldn't stop throwing up. I was not up for zero gee. It turned everything inside me upside down. Puke poured out of me. That's not sexy. So I retreated to gravity and the only other person in the centrifuge arm was this caramel-eyed girl, slender hands and long fingers, her face flickering every few moments into an unconscious micro-frown. Inward-gazing, self-loathing, scattering geek references like anti-personnel mines. Up in the hub our co-workers fucked. Down in the centrifuge pod we talked and the stars and the moon arced across the window beneath our feet.

A Brazilian miner and a London-Syriac ecologist. The centrifuge filled as freefall sex palled but we kept talking. The next day the guy I had puked over caught my eye again but I sought out Achi, on her own in the same spot, looking out at the moon. And the whirling moon was a little bigger in the observation port and we knew each other a little better and by the end of the week the moon filled the whole of the window and we had moved from conversationalists into friends.

ACHI: LEFT DAMASCUS as a cluster of cells tumbling in her mother's womb. And that informed her every breath and touch. She felt guilty for escaping. Father was a software engineer, mother was a physiotherapist. London welcomed them.

Adriana: seven of us: seven Cortas. Little cuts. I was in the middle, loved and adored but told solemnly I was plain and thick in the thighs and would have be thankful for whatever life granted me.

Achi: a water girl. Her family home was near the Olympic pool – her mother had dropped her into water days out of the hospital.

She had sunk, then she swam. Swimmer and surfer: long British summer evenings on the western beaches. Cold British water. She was small and quiet but feared no wave.

Adriana: born with the sound of the sea in her room but never learned to swim. I splash, I paddle, I wade. I come from beach people, not ocean people.

Achi: the atoner. She could not change the place or order of her birth, but she could apologise for it by being useful. Useful Achi. Make things right!

Adriana: the plain. Mãe and papai thought they were doing me a favour; allowing me no illusions or false hopes that could blight my life. Marry as well as you can; be happy: that will have to do. Not this Corta. I was the kid who shot her hand up at school. The girl who wouldn't shut up when the boys were talking. Who never got picked for the futsal team – okay, I would find my own sport. I did Brazilian jujitsu. Sport for one. No one messed with plain Adriana.

Achi: grad at UCL, post-grad at M.I.T. Her need to be useful took her battling desertification, salinisation, eutrophication. She was an -ation warrior. In the end it took her to the moon. No way to be more useful than sheltering and feeding a whole world.

Adriana: university at São Paulo. And my salvation. Where I learned that plain didn't matter as much as available, and I was sweet for sex with boys and girls. Fuckfriends. Sweet girls don't have fuckfriends. And sweet girls don't study mining engineering. Like jujitsu, like hooking up, that was a thing for me, me alone. Then the economy gave one final, apocalyptic crash at the bottom of a series of drops and hit the ground and broke so badly no one could see how to fix it. And the seaside, be-happy Cortas were in ruins, jobless, investments in ashes. It was plain Adriana who said, I can save you. I'll go to the Moon.

All this we knew by the seventh day of the orbit out. On the eight day, we rendezvoused with the transfer tether and spun down to the new world.

The freefall sex? Grossly oversold. Everything moves in all the wrong ways. Things get away from you. You have to strap everything down to get purchase. It's more like mutual bondage.

I WAS SINTERING ten kilometres ahead of Crucible when Achi's call came. I had requested the transfer from Mackenzie Metals to Vorontsov Rail. The forewoman had been puzzled when I reported to Railhead. You're a dustbunny not a track-queen. Surface work is surface work, I said and that convinced her. The work was good, easy and physical and satisfying. And it was on the surface. At the end of every up-shift you saw six new lengths of gleaming rail among the boot and track prints, and on the edge of the horizon, the blinding spark of Crucible, brighter than any star, advancing over yesterday's rails, and you said, I made that. The work had real measure: the inexorable advance of Mackenzie Metals across the Mare Insularum, brighter than the brightest star. Brighter than sunrise, so bright it could burn a hole through your helmet sunscreen if you held it in your eye line too long. Thousands of concave mirrors focusing sunlight on the smelting crucibles. Three years from now the rail lines would circle the globe and the Crucible would follow the sun, bathed in perpetual noon. Me, building a railroad around the moon.

Then ting ching and it all came apart. Achi's voice blocking out my work-mix music, Achi's face superimposed on the dirty grey hills of Rimae Maestlin. Achi telling me her routine medical had given her four weeks.

I hitched a ride on the construction car back down the rails to Crucible. I waited two hours hunkered down in the hard-vacuum shadows, tons of molten metal and ten thousand Kelvin sunlight above my head, for an expensive ticket on a slow Mackenzie ore train to Meridian. Ten hours clinging onto a maintenance platform, not even room to turn around, let alone sit. Grey dust, black sky... I listened my way through my collection of historical bossanova, from the 1940s to the 1970s. I played Connecto on my helmet hud until every time I blinked I saw tumbling, spinning gold stars. I scanned my family's social space entries and threw my thoughts and comments and good wishes at the big blue Earth. By the time I got to Meridian I was two degrees off hypothermic. My surface activity suit was rated for a shift and some scramble time, not twelve hours in the open. Should have claimed compensation. But I didn't want my former employers paying too much attention to me. I couldn't afford the time it would take to re-pressurise for the train, so I went dirty and fast, on the BALTRAN.

I knew I would vomit. I held it until the third and final jump. BALTRAN: Ballistic Transport system. The moon has no atmosphere – well, it does, a very thin one, which is getting thicker as human settlements leak air into it. Maybe in a few centuries this will become a problem for vacuum industries, but to all intents and purposes, it's a vacuum. See what I did there? That's the engineer in me. No atmosphere means ballistic trajectories can be calculated with great precision. Which means, throw something up and you know exactly where it will fall to moon again. Bring in positionable electromagnetic launchers and you have a mechanism for schlepping material quick and dirty around the moon. Launch it, catch it in a receiver, boost it on again. It's like juggling. The BALTRAN is not always used for cargo. If you can take the gees, it can just as easily juggle people across the moon.

I held it until the final jump. You cannot imagine what it is like to throw up in your helmet. In free fall. People have died. The look on the BALTRAN attendant's face when I came out of the capsule at Queen of the South was a thing to be seen. So I am told. I couldn't see it. But if I could afford the capsule I could afford the shower to clean up. And there are people in Queen who will happily clean vomit out of a sasuit for the right number of bitsies. Say what you like about the Vorontsovs, they pay handsomely.

All this I did, the endless hours riding the train like a moon-hobo, the hypothermia and being sling-shotted in a can of my own barf, because I knew that if Achi had four weeks, I could not be far behind.

YOU DON'T THINK about the bones. As a Jo Moonbeam, everything is so new and demanding, from working out how to stand and walk, to those four little digits in the bottom right corner of your field of vision that tell you how much you owe the Lunar Development Corporation for air, water, space and web. The first time you see those numbers change because demand or supply or market price has shifted, your breath catches in your throat. Nothing tells you more that you are not on Earth any more than exhaling at one price and inhaling at another. Everything – *everything* – was new and hard.

Everything other than your bones. After two years on the moon human bone structure atrophies to a point where return to Earth gravity is almost certainly fatal. The medics drop it almost incidentally into your initial assessment. It can take days – weeks – for its ripples to touch your life. Then you feel your bones crumbling away, flake by flake, inside your body. And there's not a thing you can do about it. What it means is that there is a calcium clock ticking inside your body, counting down to Moon Day. The day you decide: do I stay or do I go?

In those early days we were scared all the time, Achi and I. I looked after her – I don't know how we fell into those roles, protector and defended, but I protected and she nurtured and we won respect. There were three moon men for every moon woman. It was a man's world; a macho social meld of soldiers camped in enemy terrain and deep-diving submariners. The Jo Moonbeam barracks were exactly that; a grey, dusty warehouse of temporary accommodation cabins barely the safe legal minimum beneath the surface. We learned quickly the vertical hierarchy of moon society: the lower you live – the further from surface radiation and secondary cosmic rays – the higher your status. The air was chilly and stank of sewage, electricity, dust and unwashed bodies. The air still smells like that; I just got used to the funk in my lungs. Within hours the induction barracks self-sorted. The women gravitated together and affiliated with the astronomers on placement with the Farside observatory. Achi and I traded to get cabins beside each other. We visited, we decorated, we entertained, we opened our doors in solidarity and hospitality. We listened to the loud voices of the men, the real men, the worldbreakers, booming down the aisles of cabins, the over-loud laughter. We made cocktails from cheap industrial vodka.

Sexual violence, games of power were in the air we breathed, the water we drank, the narrow corridors through which we squeezed, pressing up against each other. The moon has never had criminal law, only contract law, and when Achi and I arrived the LDC was only beginning to set up the Court of Clavius to settle and enforce contracts. Queen of the South was a wild town. Fatalities among Jo Moonbeams ran at ten percent. In our first week, an extraction worker from Xinjiang was crushed in a pressure lock. The Moon knows a thousand ways to kill you. And I knew a thousand and one.

Cortas cut. That was our family legend. Hard sharp fast. I made the women's Brazilian jujitsu team at university. It's hard, sharp, fast: the perfect Corta fighting art. A couple of basic moves, together with lunar gravity, allowed me to put over the most intimidating of sex pests. But when Achi's stalker wouldn't take no, I reached for slower, subtler weapons. Stalkers don't go away. That's what makes them stalkers. I found which Surface Activity training squad he was on and made some adjustments to his suit thermostat. He didn't die. He wasn't meant to die.

Death would have been easier than my revenge for Achi. He never suspected me; he never suspected anyone. I made it look like a perfect malfunction. I'm a good engineer. I count his frostbite thumb and three toes as my trophies. By the time he got out of the med centre, Achi and I were on our separate ways to our contracts.

That was another clock, ticking louder than the clock in our bones. I&A was four weeks. After that, we would go to work. Achi's work in ecological habitats would take her to the underground agraria the Asamoah family were digging under Amundsen. My contract was with Mackenzie Metals; working out on the open seas. Working with dust. Dustbunny. We clung to the I&A barracks, we clung to our cabins, our friends. We clung to each other. We were scared. Truth: we were scared all the time, with every breath. Everyone on the moon is scared, all the time.

There was a party; moon mojitos. Vodka and mint are easy up here. But before the music and the drinking: a special gift for Achi. Her work with Aka would keep her underground; digging and scooping and sowing. She need never go on the surface. She could go her whole career – her whole life – in the caverns and lava tubes and agraria. She need never see the raw sky.

The suit hire was cosmologically expensive, even after negotiation. It was a GP surface activity shell; an armoured hulk to my lithe sasuit spiderwoman. Her face was nervous behind the faceplate; her breathing shallow. We held hands in the outlock as the pressure door slid up. Then her faceplate polarised in the sun and I could not see her any more. We walked up the ramp amongst a hundred thousand boot prints. We walked up the ramp and a few metres out on to the surface, still holding hands. There, beyond the coms towers and the power relays and the charging points for the buses and rovers; beyond the grey line of the crater rim that curved on the close horizon and the shadows the sun had never touched; there perched above the edge of our tiny world we saw the full earth. Full and blue and white, mottled with greens and ochres. Full and impossible and beautiful beyond any words of mine. It was winter and the southern hemisphere was offered to us; the ocean half of the planet. I saw great Africa. I saw dear Brazil.

Then the air contract advisory warned me that we were nearing the expiry of our oxygen contract and we turned out backs on the blue earth and walked back down into the moon.

That night we drank to our jobs, our friends, our loves and our bones. In the morning we parted.

WE MET IN a café on the twelfth level of the new Chandra Quadra. We hugged, we kissed, we cried a little. I smelled sweet by then. Below us excavators dug and sculpted, a new level every ten days. We held each other at arms' length and looked at each other. Then we drank mint tea on the balcony.

I loathe mint tea.

Mint tea is a fistful of herbs jammed in a glass. Sloshed with boiling water. Served scalded yet still flavourless. Effete like herbal thés and tisanes. Held between thumb and forefinger: so. Mint leaves are coarse and hairy. Mint tea is medicinal. Add sugar and it becomes infantile. It is drinking for the sake of doing something with your fingers.

Coffee is a drink for grownups. No kid ever likes coffee. It's psychoactive. Coffee is the drug of memory. I can remember the great cups of coffee of my life; the places, the faces, the words spoken. It never quite tastes the way it smells. If it did, we would drink it until our heads exploded with memory.

But coffee is not an efficient crop in our ecology. And imported coffee is more expensive than gold. Gold is easy. Gold I can sift from lunar regolith. Gold is so easy its only value is decorative. It isn't even worth the cost of shipment to Earth. Mint is rampant. Under lunar gravity, it forms plants up to three metres tall. So we are a nation of mint tea drinkers.

We didn't talk about the bones at once. It was eight lunes since we last saw each other: we talk on the network daily, we share our lives but it takes face to face contact to ground all that; make it real.

I made Achi laugh. She laughed like soft rain. I told her about King Dong and she clapped her hands to her mouth in naughty glee but laughed with her eyes. King Dong started as a joke but shift by shift was becoming reality. Footprints last forever on the moon, a bored surface worker had said on a slow shift rotation back to Crucible. What if we stamped out a giant spunking cock, a hundred kilometres long? With hairy balls. Visible from Earth. It's just a matter of co-ordination. Take a hundred male surface workers and an Australian extraction company and joke becomes temptation becomes reality. So wrong. So funny.

And Achi?

She was out of contract. The closer you are to your Moon Day, the shorter the contract, sometimes down to minutes of employment, but this was different. Aka did not want her ideas any more. They were recruiting direct from Accra and Kumasi. Ghanaians for a Ghanaian company. She was pitching ideas to the Lunar Development Corporation for their new port and capital at Meridian – quadras three kilometres deep; a sculpted city; like living in the walls of a titanic cathedral. The LDC was polite but it had been talking about development funding for two lunes now. Her savings were running low. She woke up looking at the tick of the Four Fundamentals on her lens. Oxygen water space coms: which do you cut down on first? She was considering moving to a smaller space.

"I can pay your per diems," I said. "I have lots of money."

And then the bones... Achi could not decide until I got my report. I never knew anyone who suffered from guilt as acutely as her. She could not have borne it if her decision had influenced my decision to stay with the moon or go back to Earth.

"I'll go now," I said. I didn't want to. I didn't want to be here on this balcony drinking piss-tea. I didn't want Achi to have forced a decision on me. I didn't want there to be a decision for me to make. "I'll get the tea."

Then the wonder. In the corner of my vision, a flash of gold. A lens malfunction – no, something marvellous. A woman flying. A flying woman. Her arms were outspread, she hung in the sky like a crucifix. Our Lady of Flight. Then I saw wings shimmer and run with rainbow colours; wings transparent and strong as a dragonfly's. The woman hung a moment, then folded her gossamer wings around her, and fell. She tumbled, now diving head-first, flicked her wrists, flexed her shoulders. A glimmer of wing slowed her; then she spread her full wing span and pulled up out of her dive into a soaring spiral, high into the artificial sky of Chandra Quadra.

"Oh," I said. I had been holding my breath. I was shaking with wonder. I was chewed by jealousy.

"We always could fly," Achi said. "We just haven't had the space. Until now."

Did I hear irritation in Achi's voice, that I was so bewitched by the flying woman? But if you could fly why would you ever do anything else?

I WENT TO the Mackenzie Metals medical centre and the medic put me in the scanner. He passed magnetic fields through my body and the machine gave me my bone density analysis. I was eight days behind Achi. Five weeks, and then my residency on the moon would become citizenship.

Or I could fly back to Earth, to Brazil.

THERE ARE FRIENDS and there are friends you have sex with.

After I&A it was six lunes until I saw Achi again. Six lunes in the Sea of Fertility, sifting dust. The Mackenzie Metals

Messier unit was old, cramped, creaking: cut-and-cover pods under bulldozed regolith berms. Too frequently I was evacuated to the new, lower levels by the radiation alarm. Cosmic rays kicked nasty secondary particles out of moon dust, energetic enough to penetrate the upper levels of the unit. Every time I saw the alarm flash its yellow trefoil in my lens I felt my ovaries tighten. Day and night the tunnels trembled to the vibration of the digging machines, deep beneath even those evacuation tunnels, eating rock. There were two hundred dustbunnies in Messier. After a month's gentle and wary persistence and charm from a 3D print designer, I joined the end of a small amory: my Chu-yu, his homamor in Queen, his hetamor in Meridian, her hetamor also in Meridian. What had taken him so long, Chu-yu confessed, was my rep. Word about the sex pest on I&A with the unexplained suit malfunction. *I wouldn't do that to a co-worker,* I said. *Not unless severely provoked.* Then I kissed him. The amory was warmth and sex, but it wasn't Achi. Lovers are not friends

Sun Chu-yu understood that when I kissed him goodbye at Messier's bus lock. Achi and I chatted on the network all the way to the railhead at Hypatia, then all the way down the line to the South. Even then, only moments since I had last spoken to her image on my eyeball, it was a physical shock to see her at the meeting point in Queen of the South station: her, physical her. Shorter than I remembered. Absence makes the heart grow taller.

Such fun she had planned for me! I wanted to dump my stuff at her place but no; she whirled me off into excitement. After the reek and claustrophobia of Messier Queen of the South was intense, loud, colourful, too too fast. In only six lunes it had changed beyond recognition. Every street was longer, every tunnel wider, every chamber loftier. When she took me in a glass elevator down the side of the recently completed Thoth Quadra I reeled from vertigo. Down on the floor of the massive cavern was a small copse of dwarf trees – full-size trees would reach the ceiling, Achi explained. There was a café. In that café I first tasted and immediately hated mint tea.

I built this, Achi said. *These are my trees, this is my garden.*

I was too busy looking up at the lights, all the lights, going up and up.

Such fun! Tea, then shops. I had had to find a party dress. We were going to a special party, that night. Exclusive. We browsed the catalogues in five different print shops before I found something I could wear: very retro, 1950s inspired, full and layered, it hid what I wanted hidden. Then, the shoes.

The special party was exclusive to Achi's workgroup and their F&Fs. A security-locked rail capsule took us through a dark tunnel into a space so huge, so blinding with mirrored light that once again I reeled on my feet and almost threw up over my Balenciaga. An agrarium, Achi's last project. I was at the bottom of a shaft a kilometre tall, half that wide, fifty metres broad. The horizon is close at eye level on the moon; everything curves. Underground, a different geometry applies. The agrarium was the straightest thing I had seen in months. And brilliant: a central core of mirrors ran the full height of the shaft, bouncing raw sunlight one to another to another to walls terraced with hydroponic racks. The base of the shaft was a mosaic of fish tanks, criss-crossed by walkways. The air was warm and dank and rank. I was woozy with CO_2. In these conditions plants grew fast and tall; potato plants the size of bushes; tomato vines so tall I lost their heads in the tangle of leaves and fruit. Hyper-intensive agriculture: the agrarium was huge for a cave, small for an ecosystem. The tanks splashed with fish. Did I hear frogs? Were those ducks?

Achi's team had built a new pond from waterproof sheeting and construction frame. A pool. A swimming pool. A sound system played G-pop. There were cocktails. Blue was the fashion. They matched my dress. Achi's crew were friendly and expansive. They never failed to compliment me on my fashion. I shucked it and my shoes and everything else for the pool. I lolled, I luxuriated, I let the strange, chaotic eddies waft green, woozy air over me while over my head the mirrors moved. Achi swam up beside me and we trod water together, laughing and plashing. The agrarium crew had lowered a number of benches into the pool to make a shallow end. Achi and I wafted blood-warm water with our legs and drank Blue Moons.

I am always up for a party.

I woke up in bed beside her the next morning; shit-headed with moon vodka. I remembered mumbling, fumbling love. Shivering and stupid-whispering, skin to skin. Fingerworks. Achi lay curled on her right side, facing me. She had kicked the sheet off in the night. A tiny string of drool ran from the corner of her mouth to the pillow and trembled in time to her breathing.

I looked at her there, her breath rattling in the back of her throat in drunk sleep. We had made love. I had had sex with my dearest friend. I had done a good thing, I had done a bad thing. I had done an irrevocable thing. Then I lay down and pressed myself in close to her and she mumble-grumbled and moved in close to me and her fingers found me and we began again.

I WOKE IN the dark with the golden woman swooping through my head. Achi slept beside me. The same side, the same curl of the spine, the same light rattle-snore and open mouth as that first night. When I saw Achi's new cabin, I booked us into a hostel. The bed was wide, the air was as fresh as Queen of the South could make and the taste of the water did not set your teeth on edge.

Golden woman, flying loops through my certainties.

Queen of the South never went fully dark – lunar society is 24-hour society. I pulled Achi's unneeded sheet around me and went out on to the balcony. I leaned on the rail and looked out at the walls of lights. Apts, cabins, walkways and staircases. Lives and decisions behind every light. This was an ugly world. Hard and mean. It put a price on everything. It demanded a negotiation from everyone. Out at Railhead I had seen a new thing among some of the surface workers: a medallion, or a little votive tucked into a patch pocket. A woman in Virgin Mary robes, one half of her face a black angel, the other half a naked skull. Dona Luna: goddess of dust and radiation. Our Lady Liberty, our Britannia, our Marianne, our Mother Russia. One half of her face dead, but the other alive. The moon was not a dead satellite, it was a living world. Hands and hearts and hopes like mine shaped it. There was no Mother Nature, no Gaia to set against human will. Everything that lived, we made. Dona Luna was hard and unforgiving, but she was beautiful. She could be a woman, with dragonfly wings, flying.

I stayed on the hotel balcony until the roof reddened with sun-up. Then I went back to Achi. I wanted to make love with her again. My motives were all selfish. Things that are difficult with friends are easier with lovers.

My GRANDMOTHER USED to say that love was the easiest thing in the world. Love is what you see every day.

I did not see Achi for several lunes after the party in Queen. Mackenzie Metals sent me out into the field, prospecting new terrain in the Sea of Vapours. Away from Messier, it was plain to me and Sun Chu-yu that the amory didn't work. You love what you see every day. All the amors were happy for me to leave. No blame, no claim. A simple automated contract, terminated.

I took a couple of weeks furlough back in Queen. I had called Achi about hooking up but she was at a new dig at Twe, where the Asamoahs were building a corporate headquarters. I was relieved. And then was guilty that I had felt relieved. Sex had made everything different. I drank, I partied, I had one night stands, I talked long hours of expensive bandwidth with my loved ones back on Earth. They thanked me for the money, especially the tiny kids. They said I looked different. Longer. Drawn out. My bones eroding, I said. There they were, happy and safe. The money I sent them bought their education. Health, weddings, babies. And here I was, on the moon. Plain Adriana, who would never get a man, but who got the education, who got the degree, who got the job, sending them the money from the moon.

They were right. I was different. I never felt the same about that blue pearl of Earth in the sky. I never again hired a sasuit to go look at it, just look at it. Out on the surface, I disregarded it.

The Mackenzies sent me out next to the Lansberg extraction zone and I saw the thing that made everything different.

Five extractors were working Lansberg. They were ugly towers of Archimedes screws and grids and transport belts and wheels three times my height, all topped out by a spread of solar panels that made them look like robot trees. Slow-moving, cumbersome, inelegant. Lunar design tends to the utilitarian, the practical. The bones on show. But to me they were beautiful. Marvellous trees. I saw them one day, out on the regolith, and I almost fell flat from the revelation. Not what they made – separating rare earth metals from lunar regolith – but what they threw away. Launched in high, arching ballistic jets on either side of the big, slow machines.

It was the thing I saw every day. One day you look at the boy on the bus and he sets your heart alight. One day you look at the jets of industrial waste and you see riches beyond measure.

I had to dissociate myself from anything that might link me to regolith waste and beautiful rainbows of dust.

I quit Mackenzie and became a Vorontsov track queen.

* * *

I WANT TO make a game of it, Achi said. That's the only way I can bear it. We must clench our fists behind our backs, like Scissors Paper Stone, and we must count to three, and then we open our fists and in them there will be something, some small object that will say beyond any doubt what we have decided. We must not speak, because if we say even a word, we will influence each other. That's the only way I can bear it, if it is quick and clean and we don't speak. And a game.

We went back to the balcony table of the café to play the game. It was now on the 13th level. Two glasses of mint tea. No one was flying the great empty spaces of Chandra Quadra this day. The air smelled of rock dust over the usual electricity and sewage. Every fifth sky panel was blinking. An imperfect world.

Attempted small talk. Do you want some breakfast? No, but you have some. No I'm not hungry. I haven't seen that top before. The colour is really good for you. Oh it's just something I printed out of a catalogue... Horrible awful little words to stop us saying what we really had to stay.

"I think we should do this kind of quickly," Achi said finally and in a breathtaking instant her right hand was behind her back. I slipped my small object out of my bag, clenched it in my hidden fist.

"One two three," Achi said. We opened our fists.

A *nazar*: an Arabic charm: concentric teardrops of blue, white and black plastic. An eye.

A tiny icon of Dona Luna: black and white, living and dead.

THEN I SAW Achi again. I was up in Meridian renting a data crypt and hunting for the leanest, freshest, hungriest law firm to protect the thing I had realised out on Lansberg. She had been called back from Twe to solve a problem with microbiota in the Obuasi agrarium that had left it a tower of stinking black slime.

One city; two friends and amors. We went out to party. And

found we couldn't. The frocks were fabulous, the cocktails disgraceful, the company louche and the narcotics dazzling but in each bar, club, private party we ended up in a corner together, talking.

Partying was boring. Talk was lovely and bottomless and fascinating.

We ended up in bed again, of course. We couldn't wait. Glorious, impractical 1950s Dior frocks lay crumpled on the floor, ready for the recycler.

"What do you want?" Achi asked. She lay on her bed, inhaling THC from a vaper. "Dream and don't be afraid."

"Really?"

"Moon dreams."

"I want to be a dragon," I said and Achi laughed and punched me on the thigh: *get away*. "No, seriously."

In the year and a half we had been on the moon, our small world had changed. Things move fast on the moon. Energy and raw materials are cheap, human genius plentiful. Ambition boundless. Four companies had emerged as major economic forces: four families. The Australian Mackenzies were the longest established. They had been joined by the Asamoahs, whose company Aka monopolised food and living space. The Russian Vorontsovs finally moved their operations off Earth entirely and ran the cycler, the moonloop, the bus service and the emergent rail network. Most recent to amalgamate were the Suns, who had defied the representatives of the People's Republic on the LDC board and ran the information infrastructure. Four companies: Four Dragons. That was what they called themselves. The Four Dragons of the Moon.

"I want to be the Fifth Dragon," I said.

THE LAST THINGS were simple and swift. All farewells should be sudden, I think. I booked Achi on the cycler out. There was always space on the return orbit. She booked me into the LDC medical centre. A flash of light and the lens was bonded permanently to my eye. No hand shake, no congratulations, no welcome. All I had done was decide to continue doing what I was doing. The four counters ticked, charging me to live.

I cashed in the return part of the flight and invested the lump sum in convertible LDC bonds. Safe, solid. On this foundation would I build my dynasty.

The cycler would come round the Farside and rendezvous with the moonloop in three days. Good speed. Beautiful haste. It kept us busy, it kept us from crying too much.

I went with Achi on the train to Meridian. We had a whole row of seats to ourselves and we curled up like small burrowing animals.

I'm scared, she said. It's going to hurt. The cycler spins you up to Earth gravity and then there's the gees coming down. I could be months in a wheelchair. Swimming, they say that's the closest to being on the moon. The water supports you while you build up muscle and bone mass again. I can do that. I love swimming. And then you can't help thinking, what if they got it wrong? What if, I don't know, they mixed me up with someone else and it's already too late? Would they send me back here? I couldn't live like that. No one can live here. Not really live. Everyone says about the moon being rock and dust and vacuum and radiation and that it knows a thousand ways to kill you, but that's not the moon. The moon is other people. People all the way up, all the way down; everywhere, all the time. Nothing but people. Every breath, every drop of water, every atom of carbon has been passed through people. We eat each other. And that's all it would ever be, people. The same faces looking into your face, forever. Wanting something from you. Wanting and wanting and wanting. I hated it from the first day out on the cycler. If you hadn't talked to me, if we hadn't met...

And I said: *Do you remember, when we talked about what had brought us to the moon?* You said that you owed your family for not being born in Syria – and I said I wanted to be a dragon? I saw it. Out in Lansberg. It was so simple. I just looked at something I saw every day in a different way. Helium 3. The key to the post oil economy. Mackenzie Metals throws away tons of helium 3 every day. And I thought, how could the Mackenzies not see it? Surely they must... I couldn't be the only one... But family and companies, and family companies especially, they have strange fixations and blindesses. Mackenzies mine metal. Metal mining is what they do. They can't imagine anything else and so they miss what's right under their noses. I can make it work, Achi. I know how to do it. But not with the Mackenzies. They'd take it off me. If I tried to fight them, they'd just bury me. Or kill me. It's cheaper. The Court of Clavius would make sure my family were compensated. That's why I moved to Vorontsov rail. To get away from them while I put a business plan together. I will make it work for me, and I'll build a dynasty. I'll be the Fifth Dragon. House Corta. I like the sound of that. And then I'll make an offer to my family – my final offer. Join me, or never get another cent from me. There's the opportunity – take it or leave it. But you have to come to the moon for it. I'm going to do this, Achi.

No windows in moon trains but the seat-back screen showed the surface. On a screen, outside your helmet, it is always the same. It is grey and soft and ugly and covered in footprints. Inside the train were workers and engineers; lovers and partners and even a couple of small children. There was noise and colour and drinking and laughing, swearing and sex. And us curled up in the back against the bulkhead. And I thought, *this is the moon*.

ACHI GAVE ME a gift at the moonloop gate. It was the last thing she owned. Everything else had been sold, the last few things while we were on the train.

Eight passengers at the departure gate, with friends, family, amors. No one left the moon alone and I was glad of that. The air smelled of coconut, so different from the vomit, sweat, unwashed bodies, fear of the arrival gate. Mint tea was available from a dispensing machine. No one was drinking it.

"Open this when I'm gone," Achi said. The gift was a document cylinder, crafted from bamboo. The departure was fast, the way I imagine executions must be. The VTO staff had everyone strapped into their seats and were sealing the capsule door before either I or Achi could respond. I saw her begin to mouth a goodbye, saw her wave fingers, then the locks sealed and the elevator took the capsule up to the tether platform.

The moonloop was virtually invisible: a spinning spoke of M5 fibre twenty centimetres wide and two hundred kilometres long. Up there the ascender was climbing towards the counterbalance mass, shifting the centre of gravity and sending the whole tether down into a surface-grazing orbit. Only in the final moments of approach would I see the white cable seeming to descend vertically from the star filled sky. The grapple connected and the capsule was lifted from the platform. Up there, one of those bright stars was the ascender, sliding down the tether, again shifting the centre of mass so that the whole ensemble moved into a higher orbit. At the top of the loop, the grapple would release and the cycler catch the capsule. I tried to put names on the stars: the cycler, the ascender, the counterweight; the capsule freighted with my amor, my love, my friend. The comfort of physics. I watched the images, the bamboo document tube slung over my back, until a new capsule was loaded into the gate. Already the next tether was wheeling up over the close horizon.

The price was outrageous. I dug into my bonds. For that sacrifice it had to be the real thing: imported, not spun up from an organic printer. I was sent from printer to dealer to private importer. She let me sniff it. Memories exploded like New Year fireworks and I cried. She sold me the paraphernalia as well. The equipment I needed simply didn't exist on the moon.

I took it all back to my hotel. I ground to the specified grain. I boiled the water. I let it cool to the correct temperature. I poured it from a height, for maximum aeration. I stirred it.

While it brewed I opened Achi's gift. Rolled paper: drawings. Concept art for the habitat the realities of the moon would never let her build. A lava tube, enlarged and sculpted with faces, like an inverted Mount Rushmore. The faces of the orixas, the Umbanda pantheon, each a hundred metres high, round and smooth and serene, overlooked terraces of gardens and pools. Waters cascaded from their eyes and open lips. Pavilions and belvederes were scattered across the floor of the vast cavern; vertical gardens ran from floor to artificial sky, like the hair of the gods. Balconies – she loved balconies – galleries and arcades, windows. Pools. You could swim from one end of this Orixa-world to the other. She had inscribed it: *a habitation for a dynasty*.

I thought of her, spinning away across the sky.

The grounds began to settle. I plunged, poured and savoured the aroma of the coffee. Santos Gold. Gold would have been cheaper. Gold was the dirt we threw away, together with the Helium 3.

When the importer had rubbed a pinch of ground coffee under my nose, memories of childhood, the sea, college, friends, family, celebrations flooded me.

When I smelled the coffee I had bought and ground and prepared, I experienced something different. I had a vision. I saw the sea, and I saw Achi, Achi-gone-back, on a board, in the sea. It was night and she was paddling the board out, through the waves and beyond the waves, sculling herself forward, along the silver track of the moon on the sea.

I drank my coffee.

It never tastes the way it smells.

*   *   *

MY GRANDDAUGHTER ADORES that red dress. When it gets dirty and worn, we print her a new one. She wants never to wear anything else. Luna, running barefoot through the pools, splashing and scaring the fish, leaping from stepping stone, stepping in a complex pattern of stones that must be landed on left footed, right footed, two footed or skipped over entirely. The Orixas watch her. The Orixas watch me, on my veranda, drinking tea.

I am old bones now. I haven't thought of you for years, Achi. The last time was when I finally turned those drawings into reality. But these last lunes I find my thoughts folding back, not just to you, but to all the ones from those dangerous, daring days. There were more loves than you, Achi. You always knew that. I treated most of them as badly as I treated you. It's the proper pursuit of elderly ladies, remembering and trying not to regret.

I never heard from you again. That was right, I think. You went back to your green and growing world, I stayed in the land in the sky. Hey! I built your palace and filled it with that dynasty I promised. Sons and daughters, amors, okos, madrinhas, retainers. Corta is not such a strange name to you now, or most of Earth's population. Mackenzie, Sun, Vorontsov, Asamoah. Corta. We are Dragons now.

Here comes little Luna, running to her grandmother. I sip my tea. It's mint. I still loathe mint tea. I always will. But there is only mint tea on the moon.

KHELDYU

Karl Schroeder

THE TRUCK CRESTED a hill and Gennady got his first good look at the Khantayskoe test site. He ground to a stop and sat there for a long time.

Spreading before him were thirty square kilometers of unpopulated Siberian forest. Vast pine-carpeted slopes ran up and up into impossible distance to either side, yet laid over the forest of the south-facing rise was a gleaming circle six kilometers in diameter. It was slightly crinkly, like a giant cellophane disk or parachute that had been dropped here by a passing giant. Its edges had been perfectly sharp in the photos Gennady had seen, but they were ragged in real life. That circle was just a vast roof of plastic sheeting, after all, great sections of which had fallen in the past several winters. Enough remained to turn the slope into a glittering bulls-eye of reflecting sheets and fluttering, tattered banners of plastic.

Underneath that ceiling, the dark low forest was a subdued shade of gray. That gray was why Gennady was now putting on a surgical mask.

Standing up out of the top quarter of the circle was a round, flat-topped tower, like a smoke-stack for some invisible morlock factory. The thing was over a kilometer tall, and wisps of cloud wreathed its top.

He put the truck into gear and bumped his way toward the

tumbled edges of the greenhouse. There was no trick to roofing over a whole forest, at least around here; few of the gnarled pines were more than thirty feet tall. Little grew between them, the long sight-lines making the northern arboreal forest a kind of wall-less maze. Here, the trees made a perfect filter, slowing the air that came in around the open edges of the greenhouse and letting it warm slowly as it converged on that distant tower.

"There's just one tiny problem," Achille Marceau had told Gennady when they'd talked about the job, "which is why we need you. The airflow stopped when we shut down the wind turbines at the base of the solar updraft tower. It got hot and dry under the greenhouse, and with the drought – well, you know."

The tenuous road wove between tree trunks and under the torn translucent roof whose surface wavered like an inverted lake. For the first hundred meters or so everything was okay. The trees were still alive. But then he began passing more and more orange and brown ones, and the track became obscured by deepening drifts of pine needles.

Then these began to disappear under a fog of greyish-white fungus.

He'd been prepared for this sight, but Gennady still stopped the truck to do some swearing. The trees were draped in what looked like the fake cobwebs kids hung over everything for American Halloween. Great swathes of the stuff cocooned whole trunks and stretched between them like long, sickening flags. He glanced back and saw that an ominous white cloud was beginning to curl around the truck – billions of spores kicked up by his wheels.

He gunned the engine to get ahead of the spore clouds, and that was when he finally noticed the other tracks.

Two parallel ruts ran through the white snow-like stuff, outlining the road ahead quite clearly. They looked fresh, and would have been made by a vehicle about the same size as his.

Marceau had insisted that Gennady would be the first person to visit the solar updraft plant in five years.

The slope was just steep enough that the road couldn't run straight up the hillside, but zig-zagged; so it took Gennady a good twenty minutes to make it to the tower. He was sweating and uncomfortable by the time he finally pulled the rig into the gravel parking area under the solar uplift tower. The other vehicle wasn't here, and its tracks had disappeared on the mold-free gravel. Maybe it had gone around the long curve of the tower.

He drove that way himself. He was supposed to be inspecting the tower's base for cracks, but his eyes kept straying, looking for a sign that somebody else was here. If they were, they were well hidden.

When he got back to the main lot, he rummaged in the glove compartment and came up with a flare gun. Wouldn't do any good as a weapon, but from a distance it might fool somebody. He slipped it into the pocket of his nylon jacket and climbed out to retrieve a portable generator from the bed of the truck.

Achille Marceau wanted to replace 4% of the world's coal-powered generating plants with solar updraft towers. With no fuel requirements at all, these towers would produce electricity while simultaneously removing CO_2 from the air. All together they'd suck a gigaton of carbon out of the atmosphere every year. Ignoring the electricity sales, at today's prices the carbon sales alone would be worth $40 billion a year. That was $24 million per year from this tower alone.

Marceau had built this tower to prove the plan, by producing electricity for Northern China while simultaneously pulling down carbon and sequestering it underground. It was a brilliant plan, but he'd found himself underbid in the cutthroat post-carbon-bubble economy, and he couldn't make ends meet on the electricity sales alone. He'd had to shut down.

Now he was back – literally, a few kilometers back, waiting

for his hazardous materials lackey to open the tower and give the rest of the trucks the all-clear signal.

The plastic ceiling got higher the closer you got to the tower, and now it was a good sixty meters overhead. Under it, vast round windows broke the curve of the wall; they were closed by what looked like steel Venetian blinds. Some portable trailers huddled between two of the giant circles, but these were for management. Gennady trudged past them without a glance and climbed a set of metal steps to a steel door labeled Небезпеки – 'HAZARD,' but written in Ukrainian, not Russian. Marceau's key let him in, and the door didn't even squeak, which was encouraging.

Before he stepped through, Gennady paused and looked back at the shrouded forest. It was eerily quiet, with no breeze to make the dead trees speak.

Well, he would change that.

The door opened into a kind of airlock; he could hear wind whistling around the edges of the inner portal. He closed the outer one and opened the inner, and was greeted by gray light and a sense of vast emptiness. Gennady stepped into the hollow core of the tower.

The ground was just bare red stone covered with construction litter. A few heavy lifters and cranes dotted the stadium-sized circle. Here there was sound – a discordant whistling from overhead. Faint light filtered down.

He spent a long hour inspecting the tower's foundations from the inside, then carried the little generator to the bottom of another flight of metal steps. These ones zigzagged up the concrete wall. About thirty meters up, a ring of metal beams held a wide gallery that encircled the tower, and more portable trailers had been placed on that. The stairs went on past them into a zone of shifting silvery light. The stuff up there would need attending to, but not just yet.

Hauling the generator up to the first level took him ten

minutes; halfway up he took off the surgical mask, and he was panting when he finally reached the top. He caught his breath and then shouted, "Hello?" Nobody answered; if there was another visitor here, they were either hiding or very far away across – or up – the tower.

The windows of the dust-covered control trailer were unbroken. The door was locked. He used the next key on that but didn't go in. Instead, he set up the portable generator and connected it to the mains. But now he was in his element, and was humming as he pulled the generator's cord.

While it rattled and roared he took another cautious look around then went left along the gallery. The portable trailer sat next to one of the huge round apertures that perforated the base of the tower. Seated into this circle was the biggest wind turbine he'd ever seen. The gallery was right at the level of its axle and generator, so he was able to inspect it without having to climb anything. When Marceau's men mothballed it five years ago, they'd wrapped everything vulnerable in plastic and taped it up. Consequently, the turbine's systems were in surprisingly good shape. Once he'd pitched the plastic sheeting over the gallery rail he only had to punch the red button at the back of the trailer, and somewhere below, an electric motor strained to use all the power from his little generator. Lines of daylight began to separate the imposing Venetian blinds. With them came a quickening breeze.

"Put your hands up!"

Gennady reflexively put his hands in the air; but then he had to laugh.

"What are you laughing at?"

"Sorry. Is just that, last time I put my hands up like this was for a woman also. Kazakhstan, last summer."

There was a pause. Then: "Gennady?"

He looked over his shoulder and recognized the face behind the pistol. "Nadine, does your brother know you're here?"

Nadine Marceau tilted her head to one side and shifted her stance to a hipshot, exasperated pose as she lowered the pistol. "What the hell, Gennady. I could ask you the same question."

With vast dignity he lowered his hands and turned around. "I," he said, "am working. You, on the other hand, are trespassing."

She gaped at him. "You're *working?* For *that* bastard?"

So, then it wasn't just a rumor that Achille and Nadine Marceau hated each other. Gennady shrugged; it wasn't his business. "Cushy jobs for the IAEA are hard to come by, Nadine, you know that. I'm a free-lancer, I have to get by."

"Yeah, but–" She was looking down, fumbling with her holster, as widening light unveiled behind her the industrial underworld of the solar uplift tower. Warm outside air was pouring in through the opening shutters now, and, slowly, the giant vanes of the windmill fixed in its round window began to turn.

Nadine cursed. "You've started it! Gennady, I thought you had more integrity! I never thought you'd end up being part of the problem."

"Part of the problem? God, Nadine, is just a windmill."

"No, it's not–" He'd turned to admire the turning blades, but looking back saw that she had frozen in a listening posture. "Shit!"

"Don't tell him I'm here!" she shouted as she turned and started running along the gallery. "Not a word, Gennady. You hear?"

NADINE MARCEAU, U.N. arms inspector and disowned child of one of the wealthiest families in Europe, disappeared into the shadows. Gennady could hear the approaching trucks himself now; still, he spread his hands and shouted, "Don't you even want a cup of coffee?"

The metal Venetian blinds clicked into their fully open

configuration, and now enough outside light was coming in to reveal the cyclopean vastness of the tower's interior. Gennady looked up at the little circle of sky a kilometer-and-a-half overhead, and shook his head ruefully. "Is not even radioactive."

Why was Nadine here? Some vendetta with her brother, no doubt, though Gennady preferred to think it was work-related. The last time he'd seen her was in Azerbaijan, two years ago; that time, they'd been working together to find some stolen nukes. A nightmare job, but totally in line with both their professional backgrounds. This place, though, it was just an elaborate windmill. It couldn't explode or melt down or spill oil all over the sensitive arboreal landscape. No, this had to be a family thing.

There were little windows in the reinforced concrete wall. Through one of these he could see three big trucks, mirror to his own, approaching the tower. Nadine's brother Achille had gotten impatient, apparently. He must have seen the blinds opening, and the first of the twenty wind turbines that ringed the tower's base starting to move. A legendary micro-manager, he just couldn't stay away.

By the time the boss clambered out of the second truck, unsteady in his bright-red hazmat suit, Gennady had opened the office trailer, started a hepafilter whirring, and booted up the tower's control system. He leaned in the trailer's doorway and watched as first two bodyguards, then Marceau himself, then his three engineers, reached the top of the stairs.

"Come inside," Gennady said. "You can take that off."

The hazmat suit waved its arms and made a garbled sound that Gennady eventually translated as, "You're not wearing your mask."

"Ah, no. Too hard to work in. But that's why you hired me, Mr. Marceau. To take your chances."

"Call me Achille! Everybody else does." The hazmat suit made a lunging motion; Gennady realized that Nadine's brother was trying to clap him on the shoulder. He pretended it had worked, smiled, then backed into the trailer.

It took ten minutes for them to coax Marceau out of his shell, and while they did Gennady debated with himself whether to tell Achille that his sister was here too. The moments dragged on, and eventually Gennady realized that the engineers were happily chattering on about the status of the tower's various systems, and the bodyguards were visibly bored, and he hadn't said anything. It was going to look awkward if he brought it up now... so he put it off some more.

Finally, the young billionaire removed the hazmat's headpiece, revealing a lean, high-cheekboned face currently plastered with sweat. "Thanks, Gennady," he gasped. "It was brave of you to come in here alone."

"Yeah, I risked an epic allergy attack," said Gennady with a shrug. "Nothing after camping in Chernobyl."

Achille grinned. "Forget the mold, we just weren't sure whether opening the door would make the whole tower keel over. I'm glad it's structurally sound."

"Down here, maybe," Gennady pointed out. "There's a lot up there that could still fall on us." He jerked a thumb at the ceiling.

"You were with us yesterday." They'd done a visual inspection from the helicopters on their way to the plateau. But Gennady wasn't about to trust that.

Achille turned to his engineers. "The wind's not cooperating. Now they're saying it'll shift the right way by 2:00 tomorrow afternoon. How long is it going to take to establish a full updraft?"

"There's inertia in the air inside the tower," said one. "Four hours, granted the thermal difference...?"

"I don't think we'll be ready tomorrow," Gennady pointed out. He was puzzled by Achille's impatience. "We haven't had time to inspect all the turbines, much less the scrubbers on Level Two."

The engineers should be backing him up on this one, but they stayed silent. Achille waved a hand impatiently. "We'll leave the turbines parked for now. As to the scrubbers..."

"There might be loose pieces and material that could get damaged when the air currents pick up."

"Dah! You're right, of course." Achille rubbed his chin for a second, staring into space. "We'd better test the doors now... might as well do it in pairs. Gennady, you've got an hour of good light. If you're so worried about them, go check out the scrubbers."

Gennady stared at him. "What's the hurry?"

"Time is money. You're not afraid of the updraft while we're testing the doors, are you? It's not like a hurricane or anything. We walk all the time up there when the unit's running full bore." Achille relented. "Oh, take somebody with you if you're worried. Octav, you go."

Octav was one of Achille's bodyguards. He was a blocky Lithuanian who favored chewing tobacco and expensive suits. The look he shot Gennady said, *this is all your fault.*

Gennady glanced askance at Octav, then said to Achille, "Listen, is there some reason why somebody would think that starting this thing up would be wrong?"

The boss stared at him. "Wrong?"

"I don't mean this company you're competing with – GreenCore. I mean, you know, the general public."

"Don't bug the boss," said Octav.

Achille waved a hand at him. "It's okay. A few crazy adaptationists think reversing climate change will cause as many extinctions as the temperature rise did in the first place. If you ask me, they're just worried about losing their funding. But really, Malianov – this tower sucks CO_2 right out of the air. It doesn't matter where that CO_2 came from, which means we're equally good at offsetting emissions from the airline industry as we are from, say, coal. We're good for everybody."

Gennady nodded, puzzled, and quickly followed Octav out of the trailer. He didn't want the bodyguard wandering off on his own – or maybe spotting something in the distance that he shouldn't see.

Octav *was* staring – standing in the middle of the gallery, mouth open. "Christ," he said. "It's like a fucking cathedral." With light breaking in from the opening louvers, the full scale of the place was becoming clear, and even jaded Gennady was impressed. The tower was a kilometer and a half tall, and over a hundred meters across, its base ringed with round wind turbine windows. "But I was expecting some kinda machinery in here. Is that gonna be installed later?"

Gennady shook his head, pointing at the round windows. "That's all there is to it. When those windows are open, warm air from the greenhouse comes in and rises. The wind turbines turn, and make electricity."

Gennady began the long climb up the steps to the next gallery. His gaze kept roving across the tower's interior; he was looking for Nadine. Was Octav going to spot her? He didn't want that. Even though he knew Nadine was level-headed in tight situations, Octav was another matter. And then there was the whole question of why she was out here to begin with, seemingly on her own, and carrying a gun.

Octav followed on his heels. "Well sure, I get the whole 'heat rises' thing, but why'd he build it *here?* In the middle of fucking Siberia? If it's solar-powered, wouldn't you want to put it at the equator?"

"They built it on a south-facing slope, so it's 85% as efficient as it would be at the equator. And the thermal inertia of the soil means the updraft will operate 24 hours a day."

"But in winter–"

"Even in a Siberian winter, because it's not about the absolute temperature, it's about the *difference* between the temperatures inside and outside."

Octav pointed up. "Those pull the CO2 out of the air, right?"

"If this were a cigarette of the gods, that would be the filter, yes." Just above, thousands of gray plastic sheets were stretched across the shaft of the tower. They were stacked just centimeters apart so that the air flowed freely between them.

"It's called polyaziridine. When the gods suck on the cigarette, this stuff traps the CO2."

They'd come to one of the little windows. Gennady pried it open and dry summer air poured in. They were above the greenhouse roof, and from here you could see the whole sweep of the valley where Achille had built his experiment. "Look at that."

Above the giant tower, the forested slope kept on rising, and rising, becoming bare tanned rock and then vertical cliff. "Pretty mountains," admitted Octav.

"Except they're not mountains." Yes, the slopes rose like mountainsides, culminating in those daunting cliffs. The trouble was, at the very top the usual jagged, irregular skyline of rocky peaks was missing. Instead, the cliff-tops ended in a perfectly flat, perfectly horizontal line – a knife-cut across the sky – signaling that there was no crest and fall down a north-facing slope up there. Miles up, under a regime of harsh UV light and whipping high-altitude winds, clouds scudded low and fast along a nearly endless plain of red rock. Looking down from up there, the outflung arms of the Putorana Plateau absolutely dwarfed Achille's little tower.

"I walked on it yesterday when we flew up to prime the wells," said Gennady. Octav hadn't been along on that flight; he hadn't seen what lay beyond that ruler-straight crest. "That plateau covers an area the size of Western Europe, and it's so high nothing can grow up there. This whole valley is just an erosion ditch in it."

Octav nodded, reluctantly intrigued. "Kinda strange place to build a power plant."

"Achille built here because the plateau's made of basalt. When you pump hot carbonated water into basalt it makes limestone, which permanently sequesters the carbon. All Achille has to do is keep fracking up top there and he's got a continent-sized sponge to soak up all the excess CO_2 on the planet. You could build a thousand towers like this all around the Putorana. It's perfect for—" But Octav had clapped a hand on his shoulder.

"Shht," whispered the bodyguard. "Heard something."

Before Gennady could react, Octav was creeping up the steps with his gun drawn. "What do you think you're doing?" Gennady hissed at the Lithuanian. "Put that thing away!"

Octav waved at him to stay where he was. "Could be bears," he called down in a hoarse – and not at all quiet – stage whisper. The word *bears* seemed to hang in the air for a second, like an echo that couldn't find a wall to bounce off.

Gennady started up after him, deliberately making as much noise as he could on the metal steps. "Bears are not arboreal, much less likely will they be foraging up in the scrubbers—" Octav reached the top of the steps and disappeared. Here, the hanging sheets of plastic made a bizarre drapery that completely filled the tower. Except for this little catwalk, the entire space was given over to them. It was kind of like being backstage in a large theater, except the curtains were white. Octav was hunched over, gun drawn, stepping slowly forward around the slow curve of the catwalk. This would have been a comical sight except that, about eight meters ahead of him, the curtains were swaying.

"Octav, don't—" The bodyguard lunged into the gloom.

Gennady heard a scuffle and ran forward himself. Then, terribly, two gunshots like slaps echoed out and up and down.

"No, what have you—!" Gennady staggered to a stop and had to grab the railing for support; it creaked and gave a bit, and he suddenly realized how high up they were. Octav knelt just ahead, panting. He was reaching slowly out to prod a crumpled gray and brown shape.

"Jssht!" said the walkie-talkie on Octav's belt. More garbled vocal sounds spilled out of it, until Octav suddenly seemed to realize it was there, and holstered his pistol with one hand while taking it out with the other.

"Octav," he said. The walkie-talkie spat incoherent staticky noise into his ear. He nodded.

"Everything's okay," he said. "Just shot a goose is all. I guess we have dinner."

Then he turned to glare at Gennady. "You should have stayed where I told you!"

Gennady ignored him. The white curtains swung, all of them now starting to rustle as if murmuring and pointing at Octav's minor crime scene. More of the louvered doors had opened far below, and the updraft was starting. Shadow and sound began to paint the tower's hollow spaces.

Nadine would be hard to see now, and impossible to hear. Hopefully, she'd noticed Octav's shots; even now, if she had a grain of sense, she'd be on her way back to her truck.

Gennady brushed past Octav. "If you're done murdering the locals, I need to work." The two did not speak again, as Gennady tugged at the plastic and inspected the bolts mounting the scrubbers to the tower wall.

A SIBERIAN SUMMER day lasts forever; but there came a point when the sun no longer lit the interior top of the tower. The last hundred meters up there were painted titanium white, and reflected a lot of light down. Now, though, with the sky a dove gray shading to nameless pink, and the sun's rays horizontal, Achille's lads had to light the sodium lamps and admit it was evening.

The lamps were the same kind you saw in parking lots all over the world. For Gennady, they completely stole the sense of mystery from the tower's interior, making it as grim an industrial space as any he'd seen. For a while he stood outside the control trailer with Octav and a couple of the engineers, trying to get used to the evil greenish yellow cast that everything had. Then he said, "I'm going to sleep outside."

One of the engineers laughed. "After your run-in with the climbing bears? And you know, there really are wolves in this forest."

"No, no, I will be in one of the admin trailers." Nobody had even opened those yet; and besides, he needed to find a spot where late night comings and goings wouldn't be noticed by these men.

"First, you must try the goose!" While the others inspected and tested, Octav had cooked it over a barrel-fire. He'd only made a few modest comments about the bird, but Gennady knew he was ridiculously proud of his kill, because he'd placed the barrel smack in the center of the hundred-meter-wide floor of the tower. He'd even dragged over a couple of railroad ties and set them up like logs around his campfire.

Achille was down there now, peering at his air-quality equipment, obviously debating whether he could lose his surgical mask. He waved up at them. "Come! Let's eat!"

Gennady followed the others reluctantly. He knew where this was headed: to the inevitable male bonding ritual. It came as no surprise at all, when, as they tore into the simultaneously charred and raw goose, Achille waved at Gennady, and said, "Now this man! He's a real celebrity! Octav, did you know what kind of adventurer you saved from this fierce beast?" He waved his drumstick in the air. Octav looked puzzled.

"Gennady, here. Gennady fought the famous Dragon of Pripyat!" Of course the engineers knew the story, and smiled politely; but neither Octav nor Bogdan, the other bodyguard, knew it. "Tell us, Gennady!" Achille's grin was challenging. "About the reactor, and the devil guarding it."

"We know all about that," protested an engineer. "I want to know about the Kashmiri incident. The one with the nuclear jet. Is it true you flew it into a mine?"

"Well, yes," Gennady admitted, "not myself of course. It was just a drone." Of course the attention was flattering, but it also made him uncomfortable, and over the years he'd learned that the discomfort outweighed the flattery. He told them the story, but as soon as he could he found a way to turn to Achille and say, "But these are just isolated incidents. Your whole career has been, well, something of an adventure itself, no?"

That burst of eloquence had about exhausted his skills of social manipulation; luckily, Achille was eager to talk about himself. He and Nadine had inherited wealth, and Gennady had sensed yesterday that this weighed on him. He wanted to be a self-made man, but he wasn't; so, he was using his inheritance recklessly, to see if he could achieve something great. He also had an impulsive urge to justify himself.

He told them how, when he'd seen the sheer scale of the cap and trade and carbon tax programs that were springing up across the globe, he'd decided to put all his chips into carbon air capture, "Because," he explained, "it was a completely discredited approach."

"Wait," said Octav, his brow crinkling. "You went into... that... because it had no credibility?" Achille nodded vigorously.

"Decades of research, patents, and designs were just lying around waiting to be snapped up. I was already building this place, but the carbon bubble was bursting as governments started pulling their fossil fuel subsidies. Here, the local price of petrol had gone through the roof as the Arctic oilfields went from profitable to red. But, you see, I had a plan."

The plan was to offer to offset CO_2 emissions of industries anywhere on the planet, from right here. Since Achille's giant machines harvested greenhouse gases from the ambient atmosphere, it didn't matter where they were – which meant he could sell offsets to airlines, mines in South America, or container ships burning bunker oil with equal ease.

"But then, Kafatos stole my market."

The Greek industrialist's company, Greencore, had bought up vast tracts of Siberian forest and had begun rolling out a cheaper biological alternative to Achille's towers.

"They do what? Some kind of fast-growing tree?" asked Gennady. He knew about the rivalry between Achille and Kafatos. It wasn't just business; it was personal.

Achille nodded. "Genetically modified lodgepole pines. Super-fast growing, resistant to the pine beetle. They want to turn the forest itself into a carbon sponge. It's as bad an idea as tampering with Mother Nature was – as oil was – in the first place," he said, "and I intend to prove it."

The conversation wound down a bit after this motivational speech, but then one of the engineers looked around at the trembling shadows of the amphitheater in which they sat, and said, "Pretty spooky, eh?"

"Siberia is all spooky," Bogdan pointed out. "Never mind just here."

And that set them all off on ghost stories and legends of the deep forests. The locals used to believe Siberia was a middle-world, half-way up a vast tree, with underworlds below and heavens above. Shamans rode their drums between the worlds, fighting the impossible strength of the gods with dogged courage and guile. They triumphed now and then, but in the end the deep forest swallowed all human achievement like it would swallow a shout. What was human got lost in the green maze; what came out was changed and new.

Bogdan knew a story about the 'valley of death' and the strange round *kheldyu* – iron houses – that could be found half-buried in the permafrost here and there. There was a valley no one ever returned from; kheldyu had been glimpsed there by scouts on the surrounding heights.

The engineers had their own tales, about lost Soviet-era expeditions. There were downed bombers loaded with nukes on hair-trigger, which might go off at any moment. There were

Chinese tunnel complexes, and lakes so radioactive that to stand on their shores for a half an hour meant dying within the week. (Well, that last story, at least, was perfectly true.)

"Gennady, what about you?" All eyes turned to him. Gennady had relaxed a bit and was willing to talk; but he didn't know any recent myths or legends. "All I can tell you," Gennady said, "is that it'll be poetic justice if we save the world by burying all our carbon here. Because what's in this place nearly killed the whole world through global warming once already."

The engineers hadn't heard about the plateau's past. "This place – this *thing*," said Gennady in his best ghost-story voice, "killed ninety percent of all life on Earth when it erupted. This supervolcano, called the Siberian Traps, caused the Permian extinction 250 million years ago. Think about it: the place was here before the dinosaurs and it's still here, still taller than mountain ranges and as wide as Europe." There was nothing like it on Earth – older than the present continents, the Putorana was an ineradicable scar from the greatest dying the world had ever seen.

So then they had to hear the story of the Permian extinction. Gennady did his best to convey the idea of an entire world dying, and of geologic forces so gargantuan and unstoppable that the first geologists to find this spot literally couldn't imagine the scale of the apocalypse it represented. He was rewarded by some appreciative nods, particularly for his image of a slumbering monster that could indifferently destroy all life on the planet by just rolling over. The whole thing was too abstract for Octav and Bogdan, though, who were yawning.

"Right." Achille slapped his knees. "Tomorrow's another busy day. Let's turn in everybody, and get a start at sun-up."

"Uh, boss," said an engineer, "sunrise is at 3:00 a.m."

"Make it five, then." Achille headed for the metal steps.

Gennady repeated his intent to sleep in the admin trailer; to his relief, no one volunteered to do the same. When he stepped through the second door of the tower's airlock, it was to find that although it was nearly midnight, the sun was still setting. He remembered seeing this effect before: the sun might dip below the horizon, but the lurid peach-and-rose colored glow it painted on the sky wasn't going to go away. That smear of dusk would just slide up and across the northern horizon, over the next few hours, and then the sun would pop back up once it reached the east.

That was helpful. The administration trailer needed a good airing-out, so he opened all its windows and sat on the front step for a while, waiting to see if anybody came out of the tower. The sunset inched northward. He checked his watch. Finally, with a sigh, he set off walking around the western curve of the structure. A flashlight was unnecessary, but he did bring the flare gun. Because, well, there might be bears.

Nadine had done a pretty good job of hiding her truck, among gnarled cedars and cobwebs of fungi on the north side of the tower. Either she'd been waiting for him, or she had some kind of proximity alarm, because he was still ten meters away when he heard the door slam. He stopped and waited. After a couple of minutes she stood up out of the bushes, a black cut-out on the red sky. "It's just you," she said unnecessarily.

Gennady shrugged. "Do I ever bring friends?"

"Good point." The silhouette made a motion he interpreted as the holstering of a pistol. He strolled over while she untangled herself from the bushes.

"Come back to the trailer," he said. "I have chairs."

"I'm sleeping here."

"That's fine."

"... Okay." They crunched back over the gravel. Halfway there, Nadine said, "Seriously, Gennady. You and Achille?"

"What is the problem?" He spread his hands, distorting the long shadow that leaned ahead of him. "He is restarting his carbon air capture project. That's a good thing, no?"

She stopped walking. "That's what you think he's doing?"

What did that mean? "Let's see. It's what he says he's doing. It's what the press releases say. It's what everybody else thinks he's doing... What else *could* he be up to?"

"Everybody asks that question." She kicked at the gravel angrily. "But nobody sees what he's doing! You know–" she laughed bitterly, "When I told my team at the IAEA what he was up to, they just laughed at me. And you know what? I thought about calling you. I figured, *Gennady knows how these things go. He'd understand.* But you don't get it either, do you?"

"You know I am not smart man. I need thing explained to me."

She was silent until they reached the admin trailer. Once inside she said, "Close those," with a nod at the windows. "I don't want any of that shit in here with us."

She must mean the mold. As Gennady went around shutting things up, Nadine sat down at the tiny table. After a longing look at the mothballed coffee machine, she steepled her hands and said, "I suppose you saw the pictures."

"That the paparazzi took of you two at the Paris café? There were a few, if I recall."

She grimaced. "I particularly like the one that shows Kafatos punching Achille in the face."

Gennady nodded pensively. It had been two years since Achille came across his sister having dinner with Kafatos, his biggest business rival. The punch was famous, and the whole incident had burned through the internet in a day or two, to be instantly forgotten in the wake of the next scandal.

"Achille and I haven't spoken since. He's even taken me out of his will – you know he was the sole heir, right?"

Gennady nodded. "I figured that was why you went to work at the IAEA."

"No, I did that out of idealism, but... anyway it doesn't matter.

I knew all about Achille's little rivalry with the Greek shithead, but something about it didn't add up. Achille was lying to me, so I went to Kafatos to see if he knew why. He didn't, so the whole café incident was a complete waste. But I eventually *did* get the story from one of Achille's engineers."

"Let me guess. It's something to do with the tower?"

She shrugged. "It never crossed my mind. When Achille came up with the plan for this place, I guess it was eight years ago, it seemed to make sense. He knew about the Permian, and he talked about how he was going to 'redeem' the site of the greatest extinction in history by using it to not just stop but completely reverse global warming. The whole blowup with Kafatos happened because Greencore bought up about a million square kilometers of forest just east of Achille's site. Kafatos has been genetically engineering pines to soak up the carbon, but you know that." She took a deep breath. "You also know there's no economic reason to re-open the tower."

Gennady blinked at her. "They told me there was, that was why we were here. Told me the market had turned..."

She sent him a look of complete incredulity; then that look changed, and suddenly Nadine stood up. Gennady opened his mouth to ask what was wrong, just as one of the windows rattled loosely in its mount. Nadine was staring out the window, a look of horror on her face.

A deep vibration made the plywood floor buzz. The glass rattled again.

"He's opening the windows!" Nadine ran for the door. Gennady peered outside.

"Surely not all of them..." But all the black circles he could see from here were changing, letting out a trickle of sodium-lamp light.

By the time he got outside she was gone – off and running around the tower in the direction of her truck. Gennady shifted from foot to foot, trying to decide whether to follow.

Her story hadn't made sense, but still, he paused for a moment to gaze up at the tower. In the deep sunset light of the midsummer night, it looked like a rifle barrel aimed at the sky.

He slammed through the airlocks and went up the stairs. All around the tower's base, the round windows were humming open.

Gennady fixed an empty smile on his face, and deliberately slowed himself down as he opened the door to the control trailer. He was thinking of radioactive lakes, of the Becquerel Reindeer, an entire radioactive herd he'd seen once, slaughtered and lying in the back of a transport truck; of disasters he'd cleaned up after, messes he'd hidden from the media – and the kinds of people who had made those messes.

"Hey, what's up?" he said brightly as he stepped inside.

"Close that!" Achille was pacing in the narrow space. "You'll let in the spores!"

"Ah, sorry." He sidled around the bodyguards, behind the engineers who were staring at their tablets and laptops, and found a perch near an empty water cooler. From here he could see the laptop screens, though not well.

"What's up?" he said again.

One of the engineers started to say something, but Achille interrupted him. "Just a test. You should go back to bed."

"I see." He stepped close to the table and looked over the engineer's shoulder. One of the laptop screens showed a systems diagram of the tower. The other was open to a satellite weather map. "Weather's changing," he muttered, just loud enough for the engineer to hear. The man nodded.

"Fine," Gennady said more loudly. "I'll be in my trailer." Nobody moved to stop him as he left, but outside he paused, arms wrapped around his torso, breath cold and frosting the air. Already he could feel the breeze from below.

Back in Azerbaijan, Nadine had been one of the steadiest operatives during the Alexander's Road incident; they had talked one evening about what Gennady had come to call 'industrial logic.' About what happened when the natural world became an abstraction, and the only reality was the system you were building. Gennady had fallen for that kind of thinking early in his career; had spent the rest of his life mopping up after other people who'd never gotten out from under it. He couldn't remember the details of the conversation now, but he did remember her getting a distant expression on her face at one point, and muttering something about Achille.

But it wasn't just about her brother; all of this had something to do with Kafatos, too. He shook his head, and turned to the stairs.

A flash lit the inside of the tower and seconds later a sharp *bang!* echoed weirdly off the curving walls. The grinding noise of the window mechanisms stopped.

A transformer had blown. It had happened on the far side of the tower; he started in that direction but had only taken a couple of steps when the trailer door flew open and the engineers spilled out, all talking at once. "Malianov!" one shouted. "Did you see it?"

He shook his head. "Heard it, but not sure where it came from. Echoes..." Let them stumble around in the dark for a while. That would give Nadine a chance to get away. Then he could find her again and talk her out of doing anything further.

Octav and Bogdan had come out, too, and Bogdan raced off after the engineers. Gennady shrugged at Octav and said, "I am still going back to bed." He'd gone down the stairs, reached the outer door and actually put his hand on the latch before curiosity overcame his better judgment, and he turned back.

He came up behind the engineers as they were shining their flashlights at the smoking ruin that used to be a transformer. "Something caused it to arc," one said. Bogdan was kneeling a few meters away. He stood up and dangled a mutilated padlock in the beam of his flashlight. "Somebody's got bolt-cutters."

All eyes turned to Gennady.

He backed away. "Now, wait a minute. I was with you."

"You could have set something to blow and then come back to the trailer," said one of the engineers. "It's what I would have done."

Gennady said nothing; if they thought he'd done it they wouldn't be looking for Nadine. "Grab him!" shouted one of the engineers. Gennady just put out his hands and shook his head as Bogdan took hold of his wrists.

"It's not what *I* would have done," Gennady said. "Because this would be the result. I am not so stupid."

"Oh, and I am?" Bogdan glared at him. At that moment one of the engineers put his walkie-talkie to his ear and made a shushing motion. "We found the – what? Sir, I can't hear what–"

The distorted tones of the voice on the walkie-talkie had been those of Achille, but suddenly they changed. Nadine said, "I have your boss. I'll kill him unless you go to the center of the floor and light the barrel-fire so I can see you."

The engineers gaped at one another. Bogdan let go of Gennady and grabbed at the walkie-talkie. "Who is this?"

"Someone who knows what you're up to. Now move!"

Bogdan eyed Gennady, who shrugged. "Nothing to do with me."

There was a quick, heated discussion. The engineers were afraid of being shot once they were out in the open, but Gennady pointed out that there was actually more light around the wall, because that's where the sodium lamps were. "She doesn't want to see us clearly, she just wants us where it'll be obvious which way we're going if we run," he said.

Reluctantly, they began edging toward the shadowed center of the tower. "How can you be so sure?" somebody whined. Gennady shrugged again.

"If she'd wanted to kill her brother, she would have by now," he pointed out.

"Her *what?*"

And at that moment, the gunfire started.

It was all upstairs, but the engineers scattered, leaving Gennady and Bogdan standing in half-shadow. Had Octav stayed up top? Gennady couldn't remember. He and Bogdan scanned the gallery, but the glare from the sodium lamps hid the trailer. After a few seconds, Gennady heard the metallic bounce of feet running on the mesh surface overhead. It sounded like two sets, off to the right.

"There!" Gennady pointed to the left and began running. Bogdan ran too, and quickly outpaced him; at that point Gennady peeled off and headed back. There was another set of stairs nearby, and though the engineers were there, they were huddling under its lower steps. He didn't think they'd stop him, nor did they as he ran past them and up.

Bogdan yelled something inarticulate from the other side of the floor. Gennady kept going.

"Nadine? Where are you?" She'd been running in a clockwise direction around the tower, so he went that way too, making sure now that he was making plenty of noise. He didn't want to surprise her. "Nadine, it's me!"

Multiple sets of feet rang on the gallery behind him. Gennady took the chance that she'd kept going up, and mounted the next set of steps when he came to them. "Nadine!" She'd be among the scrubbers now.

He reached the top and hesitated. Why *would* she come up here? It was the cliché thing to do: in movies, the villains always went up. Gennady tried to push past his confusion and worry to picture the layout of the tower. He remembered the two inspection elevators just as a rattling hum started up ahead.

By the time he reached the yellow wire cage, the car was on its way up. Next stop, as far as he knew, was the top of the tower. Nadine could hold it there, and maybe that was her plan. There wouldn't be just the one elevator, though, not in a structure this big. Gennady turned and ran away from the sound of the moving elevator.

He could hear somebody crashing up the steps from the lower levels. "Malianov!" shouted Octav.

He was a good quarter of the way around the curve from Gennady, so Gennady paused and leaned on the rail to shout, "I'm here!"

"What are you doing?"

"I'm right on her heels!"

"Stop! Come down! Leave it to us."

"Okay! I'll be right there." He ran on, and reached the other elevator before Octav had reached the last flight of steps. Gennady wrenched the rusty outer cage door open, but struggled with the inner one. He got in and slammed it just as Octav thundered up. Gennady hit the UP button while Octav roared in fury; but three meters up, he hit STOP.

"Octav. Don't shoot at me, please. I'll send the cage back down when I get to the top. I just need a minute to talk with Nadine, is all."

In the movies there'd be all kinds of wild gunplay happening right now, but Octav was a professional. He crossed his arms and glowered at Gennady through the grid flooring of the elevator. "Where's she going?" he demanded.

"Damned if I know. Up."

"What's up?"

"Someplace she can talk to her brother alone, I'm thinking. Reason with him, threaten him, I don't know. Look, Octav, let me talk to her. She might shoot you, but she's not going to shoot me."

"It really is Nadine? Achille's sister? Do you know her?"

"Well, remember that story I told last night about Azerbaijan and the nukes? We worked together on that. You know she's with the IAEA too. You never met her?"

There was an awkward pause. "What happened in the

trailer?" Gennady asked. "Did she hurt him?" Octav shook his head.

"She was yelling," he said. "I snuck around the trailer and came in through the bathroom window. But I got stuck."

Gennady stifled a laugh. He would have paid to see that; Octav was not a small man.

"I took a shot at her but she ran. Might have winged her, though."

Gennady cursed. "Octav, that's your boss's sister."

"He told me to shoot!"

There was another awkward pause.

"I'm sure she doesn't mean to harm him," said Gennady, but he wasn't so sure now.

"Then why's she holding him at gunpoint?"

"I don't know. Look, just give me a minute, okay?" He hit UP before Octav could reply.

He'd gotten an inkling of the size of the tower when they'd inspected it by helicopter, but down at the bottom, the true dimensions of the place were obscured by shadow. Up here it was all vast emptiness, the walls a concrete checkerboard that curved away like the face of a dam. It was all faintly lit by a distant, indigo-silver circle of sky. On the far side of this bottomless amphitheater, the other elevator car had a good lead on him. Nadine probably wouldn't hear him now if he called out to her.

The elevator frameworks ended at tiny balconies about halfway up the tower. Nadine's cage was slowing now as it neared the one on the far side.

Gennady shivered. A cool wind was coming up from below, and it went right through the gridwork floor and flapped his pant legs. There wasn't much to it yet, but it would get stronger.

He watched as Nadine and Achille got out of the other elevator. A square of brightness appeared – a door opening to the outside – and they disappeared through it.

When his own elevator stopped he found he was at a similar little balcony. There was nothing here but the side-rails and a gray metal utility door, with crash bars, in the outer concrete wall. The sense of height here was utterly physical; he'd sense it even if he shut his eyes, because the whole tower swayed ever so gently, and the moving air made it feel like you were falling. Gennady sent the elevator back down and leaned on the crash bar.

Outside it was every bit as bad as he'd feared. The door let onto a narrow catwalk that ran around the outside of the tower in both directions. He remembered seeing it from the helicopter, and while it had looked sturdy enough from that vantage, in the gray dawn light he could see long streaks of rust trailing down from the bolts that held it to the wall.

He swallowed, then tested the thing with his foot. It seemed to hold, so he began slowly circling the tower. This time, he tried every step before committing himself, and leaned on the concrete wall, as far from the railing as he could get.

Now he could hear a vague sound, like an endless sigh, rising from below. That, combined with the motion of the tower, made it feel as if something were rousing down in the wall-less maze that filled the black valley.

After a couple of minutes the far point of the circle hove into view. Here was something he hadn't seen from the helicopter: a broadening of the catwalk on this side. Here it became a wide, reinforced platform, and on it sat a white and yellow trailer. That was utterly incongruous: Gennady could see the thing's undercarriage and wheels sitting on the mesh floor. It had probably been hauled up here by helicopter during the tower's construction.

A pair of parachutes was painted on the side of the trailer. They were gray in this light, but probably pink in daylight.

Now he heard shouting – Achille's voice. Gennady tried to hurry, but the catwalk felt flimsy and the breeze was turning into a wind. He made it to the widened platform, but that was no better since it also had open gridwork flooring and several squares of it were missing.

"Nadine? It's Gennady. What're you doing?"

"Stop her!" yelled Achille. "She's gone crazy!"

He took the chance and ran to the trailer, then peeked around its corner. He was instantly dazzled by intense light – flare-light, in fact – lurid and bright green. He squinted and past his sheltering fingers saw it shift around, lean up, and then fade.

"Stop!" Achille sounded desperate. Gennady heard Nadine laugh. He edged around the corner of the trailer.

"Nadine? It's Gennady. Can I ask what you're doing?"

She laughed, sounding a little giddy. Gennady blinked away the dazzle-dots and spotted Achille. He was clutching the railing and staring wide-eyed as Nadine pulled another flare out of a box at her feet.

She'd holstered her pistol and now energetically pulled the tab from the flare. She windmilled her arm and hurled it into the distance, laughing as she did it. Gennady could see the bright spark following the last one down – but the vista here was too dizzying and he quickly brought his eyes back to Nadine.

"Found these in the trailer," she said. "They're perfect. Want to help?" She offered one to him. Gennady shook his head.

"That's going to cause a fire," he said. She nodded.

"That's the idea. Did you bring a radio? We dropped ours. Achille here has to radio his people to shut down the tower." She looked hopeful, but Gennady shook his head. "We'll have to wait for that new bodyguard, then," she said. "He's sure to have one. Then we can all go home."

The good news was, she didn't look like she was on some murderous rampage. She looked determined, but no different from the Nadine he'd known five years ago. "We can?" said Gennady. "This is just a family fight, is that it? Achille's not going to press charges, and the others aren't going to talk?"

She hesitated. "Come on, can't you let me have my moment? You of all people should be able to do that."

"Why me of all people?"

She smiled at him past smoke and vivid pink light. "'Cause you've already saved the world a couple times."

She turned to throw another flare.

"Not the world," Gennady said – only because he felt he had to say something to keep her talking. "Azerbaijan, maybe. But... all this," he gestured at the falling flares, "seems like a bit much for having your brother get into a fight with your date."

"No. *No!*" She sounded hugely disappointed in him. "This isn't about that little incident with Kafatos, is it Achille?" Achille flung up his free hand in exasperation; his other still tightly held the rail. "Although," Nadine went on, "I'm afraid I might have given brother dear the big idea myself, a couple of days before."

"What idea?" Gennady looked to Achille, who wouldn't meet his eyes.

"When he told me about the tower project and said he wanted to use the Putorana Plateau as a carbon sink, I told him about the Permian extinction. He was fascinated – weren't you, Achille? But he really lit up when I told him that though it was heat shock that undoubtedly killed many of the trees on the planet, it was something else that finished off the rest."

"What are you talking about?"

Nadine pointed down, at the disc of plastic-roofed forest below them. "You drove through it on the way up here. It's out there, trying to get into our lungs, our systems..."

"The *fungus?*"

She nodded. "A specific breed of it. It covered Earth from pole to pole during the Permian. It ate all the trees that survived the heat... *conifer* trees, tough as they were. And here's the thing: it's still around today." Again she nodded at the forest. "It's called Rhizoctonia, and Achille's been farming a particularly nasty strain of it here for two years."

Gennady looked at Achille. He was remembering how the day had gone – how Achille seemed to be building his restart schedule around prevailing winds, rather than the integrity of the tower's systems.

If you wanted to cultivate an organism that ate wood and thrived in dry heat, you'd want a greenhouse. They were perched above the biggest greenhouse in central Asia.

Nadine hoisted up the box of flares and stalked off along the catwalk. "I need to make sure the whole fungus crop goes up. *You* need to make sure Achille's engineers close the windows, or the heat's all going to come up here. See you in a bit." She disappeared around the curve of the tower; a short time later, Gennady saw a flare wobble up and then down into the night.

He turned to Achille, who had levered himself onto his feet. "Is she crazy? Or did we really come here to bomb Kafatos's forest with spores?"

Achille glared defiantly back. "So what if we did? It's industrial espionage, sure. But he screwed me over to start with, made a secret deal with the oligarchs to torpedo my bid. Fair's fair."

"And what's to prevent this rhyzoctithing from spreading? How's it supposed to tell the difference between Kafatos's trees and the rest of the forest?" Achille looked away, and suddenly Gennady saw it all – the whole plan.

"It can't, can it? You were going to spread a cloud of spores across the whole northern hemisphere. Every heat-shocked forest in Asia and North America would fall to the rhizoctonia. Biological sequestration of carbon would stagger to a stop, not just here but everywhere. Atmospheric carbon levels would shoot up. Global warming would go into high gear. No more talk about mitigation. No more talk about slowing emissions on a schedule. The world would have to go massively carbon-negative, immediately. And you own all the patents to that stuff."

"Not all," he admitted. "But for the useable stuff, yeah."

A metallic *bong bong bong* sound came from the catwalk opposite the direction Nadine had taken. Moments later Octav showed up. He was puffing, obviously spooked by the incredible drop, but determined to help his boss. "Where is she?"

"Never mind," said Achille. "Have you got a walkie-talkie?" Octav nodded and handed it over.

"Hello hello?" Achille put the thing to his ear, other hand on his other ear, and paced up and down. Octav was staring at the balloons painted on the trailer.

"What is that?" he said, assuming, it seemed, that Gennady would know.

"Looks like they were expecting tourists. Base jumping off a solar updraft tower?" From up here, you'd be able to slide down the valley thermals to the river far below. "I guess it could be fun."

"I can't get a signal," said Achille. "You," he said to Octav, "go after her!"

"You can't get a signal because you're outside. They're inside." Gennady pointed at the door in the side of the tower as Octav pounded away along the catwalk. "Try again from next to the elevator." Achille moved to the door and Gennady made to follow, but as Achille opened it a plume of smoke poured out. "Oh, shit!"

The tower had been designed to suck up air from the surrounding forest. It was already pulling in smoke from the fires Nadine had lit with her flares. And she was moving in a circle, trying to ensure that the entire bull's-eye of whitened pines caught.

"Yes! Yes!" Achille was gasping into the radio, ducking out of the smoke-filled tower every few seconds to breathe. "You have to do it now! The whole forest, yes!" He glanced at Gennady. "They're trying to get to the trailer, but they'd have to fix the transformer first and there's too much smoke, I don't know if they're going to make it."

Gennady looked down at the forest; lots of little spot fires were spreading and joining up into larger orange smears and lozenges. If Nadine made it all the way around, they'd be trapped at the center of a firestorm. "We're stuck too."

"Maybe not." Achille ran to the trailer, which turned out to be full of cardboard boxes. They rummaged among them, finding more flares – not useful – and safety harnesses, cables and crampons and, "Ha!" said Achille, holding up two parachutes.

"Is that all?"

The billionaire kicked around at the debris. "Yeah, you'd think there'd be more, but you know we never got this place up and running. These are probably the test units. Doesn't matter, there's one for me, one for you."

"Not Nadine?" Achille shot him an exasperated look. She was his own sister, but he obviously didn't care. Gennady took the chute he offered, with disgust. He would, he decided, give it to Nadine when she came back around – if only to see the expression on Achille's face.

Achille was headed out the door. "What then?" asked Gennady. Nadine's brother looked back, still exasperated. "Are you just going to walk away from your dream?"

Achille shook his head. "The patents and designs are all I've got now. I can't make a go selling the power from this place. It's the fungus or nothing. So, look, this fire might eat the tower, but the wind is blowing *in*. The Rhizoctonia on the fringes will be okay. As soon as we're on the ground I'm going to bring in some trucks, and haul away the remainder during the cleanup. I can still dump that all over Kafatos's God-damned forest. We lost the first hand, that's all."

"But..." Gennady couldn't believe he had to say it. "What about Nadine?"

Achille crossed his arms, glowering at the fires. "This has been coming a long time. You know what the worst part is? I'd made her my heir again. Lucky thing I never told her, huh."

As they stepped outside a deep groan came from the tower, and Gennady's inner ear told him he was moving, even though his feet were firmly planted on the deck. Looking down, he saw they were ringed by fire now. The only reason the smoke and heat weren't streaming up the side of the tower was because they were pouring through the open windmill apertures. Past the open door he could see only a wall of shuddering gray inside. The engineers and Bogdan must already be dead.

The tower twisted again, and with a popping sound sixteen feet of catwalk separated from the wall. It drooped, and just then Nadine and Octav came around the tower's curve, on the other side of it.

Achille and Nadine stared at one another over the gap, not speaking. Then Achille turned away with an angry shrug. "We have to go!" He began struggling into his parachute.

Octav waved at Gennady. "Got any ideas?" Neither he nor Nadine were holding weapons. They've obviously realized their best chance for survival lay with one another.

Gennady edged as close to the fallen section of catwalk as he dared. "Belts, straps, have you got anything like that?" Octav grabbed at his waist, nodded. "The tower's support cables!" Gennady pointed at the nearest one, which leaned out from under the door. "We're going to have to slide down those!" He could see that the cables' anchors were outside the ring of fire, but that wouldn't last long. "Pull up the floor mesh over one, and climb down to the cable anchor. Double up your belt and – hang on a second." Octav's belt would be worn through by friction before they got a hundred feet. Gennady ran into the trailer, which was better lit now by the rising sun, and tossed the boxes around. He found some broken metal strapping. Perfect. Coming out, he tossed a piece across to Octav. "Use that instead. Now get going!"

As they disappeared around the curved wall, Achille darted from behind the trailer. "Coming?" he shouted as he ran to the railing.

Gennady hesitated. He'd dropped his parachute by the trailer steps.

It was clear what had to be done. There was only one way off this tower. Still, he just stood there, watching as Achille clumsily mounted the railing.

Achille looked back. "Come on, what are you waiting for?"

Images from the day were flashing through Gennady's mind – and more, a vision of what could happen after the fire was over. He turned to look out over the endless skin of forest that filled the valley and spread beyond to the horizon.

He'd spent his whole life cleaning up other people's messes. There'd been the Chernobyl affair, and that other nuclear disaster in Azerbaijan. He'd chased stolen nukes across two continents, and only just succeeding in hiding from the world a discovery that would allow any disgruntled tinkerer to build such weapons without needing enriched uranium or plutonium. He'd told himself all the while that he did these things to keep humanity safe. Yet it had never been the idea that people might die that had moved him. He was afraid for something else, and had been for so long now that he couldn't imagine living without that fear.

It was time to admit where his real allegiance lay.

"I'm right behind you," he said with a forced smile. And he watched Achille dive off the tower. He watched Nadine's brother fall two hundred feet and open his chute. He watched the vortex of flame around the tower's base yank the parachute in and down, and swallow it.

Gennady picked up the last piece of metal strapping and, as the tower writhed again, ran along the catwalk opposite to the way Nadine and Octav had gone.

HE ROLLED OVER and staggered to his feet, coughing. A cloud of white was churning around him, propelled by a quickening gale. Overhead the plastic sheeting that covered the dead forest flapped where he'd cut through it. The support cable made a perfectly straight line from the concrete block at his feet up to the distant tower – or was it straight? No, the thing was starting to curve. Achille's tower, which was now in full sunlight, was curling away from the fire, as if unwilling to look at it anymore. Any second now it might fall.

Gennady raced around the perimeter of the fire as the sun touched the plastic ceiling. The flames were eating their way slowly outward, pushing against the wind. Gennady dodged fallen branches and avoided thick brambles, pausing now and then to cough heavily, so it took him a few minutes to spot the support cable opposite the one he'd slid down. When it appeared it was as an amber pen-stroke against the pre-dawn sky. The plastic greenhouse ceiling was broken where the cable pierced it, as it should be if bodies had broken through it on their way to the ground.

As he approached the cable's concrete anchor, he spotted Octav. The bodyguard was curled up on the ground, clutching his ankle.

"Where's Nadine?" Octav looked up as Gennady pounded up. He blinked, looked past Gennady, then they locked eyes.

That look said, *Where's Achille?*

Neither said anything for a long moment. Then, "She fell off," said Octav. "Back there." He pointed into the fire.

"How far–"

"Go. You might find her."

Gennady didn't need any more urging. He let the white wind push him at the shimmering walls of orange light. As the banners of fire whipped up they caught and tore the plastic sheeting that had canopied the forest for years, and they angrily pulled it down. Gennady looked for another break in that upper surface, hopefully close to the cable's anchor, and after a moment he spotted it. Nadine had left a clean incision in the plastic, but had shaved a pine below that; branches and needles were strewn across the white pillows of rhyzoctonia and made Nadine herself easy to find.

She blinked at him from where she lay on a mattress of fungi. She looked surprised, and for a moment Gennady had the absurd thought that maybe his hair was all standing up or something. But then she said, "It doesn't hurt."

He frowned, reached down and pinched her ankle.

"Ow!"

"Fungus broke your fall." He helped her up. The flames were being kept at bay by the inrushing wind, but the radiant heat was intense. "Get going." He pushed her until she was trotting away from the fire.

"What about you?"

"Right behind you!"

He followed, more slowly, until she disappeared into the swirling rhyzoctonia. Then he slowed and stopped, leaning over to brace his hands on his knees. He looked back at the fire.

Sure, if Achille had been thinking, he would have known that the fire would suck in any parachute that came off the tower. Yet Gennady could have warned him, and didn't. He'd murdered Achille, it was that simple.

The wall of fire was mesmerizing and its heat like a wall pushing Gennady back. There must have been a lot of fires like this one, the last time the rhyzoctonia roused itself to make a meal of the world. Achille had engineered special conditions under his greenhouse roof, but it wouldn't need them once it got out. The whole northern hemisphere was a tinderbox, a dry feast waiting for the guest who would consume it all.

Gennady squinted into the flames, waiting. He didn't regret killing Achille. Given the choice between saving a human, or even humanity itself, and preserving the dark labyrinth of Khantayskoe, he'd chosen the forest. In doing that he'd finally admitted his true loyalties, and stepped over the border of the human. But that left him with nowhere to go. So, he simply stood, and waited for the fire.

Somebody grabbed his arm. Gennady jerked and turned to find Octav standing next to him. The bodyguard was using a long branch as a crutch. There was a surprising expression of concern on his face. "Come on!"

"But, you see, I–"

"I don't care!" Octav had a good grip on him, and was stronger than Gennady. Dazed, Gennady let himself be towed away from the fire, and in moments a pale oval swam into sight between the upright boles of orange-painted pine: Nadine's face.

"Where's Achille?" she called.

Gennady waited until they were close enough that he didn't have to yell. "He tried to use a parachute. The fire pulled him in."

Nadine looked down, seeming to crumple in on herself. "Oh, God, all those men, and, and Achille..." She staggered, nearly fell, then seemed to realize where they were. Gennady could feel the fire at his back.

She inserted herself between Octav and Gennady, propelling them both in the direction of the lake at the bottom of the hill. "I'm sorry, I never meant any of this to happen," she cried over the roar of the fire. All I wanted was for him to go back to his original plan! It could still work." She meant the towers, Gennady knew, and the carbon-negative power plants, and the scheme to sequester all that carbon under the plateau. Not the rhyzoctonia. Maybe she was right, but even though she was Achille's heir, and owner of the technologies that could save the world, she would never climb out from under what had just happened. She'd be in jail soon, and maybe for the rest of her life.

There were options. Gennady found he was thinking coolly and rationally about those; his mind seemed to have been miraculously cleared, and of more than just the trauma of the past hour. He was waking up, it seemed, from something he'd thought of as his life, but which had only been a rough rehearsal of what he could become. He knew himself now, and the anxiety and hesitation that had dogged him since he was a child was simply gone.

What was important was the patents, and the designs, the business plan and the opportunities that might bring another tower to the plateau. It might not happen this year or next, but it would have to be soon. Someone had to take responsibility for the crawling disaster overtaking the world, and do something about it.

He would have to talk to Nadine about that inheritance, and about who would administer the fortune while she was in prison. He doubted she would object to what he had in mind.

"Yes, let's go," he said. "We have a lot to do, and not much time."

REPORT CONCERNING THE PRESENCE OF SEAHORSES ON MARS

Pat Cadigan

[Transcript: plog Rose Polat Feenixity, edited & annotated]

"WHAT *IS* THAT?" Beau asked nervously, retreating a little on the mesh in the reception grotto.

"Kidding me? It's a mobi," I said.

"It's my *ass*," he said. "What are they playing at?"

"Nothing. They're Earth people." I turned to see he'd actually climbed the netting on the wall. "Hey?"

"Does the name 'Shelob' mean anything to you?" Tiny blobs of sweat fell away in slow motion from his handsome dark face.

I blinked at him. "*The Hobbit*? Seriously?" I jerked my head at the walls where a few dozen sp(eye)ders were bouncing around the basalt mesh either relaying data or monitoring the ambience. They ranged in size from barely three centimetres across, legs included, up to critters twice the size of the average Earth tarantula. They were all half-organic, half-tech; still photos have been known to cause hysterics in the more fragile, usually Earth people. "Is this a bad time to mention you're on the web?"

"*Rose.* Tarantulas are *normal*-big. This is like something out of a horror movie! It's the size of a *Marserati!* I'm gonna have *nightmares!*"

Beau's exaggerate-itis was exacerbated by his obsession with surface racing; I knew the Marserati he was referring to and the mobi wasn't even half that size. On first sight, I'd thought it looked like an overgrown toy but now that Beau had pointed it out, I could kinda see what he meant, damn him. It *did* have an unnerving quality – eight jointed legs spread out from a centre globe with a full 360° view for the visitor/operator, whose head was displayed within as 3D hologram. All the legs ended in round pads with a plethora of tiny hairs on the bottom, possibly for climbing walls and running across ceilings. As if we could actually just give it the run of Feenixity. Most of our long-distance visitors, either from Earth or from elsewhere on Mars, came Down Here via AugmAr. Mobis are workhorses, used either on the surface or by tunnelling crews. Only a major juice box could have pulled this off but no one had seen fit to tell us who that might be. We'd just gotten a buzz to go to the south-southeast reception grotto and meet a mobi guest.

The head on display in the globe looked natural as anything for a composite. Whenever we dealt with a representative of some important Earth body, individual or corporate, it was usually an ArP designed by committee. It's how Earth people do business. An Artificial Person is easier to control than a live front with an earwig – it'll never think for itself and go off script, it doesn't need to be paid, praised, or promoted, and it won't get head-hunted. Stolen or hacked, maybe, but never lured away by a bigger salary and better perks. Or so they tell me. My own experience is – well, not limited, exactly, but skewed. I've been out of the blue and deep in the red for almost twenty Mars years and I barely remember what it's like to live on Earth any more.

Now I looked over my shoulder at Beau and signed, *Should I speak first?* He signed back *No idea.* Big help, that guy. I took a breath and bounced gently over to the mobi, stopping right in front of it.

"Welcome to Feenixity," I said cheerfully. "I'm Rose, this is Beauregard, we'll be your guides while you're here. I'm sorry to say that we haven't been briefed as to the purpose of your visit or what you want to accomplish while you're here, but we are both long-time residents and we're prepared to help you however we can." I raised my left hand and used the LED in my index finger to write my first name backwards in the air. Most Earth people prefer long-form to ideograms, at least until they get to know you better. "This is a link to our bios." And then I waited. The average gap in a Mars-Earth conversation was anywhere from fifteen to thirty minutes, depending.

The head stared blindly through me. Like most commercial ArPs, it was androgynous and ethnically ambiguous. That's a thing with Earth people, hedging their bets by trying to appeal to everyone.

After a bit, the head came to life, its androgyny tipping toward feminine as it focused on me. "I am Soledad Dimitrovich-Walker," the head told me. "I don't believe I caught your last names?"

I waited but that was all. So it was going to be like that. I swear to God, there are thousands of manuals in every freakin' language; there are videos, slide shows, even dog-and-pony shows (cartoons – they're cute) that explain how even when Mars and Earth are at their closest, it can take about four minutes for light to travel between them – that's just light, all by itself. It takes longer than that for a message to be coded by the sender, then decoded by the receiver. Then there's the time it takes for a message to be understood, considered, evaluated. Composing a reply takes more time, depending on what you're talking about, which won't be the weather, celebrity gossip, or how your day is going. Finally, the reply has to be encoded, transmitted, received, decoded, read, etc. Given all that, you have to make every transmission count on a live line, which is why most people stick to email.

I glanced at Beau; he gave me a barely perceptible nod. Creeped out or not, he had my back, one of the many reasons why I love him.

"We all have the same last name here," I said. "Feenixity. We adopted the custom almost ten years ago. Ten Mars years, that is. Other cities–"

Abruptly, the head perked up again. "Ah, we've linked your images to your resumes, thank you. I represent the Federal Government of the United States of America, under whose aegis the settlement now known as *Phoenix City* was established." The emphasis was slight but pointed.

I wasn't sure what boggled me more – an outsider telling me how to pronounce Feenixity or the fact that an authority powerful enough to force an underground visit by mobi didn't seem to know better than to speak before getting a response to their previous communication. It was the equivalent of talking over someone while they were trying to answer you in a normal conversation – not a felony but something a child would do.

"We understand that mobile units of this nature aren't customary for sub-surface visitation," the head went on in a stiffer, more formal voice, "but we have intel concerning unauthorised, even criminal activity by residents. Previous visits conducted virtually via AugmAr have been unsatisfactory. On Earth, we would simply send a delegation to investigate in person. However, interplanetary travel is not only an extreme expense but problematic time-wise." *Problematic time-wise;* I almost grinned at the antiquated expression. The US and nostalgia – heirloom tomatoes, heirloom language. "We hit on this unorthodox procedure as a compromise and sincerely hope that it will obviate any further action. I would appreciate it if you would take me directly to the Governor's office *now,* and we'll continue conversing as we go."

Beau's gaze met mine. He didn't seem at all startled; a quick glance at the scrap in my lens told me I didn't, either. When you live under constant surveillance, you learn how to keep a straight face sans Botox. Our vitals, however, were another matter. H&S didn't even bother with a ping-if-you're-still-alive.

"Talk to me, Rose," commanded the voice in my ear. My first sister, Lily; I felt a whole lot calmer immediately. Everyone in Health & Safety is pretty level-headed but even all of them agree that if you're spurting from an artery, Lily's your best bet.

I made the sign for a red-alert/defcon-one situation not involving imminent literal death, then shifted position to block the head's view of Beau while he signed the details. Not that our visitor(s) couldn't see him if they really wanted to, but tapping into our surveillance would take a lot of time and effort, things that are never cheap. Considering they'd mentioned money right away, it was probably safe to assume there was another financial crisis in progress and they were trying very hard not to over-spend. Or spend at all.

Eyemail from my supervisor appeared in my lens. *Nu sumthin ≈ this wud hapn, ⇆ ↑↓ pmp ndfns.* I almost laughed out loud. Rudi thought popping out an exercise band and pumping endorphins was the solution gateway to just about any problem. Well, it *was* the best way to play for time with Earth people; they couldn't argue about mandatory procedures to keep our muscles from atrophying and our bones from dissolving. And the Martian workout was still trending big in the west. They loved trampolines and bungee cords as much as heirloom tomatoes; still do, I hear. I slipped off my belt and did a few sets of slow push-kicks until the head perked up again.

"I see we haven't left the reception area," it said in an authoritatively displeased tone. "Is there some technical reason for this delay? We have the most recent layout onboard. You only need to plot a course for the mobile navigator. If you are unfamiliar with this particular technology, there's a help file with complete instructions."

While the head nattered on a little more about the file, I transmitted a link and then quickly composed the message it was supposed to connect with, working online so it wouldn't just come up blank if they were quick on the click. With any luck, someone there would know enough to wait for the complete text, even if they didn't seem to understand how to have an interplanetary conversation. Or maybe they did but whoever was running the head just wouldn't pay attention. That was also a thing with Earth people: they didn't take orders from us. Ever. (Sure liked to give them, though.)

Because I was working online, I knew when they got the link and when they clicked it – well, seven minutes after the fact, to be precise. I'd been mostly done by then. The only thing that would have come in while they were reading the message was my suggestion that 'Soledad Dimitrovich-Walker' review the standard guidelines for ultra-long-distance phone calls, because they weren't really like phone calls. (And then I almost sabotaged the whole thing by putting Shelob instead of Soledad. Luckily, I caught it. Even if I'd been weasel enough to try blaming Beau for putting the idea in my head, it wouldn't have helped.)

There was a much longer wait for an answer. I could imagine the vigorous discussion going on back in the blue. Lots of local phone calls and people all talking at once saying things like, *How can they get away with this?* And, *We* tried *to tell you* and *But it's supposed to be* American *soil, isn't it?* And, *Say what you will but I bet the Chinese don't have these problems with* their *people.*

Finally, the head made a throat-clearing noise. "All right, we'll do things your way, one full message at a time." *My* way? That was both laughably inaccurate and disturbingly ominous. I wished like anything I'd still been full-time in the greenhouse.

Greenhice management are all crazy but in a way that makes sense. "We have some questions. If the dimensions of the tunnels that we have been given are correct, our mobile unit will fit with some room to spare. Why then do you insist the unit is too big to move about freely, even in the grottos, which we happen to know are cavernous?

"If you insist the current hardware is unsuitable, can you supply a substitute that will meet the following requirements: free-standing, independently mobile, controlled solely by us, with a secure, unmonitored comm-link? Are you willing to allow the visit to continue until the substitute can be procured? Do you understand that if you refuse to cooperate, the consequences may be severe enough to endanger lives or worse? Reply soonest, thank you."

This time, Rudi phoned. "'I've sent them a copy of the transport regulations concerning mass and volume with the appropriate areas highlighted, and a personal note apologising for the inconvenience."

"Great," said Beau. "And if they want to argue they should be exempt from size and weight restrictions?"

"I'll be happy to debate them later," Rudi said cheerfully. "Six dogs are on their way to you. They'll disassemble the damned thing, take it to the Main Grotto, and put it back together before they can answer."

Beau didn't quite frown. "What if they think it's an AugmAr fake-out?"

"The goddam log's running," Rudi replied, the *goddam* belying his stolid cheeriness. "They'll have a perfect, authentic record of every glorious moment. Dogs comin' through now."

I hopped back to join Beau on the wall as half a dozen dogs-bodies in yellow work-suits pedalled in from the south tunnel, slotted their cycles, and went to work under a foreman only they could see and hear. From the way they went at it and what they were saying to each other, I knew Aster Li was giving the orders. Of everyone I'd ever worked for in my dogs-body days, she was my favourite. She preps every job by seeing it in three dimensions in her head and her work-plans all come out like choreography. Earth people can't get enough of her videos; her dog crews routinely get the highest number of views, and that's premieres *and* re-runs. The Firefly Murmuration video still holds the record for most paid hits on debut. Just a repair crew wearing fairy lights taking mole-bots apart in a dark grotto but even *I* love that one and I'm not much for soya entertainment these days (low-gravity isn't conducive to sitting on your ass).

Six and a half minutes later, we were all on our way to the Main Grotto. Beau and I let the crew go ahead – our cycles were set on high effort, Beau's higher than mine. I'd just done some resistance sets so I was good for a while. But my physical monitor probably figured I'd have hung back with Beau anyway and decided not to waste the effort. That's the sort of thing you really want in a fizz; it's also one of a thousand things about life in the red that they don't get back in the blue, no matter how you explain it.

"So what do you suppose the life-threatening consequences of failing to cooperate are?" I asked Beau.

"All the candy-bar people pull their sponsorship?" he wheezed, rearranging the handle-bars so he could pedal in the recumbent position. (I keep telling Transport Hardware that if they added actual wheels to these things so they weren't just handles and pedals on a pole, they'd be more a lot more fun. They always say the same thing: *Maybe someday, when there's more space and storage Down Here.*)

"Or all their candy-bars." I heard myself and stopped laughing. "What if they did? Seriously. That would be..." I trailed off, unable to think of a word awful enough to describe life without the semi-annual chocolate holidays.

"Really awful," Beau puffed, breathless.

I reached over and pulled on the back of his shirt to remind him not to lean forward, thinking that the upper body/lower body divide between men and women had never been as clear-cut as it was now, for all of us. "Worse than that. We don't have enough coca or coffee plants yet for a commercial-sized crop."

"So I guess that's at least another year without a Marsbucks franchise Down Here, then? And they dare to call this America." Beau grunted with effort. "But I don't understand where the threat to life comes in."

"Maybe they'll cut everything off," I said.

"What do you mean, 'everything'? Like–" he had to slow down to talk now. "They'd just *abandon* us? Leave us here to die?"

"If we're costing them more than they're taking in, yeah. One of the first things they mentioned was how expensive space travel is. Any time they bring up money that soon, it means it's high priority, and money's only a high priority when it's scarce." I actually wanted to stop talking because I was scaring the living fuq out of myself but I couldn't. My mind was racing, showing me a stream of pictures, none of them pretty. "I don't remember the Federal Government ever being so concerned with crime on Mars that they felt they had to intervene. Or interfere."

Beau sighed. "I opted out of the government module in favour of folklore and oral traditions, so I'm not really qualified to make any pronouncements on the matter. *But*–" he huffed mightily. "That's never stopped me before. Would they go to this much trouble to intervene – or interfere – if they were planning to cut us off?"

"Well, no," I said, feeling slightly better for all of two seconds. "But they could be taking inventory to decide which settlements to keep and which are more trouble than they're worth." My heartbeat was way up now and not just from physical effort. "During my rotation in cityhall, my mentor told me Earth is always pushing for scripted videos, for *more things happening*. One of the greenhice down south actually has a separate crew just for drama – they pretend they're having affairs or plotting to steal, I don't know, stuff, or something. The network wanted to kill off one of the characters by having another character murder them but they couldn't get anyone to go along with it. Surveillance society – somebody's always watching so it has to be worth looking at."

"Or listening to," Rudi said quietly in my ear. "Loose lips get your ass kicked, remember? Or worse, all our asses."

"And if all our asses are gonna get kicked anyway?" I said evenly.

"Don't talk like you know something when you don't," Rudi said just as evenly. "Hurry up, that thing's almost reassembled."

[Annotation... I guess; admin didn't explain all the functions on this thing very well. *(Pause #1)* Testing, testing – is this thing on? *(Pause #2)* Well, it is or it isn't. Okay, I don't see why I couldn't have done this as a standard personal log; I'd be done by now. How's *that* for an annotation?]

NOTHING TRAVELS AS fast Down Here as a scandal or a scare. Sp(eye)ders were pouring into the Main Grotto from all directions; I'd never seen so many in one place. Everybody in town must have sent one, and some, more than one. Nobody wanted to miss a thing. This was Feenixity's version of an uproar. At least it wasn't an actual crowd – climate-control would have crashed. But parts of the walls looked like they were alive and if sp(eye)ders kept on coming like this, the mass might throw the local environment out of balance, which would in turn stress other areas of Feenixity. Down Here, balance is nothing to screw around with. You can't count on a whole lot of wiggle room because there's only so much breathable air.

Local life-support is calibrated in two steps, first in general to establish gradated parameters and then continuous maintenance – [Plogger's note: Seriously? I *really* have to explain this?] which means everything's measured and balanced. Being near the North Pole, Feenixity has the advantage of easy – well, eas*ier* – access to water and oxygen. But even so, it took a while before we could start supplying plant cuttings and fresh produce to other settlements on a regular basis. Everyone says because we have the largest number of greenhice, we've got the best air. The numbers bear that out, although there isn't as much difference between our air and other settlements' now as there was even ten Mars years ago. Eventually, when the botanicals in other settlements are more mature, they'll all smell good, or at least better. But it'll be a long time before we can be spontaneous without a permit.

It's not an ideal way to live. I mean, we'd all still be under surveillance even if a gazillion people on Earth *weren't* watching us on the Reality Show Network (I hear they even watch us on the Moon; the meta must make *their* reality shows pretty static). Everything we consume/breathe is measured, going in and coming out; the ecology depends on it and our lives depend on the ecology. On Earth, if you get fed up with your job or your neighbourhood or even your whole life, you can just take off, go somewhere else and try something new. On Mars, you've already committed in advance to be where you're needed, to do what needs doing. You can express a preference and you might even get it… but you'll probably have to wait and there's no telling how long.

Which is why we're all so hobby-crazy. I got into the basalt-roving knitting thing in a big way when I first got here. Then crocheting and even lace tatting – the stuff can be as fine as hair (I still have basalt lace all over the walls of my bedroom). Being pre-disposed to fidget got me a GMO apprenticeship on the greenhouse track. It never crossed my mind to turn it down; to paraphrase an old saying, I didn't come here to say no.

* * *

ANYWAY, BY THE time Beau and I hit the Main Grotto, I had more message flags in my lens than I'd had all year. Eyemail is supposed to be more secure than email but it's an intranet, not telepathy. And even if it were, someone would probably figure out how to hack into that in less than a day.

Some people can handle eyemail while they're doing something else but my multi-tasking tree won't branch that far. I didn't have time even to tell everyone that I didn't have time to answer them so I marked myself unavailable, which bounced all the messages. That's one of those things that sounds really rude to Earth people but it isn't any more impolite than a busy signal or an answering machine. Rude would have been accepting all the messages and flushing them unread.

[Plogger's note: I'm sorry, I'm not trying to be rude now, either, but how much do I have to explain to Earth people? If anyone can tell me, don't be shy, okay?]

THE MAIN GROTTO has four levels: ground, first, second, and ceiling. The ground is mainly machinery – climate control, power, plumbing – and various kinds of micro-algae coatings. The netting on the first level is for general foot traffic and extends wall to wall. The second level nets are divided into separate sections around the perimeter for meetings or classes or other kinds of get-togethers, leaving the centre open so people can move between levels via the stiffened tethers anchored in the ceiling gym. It's not the most efficient layout but we voted to leave it as is for historical reasons. (Incidentally, all the nets are the original basalt roving. That stuff *lasts*.)

"What are you doing here?" I asked Rudi, who was still hanging around. "I thought you'd be conferring with the council."

"First, I take responsibility with my team," he said, serenely, dangling from a tether with a few dozen sp(eye)ders along a stretch just above his head. More sp(eye)ders were gathering on the net around the mobi a few metres away. The crew had reassembled it with only four legs – enough to keep it propped up for conversation but not enough to move easily. I found myself wondering if a three-legged configuration would have worked equally well to stabilise it while making even more difficult, if not impossible, to move.

"A bit too hostile," Beau whispered, reading my mind through my would-be poker face. It's the lighter gravity – like every other part of your body, your facial muscles work a bit differently with less pulling them down. Some people, like Beau, have a talent for spotting minute tells in people they know well (I think it's something to do with pattern recognition, but don't quote me).

"Ix-nay on the indreading-may," I whispered back, frowning. "Especially around you-know-what."

"FYI, I was thinking the same thing." Beau chuckled a little. "But this is okay, too. Not so Shelob, I feel better." He gave me a little push. "Go ahead, get a little closer. Before the sp(eye)ders crowd you out."

The nearest tether was closer than I really wanted to be but all the others were a little too stand-offish. I looked at the dogs, who were hanging on the wall with the other four legs. A couple of them were busily taking one apart, apparently out of curiosity. Probably career dogs, who were all compulsive tinkerers; I hoped for all our sakes they could figure out how to put it back together. I was about to ask Rudi what I'd missed when the head in the globe woke up again.

"Ah. Now can we go to the Governor's office? I would like to get started reviewing your records and scheduling interviews with the women. I would also like to consult with the Governor and whoever else can transport this mobi from one place to another about the feasibility of less formal interviews. More than that, I don't wish to say to anyone except the Governor, who must be in his office by now? Over to you."

This time, the hologram dimmed, indicating the connection had actually been broken. Everyone sighed with relief.

"Okay," I said. "Tell me what I'm supposed to do now. Do I try to explain that the Governor's office is a completely virtual construct or do I say the Governor is unavailable? If so, what lie do I tell?"

"Something with laryngitis or some other throat infection that means the Governor can't speak," suggested Beau.

"That's good. I vote for that, too," piped up one of the dogs, an ambid named Jazm. We had come out of the blue on the same transport. S/he'd gone off to pick blueberries in the Land of Opportunity. Apparently, her/his interest had shifted from rocks to machines. I sent her/him a catch-up-later ping.

"Maybe the Governor has a contingency plan?" I said, looking at Rudi.

"If he does, it's not something he's shared with me." Behind his goggles, his gaze was distant; eyemail. Rudi was one of those people who couldn't accommodate an implanted lens so he had to go around looking like he was on his way to a wind tunnel. A few moments later, he gave a short, surprised laugh. "Zeke knew they were coming."

A sp(eye)der landed on my shoulder and started to make itself at home. "No hitchhikers," I told it and it dropped away. I turned back to Rudi. "And Zeke decided to keep that to himself because... oh, he thought we'd like a surprise?"

"No," Rudi said, unperturbed. "He knew there was no way to stop them so he figured it was better not to stir everyone up ahead of time."

"And you think that was a good decision?" I said, trying not to sound disrespectful.

"Actually, yes." The circuit tattoo on Rudi's forehead puckered slightly. "In light of the furore we all know is coming, keeping things running smoothly here for as long as possible *is* the best thing to do."

Ezekiel Kebede Feenixity was a genius city-planner but not my favourite Governor. He could understand all kinds of systems objectively from the outside but he had a harder time seeing one from the inside, as part of it. Probably because he *was* thinking – over-thinking – instead of feeling the flow. His latest project was unprecedented and he'd managed to keep it quiet until it was close to completion.

Something hit the backs of my knees and I crumpled on the net. "Where *are* you?" Rudi demanded, suddenly beside me.

"Somewhere in the future." My face was burning as I bounced back up. "I've got a lot on my mind." I glanced at Beau, who winced and shook his head.

Rudi was about to say something else when Shelob woke up again. "Excuse me for communicating again before receiving your answer but readings indicate the mobi is only partially assembled. Is there some problem with the hardware or are the readings in error? Also, we have received two separate files on the layout of Phoenix City, one more extensive than the other. Neither is a complete match for the one we have. Which one reflects the current configuration? Please send another file with photographic walk-through of all habitable areas in a format suitable for viewing on a flat screen but with true-life resolution or as close to it as possible." The head dimmed again as it fell silent.

"Okay," I said, "who wants to handle that one? Don't be shy."

"We can worry about that later," Rudi said impatiently. "What I was about to tell you before I was so, uh, completely interrupted is, that's not an ArP composite. Soledad Dimitrovich-Walker is a living person, a US special envoy."

"Really." I was a bit skeptical, considering how her appearance had shifted. "Do special envoys always tinker with their looks?"

"If you still had one gee pulling your face down toward your knees every moment of every day, you'd touch up your image, too." Rudi paused, head tilted to one side.

"What?" I asked after a few moments.

"The Governor's been out of surgery for two hours. He's on his way over."

I was surprised and not surprised all at the same time. Zeke always did have a tendency to showboat.

TWO NURSES STRETCHERED Zeke in and used extra tethers to stabilise him. He looked great, considering. A little tired but his colour was good. Shelob would never guess what he'd just gone through unless he told her. I tried to bet Beau three vacation days that he would but he refused to take it; Beau likes him as Governor more than I do but he's not stupid.

Zeke was wearing the royal blue robe of office, which covered him from neck to ankles; the gold belt was sash-style, shoulder to hip instead of around his waist. The outfit's strictly ceremonial, very seldom worn. Voluminous garb in low gravity is a pain in the ass – if it's not getting caught on something, it's flying into someone's face – but it looks great on video. Earth people like to see us bounding around in capes and aerodynamic BASE-jumper flyer-suits and we go along with it despite the occasional Isadora-Duncan-esque accident (but no fatalities so far, thank Ares). We had to keep those ratings up. Ratings meant dollars and dollars meant everybody back in the blue was happy.

Right then it occurred to me that ratings might not help us now.

See, the Federal Government was quite happy when NASA started crowd-funding itself – themselves? – via entertainment. There was a lot of collaboration between the government and the Reality Show Network. The RSN pushed for a new channel completely dedicated to Mars rather than just adding us to the space channels. Both the government and NASA were skeptical at first – they weren't sure they'd get enough material from us to support an all-Mars schedule and they were worried about classified stuff getting out. Well, that was mostly the government. NASA had a different perspective – all of their people had been up, either in orbit or to the moon, which meant they were spaced out. The formal term for it is the Overview Effect. It happens when you see Earth from space as whole and undivided – no borders, no boundaries, no human-made lines dividing land masses into countries or territories.

That's a life-changing experience, nothing like merely seeing a picture of Earth taken from space, or even a super-high-resolution real-time video; believe me, I know. I still remember the initial impact – it was like taking a blow to the head with a great big stick, but from *inside* my head (it took me years to come up with that description and I'm still not sure about it). Everyone on my transport was moved in the most profound way. Some got weepy, some couldn't talk about it, some couldn't stop talking about it, and some, like me, cycled through all of the above several times.

Just for the record, our first sight of Mars was also quite affecting: our new world.

Anyway, once you're spaced out, the whole classified thing seems counter-productive. The people at NASA followed orders for the sake of their jobs – they indulged the government while they waited for opportunities to go up again, perhaps permanently. That's how it was when I left Earth, anyway – all NASA employees had to have space-flight experience. But if expenses were tight, I realised, that was probably no longer the case.

If so, it wasn't just a crying shame – it meant all of us on Mars no longer had the level of advocacy that had so often protected settlement funding when the times that were always a-changin' on Earth a-changed for the worse. When people work for money, you can never pay them enough; when they work for what they believe, they'll pay themselves.

I shook the thought away; Zeke was adjusting the stretcher so he was sitting up with restraints criss-crossing his chest so as to avoid pressure on his abdominal area. His deep brown face had a glow to it and his eyes were almost crazy-bright, if you know what I mean. But at least he didn't look like he might get teary. One of the nurses leaned in to say something to him and Zeke waved her/him away, saying, "I'm fine, I really am." He looked at the mobi and then at the masses of sp(eye)ders crawling all over the place before he turned to me, Beau, and Rudi.

"I hope they don't think we've got some kind of infestation," he said. "Would everyone who doesn't absolutely *have* to have a personal eye in here please re-call their sp(eye)ders? The bandwidth is probably so overloaded at this point, it'll run an hour behind. They'll see it back in the blue before you do. We've got plenty of surveillance – watch that. You won't miss a thing. What have I ever hidden from any of you?" he added with a chuckle.

The sp(eye)der exodus was so gradual that I wondered if everyone had decided to ignore him. But after a bit, I noticed they were dropping through the net onto the ground level, where they picked their way through the machinery and the algae beds to the vents and maintenance conduits. Not all of them, though; some of them settled down in nooks and crannies and went to sleep. Zeke noticed and I could practically see the wheels turning while he considered making the Main Grotto a no-parking zone and then decided not to. I'll say this for him, he knew when to take formal command and when to settle for just as good. (Governors who didn't insist on asserting their authority all the time always did a lot better in Feenixity than authoritarians, although I think it helps to have the occasional bossy-ass just to remind us why we don't like them.)

Beau gave me a nudge and jerked his head toward the mobi. The head was awake again, turning all the way around in the globe. "Is there some problem? We're still waiting for a response.

Please advise if there are technical difficulties on your end." It dimmed again.

"I'll handle this now." Zeke's face blanked briefly as he scanned the reports in his lens.

After a minute or two, Rudi cleared his throat. "Who else from the council will be here?"

"Besides you and Rose?" Zeke asked.

"I'm in greenhouse now," I said, "not cityhall. And I'm only on the council track. I'm not a council member yet." He knew that; had recent events actually affected his memory?

Zeke looked past me to Beau. "What about you?"

"I'm *not* on the council track," he said, "and I don't want to be."

"Ah." The Governor looked blank again. "Well, this is definitely one for oral traditions, possibly folklore." He chuckled, then tilted his head to one side. "Hello? Yes, now, Pearl. Everyone here seems to think we need more councillors in attendance. Bring anyone you can get to come with you." He straightened up. "Sorry. All right, now, for transmission." He signed *Start Message* in the air. The gesture made him wince but when the nurse leaned over to offer him something, he waved him/her away again. I saw the other nurse frown.

"Hello, I'm the current Governor, Ezekial K Feenixity. I'm sure you know that as I haven't exactly kept a low profile. I know why you're here. I'm not going to talk around this or try to obfuscate the issue. It's not a new idea. Feenixity was buzzing about it when it was still Phoenix City. That was back when I first got here, thirty-one Mars years ago. I'll let you figure out how many Earth years that is. I'm afraid we don't think in Earth time and we've recently agreed on a resolution that makes converting to any Earth measures optional. A bot can do it. In fact, our Division of Weights and Measures have several very good conversion bots for all kinds of formats from common to niche or boutique, audio and/or video and they'll give you a good rate if you buy multiple licenses. Elementary schools get a discount. Pardon the commercial. Maybe you can find a way to insert it into RSN programming as a PSA. FTR." Zeke chuckled; so did Beau and Rudi.

I had mixed feelings. I wanted to chuckle but I didn't think Zeke was doing himself or us any favours with disingenuous insolence. Besides, he wasn't talking directly to Earth people. Shelob and her posse were so far removed from the society they claimed to represent that they might as well have been from Mars, too. (Not ours, though.)

"We're not ungrateful," Zeke went on. "But we feel that we've reached a point where we must either change and grow or stagnate and die. I know every other settlement, regardless of their affiliation, feels the same. None of us will return to Earth, and not just because of the physical problems of going back to heavier gravity. We have lives here and there's much more to them than what you see on the Reality Show Network. We want even more than that. It's normal. It's human.

"What we've done – what *I've* done – some call it civil disobedience in the grand tradition of Thoreau. Personally, I'd say it's a legal loophole, in that, to my knowledge, no woman in Feenixity is pregnant or has delivered a living baby.

"We have pregnant men. I was one of them."

Zeke winced again and this time did not wave the nurse off when s/he applied an analgesic patch to the inside of his forearm. "I had a fertilised ovum implanted in my peritoneal cavity. A few hours ago, I gave birth, by surgery, to a healthy baby girl. Her name is Juno Amara Feenixity. Juno, for anyone who doesn't know, was the mother of Mars." Zeke's proud expression turned a bit sheepish. "That may be far too much to expect of a newborn so perhaps she'll go by Amara for a while. It was my wife's mother's name." He leaned slightly to one side. "Means unfading, eternal."

All at once, the nurses were stretchering him out again. The one that had given him the patch looked both furious and scared. My heart did a weird leap-up-and-sink-down move and a heavy feeling swept through me, as if I'd been instantly transported to a centrifuge running at one gee. Or two.

"He just overdid it," Beau said, putting an arm around my waist. "That's all it is. He'll be okay."

"When did you switch to the medical track?" I asked him.

"Hey, I just know my emergency first aid," he said. "His colour didn't change, he didn't get confused or delirious or pass out. He just mistook happiness for energy. Or stamina, or whatever. They don't call it labour for nothing."

"He wasn't exactly in labour. There's no birth canal leading to an exit."

"Well, metaphorically. Women have babies by Caesarean section all the time so it's not like it's all that remarkable."

"Cutting into the abdominal cavity is major surgery, for anybody. And bleeding is no joke in lower gravity–"

"His colour was *good*," Beau insisted. "You saw that yourself."

"I don't know what I saw," I said unhappily.

Rudi gave my arm a shake. "Get solid or get out," he whispered.

I looked up and saw that Pearl Bashir had arrived with Sasha Nikolai and Oren Snow. Pearl beckoned for Rudi to join them at the tethers where Zeke and his nurses had been. He hesitated, looking at me uncertainly.

"She'll be fine," Beau said, looking from him to me. "Won't you?"

I nodded, although I had no idea whether I was lying or not. But I did my best to look solid.

The councillors huddled for a fast consult, then broke apart and braced themselves for whatever was coming up next. I had a sudden mental image of everybody in Feenixity doing the same, the cultivators on duty in my greenhouse, in all the greenhice, the colorists in decor and design, the weavers in the basalt roving plant, the librarians in data management, doctors, nurses, and patients in the clinics and infirmaries, everybody in cityhall, every dogsbody on call, the newest arrivals and their mentors in orientation and training – all of us might have been holding our breath together.

In which case, we'd have suffocated *en masse*. An hour later, we still hadn't had a response.

"We have to wait them out," Pearl said finally, taking the lead; appropriate, as she was Zeke's successor. "And I'd prefer to have us all hold position here, including you." She nodded at the crew hanging on the wall with the mobi legs. "Anyone object?"

Nobody did. The crew were probably carrying at least three hitchhikers each, despite Zeke's request to free up bandwidth. But even if they weren't, no force in the solar system could have made them leave. Me, either, although I was starting to wonder if anyone had ever died of suspense, like maybe having a stroke when it ended.

When the head came to life again, everybody jumped.

"This revelation has created a crisis," Shelob said stiffly. I couldn't think of her actual name any more. "This discussion is suspended while we call an emergency summit to decide what action to take. I've been asked to read a statement from the Executive Chair.

"'This latest development has thrown the entire future of every settlement on Mars into jeopardy, not just Phoenix City. You may feel that you have made use of a legal loophole but this is a clear violation of the spirit and intent of the law. Restricting reproduction was meant to serve as a safety measure to keep the population stable until it could be determined beyond a reasonable doubt that this settlement is capable of supporting life without extraordinary intervention from Earth. At the moment, we do not feel Phoenix City is anywhere near such a state of existence.

"'Meanwhile, the support given to Phoenix City and other settlements is always costly, and must be borne by those developed nations that choose to participate in the off-planet settlement program. The US has been at the forefront financially as well as technologically. During times of austerity and fiscal crisis, it has always fallen to the US to continue bearing the burden even when other nations reduce their contributions at the behest of their own citizens, or even cut them altogether.

"'While the US has always done its best to look after her citizens no matter where they are, and to be responsible for all territories on Earth and elsewhere, it cannot condone or allow actions that would endanger everyone resident in a given territory. Unrestricted reproduction most definitely comes under this heading. Reproductive freedom is for people for whom radiation, limited breathable air, possible food shortages and/or underground cave-ins are *not* routine.

"'If it was your intention to try to reduce or even end the US's participation in your part of the off-planet program, congratulations – you may get your wish.'"

Shelob paused, seemed about to say something else, and then apparently decided not to. The head dimmed and then vanished altogether.

AFTER THAT, THERE was no keeping a lid on anything. Mars' entire pregnant population came out, along with a much smaller number of actual parents. Zeke actually seemed kind of miffed that Juno wasn't the first child born on Mars; that title belonged to a girl named Fola Adeyemi in the Land of Opportunity. Juno wasn't even the first in Feenixity. Rosco Feenixity was the first by something like twenty-four Mars days; the second was his identical twin brother Toby, who came along a few minutes later, pushing Juno Amara into third place, and seventh place over all. I suspect a few children were delivered by mothers, and there were rumours that the baby down in Huygens grew to term in an artificial womb, or a cow, or an artificial womb implanted in a cow, but I didn't give that much credence. Gossip brings out the creativity in the dullest souls.

Anyway, Zeke had to settle for being the first high-ranking political leader on Mars to bear a child, which was, in fact, no small thing. Lending the clout of his office to the Mars-Born Movement meant authorities on Earth couldn't just spin it as the product of a disillusioned few whose romantic notions of adventure on another planet had been shattered by the decidedly un-romantic, un-adventurous, and never-ending brute toil of staying alive. They tried, but nobody bought it. But that didn't mean most people on Earth, or even in the US, were on our side.

SINCE THE ESTABLISHMENT of the very first Mars base, the only way the population increased was by volunteers coming out of the blue and into the red. Among other things, it meant an all-adult population – they don't let kids get on rockets. The matter of children and space travel was still controversial and probably always will be. There are still some places on Earth where it's illegal for anyone under the age of eighteen to even take an edge-of-space sightseeing tour.

You see, it's one thing to choose a personal life without children, but an entire society without them is something else. Once you've gone from huddling up and actively not dying every day to a thriving social order with amenities, children are crucial. A society without children isn't the real thing – it's weird, it's unnatural, and it's unhealthy.

Now, everyone who qualified for lift-off had to agree to be snipped or tied or whatever they do now. Some opted for full sterilisation but most didn't; I didn't. It's not hard to reverse those procedures even on Mars and it was only a matter of time before someone did. I guess the folks back in the blue thought it would be sooner than later – every so often, we'd get a flurry of reminders that Mars settlers were legally bound not to reproduce without authorisation.

Actually, the statute, which every nation with interests on Mars signed, was quite specific: all females resident on Mars, whether on the surface or underground, were prohibited from engaging in any activity that would result in their becoming pregnant with the intention of carrying a foetus to term, resulting in a live birth, and all residents of any gender were forbidden to aid, abet, or conspire with others to cause a woman to become pregnant and deliver a child, or to conceal same.

Getting around that restriction wasn't a simple matter but not so difficult as to be completely infeasible in terms of time and/ or effort. Obviously.

THE WAY THINGS blew up on Earth was scary. Even after we managed to filter the firehose of news down to reliable sources of confirmed fact, it was scary. At first, it looked like they were going to cut off all support for every single settlement, including communications – no entertainment, no news, no email, no data of any kind – in order to re-think the purpose and practicality of funding a project threatening to run out of control when it was still a long way from delivering a reasonable return on the investment. Unquote. (In a lot of the videos we saw, people really stressed *delivering* and *delivered* and any other form of the word. Everybody seemed determined not to miss any opportunity to use a birth metaphor.) In the end, nobody cut off anything immediately, but there were a lot of dark hints/veiled threats about the near future.

No, I'm wrong – there was one supply they cut off: people. Emigration to Mars was suspended indefinitely.

As Beau's own due date drew closer, I stopped looking at any news from Earth. There were just too many stories about crazies

– the Right To Life/Anti-Abortion people didn't know whether to shit or go blind, the Campaign for Fathers' Rights started a riot in a family-planning clinic, and the La Leche Society had a major schism that I'm not sure I even understand.

And everybody had to read us the riot act. Everybody knew better. Everybody knew what we should have done instead. Everybody blamed us for needlessly stirring up trouble. Even people who claimed to be sympathetic said we were in the wrong.

I think Shelob summed it up best, in one of those sound-bites I failed to avoid: "While we can understand their point of view, the people on Mars seem to have forgotten one very important thing: we didn't send them there to lead normal lives. And that's not why they went."

If I'd still been back in the blue, I might have agreed. But being in the red gives me a different viewpoint.

When people were first exploring Earth, it wasn't because they wanted a normal life – they wanted a new one. But a new life isn't something you get – it's something you produce... and reproduce. We've always had animals and insects on Mars; the numbers are carefully limited but we get more in the usual fashion, with occasional imports to fresh up the gene pool.

Without additions from outside, the lack of diversity would eventually kill off every species. But with *only* additions from the outside, life continues without continuity; there is increase but no growth, flowering but no root.

Maybe I'll feel differently when I'm cycling home after a long day and someone in the tunnel is back-packing a baby that won't stop crying. Or Beau and I are up all night sponging vomit off the ceiling.

And – oh my God, how did I not think of this before? – toilet-training in low gravity! (If it's a boy, maybe I can off-load that to Beau.) Not everyone on Mars wants to have kids and maybe those that do will have second thoughts when they hear about things like this.

I never thought I was really cut out to be mommy myself but when Beau said he wanted to go for it, I realised it was probably the most daring thing we could ever do together. Not even crater-racing Marseratis is this audacious.

They didn't beat around the bush back on Earth when I first applied to go to Mars – they said everyone who went would die here. Well, we will. But first, we're going to live.

[P.S.: It was a boy.]

HIRAETH: A TRAGEDY IN FOUR ACTS

Karen Lord

"I FELL," SAID the cyborg, and for a moment his audience stood astounded, waiting for the larger speech, the longer explanation. None came. "I fell," he said once, and spoke no further.

"Did you not plan–?" A voice interrupted the heavy silence, courageous with curiosity. "Did you not mean to do this?"

"I wandered," the cyborg said. "I rambled and things happened and here I am."

The audience murmured, baffled but not dismayed. They would find sense in this yet.

With some effort, the cyborg thought to the days of his own curiosity and thirst for the new and undiscovered. He looked at the seeking expressions of his audience and tried to be helpful. "I was born on the Moon. That was where it began."

They brightened, as if a general sigh of relief had lifted chins, puffed out chests and raised the level of oxygen in the chamber. He smiled to see them happier and strove to continue the effect. "That was how it began. I was of the first generation born on the Moon. And I fell."

*   *   *

"How do you manage, how does *anyone* manage to fall hard enough to hurt themselves on the Moon?" his father nagged. His mother said nothing, but the tight press of her lips showed she was slightly nauseated. Both parents had been out on a research mission when he fell and failed to avoid certain unfortunately-placed shards of plastic, and now the damage had been done in more ways than one.

The doctor tried to speak reassuring words, but impatience made his voice provokingly supercilious. "Janik will recover fully. Visual implants are a very wise choice at his age. He can upgrade the components as he gets older, and then settle on a permanent replacement when he is an adult."

"Why not let his own regenerated eyes be the permanent replacement?" his father accused.

The doctor shrugged. "There have been complications with regeneration at lunar gravity. You were both absent, so I was left to take responsibility. I believe I made the best medical decision."

Janik's mother gazed sadly at him. He had not yet looked in a mirror, but he knew what cyborg eyes were like – grey, alien and cold. She was looking at him as if he had become a changeling.

"We could go back to Earth. They don't have any complications with regeneration, do they?"

The doctor took the trouble to give an empathic blink of his own mech-grey eyes and pitched his tone to something softer and kinder. "There are other complications on Earth, as you know."

Lunar gravity might keep falling objects from smashing in a satisfying fashion, but it did not prevent the smash of objects swung sideways into a wall. Janik's father destroyed one of the lamps on the doctor's desk and was about to reach for the second when the doctor unfroze from his paralysis of disbelieving horror and seized his arm in a gentle but implacable grip. His fury disintegrated into choked, desolate sobs.

Janik's mother was mortified. "Please forgive him. It's the hiraeth. It's getting worse."

"Of course," murmured the doctor, his sympathy now completely unfeigned. "I'll administer a tranquilliser."

Janik was too young to understand what this all meant, but in later years when he replayed the data in the long-memory of his eyes, things became much clearer.

THERE WERE THREE stages of hiraeth, each named for the location of greatest prevalence. It was no coincidence that hardship correlated with severity, but without a definite cause, guessing and superstition overtook logic and rational thought.

Lunar delusion was the least severe. Colonists lasted fifteen to twenty years before symptoms became noticeable. Some theorised that the visual reassurance of Earthrise, and its promise of proximity, delayed full onset of the syndrome. Others were more pragmatic, pointing out that the lunar colonies were the best-designed in the system with colonists who had developed a range of societal and personal adaptations to uniquely lunar hardships. Martian madness had an earlier onset, perhaps seven years or so, but could be put off for as long as ten years by living in the underground habitats that mimicked Earth.

Janik had the opportunity to personally observe the long melancholy and sudden manias of lunar delusion. His parents separated. His father returned to Earth, disappearing years later in the confusion of the Food Wars of America Minor. His mother eventually suffered from a milder version of the condition, but took care not to skip her encephalic adjustments and so would survive quite peaceably, if not lucidly, into her twelfth decade. Perhaps these experiences influenced him to avoid Mars as simply another version of the Moon, with the potential for the same pitfalls. Or perhaps it made him reckless and determined to seize his own brand of insanity before the universe could force it on him. Whatever the reasons, he upgraded his eyes, enhanced his limbs with a range of organic bionics, and applied to work off the debt for all his augmentation in the Rare Earth Division of CyborgAssist.

The universe, however, would not be denied. Miner's *folie*, a condition common to the asteroid belt, was harder to diagnose and more of a challenge to analyse. Should one blame mere distance, or the attempt to make a home in the extreme and unplanetary environment of a floating rock? Was it the innate instability of the risk-taking brain that brought entrepreneurs and adventurers to the asteroid pits and mines? Were both internal and external causes at play? The miner colonies were too small, too scattered and too poorly documented to offer any solid answers. Janik watched, recorded and replayed, once more looking for clarity but initially finding none.

When the miner's version of hiraeth finally seized him, he spent a week oscillating between debilitating panic and euphoric destructiveness. Both states sent adrenaline rushing through his body and brain; the difference lay only in the sound of the scream, from the discontented moan to the heart-piercing shriek. His workmates strapped him down under a bubble of armoured glass, sun-side on bare ground, so that he felt pressed between the weight of lens-sharpened light and the burden of alien rock. The crude exposure worked for a while, but by his second relapse, his superiors were worried enough to give an ultimatum. Either leave the Belt and go home (to the uncertainties of Earth politics, to the dwindling will and population of the Moon – which was home?) or submit to an experimental brain implant that would monitor and regulate his mental equilibrium.

He chose the latter.

When he went to the medical centre for a consultation before the implant operation, he had a pleasant shock.

"Doctor!"

He could not even remember the man's name, but he felt a recognition so strong it was almost like seeing family, like encountering some rarely-seen, distant cousin. It was a trivial bond made more precious by the pangs of hiraeth.

The doctor offered no name, but merely stared at him with that intensity that Janik had used himself when tracking the visual files in his memory. "Yes. Got it. The boy whose eyes I replaced when I was working on the Moon. I see you've stayed cyborg?"

"Yes," Janik replied briefly, his enthusiasm checked by the doctor's coolness.

"Good choice, good choice," the doctor said, nodding gravely. Janik noted with a glance the grey eyes of old, and the new additions – breastplate extending into an arm augmentation, partial skull plate with ear transplant, and goodness knew what else might be lying beneath the skin that moved and shone with slippery, non-organic ease.

"I have made hiraeth my speciality," the doctor explained, "and I have become more and more convinced that the only remedy is through the augmentation and modification of the human body."

Janik was distracted from his personal issues. "How so?"

The doctor's certainty faltered. He waved his hand in a manner that might have been apologetic or even self-deprecating. "There is so much superstition attached to the syndrome, but why not, when it is such a creation of the mind? The less human we believe ourselves to be, the less we yearn towards a vision of a perfected Earth. Cyborgs have shown themselves to be the most resistant to hiraeth's effects."

Janik was reminded, with some shame, of his own shortcomings. The doctor saw and tried to be kind. "You must not be so hard on yourself. You lasted six years in the Belt without contracting the *folie*, well within the statistical range for cyborgs with your level of augmentation. But if you hope to last longer, the only solution is to expand and upgrade your cerebral implants."

"I've dodged the brain stuff," Janik admitted. "It's a chancy fix, and I don't want to be like some of my workmates, dragging on with obsolete mech because they're too poor or too scared to get an upgrade."

"Oh, there's no worry where this implant is concerned. It's a new approach; the template is adaptable without need for surgical intrusion. We only have to change the command insert and the implant grows or dies off as required."

"Sounds human – even better than human," Janik laughed.

The doctor's face brightened. "Yes, yes! You understand perfectly! So you give your consent?"

A little thrill of fear fluttered in the pit of his stomach, but Janik shivered and shook it off. "Of course!"

THE OPERATION WENT smoothly. Recovery time took only a day and within the week Janik was eager to return to work.

"Patience," the doctor advised. "What you feel now is merely the excitement of a new augmentation. It will soon wear off and the hiraeth will take over once more. Only later, when the implant begins to extend and self-calibrate, will you truly begin to feel the cure."

Janik obediently returned to his isolation bubble and waited for the hiraeth. When it came, with all attendant palpitations, perspirations, alarums and excursions, curiosity kept a part of his mind sufficiently free to observe as the implant started its work. It was like watching a master builder construct a high, thick wall that curved around to make an enclosure, then arched over and under to make a sphere, and within the sphere, made quiet at last, was all the yearning, screaming hollowness of hiraeth.

Naturally, he was incredibly happy, but not as happy as the

doctor. "Isn't this amazing?" he all but sang as he pointed out to Janik the mysteries of several medical scans arrayed on a luminous wall. "Do you see how the filaments have rooted with no rejection whatsoever?"

Janik smiled uncertainly at the images flitting past the doctor's fingers. There was only one thing he understood, and he clung to it. "Rejection?"

A mere moment's pause, long enough for a fist to clench convulsively with enough force to make knuckles crack, and the doctor was answering. "A side effect of earlier versions of the implant. No need to worry: your lunar origins and your early exposure to cyborg augmentation greatly improved your tolerance for this procedure."

Janik glanced at the still-clenched fist resting over the glow of the medical scans, and continued to look worried.

"I assure you, I am delighted with the results, so much so that I plan to replace my present skull implant with one identical to the model you are presently pioneering."

Janik blinked. Of course.

"Yes," the doctor murmured. "I have been fleeing hiraeth for many years now. I hope this will be the final step."

THE DOCTOR MOVED on, travelling from asteroid to asteroid to other mining stations farther out in the Belt. In time, follow-up assessments were no longer needed and Janik gradually lost touch. There were plenty of other things to distract him. CyborgAssist became CyborgAdvance, and then simply CA. The Martian branch downsized in the wake of the failure of the Terraform Project, pulling all human and cyborg personnel and leaving only robots and remote systems to maintain a presence on the planet. Directives from the lunar headquarters arrived with increasing sluggishness, until at last news came that the lunar colony had also been declared a failure. Scientists still lived and worked on the Moon, but the days of true settlement and Moon-born children were over. The CA office on Vesta took over the mining stations, thus making CA the first truly autonomous extraterrestrial corporate entity in the solar system.

It was a landmark occasion. It was also the spur for a fresh surge of hiraeth.

Information about Earth was scarce. Extraterrestrial colonial dreams had been severely tempered, and most of the first wave pioneers had returned to face the task of salvaging their first (and now perhaps only) home. No-one knew whether they were succeeding, but the majority of the non-cyborg and minimally augmented humans quit CA and also fled to Earth, beaten at last by a quirk of psychology or spirit that no-one fully understood. Janik remained unaffected, a walking advertisement for brain augmentation. CA shrewdly upped the price for the implant, causing several of Janik's workmates to be stuck in a debt extension that was unlikely to expire before they did.

Some of the lunar-born children, too young and too alien to be deterred by the first faint stirrings of hiraeth, went in the opposite direction – beyond the Belt. Janik began to hear tales about the moons of Jupiter, distant planetoids beyond Neptune, and roving space-stations with solar wings sailing in the vastness between the dwarf planets of the outer reaches. He encountered a few outbound pilots during his assignment with CA security. They always needed supplies and always had news to share, and CA policy was to be friendly as long as they were not trying to pilfer company resources.

Lee was not the first unaugmented traveller he had met, but she was the most aggressively so. Her second-in-command and sole travelling companion was pure robot and bore all the accessories that could have made her life easier: broad-spectrum vision, direct data access, communications add-ons – the works. She didn't even have the smallest of brain implants, something which had become standard for all those seeking to delay or reduce hiraeth.

Janik asked why. She looked both embarrassed and defiant. "What's the point of it if there isn't a bit of hiraeth to fight against?"

Janik revised his view. Not merely an adventurer to the farthest distance, but an endurance enthusiast sprinting outwards as fast as she could before hiraeth stopped her, like a diver pushing to the limit of her lungs. He touched the smooth walls of the sealed pearl of hiraeth that his brain still kept, a habit that had started out of anxiety as he looked for cracks in the protection, but was now a soothing tic, like caressing a prayer bead.

"And then what?" he asked.

She shrugged.

"Back to Earth, perhaps?" he suggested. "What is it like there?"

He should not have asked. Everything in the Belt was under watch; his own eyes were complicit as his on-duty data was owned by CA and could be requisitioned as needed. The crooked smile she gave him told him she knew it well.

"So many stories from so many sources! Earth has fallen. Earth is recovering. Earth is in a new age, back from the brink of disaster and on the path to becoming a paradise. But then again, CA is bankrupt and obsolete. CA is the only surviving tech company. The CA cyborgs represent the last bastion of humanity in the solar system. It all depends on who you talk to, doesn't it? You're strange. I've never heard of a CA cyborg asking about Earth. Would you go back to Earth?"

Janik lowered his head. It disturbed him that the more augmentation-addicted his workmates became, the harder it was to hold a conversation with them that did not involve work and CA. It disturbed him even more that this was now common knowledge beyond the Belt. Fortunately his communicator buzzed and gave him reason to avoid replying. He excused himself and went to the neutral ground of the entrance hatch to take the routine communication.

The roster computer spoke as courteously as usual, but this time it sounded almost apologetic that the news was not good. "CA3546 Janik, report for transfer to Pit N75A within the next 172 kiloseconds."

He froze. He was being sent to one of the most dangerous pits, located on a fragmenting asteroid with a hot core, and subject to unpredictable seismic activity. He protested.

"All cyborgs above level five are cleared for Pit N75A," the soothing voice of the roster computer told him. "Resuscitation and reboot in case of demise will be provided free of charge."

"I'm an early adopter level seven," he tried to explain. "No chance of resuscitation. When I die, I die."

The roster fell silent as it carried out a search on his personnel files. "Level seven early adoption is resuscitation compliant when CA-approved command inserts are employed–"

"I was the first," he insisted, growing impatient. "There were no CA-approved command inserts back then. I use the prototype."

Another pause, shorter than the first, then the roster said, "Please update using this cycle's CA-approved level seven command insert and report for duty at Pit N75A within 172 kiloseconds of reboot. Cost of command insert is ¢@ 85,000 which will be deducted from your wages over the next 0.317 gigaseconds."

Exasperated, he scanned the update files attached to the final communication, but what he saw made him pause. The most recent command insert depended on the changes made via a previous insert's commands, which was in turn tied to an earlier update. Janik calculated that he would have to endure five cycles of updates totalling ¢@ 297,6700, which would shift his debt period from one decade to nearly four.

Caveat emptor, especially when buying from CA.

He hopped back into Lee's control room. "Quick," he said. "Can you take me with you? I can pay – proper minerals, not CA currency – and I can be useful."

Lee considered swiftly, but from the mischief growing in her eyes and the smile that twitched up the corner of her mouth he could see that she had already decided. Lucky for him that he had piqued her interest, asking about Earth. "You'll have to shut down so they can't detect you."

He thought about explaining again about his prototype implant and how it was distinct from the rest of CA, but time was short and he merely nodded.

"Go to cargo – you'll find a life-support module there. Settle in."

Janik did so, stopping just long enough to compose a time-delayed resignation note that would reach CA in approximately 0.317 gigaseconds, by which time he hoped to be far beyond any CA branch office or outpost on the outer fringes of the Belt. Then he sealed the cover and let the long sleep bury him and his pearl together.

WAKING UP WAS not what he expected.

There was a faint cheering in his ears. His eyes were open, but his sight was blurred. He was standing up, but leaning against a wall. His head felt too full. He had never experienced a hangover – no cyborg would, given their basic antitoxin functions – but he imagined it would feel like this: uncalibrated, out of focus, and off-balance.

"Congratulations!' The word was strangely pronounced and stilted, as if voiced by a bad translation programme, but the emotion was genuinely cheerful.

He fought his sluggish senses and tried to remember his own name. "What?" His lips moved; no sound came out.

"You are the first human to overcome hiraeth long enough to sail out of the solar system! That we know of! That we have been able to communicate with! Congratulations!"

Slowly he absorbed what was happening. He was still in

the life support module, but gravity pulled at his feet, making him lean slightly against the lid. His sight was blurred because the light mist activated to raise the module's humidity was mostly spraying into his face. His head felt full because... His consciousness blossomed, making him aware of the strangeness that was the inside of his skull. His implant had been... *busy*. He felt less like Sleeping Beauty and more like the thorny, overgrown wood. And where was his pearl?

The mist subsided, the air cleared. A small dip of motion outside the module caught his attention. It was a hovering sphere, about the size of a human head, made of some dark metal with irregular, illuminated chips pitting the surface. It looked like a hallucination.

"Oh," it said in disappointment. "It's only an old cyborg."

It sounded like a hallucination too.

"No, it's not," it argued with itself. "See the readings? The implant's still an overlay, not an integrant."

He was scanning his own brain even as they spoke. The implant had run wild and was now twisted past pruning and partly tangled into the mechanism of the life support module. He went deeper... hoping, yearning. There was the hiraeth, kept safely alive and buzzing behind thinning walls.

Meanwhile, the sphere was speaking excitedly in a language he could not understand. He waited patiently for it to notice him again.

"We're not sure that you're human," it said at last, "but whatever you are you're more than just a cyborg and everyone should know about this!"

"The pilot. She's human.' He guessed, but he needed confirmation.

"You are the only one alive on this ship," the sphere said sadly.

He wondered what could have happened to Lee that she had not even tried to wake him. Perhaps the ship's records had some information. He tried to access the central data system but was distracted by a strange noise. The sphere was giggling. "This is so exciting!"

In the blink of an eye, his view of the cargo area changed. A small group of spheres crowded above, spilling light which coalesced into various images, a patchwork that stitched together into an audience of human figures represented by half-sized holograms. None was cyborg as far as he could see, but some had robot familiars perched on shoulders or wrists. All faces were turned avidly to him. The central data system came online with a sudden burst of output, flooding his already taxed brain with names and titles and dates and places. He bit his lip against rising nausea and tried to organise the deluge, but only ended up feeling as groggy and uncoordinated as when he first woke.

"Have a little respect." Two children, slender as lunar-born and dark as Earth-raised, stood beneath the original sphere and chided their elders. "Remember he's human and needs time to adjust."

The intrusion stopped suddenly and was replaced by a gentle probing.

"No," someone countered. "He *is* a cyborg, but a very odd one. He still holds hiraeth within."

Murmurs of interest and disbelief. "Impossible." "Augmentation is a dead end for humanity." "But imagine – a human cyborg with hiraeth? He could tesser farther and faster than any of us and always have a beacon to navigate home!"

"Hush," said a voice reverently. "He is crying."

Of course he was crying. The stress of waking, the burden of information, the shock of communicating with others after so long... it all came together in an incredible pressure that pushed at the thinnest part of the wall, cracked the containment, and let hiraeth leak through. His implant was overloading and his other augmentations were slowly beginning to malfunction.

He did not have much time.

The babble quieted and a sole voice took over. "Our apologies. We have so many questions, but perhaps we should let you speak. Tell us, how did you come to be such a unique cyborg?"

My name is Janik. I once had eyes that truly cried, not these imitations. I once feared hiraeth, then I grew to love it, and now it will kill me.

He began as best he could. "I fell."

AMICAE AETERNUM

Ellen Klages

IT WAS STILL dark when Corry woke, no lights on in the neighbors' houses, just a yellow glow from the streetlight on the other side of the elm. Through her open window, the early summer breeze brushed across her coverlet like silk.

Corry dressed silently, trying not to see the empty walls, the boxes piled in a corner. She pulled on a shirt and shorts, looping the laces of her shoes around her neck, and climbed from bed to sill and out the window with only a whisper of fabric against the worn wood. Then she was outside.

The grass was chill and damp beneath her bare feet. She let them rest on it for a minute, the freshly-mowed blades tickling her toes, her heels sinking into the springy-sponginess of the dirt. She breathed deep, to catch it all – the cool and the green and the stillness – holding it in for as long as she could before slipping on her shoes.

A morning to remember. Every little detail.

She walked across the lawn, stepping over the ridge of clippings along the verge, onto the sidewalk. Theirs was a corner lot. In a minute, she would be out of sight. For once, she was up before her practical, morning-people parents. The engineer and the physicist did not believe in sleeping in, but Corry could count on the fingers of one hand the number of times in her eleven years that she had seen the dawn.

No one else was on the street. It felt solemn and private, as if she had stepped out of time, so quiet she could hear the wind ruffling the wide canopy of trees, an owl hooting from somewhere behind her, the diesel chug of the all-night bus two blocks away. She crossed Branson St. and turned down the alley that ran behind the houses.

A dandelion's spiky leaves pushed through a crack in the cement. Corry squatted, touching it with a finger, tracing the jagged outline, memorizing its contours. A weed. No one planted it or planned it. She smiled and stood up, her hand against a wooden fence, feeling the grain beneath her palm, the crackling web of old paint, and continued on. The alley stretched ahead for several blocks, the pavement a narrowing pale V.

She paused a minute later to watch a cat prowl stealthily along the base of another fence, hunting or slinking home. It looked up, saw her, and sped into a purposeful thousand-leg trot before disappearing into a yard. She thought of her own cat, Mr. Bumble, who now belonged to a neighbor, and wiped at the edge of her eye. She distracted herself by peering into backyards at random bits of other people's lives – lawn chairs, an overturned tricycle, a metal barbecue grill, its lid open.

Barbecue. She hadn't thought to add that to her list. She'd like to have one more whiff of charcoal, lit with lighter fluid, smoking and wafting across the yards, smelling like summer. Too late now. No one barbecued their breakfast.

She walked on, past Remington Rd. She brushed her fingers over a rosebush – velvet petals, leathery leaves; pressed a hand against the oft-stapled roughness of a telephone pole, fringed with remnants of garage-sale flyers; stood on tiptoe to trace the red octagon of a stop sign. She stepped from sidewalk to grass to asphalt and back, tasting the textures with her feet, noting the cracks and holes and bumps, the faded paint on the curb near a fire hydrant.

"Fire hydrant," she said softly, but aloud, checking it off in her mind. "Rain gutter. Lawn mower. Mailbox."

The sky was just beginning to purple in the east when she reached Anna's back gate. She knew it as well as her own. They'd been best friends since first grade, had been in and out of each other's houses practically every day. Corry tapped on the frame of the porch's screen door with one knuckle.

A moment later, Anna came out. "Hi, Spunk," she whispered.

"Hi, Spork," Corry answered. She waited while Anna eased the door closed so it wouldn't bang, sat on the steps, put on her shoes.

Their bikes leaned against the side of the garage. Corry had told her mom that she had given her bike to Anna's sister Pat. And she would, in an hour or two. So it hadn't really been a lie, just the wrong tense.

They walked their bikes through the gate. In the alley, Corry threw a leg over and settled onto the vinyl seat, its shape molded to hers over the years. Her bike. Her steed. Her hands fit themselves around the rubber grips of the handlebars and she pushed off with one foot. Anna was a few feet behind, then beside her. They rode abreast down to the mouth of the alley and away.

The slight grade of Thompson St. was perfect for coasting, the wind on their faces, blowing Corry's short dark hair off her forehead, rippling Anna's ponytail. At the bottom of the hill, Corry stood tall on her pedals, pumping hard, the muscles in her calves a good ache as the chain rattled and whirred as fast and constant as a train.

"Trains!" she yelled into the wind. Another item from her list.

"Train whistles!" Anna yelled back.

They leaned into a curve. Corry felt gravity pull at her, pumped harder, in control. They turned a corner and a moment later, Anna said, "Look."

Corry slowed, looked up, then braked to a stop. The crescent moon hung above a gap in the trees, a thin sliver of blue-white light.

171

Anna began the lullaby her mother used to sing when Corry first slept over. On the second line, Corry joined in.

I see the moon, and the moon sees me.
The moon sees somebody I want to see.

The sound of their voices was liquid in the stillness, sweet and smooth. Anna reached out and held Corry's hand across the space between their bikes.

God bless the moon, and God bless me,
And God bless the somebody I want to see.

They stood for a minute, feet on the ground, still holding hands. Corry gave a squeeze and let go. "Thanks," she said.

"Any time," said Anna, and bit her lip.

"I know," Corry said. Because it wouldn't be. She pointed. The sky was lighter now, palest blue at the end of the street shading to indigo directly above. "Let's get to the park before the sun comes up."

No traffic, no cars. It felt like they were the only people in the world. They headed east, riding down the middle of the street, chasing the shadows of their bikes from streetlight to streetlight, never quite catching them. The houses on both sides were dark, only one light in a kitchen window making a yellow rectangle on a driveway. As they passed it, they smelled bacon frying, heard a fragment of music.

The light at 38th St. was red. They stopped, toes on the ground, waiting. A raccoon scuttled from under a hedge, humpbacked and quick, disappearing behind a parked car. In the hush, Corry heard the metallic *tick* from the light box before she saw it change from red to green.

Three blocks up Ralston Hill. The sky looked magic now, the edges wiped with pastels, peach and lavender and a blush of orange. Corry pedaled as hard as she could, felt her breath ragged in her throat, a trickle of sweat between her shoulder blades. Under the arched entrance to the park, into the broad, grassy picnic area that sloped down to the creek.

They abandoned their bikes to the grass, and walked to a low stone wall. Corry sat, cross-legged, her best friend beside her, and waited for the sun to rise for the last time.

She knew it didn't actually rise, that *it* wasn't moving. They were rotating a quarter mile every second, coming all the way around once every twenty-four hours, exposing themselves once again to the star they called the sun, and naming that moment *morning*. But it was the last time she'd get to watch.

"There it is," Anna said. Golden light pierced the spaces between the trunks of the trees, casting long thin shadows across the grass. They leaned against each other and watched as the sky brightened to its familiar blue, and color returned: green leaves, pink bicycles, yellow shorts. Behind them lights began to come on in houses and a dog barked.

By the time the sun touched the tops of the distant trees, the backs of their legs were pebbled with the pattern of the wall, and it was daytime.

Corry sat, listening to the world waking up and going about its ordinary business: cars starting, birds chirping, a mother calling out, "Jimmy! Breakfast!" She felt as if her whole body was aware, making all of this a part of her.

Over by the playground, geese waddled on the grass, pecking for bugs. One goose climbed onto the end of the teeter-totter and sat, as if waiting for a playmate. Corry laughed out loud. She would never have thought to put *that* on her list. "What's next?" Anna asked.

"The creek, before anyone else is there."

They walked single file down the steep railroad-tie steps, flanked by tall oaks and thick undergrowth dotted with wildflowers. "Wild," Corry said softly.

When they reached the bank they took off their shoes and climbed over boulders until they were surrounded by rushing water. The air smelled fresh, full of minerals, the sound of the water both constant and never-the-same as it poured over rocks and rills, eddied around logs.

They sat down on the biggest, flattest rock and eased their bare feet into the creek, watching goosebumps rise up their legs. Corry felt the current swirl around her. She watched the speckles of light dance on the water, the deep shade under the bank, ten thousand shades of green and brown everywhere she looked. Sun on her face, wind in her hair, water at her feet, rock beneath her.

"How much of your list did you get to do?" asked Anna.

"A lot of it. It kept getting longer. I'd check one thing off, and it'd remind me of something else. I got to most of the everyday ones, 'cause I could walk, or ride my bike. Mom was too busy packing and giving stuff away and checking off her own lists to take me to the aquarium, or to the zoo, so I didn't see the jellies or the elephants and the bears."

Anna nodded. "My mom was like that too, when we were moving here from Indianapolis."

"At least you knew where you were going. We're heading off into the great unknown, my dad says. Boldly going where nobody's gone before."

"Like that old TV show."

"Yeah, except we're not going to *get* anywhere. At least not me, or my mom or my dad. The *Goddard* is a generation ship. The planet it's heading for is five light years away, and even with solar sails and stuff, the trip's going to take a couple hundred years."

"Wow."

"Yeah. It won't land until my great-great – I don't know, add about five more greats to that – grandchildren are around. I'll be old – like thirty – before we even get out of the solar system.

Dad keeps saying that it's the adventure of a lifetime, and we're achieving humankind's greatest dream, and blah, blah, blah. But it's *his* dream." She picked at a piece of lichen on the rock.

"Does your mom want to go?"

"Uh-huh. She's all excited about the experiments she can do in zero-g. She says it's an honor that we were chosen and I should be proud to be a pioneer."

"Will you be in history books?"

Corry shrugged. "Maybe. There are around four thousand people going, from all over the world, so I'd be in tiny, tiny print. But maybe."

"Four *thousand?*" Anna whistled. "How big a rocket is it?"

"Big. Bigger than big." Corry pulled her feet up, hugging her arms around her knees. "Remember that humongous cruise ship we saw when we went to Miami?"

"Sure. It looked like a skyscraper, lying on its side."

"That's what this ship is like, only bigger. And rounder. My mom keeps saying it'll be *just* like a cruise – any food anytime I want, games to play, all the movies and books and music ever made – after school, of course. Except people on cruise ships stop at ports and get off and explore. Once we board tonight, we're *never* getting off. I'm going to spend the rest of my whole entire life in a big tin can."

"That sucks."

"Tell me about it." Corry reached into her pocket and pulled out a crumpled sheet of paper, scribbles covering both sides. She smoothed it out on her knee. "I've got another list." She cleared her throat and began to read:

Twenty Reasons Why Being on a Generation Ship Sucks, by Corrine Garcia-Kelly

1. *I will never go away to college.*
2. *I will never see blue sky again, except in pictures.*

3. *There will never be a new kid in my class.*

4. *I will never meet anyone my parents don't already know.*

5. *I will never have anything new that isn't human-made. Manufactured or processed or grown in a lab.*

6. *Once I get my ID chip, my parents will always know exactly where I am.*

7. *I will never get to drive my Aunt Frieda's convertible, even though she promised I could when I turned sixteen.*

8. *I will never see the ocean again.*

9. *I will never go to Paris.*

10. *I will never meet a tall, dark stranger, dangerous or not.*

11. *I will never move away from home.*

12. *I will never get to make the rules for my own life.*

13. *I will never ride my bike to a new neighborhood and find a store I haven't seen before.*

14. *I will never ride my bike again.*

15. *I will never go outside again.*

16. *I will never take a walk to anywhere that isn't planned and mapped and numbered.*

17. *I will never see another thunderstorm. Or lightning bugs. Or fireworks.*

18. *I will never buy an old house and fix it up.*

19. *I will never eat another Whopper.*

20. *I will never go to the state fair and win a stuffed animal.*

She stopped. "I was getting kind of sleepy toward the end."

"I could tell." Anna slipped her arm around Corry's waist. "What will you miss most?"

"You." Corry pulled Anna closer.

"Me, too." Anna settled her head on her friend's shoulder. "I can't believe I'll never see you again."

"I know." Corry sighed. "I *like* Earth. I like that there are parts that no one made, and that there are always surprises." She shifted her arm a little. "Maybe I don't want to be a pioneer.

I mean, I don't know *what* I want to be when I grow up. Mom's always said I could be anything I wanted to be, but now? The Peace Corps is out. So is being a coal miner or a deep-sea diver or a park ranger. Or an antique dealer."

"You like old things."

"I do. They're from the past, so everything has a story."

"I thought so." Anna reached into her pocket with her free hand. "I used the metals kit from my dad's printer, and made you something." She pulled out a tissue paper-wrapped lump and put it in Corry's lap.

Corry tore off the paper. Inside was a silver disk, about five centimeters across. In raised letters around the edge it said SPUNK-CORRY-ANNA-SPORK-2065. Etched in the center was a photo of the two of them, arm in arm, wearing tall pointed hats with stars, taken at Anna's last birthday party. Corry turned it over. The back said: *Optimae amicae aeternum.* "What does that mean?"

"'Best friends forever.' At least that's what Translator said."

"It's great. Thanks. I'll keep it with me, all the time."

"You'd better. It's an artifact."

"It is really nice."

"I'm serious. Isn't your space ship going off to another planet with a whole library of Earth's art and culture and all?"

"Yeah...?"

"But by the time it lands, that'll be ancient history and tales. No one alive will ever have been on Earth, right?"

"Yeah..."

"So your mission – if you choose to accept it – is to preserve this artifact from your home planet." Anna shrugged. "It isn't old now, but it will be. You can tell your kids stories about it – about us. It'll be an heirloom. Then they'll tell their kids, and–"

"–and their kids, and on down for umpity generations." Corry nodded, turning the disc over in her hands. "By then it'll be a relic. There'll be legends about it." She rolled it across her palm, silver winking in the sun "How'd you think of that?"

"Well, you said you're only allowed to take ten kilos of personal stuff with you, and that's all you'll ever have from Earth. Which is why you made your list and have been going around saying goodbye to squirrels and stop signs and Snickers bars and all."

"Ten kilos isn't much. My mom said the ship is so well-stocked I won't need much, but it's hard. I had to pick between my bear and my jewelry box."

"I know. And in twenty years, I'll probably have a house full of clothes and furniture and junk. But the thing is, when I'm old and I die, my kids'll get rid of most of it, like we did with my Gramma. Maybe they'll keep some pictures. But then their kids will do the same thing. So in a couple hundred years, there won't be any trace of me *here*–"

"–but you'll be part of the legend."

"Yep."

"Okay, then. I accept the mission." Corry turned and kissed Anna on the cheek.

"You'll take us to the stars?"

"You bet." She slipped the disc into her pocket. "It's getting late."

She stood up and reached to help Anna to her feet. "C'mon. Let's ride."

TRADEMARK BUGS: A LEGAL HISTORY

Adam Roberts

THE FOLLOWING DISCUSSION document has been produced by a working group comprising academics from the UK's Royal Psychological and Somatic Law Institute (Birmingham) and the Russian Federation's Academic Law University (Академический правовой университет, АПУ). It aims to summarise the legal position with respect to so-called 'Trademark Bugs', and is **not** intended to have the force of a policy proposal or political statement. The management board of the АПУ in particular wish to distance themselves from the conclusion in section 5. For more discussion on these matters see Kokoschka et al 2099.

The Three 'Porter Rules'

THE FIRST COURT CASE directly relevant was filed under UK legislation, not because the first Trademark Bugs were developed or distributed in that country, but because the UK's unilateral renegotiation of their national relationship to the 'Madrid System' (which was in turn part of their withdrawal from EU copyright jurisdictions) created a more favourable balance of proof for INTA, USPTO or WIPO prosecution. Protocols governing the dissemination of these new products meant that the bugs were not at first distributed in areas that had suffered calamitous natural disaster (earthquake, tsunami, plague) in the previous five years, although this was later reduced to 12 months and subsequently – as of 2031 – abandoned altogether. As a consequence of this, Porter-addend.2031d clarifies the extent to which the original Rules must be considered consonant with international law.

PORTER'S ORIGINAL RULING laid down the so-called three 'Porter Rules' for Trademark Bugs. These are:

- That the pathology itself must not be 'excessively physically distressing' or entail any long-term hazard to health, wellbeing or longevity. These latter terms, of course, have proved hard to define precisely as salients under legal challenge.

- That the pathology itself must be no *more* virulent than the baseline virus or bacterium, prior to any genetic adaptation. This applies the legal principle, common from other aspects of EU Genetics Law, of balanced hazard equilibrium.

- That the pathology itself must be *preventable* by some means (later modified to 'at least one mean') *not trademarked* to the distributing company. The meaning of *preventable* in this context has generated a great deal of discussion, with legal authorities divided between interpreting this so-called 'Third Porter Rule' either (a) strictly, in terms of legal consent – briefly, that plaintiffs need only show that they did not knowingly and competently *opt-in* to the relevant pathology; or (b) broadly, in terms of *reasonable precaution* – the argument advanced by Goober, Thwaite and Associates, known popularly as the 'soap and water' test. This latter holds that, as with the common cold, everyday precautions such as washing one's hands with soap and water should be enough to avoid infection, for it to come within the meaning of the act. Accordingly people who, compos mentis and of legal majority, elect *not* to take such common-sense precautions have ipso facto given consent to being infected by Trademark Bugs. The rulings of Ito (Ito-2025c) and Carallan (Carallan-2024d-2025a) confirmed the 'broad' definition to have legal grounding. Since 2034 this has only been challenged in court once (Boothby-2037b-d), a case which eventually tested the legal status of all three of the Porter Rules. The 'broad' interpretation of Rule 3 was eventually upheld.

SEVERAL EARLY LEGAL challenges stalled because the plaintiffs exhausted their funding. It is worth noting this fact because there is a widely held though erroneous belief that the case of Lukacs vs. Glaxco (Reinhart-2029a-d) established any legal precedent. Passages from the speeches delivered in court by Milo Lukacs have passed into popular currency *as if* they had legal basis; although in fact the case was later suspended for non-disbursement of legal stipends and no judgment was arrived at.

Let us not lose sight of the key issue: corporations are not only *manufacturing* genetically tweaked versions of the common cold, they are *releasing* them into the environment via multiple vectors. We have not yet been able to prove in court that such releasing itself constitutes corporate delinquency, but we do know this: polls have consistently shown that the general public thinks of these actions *in exactly those terms* – as delinquency, quasi-criminal activity and worse. People are getting sick with genetically tagged flu viruses for which the only cure is manufactured by these same corporations! People are being forced into the position where they *have* to purchase medication, manufactured by the same corporations that made them sick, in order to bring them back to the baseline position of health. This practice is profoundly inhumane, unethical, and monopolistic. This practice is wicked.

LUKACS ALSO PUT before the court various financial estimates that have been contested. He claimed that over the tax-year '28-'29, the three biggest pharmaceutical companies made €875 billion profit on Trademark Bugs alone; and that over the previous five years the profit from Trademark Bugs was double that of all other pharmaceutical sales combined. These claims were themselves the cause of two legal challenges: one on the grounds of their inaccuracy (it was argued in court that the €875 billion figure was gross, not net; although a countersuit [Abnett-2030a] sought to show that, when EU tax-incentives for medical research and charitable donations were included, the tax rate on this profit was zero) and on the grounds that disclosure of profits violated the corporations' legal rights (legally functional as 'individuals') to privacy. This was upheld by Rinn-2031b, but without retrospective force. Accordingly all sums cited for post-'31 profits, including ones included in this paper, are estimates (legally permitted under the Corporate Oversight Act of 2035) and in no way intended to intrude upon the privacy of corporations qua individuals.

BALANCE REQUIRES US to quote from the chief legal representative for Glaxco, Magrat Helmansdottir KC, who said:

The soap-and-water test is no mere legal fiction, but an actual, measurable social good. Drugs have their part to play in humankind's perennial war against illness, but it is a small part compared to the role played by simple hygiene. Hygiene has saved more lives than all the drugs ever produced. The distribution of Trademark Bugs (free at point of issue, I might add) is an actual, measurable and positive incitement to people to live more hygienic lives. Glaxco themselves sell one-cent bars of proprietary soap through all the major supermarkets; and expend considerable sums advertising the need to wash hands every hour and avoid spreading infections – *all* such transmissible infections, not merely those bugs Trademarked to Glaxco. Furthermore, Glaxco has invested €1.1 billion in the science of Epidemiology, including endowing the Glaxco Chair in Epidemiological Science at Harvard, and funding forty annual PhD scholarships in the discipline. It is no exaggeration to say that this investment is the single most significant investment in this science *ever made*. What the prosecution are calling for would devastate the advances made in medical science and materially diminish human wellbeing. Quite apart from our moral duty to uphold the laws protecting the sanctity of commercial free enterprise and encouraging self-reliance and independence in consumers – quite apart from that, what the prosecution proposes would have a measurably negative impact upon world health.

OUTSIDE THE COURTROOM, during media interviews, Helmansdottir added: 'I appreciate it sounds counter-intuitive; I understand that many people feel that these corporations are deliberately infecting them with designer germs in order to increase their profits by selling them the cures – but the facts are the facts. None of that *is true*. Trademark Bugs have made the world cleaner and healthier. We can't afford to undo the advances we have made.' She later – successfully – resisted a prosecution petition that this speech be entered into evidence, arguing that the clause '*these corporations are deliberately infecting them with designer germs in order to sell them the cures*', abstracted from context, would be prejudicial to the legal process.

* * *

FOLLOWING THE COLLAPSE of Lukacs vs. Glaxco (Reinhart-2029a-d), 47 private prosecutions were brought against various corporations by individuals who claimed they had caught Trademarked diseases and suffered, in one way or another, *in excess of* the discomfort permitted by the Porter Rules. All but one were conducted under the no-win-no-fee remit. Of these 5 were abandoned, 3 went to court (the plaintiffs losing in each case) and 39 were settled out of court. The next legal milestone was Glaxco vs The Guardian (Gesswyn 2033a), when the company successfully sued the UK-based media conglomerate for repeating claims that eleven distinct strains of Trademark Bug were 'monopolistic'.

THE EDITOR AT the time, Jean Ebner, conceded that this defeat 'stung and enraged' her senior staff. After a popular campaign and fundraising effort ('Goldenbugs') the Guardian took Glaxco to court under US legal jurisdiction (presiding justice Natch Greys, Guardian Corps v. Glaxco, 676 F.3d 854, 862 (9th Cir 2036); [EU citation format: Greyes-2036c-2039a]). The grounds of the suit were ingenious: a Guardian reporter, Po Lok Tam, deliberately contracted one of Glaxco's most widely disseminated Trademark Bugs, a common-cold tweak called 'Sapphire Sniffles', the cure for which – 'Azure 7' (available as pill, or nanoneedle diffuser) – was amongst the cheapest in the Glaxco range. The symbolic significance of the 'four-shots-a-dollar' cure was part of the intended effect. Po Lok Tam refused to buy the cure and suffered the symptoms of the bug: raised temperature, headache, runny nose and sore throat, advertised as 'lasting depending on the state of the sufferer's immune system between three and eight weeks'. There were, she claimed, other symptoms; but only the ones specified in the Glaxco promotional material were entered into evidence without dispute from either side. The force of the Guardian suit was that the sore throat, by impairing the ability of the plaintiff to speak, illegally restricted her first amendment rights to free speech under the US constitution.

Guardian v. Glaxco (2036-39): a summary

INITIAL REPORTS OF this trial expressed the opinion that it would soon be thrown out of court: none of the symptoms breached Porter Rules, and neither side denied that Ms Po could still express herself in writing – in previous cases concerning the right to freedom of speech (see Grohmann, 2088 for a summary of this legal history) this had been deemed sufficient to satisfy the constitutional requirement. In fact, Guardian v. Glaxco became one of the longest, most fiercely fought and expensive cases in the history of Trademark Bug law. We can only provide the merest sketch of the arguments and counter-arguments, here (Malahat 2090 has a more detailed account). The main theses and antitheses can be summarised as follows:

• A first move by Glaxco to dismiss the case as lacking prima facie validity (the plaintiff having unimpeded access to text-based modes, including an artificial voice app on her phone, was able fully to actualise her first-amendment rights, irrespective of her sore throat). Motion was denied.

• A move to early resolution by the plaintiff on the grounds that Ms Po gave no explicit consent to losing her voice. Denied, after the Glaxco team satisfied the court that Ms Po had, intentionally, gone out of her way to catch the bug.

• Glaxco legal team attempted to prove that, since many other Trademark Bugs produced symptoms that left the throat and voice unaffected – and since the plaintiff could have elected to catch any of these – she had no legal right to complain about loss of voice following a Bug she specifically elected to catch.

• Over several months, the Guardian team attempted to persuade the court that Trademark Bugs diminished or denied not only first amendment rights, but basic constitutional rights to life liberty and the pursuit of happiness. Since Ms Po's life was not in danger, the legal debate concentrated on the criteria of 'liberty' and 'happiness'. The Guardian attempted to bring before the court testimony of hundreds of sufferers of common colds who had, by their own admission, been left 'housebound', hoping to show that this impaired their liberty. They also argued that being ill contravened the right to happiness, on the grounds that being ill makes people unhappy. Glaxco counter-argued that being ill did not prevent an individual from *pursuing* happiness, if they so chose; and that it was this latter right that was constitutionally guaranteed. Justice Greyes concurred.

• One woman (Paula de Chirico, from Waco, TX) gave evidence for sixty days, after Justice Greyes admitted her evidence. Having caught a Glaxco bug called 'Nosy Rudolf' she had ordered the cure ($9.95 for three tablets) online, but delivery was held up by a postal strike. She had gone to work mildly ill, and had inadvertently sneezed on her boss, who had thus also caught the bug. The boss had fired Ms de Chirico. The Guardian sought to argue that this demonstrated that Glaxco Trademark Bugs had interfered with Ms de Chirico's constitutional rights. The court debated for several weeks on the admissibility of a completely different Trademark Bug; the relevance of an individual other than the plaintiff; and the relative liability of the postal company. Eventually Justice Greves ruled that the burden of liability rested with de Chirico, for not maintaining hygienic practice with respect to her own contagion or spreading her contagion to others.

• Following this, many of the plaintiff's claims were rolled back. Glaxco again moved the case be dismissed.

• The Guardian pressed the freedom of speech angle. At the heart of this was their claim that for eight days in the first instance, and for a later 12-hour period, Ms Po had been denied her right to free expression by Glaxco's bug. The Glaxco team brought in expert witnesses to show that Ms Po had received far greater media exposure during those three days than at any other time in her career.

• There was a long discussion as to whether 'media exposure' amounts to 'freedom of speech'. Dozens of expert witnesses were called by both sides. This debate was eventually parked by Justice Greves, as ingermane and vexatious.

• The final months of the case were characterised by a series of increasingly complex blocking motions by the Guardian. Eventually Justice Greve guillotined further blocking, and ruled in favour of Glaxco. In his summing up, he declared: 'there may yet be a legal challenge that could be mounted on the grounds that Trademark Bugs violate a citizen's first amendment rights; but such a challenge will need to take as its plaintiff somebody other than a professional journalist mounting a clear and exploitative publicity stunt'.

• Seven different appeals followed, on grounds both of the due process and the Justice's final summing up. Two of these were unresolved or abandoned for financial reasons. Five upheld the judgment.

'This is a bad day for democracy,' Jean Ebner declared

from the courthouse steps. 'The judge has said, in effect, that people who work for the media cannot challenge these wicked corporations, and their terrible diseases, *because* they work for the media! He has left open the possibility that so-called "ordinary citizens" could mount a legal challenge, but how will they ever be able to afford it?'

'WITHOUT THE SUPPORT of the Guardian and the public fundraising campaign,' Ms Po added, 'I would never have been able to bring my case. This judgment puts corporate profit above the needs of common human decency.' It was not obvious at the time (although posterity has made clear) that this court case was the last serious legal challenge to the marketing of Trademark Bugs. The Guardian Conglomeration never recovered from the expense of mounting and then losing the suit, and ceased trading two years later.

THROUGHOUT THE EARLY 2040s there were several attempts to raise the funding necessary to challenge the big Trademark Bug manufacturers in courts; but none of these progressed beyond initial stages. The 'big three' pharma companies – Pfizer-Novartis, Glaxco and Bayer – expanded operations. Bayer developed anti-addiction medication, which it sold alongside its own-brand tobacco, stimulant and euphoric products. PN developed respirant illnesses that spread what it called 'one-quarter-asthma' (this label has been several times challenged in court as deliberately misrepresenting the degree of respiratory distress experienced by sufferers) alongside several models of 'fashion accessory inhalers'. The marketing of these to children resulted in a fad for carrying the devices, often expensively personalised, across much of Europe, South America and East Asia during the later 2040s.

Change in generational attitudes

EVIDENCE THAT YOUNGER generations had a different attitude to Trademark Bugs than their parents and grandparents has been gathered by Rakesh Bandari (Bandari 2089).

For people growing up in the '40s and '50s most of the diseases that had afflicted humanity for millennia had been cured. Nobody expected those cures to be distributed free. Moreover, the sense that 'disease' in the abstract still had a place in the ontological ecosystem of human life was deep-rooted, and many young people found it easy to accept that the Big Three pharma companies filled a niche that would otherwise be supplied by unpredictable feral viruses and bacteria. The situation was helped by canny PR by all three: PN and Glaxco by 2053 (and Bayer by 2055) guaranteed student loans at 1% under the bank rate to all university students. A mass-market campaign established them as 'cool' with younger demographics. Sports events, game and music products and TV – all of it was heavily subsidised by pharma money. Advertising presented the Trademark Bugs as a way of unofficially 'taxing' those too old and foolish to follow simple hygiene regimens, syphoning their money for the benefit of the young. That the young (especially the very young) were disproportionately affected by Trademark Bugs did not adversely affect this impression. By 2055 pharma companies overtook munitions companies as the largest donors to political parties; and after the '58 reforms they donated huge sums to legal infrastructure too. By 2060 few could deny that the industry as a whole, and the Big Three in particular, represented the most politically powerful group on the planet.

*   *   *

THIS CAN BE illustrated by Glaxco's development of 'Faceshapers', bugs that cause non-metastasising tumours to grow on various areas of the upper body and skull. The drugs necessary to reverse these growths were not cheap; and some people (especially in the climate-change affected equatorial areas) were compelled to live with the deformities. But many young people in the affluent west actively embraced this Bug, going so far as arranging Trademark Bug Swap Parties. The aim was to alter the body in ways deemed 'cool'. Particularly valued were horns of bone growing under the skin on shoulders and collar-bone, or so-called 'Klingon' or 'Publikumsbeschimpfung' growths on the forehead and cheeks.

LEGAL CHALLENGES WERE sometimes mounted against the new strains of bug, but without success. The big court cases of the '60s went, as it were, the other way: in particular PN v. Raj Choudhury (Schwarz-Gardos 2065c). Choudhury had made a personal fortune in IT, and set up a company that bought medication from Glaxco, PN and Bayer in bulk, and then distributed it free at clinics in the Third World. PN agreed to Glaxco and Bayer to take on the task of challenging this in court, as restraint of trade and violation of the terms of sale. The case lasted three weeks, in which Choudury's main defence – humanitarianism – was legally demolished. Choudhury was fined, and imprisoned after refusing to pay. His assets were seized and distributed to the plaintiff.

THROUGH THE EARLY '70s the Big Three confined their new products to cosmetic and minor afflictions. Bayer had a hit in '74 with their Kahlkopf product. Male-pattern baldness having been cured in the '40s, the effect of this Bug – it affected both men and women with rapid-onset alopecia – was extraordinary.

Sales of the cure pushed Bayer into the top position, profit-wise. Bayer were also the first of the Big Three to break the €10 trillion annual profit barrier (PN currently hold the all-time record, with their one-year profit of €74 trillion, although these figures do not include monies made that are tax-deductible under charitable, educational and defence budgets) [Figures estimated under academic 'fair use' rules].

Tax consequences of Big Three success

Big Three annual profits began outstripping the GDPs of even the world's largest countries in the early '60s. By the '80s it was clear that these commercial organisations were, simply, doing a better job of 'titheing' the population than nation-states had previously managed with old-fashioned tax collection paradigms. The use of the term 'tithe' was forwarded by the various financial restructuring proposals of '83, and challenged in court. The Russian Federation fought the longest legal battle on this (see Brohstein 2090 for a detailed account), but by the middle of the decade the only countries that retained a 'traditional' old-style tax regimen were few and small-scale. The bigger countries all passed over to systems where income tax and sales taxes were reduced to between 2% and 5% – and in some cases abolished altogether (less than 2% did not provide enough income to cover the expense of gathering the tax). Where previous generations had worked and then paid tax on work income, the new generations quickly adapted to receiving their salaries effectively tax-free, but paying money instead to maintain baseline levels of health and productivity.

The balance was simple: (a) pay the Big Three for the so-called Omnipills, that protected against all the traditional Trademark Bugs – as an expense, this averaged 17% of average income in most countries, although (being price rather than index-determined) it was flat-rate, benefitting the wealthy at the relative expense of the poor. Or (b) elect not to buy health, and attempt to work through whatever illnesses ensued. The 'soap-and-water' test was tested in court in 2086, when it was claimed that the Bayer Bug 'Emerald Rash' survived soap. The outcome (Kawasaki-86d) was that 'soap' was taken, legally, to include a variety of proprietary antibacterial washes and wipes. 'It is clear,' writes Bandari, 'that this would not have been accepted by the courts of the '30s and '40s. But public attitudes to the role of Trademark Bugs in society had shifted' (Bandari 2089).

THE BIG THREE funded national programmes of education, policing and crime; and sponsored infrastructure programmes. Many countries retained 'traditional' tax only in order to fund their military, although EU, South American and East Asian nations were happy to have the Pharma companies supply defence needs as well. Faced with an impending legal challenge on the 'no taxation without representation' principle, Bayer and Glaxco created a second variety of publically tradable share – giving the owner the right to vote on public policy, but not commercial or proprietary, matters. By 2090 PN followed suit, and by the century's end – at time of writing – democracy has adapted to the new model across much of the globe. 'Voting' is now something a citizen does if they opt-in to the political process by buying voting shares. If s/he chooses not to do so they are deemed, legally, to have surrendered their democratic rights.

Legal Implications of Combat

IT IS HARD to assess the long-term impact of the financial success of Trademark Bugs, and is beyond the scope of the present paper. The purpose of this final section is to consider the potential consequences of on-going litigation pertaining to the Bangladeshi Conflict. The high casualty figures of this conflict, as much as the central role played by pharma companies, render it a test-case for the on-going development of Trademark Bugs in the future of international relations. What is clear is that conflict represents a significant legal test-case for what amounts to a radically revisioned basis for civic and legal management of Trademark Bugs, up to and including a complete restatement of the Porter Rules for their commercial exploitation.

DESPITE BEING OFFICIALLY termed the 'Bangladeshi War', the conflict has spread across a much larger area than the Bay of Bengal. At the same time it is also true that the Battle for the port of Chaṭṭagrama – in Bangladesh – has been one of the biggest of the war so far. The whole region has suffered much more markedly from climate change than other areas on the globe, and economic growth of an averagely consistent 3% per 5 years has been diluted by outstripping population increases. The whole area shares with central Mexico the distinction of the world's highest rates of untreated Trademark Bug infections. At the same time, the Big Three have directed in excess of €5 billion humanitarian aid, including €220 million worth of free antiseptic soap, dispersed in the area since 2091.

THE MAIN ANTAGONISTS in the war (despite the use of nation-state shell identities) are generally agreed as being Bayer on the one hand, and on the other an alliance of smaller, ambitious and emergent pharmaceutical companies, led by the Myanmar Pharmaceutical Manufacturers Union (MPMU). The latter brought together troops from Myanmar, Malaysia and India; the former deployed armies from Russian Federation and

EU states. The specific flashpoints – control of the lucrative industrial centres positioned along the Karnaphuli River – are less relevant to our present discussion than the way the war has been prosecuted.

A rapid conventional phase shifted suddenly in June 2098 with the release of weaponised pharma. The poisoning of the Ganges aside (not a matter of strictly legal relevance) this led to two large-scale lawsuits. One was lodged by the MPMU Alliance in the EU Supreme Court, arguing that Bayer's pharmaceutical ordnance, deployed to cause harm and death to opposing troops, was in clear breach of the Porter Rules. Bayer's legal defence team counter-argued that the Porter Rules were never intended to apply to a warzone. The court was told that Bayer did indeed hold reserves of meds to cure such soldiers who had not already died, and that they were prepared to release these when a peace treaty was signed.

THE MPMU TACITLY conceded this suit by releasing its own weaponised pharma. Bayer filed a countersuit against the MPMU conventional weapons, on the grounds that the companies held no 'antidote' materiel to counter the effects of bullets and shrapnel. In peacetime this suit would almost certainly have been dismissed as vexatious litigation, but under the extraordinary circumstances it was allowed to proceed. It was, in fact, accepted by many as an attempt to reconfigure the nature of war along more humanitarian lines ('our aim is legally restraining more destructive conventional weaponry in favour of less destructive pharmaceutical weaponry', was the official Bayer court statement). This suit is on-going. Recently, Bayer has undertaken pre-emptive strikes against the factories of the MPMU, following intelligence reports that they were working on trademark-infringing cures for the weapons of the Bayer forces. 'Killing and maiming is one thing,' said Bayer vice-chairman Hester Lu. 'Wars have entailed that for thousands of years. But violating commercial copyrights and trademarks is quite another, and such behaviour will not be tolerated, in peace or in war'. Retaliation has brought long-range missile strikes to the European base of Bayer manufacture, and threatens to spread the conflict further.

IT IS POSSIBLE that further pharma conflicts will develop around the world. As such, it is necessary to establish legal protocols that go beyond the Geneva Convention in order to structure and horizon belligerence. At this point the joint-working team on the present paper have failed to find unanimity, and instead have agreed to position two alternate concluding paragraphs. For legal reasons, these are personalised with the names of team-leaders, although the sentiments they express were collectively agreed by the team-leaders' respective teams.

Conclusion 1:

Rachel Statton-Cummings, RPSL: The financial power and influence of the income associated with Trademark Bugs has resulted in seismic changes in the political and therefore social structures of our world. Democracy has, broadly, shifted from a flat-rate one-person-one-vote model to a corporate, buy-as-many-votes-as-you-like model. Democratic engagement is still open, at least for those who can afford to buy votes, but there is no guarantee it will stay this way (US and EU sets a maximum price for voting shares at $5/€3 each; but legislation currently being debated will remove maxima and allow the market to determine rates). Freedom of speech, once a necessary plank of democracy, has been reoriented around the axis of copyright and trademark law. Above all, what could have been the greatest single step towards collective human wellbeing in the world's history – the development of effective treatments for almost all cancers, all bacterial fevers, all GTI and skin diseases, all influenzas and even the myriad forms of the common cold – has instead been diverted into the artificial maintaining of these diseases in the general population solely to generate profits for three large and fifty-five smaller pharma companies. Trademark bugs go routinely untreated in poorer countries, causing unnecessary distress – and, since the leakage of weaponised pharma from the Asian War, often provoke long-term harm and even death. This whole situation can only be described as a collective moral wrong on a massive scale; and the international Law needs to be mobilised to address its consequences.

Conclusion 2:

Aleksandr Aleksandrovich Golumbovsy, АПУ. There are areas where the commercial handling of Trademark Bugs could be reformed and improved, especially with respect to medical access in poorer nations. But we as legal theorists must not overlook the very powerful good that the Big Three pharma companies have accomplished in the space of less than seventy years.

Having invested trillions of dollars in research and development, these three companies developed cures for pathologies that had plagued humanity for hundreds of millennia: plague, cancer, auto-immune diseases, influenza, malaria, TB, diphtheria, cholera, typhus, myriad genetic conditions and fevers. This, in a sense, is what these companies existed to do; and whilst these cures represented a massive humanitarian good, they also embodied the power of commercial self-interest. Having achieved this set of goals, it is not realistic to believe that these companies would simply roll-themselves-up and cease trading.

Indeed, under the well-established legal rule of corporate individuality, it would not be licit to expect them to commit suicide in this fashion. The distribution of Trademark Bugs – in every case, much milder diseases than the 'feral' illness that previously afflicted humanity – provided a viable commercial model by which these companies could continue to trade, with all the benefits that entailed in terms of employment, economic stimulus and so on.

The success of these Bugs was a function of two factors. One was the competitive pricing model adopted, whereby mild colds could be cured with cheap medicines, and only rarer, more serious illnesses required more expensive pharmaceuticals. Two was cultural inertia: people were used to getting sick with colds and flus, and they continued getting sick with these illnesses. The difference was that now they could be cured for a small financial outlay. High-profile media campaigns argued that if the companies ceased distributing their new modified bugs then the illnesses would stop happening altogether; but these failed to make significant inroads in many areas. Like taxation (discussed below), people broadly accept a degree of disease in their lives, provided only that the proportion does not rise too high.

The broader ethics of this practice are a matter for philosophical discussion; but on the practical plane the practice has been bedded-in as a fait accompli by its prodigious financial success. This money has altered the structure of global society in ways that are (arguably) both bad and good. It is worth, however, stressing the good.

The global spread of Trademark Bugs created the circumstances for titheing, which in turn shrunk nation-state tax collection. The Big Three are now, broadly speaking, responsible for the infrastructure, health, educational and military provision that used to be the preserve of countries. In effect the tax take has shifted from governments to these corporations. This is more ethical – since nobody is obliged to purchase the company cures, nobody is forced to pay 'tax' – *and* more practical. The 'tax' base has widened (since everybody is liable to infection) and consequently the actual rate has reduced from an average 17% of income (by-total-population) to an average 9% [Engell 2098]. Both these outcomes are improvements. More, previously people paid tax to government and often resented it; now people pay 'tax' for the immediate somatic relief of freedom from a pressing illness, and are grateful. There are compelling arguments [Iglesias 2098, Kaufmann, 2099] that corporations not only collect less tax, but disburse what they do collect more efficiently than did the old governments.

There is nothing immutable about any particular social model of structure of government. The only salient is that people are governed predictably, fairly and effectively. Attachment to the old systems merely for the sake of nostalgic attachment to tradition is illogical. The Big Three have effected a bloodless revolution and left the world, broadly speaking, better off.

Bibliography

Bandari, Q., *Pharma: the Social Revolution* (PN Press 2089)

Brohstein, L., *Efficiency, Inefficiency, Mortality and Disbursement: an Account of Russian Federation Tax Affairs 2082-88* (Glaxco Press, 2090)

Engell, J., *Global Tax Take: a Quantitative History 1600-2100* (Bayer University Press 2098)

Gharzai, M., *The First Asian War: One Million Casualties and Counting* (Scorpion Press 2099)

Gharzai, M., *Corporate Responsibility: the Limits of Genocide* (Independent Distribution 2100)

Grohmann, *Freedom and Restriction of Speech: New Commercial Paradigms* (PN Press 2088)

Iglesias, M., *Tax Disbursement in an Age of Mass Casualties: Commercial and Nation-State Paradigms Compared* (Oxfam 2098)

Kaufmann, S., *The Metaphysics of Taxation* (Glaxco Press, 2099)

Kokoschka L, Maass G., Truman Q and Wellek R, *Legal Discussion, Discourse and Social Policy: the Anglo-Russian Collaborations* (5th edition, EU 2099)

Malahat, M., *An Elongated Summary of Guardian v. Glaxco, 2036-39* (Bayer Press 2090)

Trebuchet, A., 'Unlogged and Unplanned Feral Mutations to Trademark Bugs in the Field: a Catalogue and Assessment of Future Risk', *Journal of Independent Epidemiology* 12 (Fall 2096), 55-109

ATTITUDE

Linda Nagata

Our Only Export is Entertainment

THE ANNOUNCER'S VOICE boomed across the arena as I plummeted feet first toward the alpha fin of the central pylon. I caught my name – Juliet Alo – but nothing else because I was playing Attitude, and in the climactic seconds of the championship round, all my brain power was consumed with calculating trajectories across the three dimensions of zero-gee.

I was only a rookie, but I could extrapolate a player's destination a moment after launch. Sometimes I knew where players would go before they did – and that gave me time to evade them.

I reached the alpha fin and kicked off again with the ball of my foot, extending into a needle posture to shoot across the zero-gee arena with my arms pressed to my sides, legs straight, toes pointed in an aerodynamic configuration aided by the smooth lines of my gold bodysuit. An opposing player in the dark-purple suit of Team August streaked in to intercept my trajectory – too late. Frustration lined a face framed by the gel-padded bars of his helmet as I whispered past his outstretched fingertips on my way to a calculated rendezvous with the ball.

The arena we played in was a vast oval, sixty meters in length and caged by softly glowing red filaments that flared a penalty if touched by a player or by the ball. Up and down had no real meaning, but we oriented anyway with a gradient from deep-water blue at the base to brilliant white at the summit. The central pylon was an irregular corkscrew studded with fins small and large and set at random angles in an array that changed every quarter, never twice the same. Goal rings were hung at the base and the summit.

The number of spectators present in the zero-gee hub of Stage One was small – just the players from other teams, the Stage One staff, and, for every game, at least four 'special guests' – Attitude fans flown to LEO at the A-League's expense, because 'Attitude is for everyone.'

It was a slogan, but the A-League took it seriously. Fans around the world could watch sponsored showings at home or they could spend a little to purchase admission to live, 3-D renderings of the game in theaters, sharing the experience with hundreds of others, at a ticket price that shifted with a region's median income. And of course there was gear, and gambling, and commercial endorsements, but there were also prizes and scholarships and a network of authorized trainers around the world sponsoring camps and competitions for future players. Though only in its fifth year of existence, Attitude had become one of the most popular spectator sports in or off the world.

I played for Team November. We'd won three of five games in the final series against Team August, and with time running out in Game 6, one more score would give us the championship.

I pulled in my knees, executed a flip, and hammered my feet against the jelly membrane of a static drum, arresting my momentum just as the spindle-shaped A-ball slammed into my hands.

Min Tao had thrown it hard, with so much spin it almost tore out of my grip. Fierce screams rose up from the arena audience and after a delay of a fractional second – the time required for the crowd noise generated by the nearest theaters to reach us

– there were groans and gasps and then a deafening cheer as I secured my grip on the ball.

Team August players in their dark uniforms raced to set up a defense as I cocked my arm and passed for the goal–

Fake passed.

I pumped my arm but held onto the ball, drawing out an opposing player who'd been lurking for a chance to intercept. He dove toward me, blocking my line to the goal ring – but I never meant to go straight in anyway. I counted silently, the same count Min Tao was keeping as he clung to a nearby fin, gleaming in Team November's gold uniform – and at zero we both launched.

Our trajectories met in wide-open air. The screams of the crowd reverberated around us as I flat-handed off Min Tao's shoulder, shifting my trajectory toward the goal ring as my teammates converged from all sides to block Team August's players.

I scanned the moving field, assuring myself no one could block me before I shot through the goal ring and scored. The game was mine to win.

Then I saw Cherise Caron moving – a third year veteran and Team August's best player. She relayed with a teammate, picking up momentum from the exchange along with a trajectory shift. In my head I extrapolated her course. Cherise would hit a summit fin where she would have to align and launch again to block my goal. I'd studied every play she'd made over three seasons and knew she had the skill to do it, but she did not have the time.

The score was mine. The game, mine. The equation was set and nothing could change my flight so I relaxed, turning my head to watch her as she reached the fin.

Something happened then that I could not explain. Her momentum reversed so quickly it was as if a digital record skipped in time. All my calculations were thrown off by at least three-tenths of a second as she darted to intercept me, and before I could twist to protect the ball it was gone from my hands. She passed the ball on the fly, hurling it to a teammate waiting halfway to blue. Our backfield was left playing catch-up as Team August relayed the ball past fins and static drums. Then they blocked our lone defender before a player took the ball through the goal ring for an easy score.

The crowd roared, half in outraged disbelief, half in astonished joy.

The coaches liked to remind us that the only thing Stage One exports to Earth is entertainment.

We did a raging business that game.

Integrity is Everything

I CAME UP to Stage One nine months ago, debarking from the space plane as a wonder-struck recruit. After the first ten minutes I was so nauseous I lost my lunch, heaving into a specially designed barf bag – and that was the only time I ever questioned my decision to play for the Attitude League.

The coaches and the medical staff helped us with the transition, and then we were herded into the huge arena – all of the season's first-year players together, with the veterans beside us. I want to say it was dreamlike, but if so it was a disturbing dream in which I foundered, nearly helpless in zero gee, bumping into other lost and frightened rookies just like me, while breathing in chill air laden with the stink of vomit and sweat and plastic volatiles. I felt lost, vulnerable, nauseous – but triumphant too because I'd made it.

Against all odds I'd won a place in the A-League and a home in low Earth orbit as a probationary citizen of Stage One.

Zaid Hackett came to speak to us. Known around the world simply as 'Zaid,' she was CEO of Stage One and the architect of this house of dreams. A small woman, already seventy years old, with close-cropped curly silver hair, light-colored eyes, and striking dark, red-brown skin. That day she wore knit pants and a short pullover that didn't quite hide a paunch, and though she spoke to us in a soft, husky voice, everything she said had resonance, as if the pent-up energy inside her escaped as a low vibration in every word, spilling purpose into the world.

Who else could have established Stage One? Though we were still under construction, with a build-out that would take many more years, we were the first-ever city in space. Other habitats existed in low Earth orbit, but we were the only one to rotate, generating a half-gee of pseudogravity at the end of the spokes that circled the zero-gee core. Donations had financed the initial startup, but every stage since had been paid for with revenue generated by the A-League. Our fans financed the future, creating a permanent foothold in space for the people of Earth.

Zaid Hackett was a visionary, but she was a realist too who reminded us of the hard truth: "Given the cost of access to space, only a few people will ever be privileged to go up. Those of us who are here carry with us the hopes and dreams of millions who will never have the chance to go forward into a wider future. Remember that. Remember them. Our fans will support us only so long as we are worthy of their support. In the Attitude League, integrity is everything."

MY TEAM, TEAM November, had lost Game 6 and I was furious. We left the victors celebrating in the arena and sculled in sullen silence through the short passage to our locker room – a small chamber curved to fit within the rim of the core. The twelve of us gathered there, floating with knees folded, our gold uniforms damp with sweat but still bright – a sharp contrast to our dark, disbelieving murmurs.

Coach Szarka came in last. He was a passionate, determined man and I'm sure he would have delivered a memorable speech about how we would return, stronger for our loss, to win both Game 7 and the season championship – except I didn't give him the chance. If I let my anger cool I would talk myself into doing nothing. So as the door closed I held fast to a wall loop and blurted what I knew to be the truth: "We were cheated out of a victory! Cherise could not have done what she did without over-enhancing. I wasn't the only one counting off the time. Everyone here knows I'm right."

Dead silence followed. Never before had there been an accusation of cheating in the A-League. My heart beat once, twice, three times as Coach stared at me, too stunned to speak. My face, already puffy in the absence of gravity, swelled a little more as I flushed, overtaken by an emotion somewhere between shame, terror, and outrage.

I turned to my teammates for support. Several looked frightened. Bruna Duarte, a first-year like me, looked confused. But Min Tao – who was both team captain and our top player – encouraged me with a nod, so I turned back to Coach and made my argument, pretending I didn't hear the quaver in my voice:

"We've all enhanced our response times. That's no secret. We operate at the maximum allowed by the League – which means we all know the exact time it should have taken Cherise to perform that V-launch. But she beat that time – and the only way she could have done that was by cheating. She over-enhanced."

Min Tao hooked a foot under a loop and straightened his lean, compact body. "Juliet's right. I counted too and Cherise could not have *legally* moved that fast."

It was as if he'd given the team permission to see the truth. Everyone started talking, insisting they'd suspected too. I raised my voice to be heard. "I want to file a protest."

Bruna scowled at me, but others agreed:

"Juliet's right."

"If we're going to file a protest, we need to do it now."

"I *knew* something was off."

Coach listened and nodded, looking grim. "It's our duty to report it. I'll take it to the league."

The Millions

WE FILED OUT, eager to get up the spoke to Stage One's rotating rim before Team August left the arena. With towels in hand to mop up our game sweat, we mobbed the portal. The transit pod carried only six passengers at a time, so I made sure I was at the front of the crush.

I was frightened by what I'd done. No one was going to be happy about it. Not even my teammates, not even if we were given the victory, because no one wanted to win the championship like that, post-game, on a technicality. Team August would hate me for it, and the league officials would be furious that I'd cast doubt on the integrity of the A-League. Would my career even survive?

The portal door slid open. I launched myself into the waiting pod right behind Bruna, following her to a backseat and buckling in. The transit pod was a rectangular brick with a transparent canopy. Blue Earth loomed overhead, but I only glanced at it before my gaze shifted to the oncoming gray wall that was Spoke-1. It swept toward us, huge and remorseless, one of only two complete spokes in our partially built city. Stage One would eventually grow into a spoked ring of habitable spaces, but we were still building the frame of the ring and so far our 'city' occupied less than thirty degrees of arc at the end of Spoke-1, with an empty habitat as counterbalance at the end of Spoke-2. There was not room or resources to house a separate construction crew, so it was the players who did the work, putting in hours outside every day before practice.

The other four seats filled, the pod door slid shut, and behind it the portal closed.

"Why would she do it?" Bruna asked, loudly enough to include everyone.

Angelo answered her, a second-year player with an ego that outran his game skills. "So she can *win*. What do you think?"

"We all want to win," Min Tao said from his seat in the front row. "But we don't cheat. I've played against Cherise three seasons and she's never cheated before. Why now?"

"Money," Angelo said. "Why else?"

Money

As PLAYERS, WE earned a respectable salary, but no one expected to get rich playing Attitude. Though the A-League took in vast sums of money, nearly all of it went into the maintenance and expansion of Stage One. As players, it was our privilege to be part of that. The league allowed us three seasons of play. At the end of that time, our names would go to the top of the list for subsidized family housing.

But bringing family up? We had to pay for that.

So money still mattered. Money always does.

As SPOKE-1 REACHED us, we launched, the pod dropping onto the spoke's track in what felt like a sudden, sharp fall into gravity – or at least the pseudogravity generated by the centripetal force of the station's spin. We plummeted down the track, and a few seconds later an automated docking process synced us with the rim portal.

I was out of the transit pod as soon as the doors opened. The half-gee pull meant we walked, all of us hurrying because we had only a little time to shower and dress before the losers' post-game press conference – but as I neared my apartment I was distracted by a faint buzz, a sound I couldn't place.

"Hey!" Bruna said behind me. "Is that a fly? How did a fly get here?"

I ducked and backed against the wall as a silver insect buzzed above my head.

But it wasn't an insect. Though no bigger than a housefly, it was something mechanical, humming on iridescent wings that supported an oblong body, gray and hard to focus on.

"Crush it!" Min Tao shouted. He bounded past Bruna and jumped at the thing. It swerved, but Min Tao was faster. He flattened it against the ceiling, landing in a graceful crouch.

"Brutal," Bruna said. "Was that your lost toy?"

Min Tao held the lifeless thing in his palm for us to see. "Mech-skeeter. Someone smuggled a swarm of them up my first year."

The body of the device was an array of tiny, feathery plumes; from the sheen of its crushed wings, I suspected it was powered by light.

"So what's a mech-skeeter?" I asked.

"An assay device, to analyze air quality. Hypersensitive. Gambling operations use them to track the physical condition of athletes. Breathe on it" – he did – "and it'll ID you and measure your fitness by reading the chemicals in your breath." He looked up with a grin that made me wonder if he was joking. "Kill them," he advised as he opened the door to his room. "Or all your secrets are lost."

I STOOD BENEATH an endlessly recycling stream of hot water in the shower's tight confines, keeping my elbows close to my body as I washed my short hair. A scroll tacked to the shower wall showed the victors' post-game interview, with the twelve Team August players in their locker room, ready to answer questions from around the world. Most of the questions though went to their star player.

"Cherise, how do you explain your phenomenal performance?" Cherise was a striking, sharp-featured woman of twenty-five, her skin smooth and made milky by an absence of sunlight. "Three years of hard work," she said as I tapped the scroll to activate a facial analysis program. No alerts went up. She wasn't lying, but then the proper question hadn't been asked. "But also, the entire team is hungry to do what's never been done before, to win the Attitude championship two years in a row. We *can* do it. We *will* do it, now that we've made it to Game 7."

"Cherise, many of your fans wondered if Game 6 would be the last you ever played. Now you've earned one more, but this must be an emotional time for you, so close to the end of your career. Can you share your feelings with us?"

"It's tremendously sad. My time on Stage One has been the most meaningful of my life, and it will be hard to go home."

Her teammates gasped at her answer. I caught my breath, shutting off the water so I could hear better as the press corps fired off questions:

"Cherise, are you saying you're returning to Earth?"

"Are you saying you won't stay aboard Stage One?"

"Are you giving up citizenship?"

We were all shocked. Several players who'd finished their allotted three seasons had chosen to give up their claim to permanent housing and return to the world, but it was different with Cherise. She'd become the face of Attitude, widely considered the best who'd ever played. For her not to stay... it was as if a queen should abdicate her throne.

I toweled off, taking the scroll with me as I stepped out of my tiny bathroom into my tiny apartment. The bed was a narrow platform accessed by a ladder, with storage underneath. A narrow desk was built into the opposite wall. There was nothing else, but it was enough.

I slapped the scroll against the wall, continuing to watch

while I pulled on leggings and a team jersey. I was combing my black hair into neat lines when Team August signed off with a rousing cheer, "*August for the win!*"

I watched Cherise as she pumped her fist in the air along with the rest of the team, and I saw an imbalance in the gesture, as if her shoulders, elbows, and wrists were not quite synchronized. It was subtle, something I could see only because I'd studied her so closely for three years, but it was enough to convince me my protest had not been a mistake.

The league established a limit on neural enhancement because anything greater resulted in painful damage to joints and nerves that presented first as a loss of coordination. It horrified me to imagine Cherise crippled, and for what? To play just one more game? To win the championship bonus? And what was that worth? I knew the answer: one flight, one-way, on the space plane. That was all. Not enough to sacrifice your reputation and your health.

BRUNA AND ANGELO were waiting for me in the corridor.

"Did you see the way she moved?" Bruna asked, her dark eyes and charcoal skin in contrast with close-cropped hair that she colored gold like our uniforms.

I nodded. "I can't believe she would do it, just for a chance at the bonus."

"It's not the bonus," Angelo said. He was petite and brown, with big hands, a sharp nose, and an annoying certainty about all his opinions, but I always listened to him anyway, because mostly he was right. "Half the world knows her name. If she retires with two championships in three years of play, the endorsement fees she'll command–"

"In the *millions*," I realized.

"That's right, baby girl," Angelo said. "Integrity is everything, right up until the day you leave Stage One."

*   *   *

Sportsmanship

BRUNA, ANGELO, AND I were the last of the team to arrive in the press room. We walked into an ominous silence. Everyone else was already seated behind a long, elevated table, with Team November's hawk logo projected behind them. Facing the podium was a wall monitor used to stitch together the faces of media personalities from around the world to create an illusion of a collocated audience – except no one was there. The monitor was a neutral gray. Coach Szarka stood near it, his back turned to us, head bent in a whispered conference with Dob Irish, the League's marketing director. Both looked up as we came in.

"Take a seat," Coach said.

I went first, sitting next to Min Tao, who met my gaze with a grim expression.

Dob Irish took over. "The press conference is cancelled," he announced in a blunt, angry voice. He was a small but broad-shouldered man of florid complexion, outgoing, and well-known for his abundant smiles. I'd never seen him angry before – but cheating scandals were new to the A-League, and I approved of his outrage. "Marketing has been charged with containing the damage generated by today's sorry incident. The A-League prospers only so long as we maintain our reputation for fairness and respect for one another, but the poor sportsmanship displayed here today puts us all at risk."

Beside him, Coach Szarka's scowl became so deep his eyebrows met. "That is enough, Dob. You may not like it, but we had a legitimate reason for doubt. It was our *duty* to file a protest–"

"Tarnishing the reputation of our most beloved player because she snatched the championship away from you."

"Get out, Dob, before I do something we'll both regret."

Dob opened his mouth, reconsidered, and disappeared out the door.

I was so shocked, I could hardly breathe. I felt worse when Coach Szarka turned his scowl on us, because I knew what was coming.

"In response to our protest, Cherise's reaction time was tested by Dr. Kyre immediately following the locker-room interview. She passed that test. So August is the legitimate winner of Game 6. The A-League requests all players refrain from discussing the incident or responding to any questions about over-enhancement. Dismissed – all but you, Juliet. I want a word with you."

I felt cold and hot all at once, exposed and ruined and betrayed – because I knew what I'd seen. "They're covering it up," I whispered.

Min Tao put his hand on mine. "We'll talk later," he said as our teammates filed behind us, eager to escape.

I nodded, not even noticing when he disappeared. Quiet descended and I was alone behind the podium, staring at Coach Szarka. He said, "I'm not going to yell at you. I think we did the right thing. It's important we all police the integrity of the league – but this time we were wrong. Zaid has asked that you visit Cherise and offer your apology. I advise you to do it. A reputation for poor sportsmanship is not going to help you make it to your second season."

My hot flush was gone and all I felt was cold. "I was not the one who cheated."

"No one cheated," Coach insisted. "Apologize, Juliet, and hope we can put this behind us."

FROM THE DAY I first heard of Stage One, I wanted to be part of it, this daring future aimed at building a city in space through the enthusiasm and the contributions of all the people of Earth. A city on the edge of the high frontier.

Skeptics had laughed at the business plan and called it a scam. Finance an orbital habitat from the revenue earned by a professional sports league? It could never happen!

But I was sixteen, not yet conquered by cynicism, and I thought, *Why not?* For decades professional sports had built mega-corporations, luxury stadiums, athletic complexes, and individual fortunes all around the world. What if all that money was channeled instead into Stage One?

I read the player qualifications, and knew they were within my reach. I'd gone from champion gymnastics in childhood to a national ranking in volleyball as a teen, so I had the necessary athleticism. Fluency in two languages was required. I was a native English speaker, knew Spanish, and had an acquaintance with Mandarin. My lack of height, which had limited my prospects in volleyball, was an advantage in the A-League, where the height restriction was 178 centimeters, because smaller people consume fewer resources and require less living space.

I applied three times before I was accepted. Afterward, I did a hundred interviews, bubbling with joy through every one of them, knowing I was one of the luckiest people in the world.

I DID NOT apologize.

I returned to my apartment instead, feeling sick. I still believed I was right, that Cherise could not have done what she did without cheating, but it was a scandal the league did not want to pursue because integrity is everything – or the illusion of it anyway. For the first time I wondered if the skeptics were right: *was* Attitude a scam? Was the league's goal really to build a city in space? Or were we here to make a handful of players and the investors who sponsored them ungodly rich?

I changed out of my jersey, determined to go to dinner, not because I was hungry, but because I was afraid to go; afraid of what the other players would say, what they would do – and I hate being afraid.

SCENTS OF COOKED fruit and spices seeped out of the dining hall, along with a low burr of sullen conversation. I hesitated in the open doorway, staring in at a packed room. It looked like every player and every coach had come to dinner at the same time. Faces turned in my direction and the volume of conversation dropped.

I squared my shoulders and entered, weaving between the tables, all too conscious of the cold glares that followed me. And though I pretended not to hear, I was offered thoughtful advice–

"Next time play harder. You can't win by complaining."

"Even rookie stars can't win every game, Juliet. Deal with it."

"What did Cherise ever do to you?"

I kept my eyes straight ahead. Reached the buffet and filled up my plate and then wondered if there would be a place for me to sit.

Angelo rescued me. He caught my elbow, steering me to a table shared by Bruna and Min Tao, and on the way he whispered in my ear, "Guess who's not here tonight?"

I scowled at him. He returned a toothy smile. "Cherise has not come out to celebrate her victory. There's a rumor going around she's caught a mild flu."

"From where?" I asked skeptically. "Bit by a mech-skeeter?"

He shrugged. "All sorts of things come up on the space plane." As we reached the table, he pulled out a chair for me. "Dr. Kyre has ordered bed rest in her apartment. At least three days."

"Three days out of sight?"

"Exactly."

*　　*　　*

Discretion

BY THE NEXT morning, I decided to do as I'd been told and go to see Cherise. I wasn't intending to apologize though; I just wanted to learn what I could about her 'flu.'

Skipping the lift, I took the steep stairs down to the next level, but I hesitated at the door, alerted by a faint buzzing. It was another mech-skeeter venturing up the stairwell from somewhere below. The tiny device hovered out of reach, so I turned my back on it and opened the door. It darted through to the corridor – but to my surprise it reversed course right away, and tried to return to the stairwell. I didn't let it. As it passed, I knocked it out of the air, crushing it against the floor with my foot.

I looked up to see Dr. Kyre, hesitating on his way out of one of the apartments – Cherise's apartment, I realized. He was watching me with a half smile. "We've been invaded," he said. "It happened a couple years ago too, just before the final game."

Kyre was an older man, sixty-two, a fact I knew because I'd read his profile, not because he looked it. He was the physician for Teams July, August, and September, but not for November, so I didn't know him well.

"Have you come to see my patient?" he asked. "I was told you might."

"How is she doing?" I asked, hoping my nervousness didn't show.

He spread his hands. "She's been better, but she's determined to play in the final game."

"She *is* a champion."

"I'm sure she'll welcome your company," he said, leaving the apartment door ajar.

I tapped on the door, pushed it wider, and then stepped inside. The apartment was like mine, with a tiny bathroom just inside the door, a bed beyond it, and the desk opposite, separated by a narrow strip of floor space. Cherise occupied that space, sitting in the desk chair, her feet resting on a foot stool concocted from a plastic box.

Her gaze challenged me. "I don't think you've come to apologize."

I slid the door shut. "Should I?"

As an answer she stood up. This simple movement was awkward and slow. She raised her arm. Her wrist flopped twice before she managed to hold her hand up. Watching her, a shudder of dismay ran down my spine.

"You see?" she asked. "This is what's been done to me."

So I had been right. She returned to her chair with such painful effort I wished I had been wrong. The way she sat – so stiff and motionless – it frightened me.

"You need to get treatment," I said stupidly.

"I am getting treatment." Her lips barely parted as she spoke. "Believe it or not, I'm better now than last night. Kyre swears he's treated cases like this before. He assures me it's not permanent and has promised I'll be fine by game day."

"I don't understand. Why did you–"

"I didn't do it! I didn't even suspect it. I was so angry with you for pissing on the best game I'd ever played, but as soon as I started to cool down I felt it, shooting pains in my arms and legs, a burning in my joints." She spoke with a bitterness I could easily understand. "You were right. It wasn't me playing that game. It was some jacked-up version of me."

"But how did you pass the test?"

"Cheated. Kyre did the test. He protected me."

"And the league knows that?"

"I don't know what the league knows. I just know that no one but you is asking questions, which seems very strange until you consider how much more revenue comes in if the series runs to seven games. August must have been predicted to lose, so someone decided to help me – and so what if I got burned? I'm done anyway, right?"

I wanted to believe her, to believe she had nothing to do with it, but Cherise had her own back story. "Is it true you have an endorsement deal?"

"Oh yes. And it's also true I'll get paid a whole lot more if I help August take the championship. So… maybe I did this to myself?"

If she had, it was a stupid gamble – and Cherise was not stupid. "August isn't going to win Game 7 if you're not in top form."

"There won't be a Game 7 if you report me. I didn't do anything wrong, Juliet, but if this gets out, I lose everything."

"But if the A-League is involved in this–"

Her voice shot up an octave: "*No!* What is that thing doing here?" She glared at the desk, where a mech-skeeter had alighted. "I saw those in my first year."

"Min Tau thinks they're feeding information to a gambling network."

She stared at the device like it was a pile of shit, freshly fallen and steaming. "A gambling network?"

"Yes."

I smashed the skeeter so it could not betray her true condition – and I hoped there were no more in the room.

DR. KYRE MUST have reported my visit, because Dob Irish was outside waiting for me when I left Cherise's room.

Yesterday, the marketer had accused me of poor sportsmanship, of lodging a frivolous protest because I was disgruntled. It was an insult that had left us mutually wary.

"It's gotten a little crazy around here," he said in an apologetic tone. "I stepped over the line yesterday. It's just that Cherise is such a popular player. For her to be… well, it's not just *her* public image that's been hurt."

"I'm the bad guy, right?"

His thin shoulders rose in a half-hearted shrug as a mech-skeeter glided between us. "There's work to do to repair your image."

I didn't answer this, allowing him to move on to what was really on his mind. "Were you able to discuss the cheating incident with Cherise?"

I wondered how much he knew. "The league has stated there was no cheating incident."

"And... do you agree with that?"

He was fishing for a statement.

I resolved to give him one. "I was mistaken. Cherise did not cheat."

He smiled and nodded, knowing he could spin that handful of words to everyone's advantage. "Misunderstandings have to be expected when emotions run high."

"And still, integrity is everything–"

"Absolutely."

"– no matter how many millions of euros are riding on the outcome of this game."

His smile collapsed into a dark glare. "I'll edit that out and release the rest. It'll help, but you need to consider what you can do to salvage your image, or I'll be writing a negative assessment of your marketing potential for next year."

Like everyone else on staff, Dob received a flat salary. I wondered: had he begun to believe he deserved a little more?

Don't Ever Get Complacent

THINGS HAD GOTTEN crazy, but I was still expected to work my shift.

It was a surreal truth that hundreds of millions of euros – maybe a billion – would be in play with the last game, but we were still working stiffs, putting in our hours on the construction and maintenance of Stage One. That was one of the marketing draws of Attitude athletes. We were sold as unassuming superstars who worked hard all week just like our fans. The only difference, we got to enjoy a little glory on game day.

The assignment that day was mundane. The space plane had just docked and I was on a team assigned to unload construction materials, brought up at enormous cost.

Immense sums of money, forever swirling around us.

I suited up along with Bruna, Min Tao, and three others from November. I didn't tell them about my visit to Cherise. I was no attorney, but I was fairly sure I had an obligation to report what Cherise had told me. By keeping quiet, I'd become part of a conspiracy to hide the truth and I didn't want to include my friends in that.

With Min Tao and Bruna, I squeezed into the airlock, our faces hidden behind the reflective gold sheen of our visors. The inner door closed and sealed.

When we first trained to go outside we were warned, *Don't ever get complacent.*

Always, we followed procedure.

I hooked my tether to a wall loop and then reported to the gate marshal: "Secured and ready for depressurization."

"Secured," Min echoed. "Also ready."

And then Bruna, "Secured and squared away. Let's go."

"Status affirmed," the gate marshal answered. "Commencing depressurization."

My suit inflated as air was evacuated from the lock, but even in vacuum, the finely engineered joints slid with mechanical ease.

"Suit pressures steady," the gate marshal intoned. "Oxygen levels nominal. Are there any anomalies to report?"

We responded in turn, "Negative. All's well."

"Egress approved."

I turned the manual lock, pushed the door aside, and then

took a moment to admire the view: Earth looming above us as night reached the mid-Pacific, with a tiny gleam of golden lights marking the islands that were my first home.

Reaching outside, I hooked a second tether into a track ring. "Secure on two."

"Release on one," the gate marshal answered. "Transferring you to the shift marshal's control."

The shift marshal acknowledged the transfer as my first tether automatically released, leaving me free to transit outside.

The space plane was docked to the core, illuminated by artificial lights. Passengers exited through a gate, but construction materials were offloaded directly from the depressurized hold, its doors standing open, the interior illuminated by docking lights. Inside was a precisely fitted row of cargo containers. Our task was to connect each to a sled that would extract it and ferry it to an assigned construction site.

Min Tao and Bruna followed me outside.

I should have proceeded directly to the sled rack, but I was distracted by a faint, whining buzz, both familiar and mysterious. My heart rate ramped up. Was something wrong with my suit?

Within the bubble of my helmet I turned my head, trying to locate the source of the sound, and as I did the buzzing grew louder until, to my shock, a mech-skeeter flew in front of my face. It bounced off the smooth curve of my visor, then landed on my lip. In instinctive panic, I shook my head, sending the device humming away, to buzz somewhere unreachable, behind my ear.

I announced my dilemma on a general channel. "There's a mech-skeeter in my suit!"

"I've got one too," Bruna said in disgust.

But we couldn't go back inside, because the other half of our offloading team was still in the airlock, and before the lock finished its cycle, two of them realized they shared our predicament. The gate marshal readmitted them, while Bruna and I were forced to wait, me with a mechanical insect walking up the back of my neck.

I was paying attention to that, not to Min Tao, when he announced, "I'm going to go ahead and do the inventory."

He kicked off toward the space plane's cargo hold, his tether extending behind him – and I looked away.

"Hey!" Bruna said. "Min Tao, why did you unhook?"

"I didn't! My tether snapped!"

I looked up, startled by the fear in his voice. I looked around, but I couldn't see him. So I pushed off the wall, pivoting until I glimpsed him as he vanished into an inky shadow beneath the space plane. Clumsy in the suit, he'd missed his jump, and now only the trailing end of his loose tether remained in the light.

"Bruna, make sure my tether doesn't slip!"

I launched myself after him with all the velocity I could generate, catching the end of his tether just before it glided out of reach.

WE CYCLED BACK through the lock to a warm reception. Min Tao was mugged by our three teammates and they tried to mug me, but Dob Irish – as happy as anyone – was there too. As I got my helmet off, he pulled me away.

"Brilliant!" he whispered so only I could hear. "You handled that perfectly. Your name is already trending, and you're regaining audience sympathy."

I grabbed his arm with my thick glove, icy cold from being outside. "What are you talking about? You're not saying that was a setup? Just to boost my image?"

Dob looked annoyed. "Come on. If it was real, then Min Tao–" He frowned, thinking it over, while a mech-skeeter passed above our heads.

Behind me I heard the laughing voices of my teammates.

If I'd missed grabbing the loose tether, maybe Bruna could have gone after Min Tao with a sled, I don't know. But thinking about it, I started to shake. I imagined him floating alone out there, faced with a slow death when his air ran out – and my grip on Dob's arm tightened. "Tell me what's going on."

He shook his head, looking stricken. "It must have been an accident."

Or the A-League had betrayed us, betrayed Min Tao, betrayed Cherise, to feed a tabloid narrative designed to boost our ratings and our revenue. If so, I intended to be on the space plane when it returned to Earth.

I wriggled out of the cumbersome suit.

"Hey," Bruna said, "we still have to unload the plane."

"Check with the gate marshal. If she lets you outside before there's an investigation, then we all need to resign right now and go home."

A TRANSIT POD was already in the cradle when I reached the Spoke-1 gate. I climbed in, followed by a mech-skeeter, which settled on the transparent canopy just out of my reach. I wanted to crush it, an outlet for my anger at all that had happened, but I'd have to take off my harness to do it, so I reached for the button to close the door instead.

"Hold the pod!" a man shouted. "One more coming!"

And Dr. Kyre tumbled in with a grin.

His eyes widened as if he was surprised to find me there. "Juliet! I heard what happened outside."

He pulled himself into the seat beside me and strapped in, while the mech-skeeter decided to leave, gliding out just ahead of the closing door. It was the second time I'd seen one retreat when Kyre showed up; the first had been outside Cherise's room.

"I'm getting worried," Kyre said. "Real worried. What happened to Cherise was about ensuring a seven-game championship. What happened to Min Tao–" He pursed his lips, frowning at Earth's glittering nightside floating overhead. "I think you were right. Irish set Min Tao up."

"You talked to Irish?"

"It's the money," Kyre said in soft concern. "It makes people crazy. You need to keep that in mind, Juliet. You need to be careful."

We docked and locked and the doors opened. A group of Team August players was waiting for the pod, all of them dressed for practice. Dr. Kyre smiled, greeting each by name as he got out. I slipped past him, forgotten, and grateful for it.

Face Off

I'D NEVER BEEN to our CEO's office before; I'd never had cause. I was surprised to find it defended by a middle-aged receptionist who I knew to be Zaid Hackett's wife.

"I need to see her," I said.

We did the dance:

"She's busy."

"This is important."

"If you make an appointment–"

"I need to see her now."

"She's in a phone conference."

"Min Tao could have died."

That got her attention. She went to the office door, slid it open a few centimeters, and peered inside. "Zaid? Juliet Alo is here."

I was allowed in.

Zaid was seated at a desk, a fierce scowl on her face as she talked onscreen with a man I recognized as the station's chief engineer. "Of course, I agree!" she said. "Absolutely. All work outside stops until we find out what happened. Sid, I need to talk to someone. I'll check in with you in a few minutes."

The screen shifted to neutral as she turned to me. "Dob Irish thinks you and Min Tao might have manufactured the incident outside."

A mech-skeeter floated past, and then another. I sat down in the guest chair without being asked. "Integrity is everything. Was that always a lie?"

Her expression, already dark, grew ominous. "Did you manufacture the incident, or not?"

"I did not."

"But you falsely accused Cherise Caron."

"You should visit Cherise Caron."

Zaid studied me... and looked less certain. "I was in Paris when the scandal broke. I came up on the next flight. Haven't been here an hour." She frowned at her monitor, then at me. "I think you should tell me what's been going on."

I heard the door open behind me, and turned. Zaid's wife was there, peering in through a narrow gap. "Now Dr. Kyre is here. He says it's urgent."

I shook my head at Zaid.

She looked suddenly tired. "Not now, Helma. Thank you." As the door slid shut, she touched her monitor. "Security to my office now, please."

I rose in alarm, but Zaid waved me back to my seat. "Kyre can be... insistent. And I want to hear what you have to say. So speak."

"You first, ma'am. I asked a question. I need an answer."

Her lips came together in an angry line. Zaid Hackett had the respect of the world, and yet here I was, a first-year player, calling her out. Maybe she saw the irony, because she sighed and leaned back in her chair.

"Our house is in disorder. We've come to see even millions of euros as trivial, forgetting that money represents the labor of thousands of people. Real people with real lives."

"Yes, ma'am."

"What we're doing here matters, Juliet. It is *not* about the money. It's about what the money can build." She gestured at the ceiling. "This great monument, a hopeful experiment, and only the first stage of what will come. So to answer your question, integrity *is* everything. It has to be, to survive the long term, and I intend that what we build here should last for the long term. Now please, tell me what's gone wrong."

KYRE HAD HIS audience after me. I don't know what was discussed.

I was called back to my shift to help deploy a mesh around the space plane – an extra layer of safety while the cargo containers were unloaded – and after that I went to practice, worried that nothing would be done.

But I was wrong.

Two days later the space plane returned, bringing with it a team of three investigators. They questioned both players and staff, rumors ran wild, but it was the mech-skeeters that provided the critical testimony: it turned out that all the data collected by the ubiquitous little devices left the station through Dr. Kyre's account. Unknown to Cherise, her agent was paying him to make sure Team August took the championship.

The cause of Min Tao's accident could not be decisively proven, but with Kyre gone, we all feel safe again.

Cherise and I both endured a brief hearing in which our actions were examined and, ultimately, excused. She lost her endorsement contract, but she's confident she'll get another, especially if Team August takes Game 7.

As much as I admire her, it's my job to make sure that doesn't happen.

We face off tomorrow.

I intend to win.

INVISIBLE PLANETS

Hannu Rajaniemi

(with apologies to Italo Calvino)

TRAVELLING THROUGH CYGNUS 61, *as it prepares to cross the gulf between the galaxies, the darkship commands its sub-minds to describe the worlds it has visited.*

In the lives of darkships, like in the journeys of any ambassador, there always comes a time that is filled with doubt. As the dark matter neutralinos packed tight like wet sand in the galactic core annihilate each other in its hungry Chown drive heart and push it ever closer to the speed of light, the darkship wonders if it truly carries a cargo worthy of the Network and the Controller. What if the data it has gathered from the electromagnetic echoes of young civilisations and the warm infrared dreams of Dyson spheres, written onto tons upon tons of endlessly coiled DNA strands that hold petabytes in a single gram, is nothing more than a scrawled message in a bottle, to be picked up by a fisherman on an unknown shore and then discarded, alien and meaningless?

That is why – before the relentless hand of Lorentz squeezes the ship's clocks so thin that aeons pass with every tick and the starry gaze of the Universe gathers into a single blazing, blue-shifted, judging eye – the ship studies its memory and tries to discern a pattern subtle enough to escape entropy's gnawing.

During the millennia of its journey, the darkship's mind

has expanded, until it has become something that has to be explored and mapped. The treasures it contains can only be described in metaphors, fragile and misleading and elegant, like Japanese street numbers. And so, more and more, amongst all the agents in its sprawling society of mind, the darkship finds itself listening to the voice of a tiny sub-mind, so insignificant that she is barely more than a wanderer lost in a desert, coming from reaches of the ship's mind so distant that she might as well be a traveller from another country that has stumbled upon an ancient and exotic kingdom on the other side of the world, and now finds herself serving a quizzical, omnipotent emperor.

The sub-mind gives the ship not simulations or mind-states or data but words. She communicates with symbols, hints and whispers that light up old connections in the darkship's mind, bright like cities and highways seen from orbit, maps of ancient planets, drawn with guttural monkey sounds.

Planets and Death

THE RULERS OF the planet Oya love the dead. They have discovered that corpses in graveyards are hosts to xenocatabolic bacteria that, when suitably engineered and integrated into the gut microbiome, vastly prolong the Oyan lifespan. Graveyards on Oya are fortresses, carefully guarded against the Resurrection Men, those daring raiders who seek more immortality bugs in the fertile soil fed by the long dead. The wealthiest Oyans – now only vulnerable to accidents or criminal acts – who still cling to traditions of burial are interred in secret places together with coffin torpedoes, elaborate weapons and traps that guard their final resting places from prying fingers.

The wealthiest and the most ambitious of all Oyans is not buried on Oya, but on Nirgal, the dead red planet that has called to the Oyans since the dawn of time. Liberated from the shackles of age and free to fill his millennia with foolish projects without the short-sightedness that plagues mortals, the Oyan constructed rockets to journey to Nirgal and built a great city there, in deep caves to guard it against the harsh rays of the sun.

But others never followed, preferring to spend their prolonged existence in Oya's far gentler embrace, and thus, in the uncountable years of our journey that have passed since, Nirgal itself has become a graveyard. It is populated only by travellers who visit from other worlds, arriving in ephemeral ships, visible only as transparent shapes in swirling red dust. Wearing exoskeletons to support their fragile bodies, the visitors explore the endless caves that glitter with the living technology of the Oyans, and explore the crisscrossing tracery of rover tracks and footsteps in Nirgal's sands, careful to instruct their utility fog cloaks to replace each iron oxide particle exactly where it was, to preserve each imprint of an Oyan foot forever. But even though they leave Nirgal's surface undisturbed, the visitors themselves carry home a faint taste of despair from the grave of the immortal Oyan, a reminder of their own ultimate mortality, however distant.

Yet Nirgal itself lives, for the hardy bacteria of the Oyan's body burrow ever deeper beneath the red planet's surface and build porous cities of their own in its crust. Stolen from the dead, they are slowly stealing Nirgal for themselves.

Planets and Money

ON LAKSHMI, YOU know that the launch day is coming when the smell of yeast is everywhere, that sticky odour of alcohol the day after, even before the party itself starts. The stench comes from bacteria that churn and belch rocket fuel in stills and bioreactors in garages and backyards, for everybody on Lakshmi builds rockets, shiny cones made from 3D-printed parts and emblazoned with bright neon colours, designed with eager thoughts and gestures by teenagers wearing headsets, their eyes flashing with the imaginary interfaces of superhero movies.

When it gets dark, the rockets will go up like paper lanterns in a hurricane, orange and bright, fiery golden ribbons flowing and dancing, their sonic booms like cannons, delivering their payloads to Lakshmi's growing man-made ring that the planet now proudly wears around its waist. The people of Lakshmi will only watch them for a moment, for as soon as the rocket tails disappear from sight, everyone reaches into their pockets and the night is suddenly full of hungry faces illuminated by the paler, harsher fire of smartphone screens, showing numbers going up.

The rocket girls and boys of Lakshmi do not build their machines out of sense of wonder or exploration, but out of sheer greed, for in Lakshmi, all things are bought with quantum cryptocurrencies, imaginary coins mined by small machines in orbit or by autonomous dirigibles in the stratosphere. The quantum mints eat cosmic rays and send money to their owners in bursts of light, each quantum coin stamped with a dice roll by God.

Unforgeable and anonymous, each light-coin vanishes when it is measured and verified, so unless you are one of the entanglement bankers who constructs complex instruments like inverse telescopes that allow coins to interact and stay connected forever, the only way to live on Lakshmi is to devote all your efforts to the art of building rockets or mints, and hope that it is your very own coin, stamped with your quantum signature, that becomes the currency that everyone wants. Even a traveller arriving at Lakshmi soon finds herself going hungry, unless she builds a rocket of her own to launch a personal mint to join the growing Mammon ring around the planet.

The people of Lakshmi consider themselves to be truly free, free of centralised systems and governments, free of the misguided dreams of the past, free from starships, from galactic empires, from kings and emperors, agreeing only on the constant striving for universal abundance and wealth.

The truth is that they are right. For were the Lakshmians to look deeper into the tangled financial relationships amongst the countless light-mints and entanglement banks that orbit their planet, they would uncover deep relationships between quantum mechanics and gravity, a way to measure the motion of Lakshmi in the primordial inertial frame of the universe, and ultimately a new theory for building machines that alter gravity and inertia, machines that could lift the very cities of Lakshmi towards the sky and beyond. But that old dream is hidden too deep in the brightness of the many currencies of Lakshmi to be seen, drowned in the thunder of the rockets of the next launch day.

Planets and Gravity

WHEN A TRAVELLER from the planet Ki visits another world, at first, she feels flattened, less, confined to two dimensions, a prisoner of gravity, every now and then trying to take off like a helpless fly. But after a while, she finds her gaze drawn irresistibly to the horizon and stands rapt and still, watching the edge of the world, the circular boundary that surrounds her in all directions.

Ki itself has no horizons. It is a planet that has become truly three-dimensional. It is hard to say where Ki begins or ends: it is smudged, a stain of ink that spreads on the paper of space and encroaches on the gravity wells of other worlds. The people of Ki are born with personal flight units: thought-controlled jetpacks powered by carefully focussed phased-array microwave beams from the vast solar panel fields that cover the planet's entire neglected surface. The cities of Ki are at constant war with gravity, built on top of pillars that are made of electromagnetic fields and iron pellets, so high they reach out through Ki's atmosphere. Other cities encircle Ki along orbital rings, yet others float in the sky, every building a buckyball tensegrity structure lighter than air. Space elevators reach to Ki's Lagrange points, and skyhooks hurl a constant stream of ships and matter out of Ki, dipping in and out of the atmosphere, bending like a fisherman's rod.

Growing up on Ki, you immediately comprehend the nature of the three spatial dimensions, watch the inhabitants of other two-dimensional planets crawl on the surfaces of their worlds without ever looking up, and naturally start to wonder if there are dimensions that *you* cannot see, other directions that remain to be conquered: and to your delight, the scientists of Ki tell you that there are many left to explore, ten, eleven or even twenty-six.

However, they add that as far as they know, only the familiar three dimensions are actually infinite: all the other dimensions are curled up into a tiny horizon like the Flatland of the planetary surface, with no room for towers or flying cars or jetpacks, and the only thing that can penetrate into the forbidden directions is gravity, the most despised of all forces on Ki, the great enemy of flight.

That is why the people of Ki have now turned all their energies to conquering the remaining boundless dimension, time, building great ships that will climb ever upwards through aeons, carrying a piece of Ki to timelike infinities.

WITH EACH PLANET *that the sub-mind describes, the darkship's doubt deepens. It has no recollection of these worlds, yet merely by rearranging symbols, the sub-mind brings them to life. Is it possible that she is a confabulatory agent, a remnant of some primitive, vestigial dreaming function in the darkship's cognitive architecture, and her planets are made of nothing more but the darkship's dreams and fears? And if so, how can the darkship know that it is carrying anything of value at all, or indeed if itself is merely a random mutation in some genetic algorithm that simulates darkships, creating and destroying them in countless billions, simply to find one that survives the empty dark?*

Yet there is something familiar in each planet, a strange melancholy and a quiet joy, and so the darkship listens.

Planets and Eyes

ON THE PLANET Glaukopis, your most valuable possession, are your eyes. From birth, you wear glasses or contact lenses or artificial eyes that record everything that you see, and furthermore allow others to see through your eyes, and you to look through theirs. As you reach adulthood, you inevitably choose to focus on a point of view that is not your own, trading your own vision for someone else's. For in Glaukopis, material abundance has been achieved long ago, so that a viewpoint, a unique perception of reality, is the only thing that is worth buying or selling.

Over the centuries of such eyetrade, the viewpoints of Glaukopis have been so thoroughly shuffled amongst ten billion bodies that no two lovers have ever seen each other with their own eyes, no mother has ever held her own child, or if they have, it has only been in passing, an unrecognised flash in the kaleidoscope of Glaukopian vision.

A few select dreamers of Glaukopis choose to give their eyes to machines instead: they allow the connectome of their visual centres to be mapped by programmed viruses and DNA nanomachines so that the machines can recognise faint echoes of life in the spectroscopy of distant extrasolar planets in the same way that you recognise your grandmother, with the same instantaneous, unquestionable clarity. In return, they are allowed to look through the eyes of machines, and so they alone have seen what it looks like to fly through the thousand-kilometre water fountains rising from the surface of a faraway moon that teem with primitive life, and the true watercolour hues of the eternal eyestorm that swirls in a gas giant's southern pole. But because they can no longer afford to share these visions with other Glaukopians, they are mocked and scorned, the only blind in the kingdom of the all-seeing.

It is easy for us to mock Glaukopis, having seen the unimaginable visions of our journey, to think them forever lost in an infinite corridor of mirrors. But we would do well to remember that Glaukopis is long gone, and all that remains to us is what their eyes saw. Perhaps one day a machine will be built that will take the sum of the visions and reconstruct the minds and the brains that saw them. Perhaps it will even solve the puzzle of who saw what, solve the Rubik's cube made of eyes that was Glaukopis.

Planets and Words

SESHAT IS A planet of books, of reading and writing. Not only do the people of Seshat document their every waking moment with words, they also build machines that write things into existence. On Seshat, a pen's ink can be stem cells or plastic or steel, and thus words can become flesh and food and many-coloured candies and guns. In Seshat, you can eat a chocolate soufflé in the shape of a dream you had, and the bright-eyed ancient chocolatier may have a new heart that is itself a word become flesh. Every object in Seshat writes, churning out endless idiot stories about what it is like to be a cow, a pill jar or a bottle of wine. And of course the genomes of living beings are also read and written: the telomeres in Seshatian cells are copied and extended and rewritten by tiny molecular scribes, allowing the people of Seshat to live nearly as long as their books.

It is no surprise that Seshat is overcrowded, its landfills full of small pieces of plastic, its networks groaning under the weight of endless spambot drivel, the work of fridges and fire alarms with literary aspirations, the four-letter library of Babel that flows from the mouths of DNA sequencers, with no end in sight.

Yet the Seshatians hunger for more things to read. They have devised books with golden pages that the Universe itself can write in: books where gold atoms displaced by dark matter particles leave traces in carefully crafted strands of DNA, allowing the flows and currents of the dark to be read and mapped and interpreted. And over the centuries, as the invisible ink of the neutralinos and axions dries and forms words on the golden pages, hinting at ships that could be built to trace every whirl and letter out in the void and turn the dark sentences into light, the people of Seshat hold their breath and hope that their planet will be the first line in a holy book, or at least the hook in a gripping yarn, and not the inevitable, final period.

Planets and Ruins

ZYWIE IS A silent planet. Its empty cities are glorious ruins, full of structures higher than mountains: space towers, skyhooks, space fountains, launch loops, mass drivers, rail guns, slingatrons, spaceplane drones, sky anchors, the tarnished emitters of laser propulsion systems, still maintained by patient machines but slowly crumbling.

It would be easy to think Zywie nothing but a dried placenta of an ancient birth. Yet in the ocean floors, in a landscape grey and colourless like a reflection of lunar surface, twisted fragments of great engines are turning into coral castles, their hard sleek lines softened and broken by ringed polyp shapes and multicoloured whorls.

On the continents of Zywie, huge puffed-up balls of precious metal drift down from the sky every now and then. They are platinum, mined in the asteroid belt by tireless robots, melted with sunlight in zero gravity, coalesced into porous spheres like a metal giant's bezoars, and launched at Zywie, where they fall at a leisurely hundred miles an hour, into rainforests and oceans and the silent, overgrown cities. They settle on the ground with a gentle thump and become habitations of insects, birds, moss and lichen.

Beneath Zywie's surface and oceans, endless glass threads are full of light, and the thoughts of ancient machines travel along them, slowly becoming something new.

Zywie's ruins are a scaffold. One day, life will climb up along its struts again, reach up and leave its own ruins behind for others to use, just another stroke of the pen in Zywie's endless palimpsest.

"IT SEEMS TO *me*," *the darkship tells the sub-mind, slowly understanding, "that all the planets you describe have something in common. They are all Earth, each defined not by what you speak of but by what is left unsaid."*

The sub-mind smiles in the desert of the darkship's mind, and in her eyes there are white clouds and blue oceans and endless green.

"Are you the part of me that still longs for home?" the darkship asks. "The part that defines all things by what it has left behind, by the lost pluralities of what might have been?"

The sub-mind shakes her head.

"To be an ambassador," she says, "you ever needed to carry one thing."

She embraces the darkship's primary mind. Her skin smells of sand and exotic spices and sweat and wind and is warm from the sun. She dissolves in the darkship's mindstream, and suddenly the ship is full of the joy that the traveller feels when glimpsing purple mountains in a new horizon, hearing the voices of a strange city for the first time, seeing the thunderous glory of a rocket rising in the dawn, and just as the dark fingers of Cygnus 61's gravity cast it into the void between galaxies, it knows that this is the only thing truly worth preserving, the only constant in the shifting worlds of the Network made from desires and fears, the yearning for infinity.

WILDER STILL, THE STARS

Kathleen Ann Goonan

MEMORIES ARE STONES across a swift-running creek. I teeter on
one and leap to the next, breathing in the scent of life-giving
water, hearing the roar, the rush, of time.

Beneath them, the abyss.

MY ROMANCE WITH space began when I was four, when I visited
the Naval Observatory in Washington D.C. At least, that's the
first visit I remember.

And do I, really? I am one hundred and thirty years old. More
or less.

I rub my thumb over the smooth groove across the middle of
a palm-sized stone in my hand.

A FRIGID, MOONLESS night in January, 1954. Dad bundles me
up in so many sweaters, tights, and snow pants that I waddle.
The storm hit after my mother left for the Naval Observatory
that morning, and ceased suddenly at dark, leaving two feet of
snow.

The city is deserted; enchanted. Stranded cars buried in snow
loom like small hillocks. Big wind flings fine, stinging pellets
of ice against my face. Dad scoops me onto his shoulders and

trudges up the plowed center of Massachusetts Avenue, which steepens as it winds up Observatory Hill.

I have seen the graceful iron gates of the Naval Observatory in Washington, D.C. hundreds of times since then, flanked by black obelisks embossed with the seal of the USNO: a woman flies through the air, holding a planet aloft in both hands.

That first time the gates swung open, it seemed like I was entering fairyland. And indeed, I was: space was an unattainable place to which I could never travel, filled with wonders stranger than I could imagine.

My father speaks into an intercom. A man in a crisp white Navy uniform steps out of the guardhouse to welcome us. "Hi, Ed. And little May – you've grown! I broke a path. Dr. Jainkuru is waiting."

As we climb the final curve to the highest point in D.C., I am like the prince climbing the glass mountain, except that it is ice. The deep voice of the wind is that of a ravening beast. Ancient trees, flailing like mad creatures, reach out to grab me with gigantic, crabbed arms. The otherworldly dome, gleaming white by day but now dim as a shadow, gradually emerges as we round the hill.

My mother stands in the open doorway, waving us in. For a moment, she does not even seem like my mother, for she wears a long, dressy coat and low heels. When we bustle inside she peels off my mittens and stuffs them into my pockets so they won't get lost, and she is Mom again. "Brrr. Keep your coats on!" She laughs. "Only two hardy souls came for my talk. We have plenty of goodies to take home."

We climb a graceful curved stairway to a domed room. The ceiling divides, revealing a slice of space. My mother raises the floor, but I still must climb a ladder to look through the telescope.

"That's Saturn."

At first, all I see is a shifting blob. It sharpens into a brownish sphere, encircled by a flat ring that looks good for running around and around on.

"I want to go there."

"Maybe someday," says my mother.

"Where's the sun?"

"It's on the other side of the earth right now. You know that – remember? But you saw thousands of suns when you walked here tonight. The stars are suns."

"They're too little."

"Earth is very close to the star we call the sun. That's why it looks so big. Those other suns might have planets too, with life. But they're very far away. Too far to go to." She smiles. "Except, maybe, in science fiction."

"I want to go to the other suns, too."

"Maybe you can figure out a way when you grow up. A lot of people have the same dream."

The planets and their moons, shrouded in ice and gas, are enticingly bizarre. I grow to know them like people, catalogue their characteristics, study them fervently.

They are pure wilderness. I write in a notebook, in my childish hand: Wild, the planets. Wilder still, the stars.

WE CALL IT *Stardust*.

MY PARENTS HAVE died, so I live with my cousin Irene near the Blue Ridge. We are ten. Our china horses gallop on board the space ship. *Stardust* reads the minds of the china horses, which are much smarter than the real horses we ride across the white-fenced pastures of Blue Ridge Farms, the old-money estate of Irene's family. That is because real horses hide their brilliance. But *Stardust* knows and understands them. They must flee the Earth. It grows pristine fields, mountains, and rivers, and finds the perfect sun, out of all the suns we can see at night. As they travel to Horse Planet, they will be wild and free; the ship will care for them. When they arrive at Horse Planet, they will rule the world.

Sounds like a plan.

Forty years later, Irene and I form Infinity Tech and begin R&D.

SLEEPING PORCH: SAGGING, third floor, delightful. July: overpowering scent of roses. Almost my 130th birthday – July, 2080.

IN THE DIM just-dawn, I wake, but do not cloud, ears filled with finches in sudden chorus, susurrating white oak leaves that let moving light-specks dapple the walls, and the oak limb I should cut down scraping against the roof.

People now don't grasp the irony of the term clouding, which caught on such a long time ago that its origin is the stuff of crossword puzzle clues. Though I'm sharpened by data when I connect with it, clouding clouds my self. I must allow that nameless, mysterious *something* its daily time. If I don't practice, I go barking mad.

I am aware that many consider stark barking mad to be my constant state.

After sitting, I don my data bracelet, walk through my decrepit, beloved mansion, let out Sybil, my old-fashioned unenhanced mutt, and sort through neurology studies at my kitchen table. Right now, I'm working for a company that needs expert testimony in court.

A few hours later, I sip midmorning tea, data bracelet tossed next to a vase of pink peonies that copiously shed petals, and consider that my birthday, fast approaching, might be a lonely affair. After 130 years – hell, after a hundred years – one begins to think seriously about one's brand spanking new oldness. I am healthy, despite my trips to Mars and to the Moon, but am I wise? Assuredly not.

I've worked hard at maintaining relationships, but life is a lot more comfortable if you have people around who share your referents. Most of my dear friends died tragically young, on the cusp of medical advances that would have let them live. Progress to my present age was not one of smooth acceleration. There were cliffs of near-death, bullets dodged, economic hurdles overcome, and reprieves granted at the last minute after years of debilitation. People as old as myself are not common, but will be in the future. Most people born after 2020 will probably live to be 160 or older.

I've had the time and resources to follow all of my interests, which is the best thing about living a long time. My first degree, predictably, was astronomy, but I tasted astrophysics and other engineering disciplines before settling on neuroscience, at least for several decades now. I never followed a straight path.

My big achievement? Irene and I developed a new kind of space vehicle – flexible, one that could adjust to changing conditions on very long voyages.

Stardust. Ahead of its time, mothballed for twenty years for lack of funds. My fault. I probably can't even think in that league now, no matter what neuroplasticity drugs I might try.

Well. I'll just have a birthday party. I decide to invite my zen friends, the other three-quarters of my jazz quartet, and one of my next-door neighbors, a woman who has gone Cat – Siamese, to be exact, with beautiful ivory face-fur, who long ago tired of her apparently unrescindable choice (she as much as told me she ate my koi) – farmers from the Market, Irene (though she probably will not have time to come), and all of my children, grandchildren, and great-grandchildren. I throw in some new acquaintances.

Already, I am cheered. I know lots of people. I'm normal. Well-adjusted.

You gotta have a dream.

I decide to get out of the house for lunch.

BLACK, DEEP COLD. I do not know how long it lasts. A second. A light-year.

I MEET AMANDA in a café a few blocks from my house.

"Hello. I am your server." Gazing down at me with blue eyes, her face perfect as that of a china doll, she exudes a strange smell – nine parts homelessness and one almost-disguised part Artificial Person. Newer AP's lack this smell, which is like the undertone of a complex perfume.

"How's the special today?"

"Great." Her voice is toneless.

As she bends her head over her device to put in my order, I take a deep breath. Relax. Let go of your anger.

Right. That never works for me, either.

I'm sure that the restaurant isn't paying Amanda. She probably sleeps on a pallet, eats scraps, and doesn't know to complain – and if she does know, is afraid to. In a word, AP's are childlike.

No one befriends them or interacts with them. Help groups are often a front for manufacturers, who want to reel in their lost, discarded, or runaway products before someone else figures out their secrets, the government, which wants to use them to indict manufacturers and owners, or vigilantes, who simply want to rid the world of this new affront to human dignity. Dozens are on Mars, where they help maintain Giovanni, the colony, which withers while countries and corporations spend fortunes and years arguing over ancient treaties and agreements.

Creating an AP is horrendously expensive. Using standardized

DNA printing templates created for legal medical research, artificial and recombinant DNA, and other bio advances, blank adult humanoids – fully functioning but comatose humans – are infused with virus-borne agents that initiate and accelerate neural development a millionfold. The pre-AP is stimulated with the language of choice, and certain parts of individual brains are more intensely oxygenated, depending on the use to which the AP is committed. Content organizes the brain. Sessions of intensive, finely targeted fine and large motor control exercises give them a developmental kick. I have no doubt that many of them die in the process, or soon after awakening.

I feel responsible. Some of my neurology research fed into the possibility of Amandas.

"My name is May," I tell her. "Is Amanda your real name?"

She looks down at her uniform pocket, twists it with both hands. "Yes."

"Would you like to come home with me, Amanda? You can eat, bathe, and decide what you want to do."

"Okay," she says, obviously not even imagining that I might harm her. Her blue eyes, her hesitant smile, are dazzling. I take her hand.

We have almost reached the open front door when a woman steps in front of us. "Where do you think you're going with my J?" J is short for jiang-shee, Chinese for zombies, because they first showed up in China about two years ago. Then, almost overnight, they were everywhere. Criminals love them. They can do the dirty work. Some appear only intelligent enough to perform very simple, repetitive jobs, but often, they have savant-like capabilities. APs are one among thousands of technological wonders that seem to manifest suddenly, the way smartphones became ubiquitous in the early century, so indispensible and seductive that everyone surrendered.

I bluff. "This woman does not belong to you. I'm a tracker."

"What?"

"This AP is the property of my boss."

"I have no idea what you're talking about." But she lets us pass. Her next step might be to call and turn us in, but I'm gambling she won't.

Outside is a pleasant, tree-shaded sidewalk where people shop, lunch, stroll. I signal for a pod, and she gets in, again, unquestioning. I tell it, "The Washington Monument," and the pod moves off, self-driving, silent except for the light tone that proclaims its presence and harmonizes with the other pods and small busses that fill Connecticut Avenue. They flow around bicycles and pedestrians. The terrible carnage of bicyclists, pedestrians, and automobile passengers is a horror of the past, inexplicable to those born since it ended.

I study the perfect profile of this manufactured human as she stares out the window, wondering who she truly is.

I think about what to ask her. *How old are you?* That would be a good question. I fear they have pre-programmed short lives to create a market for new, improved models and, perhaps, to keep them from developing into something uncontrollable. However, she probably can't answer honestly. Most are engineered so that it is impossible for them to understand that they are AP's; thus, they cannot betray their origin and get their manufacturer or owner in trouble. Or agitate. They are similar, in this regard, to some right-hemisphere stroke victims. One possible result of a right-hemisphere stroke is left-side paralysis, coupled with the stroke victim's inability to understand that their left leg does not work. They believe they can walk, try to walk, and even though they always fail, they never learn that walking is impossible. In the same way, AP's cannot acknowledge that they are created. They believe that they are normal humans.

How about *Are there others like you? A community, someone you can turn to?* But all AP's are unique. Expensive, created by different entities for different reasons; chock-full of heavily guarded biological trade secrets.

"Where do you live?" I ask.

"Here. I live here."

"Where is 'here'?"

She smiles and gestures. "All around. Here."

I'd vaguely planned some elaborate hugger-mugger: mingle with tourists, take the Metro, grab a d-meter at a kiosk – the only way to tell if tiny drones are locked onto you. Drones were made completely illegal in D.C. in 2025, but droners are always one step ahead of the law. They can be anywhere, anything. Because I don't reflexively cloud every time I turn around – in fact, I left my data bracelet at home – I can't be tracked. But Amanda probably can be.

I realize: maybe she knows. "Are you being tracked?"

"No."

"Why not?"

"I turned it off."

She is more aware of her situation than I first surmised. "The YouTel," I say, deciding to believe her.

We get out at the snazzy YouTel, where you design your own space with nanotech – the limited, heavily regulated nanotech that has become the civilian norm, though military and space programs can do anything they please – and pass the French Embassy. After a few blocks, we enter the cul-de-sac where the local Victorian embarrassment no one has the power to change overpowers newer faux-Classical homes that cower at both sides, the owners of which probably plot my death.

Huge New American Chestnut trees shade the dark green, turreted mansion my parents fell in love with over a century ago, and it was old then. My acre is rich with generations of gardens gone wild. I wish that I could afford to keep it up. I get a bit of money from Infinity Tech, but about twenty years ago I sold most of my stock to help one of my sons, which was a fiasco any way you look at it. Irene spent years buying it all back. My son lost the money.

My house needs... everything. Sometimes I'm almost ready to succumb to nanotech plumbing, wiring, roof. A huge investment up front, but touted to last "forever." I would lose my historic tax exemption, though. It's expensive to live a long time, and I have not invested wisely. To say the least.

I give Amanda the ten-cent tour.

"The kitchen." Most people swoon at the high, glass-door cupboards, the marble table in the center of the vast room, the tiny black-and-white tiles on the floor, and the fireplace, and I explain that in its heyday the Big Green One had a large kitchen staff. Breakfast in bed for sir and madam and fifteen house guests? Dinner party for twenty-five? No problem.

Amanda just nods.

I open the French doors of the morning room, filled with musical instruments, and she catalogues them. "Chickering grand piano, 1921. Martin guitar, 1945." She continues with the saxes, clarinets, mandolins until I open the pocket doors.

"The drawing room, where I paint."

"The original floor plan has been changed."

"What?"

"It was filed with the city in 1894. This room was a doctor's office, and was accessed through the foyer, not through a pocket door."

"I thought you were disconnected."

"I am. I remember. I know the permitting history of all the properties in Northwest Washington. A job – development opportunity search. The houses on both sides were built by the same builder, in 2072, after older homes were torn down."

Definitely an AP.

I show her the wide back porch with run-down wicker furniture, where my overgrown 'wildflower garden' sweeps onto the lower steps like the waves of an oncoming storm. "Do you like gardening?"

"I don't know."

When she sees the long-unused business suits in my closet (I freely admit that I keep old things, and lots of them) she beams. "May I borrow the dark blue one? Maybe I could get my job back." She plucks an expensive scarf from a hook, knots it artfully around her neck, and pirouettes before the mirror.

"Where did you work?"

"At... um, somewhere down on K Street."

"What did you do?

"Analyzed data. Gave presentations."

"What happened?"

"I woke up in a park. I don't know how I got there."

A castoff: reasons, unknown.

"Amanda," I say gently, "I don't think you can get your job back by wearing the right suit."

"Oh, yes, I can. How you look is everything. They made me wear yellow. It's wrong for my complexion."

"How did you get the restaurant job?"

"That was a job? There was nothing to do. There wasn't any feed."

"Feed?"

"Where you sit and they hook you up and feed you."

"What do they feed you with?"

"I'll show you." She taps one of the faded hydrangeas on my wallpaper.

"It's not there."

She looks baffled.

"I only have it in one room." It, the cloud, whatever.

She follows me to a room on the third floor. Walking through the arched doorway activates the Wall. It is continuously updated, but I don't wear it, implant it, or have it in every room. I don't love it or hate it. Like my bracelet, it's a tool.

I flop down on some floor pillows. She stands, intense, before the wall and gestures.

Numbers flow down the screen so fast that they form a moving pattern. "It's relaxing, isn't it? It's not in my brain. But it's better than nothing."

I open my mouth to tell her that I have the kind of interface she craves – a device that looks like a skullcap – when she reaches out and pulls the numbers from the wall in long shining strands, shapes them, hugs them, and then, to my surprise, throws off her clothes and lurfs them in big luminous blobs over her body with her hands, splashing herself with information.

She seems happy.

I walk to the end of the hall, open a screen door, and sit on a small, dangerously rickety balcony that overlooks a koi pond, now empty of carp but rich with algae.

My old colleagues have gone off the rails.

They, apparently, are the ones who are barking mad. They have sold out; released this delicate woman into the dangerous wilderness of us.

I begin to feel steely. Invigorated.

I can outbark them any day.

GENTLE WHISPER: DOING okay? Good.

I FIND THAT Amanda was 'let go' – really let go, like you might boot a stray dog back into the street – from Smith-Erikson, a gargantuan investment firm. I learn how to access her information via her cloud-stored data. I watch the entire illegal action, as well as her three-year-long life, in fast-forward. They kept her in special AP barracks, where she and her companions were fed, exercised, and allowed to watch movies. I surmise that Smith-Erikson had no idea that she could make this kind of record, which, of course, the manufacturer could watch. I ask Amanda if she can turn off the record or make it private and she says, oh, I made it private last week. She burns it out of the cloud.

"Did you make it private when you left Smith-Erikson?"

"Yes."

"Why?"

"They were mean."

When I was a teenager, I had two show-quality collies, a breed that, at the time, were all the rage. I sold their first litter. It was agony. I hated to let any of those defenseless pups out into the void of potential abuse, loneliness, injury. I had my dogs neutered.

Amanda reminds me of those puppies.

WHY NOT USE computers for AP tasks? One reason is that the human brain is the most powerful and intricate computing device known. Our brain performs billions of transactions a day; synchronizes information seamlessly behind the scenes of consciousness. People-like beings can easily sit in on meetings and in negotiations without the opposition being any wiser. Accusing someone of not being a person is lucratively actionable. Amanda could strut into a room, slide into a seat at a long, polished table, speak the language of statistics with charming ease, and close immense, complex deals.

You give them benefits, on paper, but when the AP disappears, after documentation about deep emotional problems or non-performance, those funds are easily re-absorbed by the Corporate Person. For the most part, they are curiously, alienly egoless. They will never demand pay, much less a raise – at least, not until they grow up. Not unless some barrier is broken.

They are new and shiny.

It's the Wild West. Impossible to regulate.

If anyone can break that barrier and give them a sense of self, it's me.

It's something to do. I'm not sure that it is a good thing to do, because I don't know what it will mean for them; to them.

I hesitate.

But my mother always said you needed something to look forward to. It would be good to look forward to a nice, new study. A new wilderness.

Amanda is asleep on the floor, in front of the darkened Wall. I bring her the suit she liked, that uniform that got locked into our brains in the early 1900's, and leave it beside her, with a note to find me in the kitchen when she wakes. The suit will be tight, but tight will look great on her. The next day, I give her the run of my closet, but she wears the suit, with heels that must pinch, for a week before she gives it up.

That's when a fleet of boxes arrives – beautiful nanotech clothes that I know are very expensive. Cheap as dirt to make, but the formulas are proprietary.

"You will have to return them," I say. "I can't afford them."

"No one has to pay for them. I hacked them."

"Amanda, that's wrong."

"Why?"

My lecture on how she is undermining capitalism, the arts, and the economic structure of the world is met with a shrug. "That's crazy."

Considering that her very existence may be doing the same damage, I suppose she's right.

A STAR-MAP. One star slides toward me until its leaping gas-arcs splash and twist against velvet infinity. Slide back, change view to schematic: planets orbit; moons abound. Habitable? Inhabited? Voices murmur. A stone with a smooth groove in the center rests in my palm. I grasp it tightly.

*　　*　　*

TREES, POTATOES, STORMS, planets, and me. We all have eyes.

ONCE I AWAKEN, they are easy to see. I notice Jack in Farragut Square. He seems mute. Thin, tall, with long, dark, greasy hair and a long nose, he gesticulates with a combination of broad and tiny gestures, animated, clear-eyed, and filthy, wearing a too-large tweed jacket open over a bare chest, shorts, and no shoes. I run a search revealing that he speaks no known sign language. Crowds flow past him, ignoring him as they ignore any bum.

I sit beside the statue of Admiral Farragut on his mighty steed, sword drawn, for hours before I rise, muttering Farragut's Civil War battle cry, carved on the base of the statue: "Damn the torpedoes! Full speed ahead!"

I take the man's hand, and call for a pod. He is compliant and, when we get home, extremely hungry. He is not deaf, yet he only speaks with signs. He emerges from his shower clean-shaven, long hair combed. He seems to like his little bedroom, and loves the Wall, where his motions splatter the surface like paint, which resolves into equations. Beyond me, certainly. But he quickly finds others with whom he can communicate; women and men from all over the world. They splat upon one another's work in a rainbow of colors, nodding, applauding. I hear him laugh, but never hear words. He and Amanda battle for Wall time, so I surrender a few more walls to data. I have plenty of empty bedrooms.

Xia is a bike messenger by day – kinetic; valuable, as she streaks through G-town like the visual trail of an acid trip – and by weekend a Harley sailor, leaning into the curves of the Blue Ridge Parkway motorcycle lane with such fierce, acutely tilting joy that she scares the bejeezus out of me the one time I go with her. She has maps in her head, loves speed, has excellent reflexes, perfect vision, and is strong as a horse. She can also operate and repair any machine.

I find Olek sleeping on a grate near American University. He is long-limbed, ebony-black and has a British accent. He says that he worked there but that one day when he went back his ID didn't work, and he couldn't get another. "In fact, no one seemed to know me any longer." He speaks beautifully and at length, a loquacious contrast to Jack. "What did you do there?" I ask. "I made vids." In fact, I find him on thousands of vids, through a face-matching program. He delivers lectures about the history of physics and chemistry, up to and including the latest nanotech endeavors. I am watching one of them, a lecture on the discovery of the Higgs Boson, when he enters the room and sits beside me. "You have paid for that. There is no need." He recites it verbatim, then answers my questions about dark matter until I reach the limit of my ability to ask.

They are all amazingly kind, empathic, and seem almost telepathic, but they are created to serve. I'm not sure how deep these behaviors, or any of their behaviors, go. They have vague ethnic facial characteristics – Amanda and Jack, mainstream American; Olek, Maasai; Xia, Chinese – but no culture; no depth. Being human is a culture in and of itself and they lack all but the most obvious human culture. I can see them replacing one's beloved, but perhaps in a more compliant mode. A million nightmares dating from the Golem have finally come true.

Is it humane to deny them understanding of who and what they are? Of course not. I will find the key. And shouldn't they at least have a normal lifespan? I will unlock their humanity.

I sit in my living room one evening after we have cleaned up the kitchen and reflect on what I'm doing. What *am* I doing? In the strange, roiling humansphere, what is now normal? We are constantly knocked flat by massive waves of the New that seem to come out of nowhere, tsunamis of powerful change that deposit some of us on high ground and leave the littoral strewn with those who didn't make the grade.

It is said that some of the things that make us human are that we have language, we use tools, and we are creative. I have another qualifier: we are irrational. We constantly draw on irrationality, whether we know it or not. I would be heartened if they behaved irrationally. Playfully. Humans play. When was the last time I played?

They will be my play.

Working together, they assemble a pure white two-thousand-piece jigsaw puzzle in twenty minutes. It takes them that long because a certain amount of time is needed to physically move each piece. I give them a box from the attic full of an antique Underwood typewriter my charming grandchildren dismantled one rainy day. Not even knowing what it is, it only takes them a few hours to reassemble it, minus the platen and a few screws. They do not react to music by saying they like or dislike it – indeed, they are puzzled by my question, though they all have perfect pitch.

I get out sheet music and elementary exercise books for the piano. I'm pretty rusty – the sax is my instrument of choice, right now – but keep at it for a week, an hour a day, and soon, to my delight, I can play my old Grieg, Bach, and dreamy Chopin. I am not surprised when, a few days later, I hear perfectly rendered Beethoven ringing down the hallway. I peek through the door and see that it is Olek, and that there is no music.

When he winds up, I applaud. "You heard that somewhere and could just remember it?" He tilts his head and narrows his eyes. "What do you mean, just?"

"It's unusual for humans to be able to remember every note of a complex composition after hearing it once. It would be easy for an AP, I suppose."

"I know a lot of them. What would you like to hear?" he says, leaving the question open.

I do the same thing for all kinds of arts: jazz, the core of which is improvisation; painting; dance. They copy effortlessly, but cannot seem to create anything new, or collaborate on a jazz improvisation.

Nevertheless, I keep trying, thinking of ways to help them make that leap.

If they can.

I don't know that they aren't creative, but if they are, or can grow to creativity, that might be one way to humanize them for the public.

If they knew the difference, would they want to be only human? The question is tiny, fleeting, in the big, booming satisfaction of my own salvation-through-helping. Do they want to wage war, be cruel, think of how to create creatures like themselves?

Feh. You gotta have a dream.

SPADES: CARDS CLING to the table and collapse into a small, light game-cube filled with an infinite number of games. Programmable. We have fun thinking up fiendish new games.

"I HATE PULLING weeds." Amanda leans back on her heels and wipes sweat from her forehead with the bottom of her t-shirt.

Olek says, "Try pulling dinner duty for a change." He is perfectly beautiful. They all are. His long, bare legs are stretched out, ankles crossed, on the rubble with which we will build walkways through the garden. He sips green tea, having just finished ingesting international news from a thousand feeds. "Big to-do about J's today. Their rights."

They are conversing more frequently and more fluently, except for Jack.

"All of you are J's," I say.

Amanda studies the plants. "Why do they call these weeds?

They have flowers." She lowers her eyelids a second, then says, "It's purslane. Hmmm. Many uses."

Olek clasps his hands behind his shiny, bald head. "I wish J's the best of luck. It's wrong to deny that they're human. Even though they really aren't."

"They are!" says Amanda. She crawls around on her hands and knees, piling up purslane.

"What's different about them and humans?" I ask.

Olek says, "They are transgenic. And their brains are engineered to handle big data. Most humans can't do that. I gather that it scares a lot of people."

"How do you think we could help them?" I ask.

"Educate people," says Olek.

"And make their brains more normal," says Amanda. "Poor freaks."

Yes, they converse now. The rest of the time, who knows what they're thinking, even between the words.

I suspect we'll have purslane for dinner. Next week we'll probably be wearing it.

Creative. In my opinion. Economical, too.

TIME TO WAKE up! The faces of my dear friends surround me. I vomit.

WITH THEIR PERMISSION, Amanda wipe out all of their cloud-records as soon as they arrived, so we are out of sight, and out of Mind. I hope. I don't want to risk raising their profile by trying to get brain scans. No health-industry machines are standalones, unattached to the cloud.

They never question my authority. Not one of them ever says "Who made you God," as would happen in any normal mix of humans, particularly those to whom I have rented rooms. I never lay down the law. We have no formal organization. I can discern no pecking order among them.

They mate like rabbits. With restored fertility, what would their children be like?

One of their outstanding characteristics, their physical perfection, would ring through you like a bell if you were to see them as a group. On the other hand, the science and business of physical beauty has advanced spectacularly since I was young, so, taken singly, they are not all that noticeable.

I stock all the baths with powerfully scented soaps.

I continue my study. The better I get to know them, the more difficult it is.

ON AUGUST 9TH, I'm in the kitchen, working on a big pan of party lasagna, when Olek comes in. "I can help." He grabs some garlic from my cluttered windowsill and says, "Why do you have all these stones here?"

"They're pretty, aren't they? This chunk of white granite is from Nepal. Here's a pebble from the shore of the Ganges."

"Which is your favorite?"

I pick up a pale, irregular, sandy stone with a curved, inch-long indentation on one side. "I found it in Rock Creek Park when I was a little girl. It's the fossilized trail of a prehistoric creature. Maybe a snail. It reminds me that we're all made of stardust, that life has changed again and again over periods of time so vast that we can't even imagine them."

He nods, and bursts a garlic clove with the flat of his knife.

Amanda enlisted everyone to help in the garden, along with my hired hands, who I made sure were as newsless and politics-free as one can be, now, unlikely to even know or even care about APs.

As the sun sets, the last rays intensify the yellows, purples, and reds of gladiola. Brash dahlias and sophisticated lilies, divided by peony bushes and ornamental grasses, enclose small, private alcoves, some with fountains. Stands of strange new flowers that I think Amanda must have invented punctuate the bloomscape; her Wall time shows intensive genetic work. Tiny solar-powered spheres, flung like confetti, cling to the trees, and the heavenly scent of night-blooming jasmine will soon infuse the evening.

One of the zenners brought a keg of homemade beer, and we cheer when it froths from the tap. Bertha Smith, my Siamese neighbor, eyes my new koi as they weave sinuous paths beneath water lily pads on the renovated pond. I shake my head at her and mouth *No*. My jazz friends and I are setting up when someone taps me on the shoulder.

"Irene!" We hug madly, kiss, and hug again. Wipe away tears. Irene is tiny, blonde, and the President and CEO of Infinity Tech, roaming the world to oversee launches and get more contracts, riding herd on a passel of brilliant engineers, piling up patents.

"Gosh." She gazes at the yard. "It's as lovely as when your parents were alive. Is that gazebo still back there?" She grabs my hands and pulls me along the curving paths. "It was a sailing ship. A frontier cabin. A covered wagon. A... a space ship." She stops for a moment. "You are doing okay, aren't you? This must have taken some cash."

"Doing a bit better. Infinity Tech is doing pretty well too – my monthly cash infusion has increased lately."

"We are," she says. "In fact, I'm on call for a Russian launch right now, but sent my best backup." In the gazebo, we settle in wicker chairs. "Tonight, I declare this the *Stardust*!"

We clink raised glasses to the dream that nearly destroyed us. I say, "I wish–"

She puts her hand on my arm. "May, I came to apologize. I'm sorry about everything. I should have been more understanding."

"There's no need for any apology from you, Irene. God, I should have been on mood drugs or something."

"I should have told you how much I'd invested in that drive research, how little money we had to spare right then." She shakes her head. "Two fools and their money. But we've pulled out of it at last. You know, we never wanted other investors – never wanted them to know what we were doing. What we had. We are completely in the clear at last. That's one of the things I came to tell you."

"Thanks you, Irene. I wish I'd done more to help. It seemed like the most helpful thing I could do was stay away. What else?"

"I–"

Xia and Amanda meander past, carrying champagne flutes, bending to examine plants in the fading light. Irene stares at them. When they are past, she says, "Christ on a stick, woman! How long–?"

I give my head a slight shake, not wanting to talk about harboring APs. "You're right! I haven't been out to the farm in ages."

She gets it, of course. "You'll have to come..." she looks on her arm, where two months of her calendar manifest in curved, glowing blue and green. "Well. Looks like late October. I'll have my secretary do some rearranging." She tilts her head, listening. "Crap. My backup isn't doing very well. We should have used Broglio Port in Kenya. I'll have to take the tunnel to London. Only takes an hour. Then... well, more travel."

I walk her through the house. Her pod waits on the street. She says "Bye, sweetie. It is so good to see you! We wasted so many years. I wish–"

"At least there's plenty of time in the future," I say, and hug her. She turns, tears in her eyes, jumps into her pod, waves, and is gone, leaving me bewildered and happy as all get out. The best birthday present I could have ever asked for.

My cohorts are on the front porch.

Obek says, "Who was that?"

"My partner, Irene."

"Why was she crying?"

"We haven't seen each other in a long time, and she had to leave suddenly."

Amanda asks, "Do you love each other?"

"Yes, we do. Very much."

I shake off my yearning for more Irene. About now, we would be laughing hysterically.

The party is a great romping success. The Jump for Joys, our jazz quartet, rings swing and bop through the neighborhood, and more people drop in, drawn by the music.

Everyone delights in the apparent strangeness of my new friends. I doubt that any guests make the connection between them and the sinister, inhuman J's portrayed in the media, or would have cared if they did. We make merry until dawn. All remnants of ennui run off and hide.

METHANE RAIN FILMS my porthole.

WE ARE RAMBLING on one of those fine, brisk autumn days when it seems as if the entire sky has taken flight. Leaves wrenched from trees, flocked by the wind, dash downward to scud along street. Thin sunlight makes dog-walkers, stroller-pushers, stately embassies, and high, white clouds sharp-edged, yet almost transparent, as if the world and we are flimsy as watercolors, and as dissolvable.

My memory, at 130, is a kaleidoscope, a vast rich cape swirling round me, coloring all I sense. Every new snip of sensorial input shifts the colored chips to line up in unique configuration, fed by bits of time. How are these visions brought forth; how summoned? Not by me; not by my conscious self. However it works, memory is definitely one of the things that makes me human.

"What's that?" asks Olek, pointing to a long, winding drive guarded by a two-sided wrought-iron gate that opens in the middle.

The kaleidoscope shifts, then holds. We are on Massachusetts Avenue, my personal lifelong memory treasure-trove. "Why, we're at the Naval Observatory! I worked here as an astronomy grad student, about a hundred years ago. One of my first memories is coming here as a child. That night was magical. There was a blizzard. My father brought me; we had to walk. My mother worked there. I saw the Moon; Mars; the rings of Saturn."

They gather round the black obelisks that anchor each side of the gates, and touch the round USNO Seal. "A woman holding a planet while she flies through the air," says Amanda, "her clothes all rippley from the wind. It says" – that half-closing of her eyelids, so swift that it is barely more than blink – "'Adde gubernandi studium: Pervenit in astra, et pontum caelo conjunxit.' 'With the captain's care, the stars are measured, the sea and heavens married.' The woman is Urania, muse of astronomy."

"Beautiful, isn't it?" I say.

"Beautiful," she echoes. I can hear that she still wonders what beautiful really means and what else might be beautiful.

Jack stares at Amanda for a long moment, and then, with a jerk, his feet are moving, and then, his hands and head. He looks like a perky marionette. I can see him dancing a hornpipe on deck, long ago, while the Captain marries the time and space using perfect time, as determined by the Naval Observatory, and a sextant, then commands *Two degrees south by southwest*!

Xia mimics him, and then they all do, as if they are a chorus in an old Broadway musical. A few passers-by clap; someone tosses us a few bits. I am laughing in the autumn afternoon; laughing, as the transparent phenomenal world pulls me too into the dance.

And then, by degrees, back into the sky. Back to space, where it all started, for me, wondering, *How does one navigate spacetime?* Who does the perfect measuring? And what, exactly do they measure?

What will the touchstone be, in the future?

I HAVE FELT this much joy only when my children were born. But where *am* I?

THE USNO DIRECTOR and I are old friends. I give my kids a private tour. Washington, D.C. is not the best place to observe space, but conservation efforts have lessened light pollution tremendously in the last century, and cleared the sky of chemical pollutants.

Xia is all over the ancient 26-inch Alvin, turning the huge gears, sectioning it in her head, I am sure, into a series of infinitely finely shaved views, rotating it, inferring the insides – correctly, of course – by what the outside does, from the evidence. She could take that memory to the market, and, though it would be massively expensive, and a long, slow process, she could print out another 26-inch Alvin.

"Jack, look at Mars. Asaph Hall used this very telescope to discover the moons of Mars in 1877."

"I would like to go to Mars." He has a nice tenor voice and perfect diction.

I notice that no one but me is surprised that he is talking.

DISORIENTING, TO HAVE more room.

"TIME FOR THE bedtime story," Xia announces, striding through the house rattling a tambourine.

"Knock it off," yells Amanda, but they all gather in the living room with wine or tea. Olek lights candles. In the distance, a bicycle airhorn blares. A dog barks.

On the first night, I begin with, "On Europa, there is a geyser a hundred miles high," one of my mother's stories.

"No! You went to the Moon. To Mars. Tell us about that!"

Over the next few months, we discuss space travel. How to make more of our solar system's planets and moons habitable: Enceladus, Europa, Titan. How long it might take to get to a habitable exoplanet, how we can predict what conditions would be like and how to prepare for all contingencies in many different environments. What an expedition would need in its tool kit to cover all the possibilities.

They absorb information swiftly, voraciously – science fiction, science, documents and videos about past and present space exploration and colonies. The most recent research, the most cutting-edge bionan applications. Fictional ships that are like neural networks, wombs that supply everything the intrepid space explorer might need to travel to likely exoplanets at just-below-lightspeed. A briefer jaunt to Europa might use laser propulsion or, as a backup, massive self-mending nets that collect matter to be used as fuel. Olek says, "Dark matter collection might be the ticket." I am really not surprised how easily, casually, and, I'm pretty sure, undetectably they hack into the separate top-secret nanonets of all the industrialized nations, where military and manufacturing secrets are stored.

"Velcro ourselves to spacetime somehow... it moves past us."

"No, no... change to light..."

"We are light..."

"Not what I mean..."

"Maybe we're there and back already..."

"Not funny."

"Listen! With this warp drive, we stay in the same place... get in touch with this woman at Georgia Tech."

"Amanda, would you mind helping with this genetic work?"

"I'm already doing most of the..."

I'm dizzied and dazzled. They ignore my question. I'm not here. I'm some kind of slow matter.

I am the superfluous human.

The not-at-all impartial observer.

The walls, floors, and ceilings of several emptied rooms are now completely committed to astronomy, physics, and engineering classes, many of them Olek's, only run and absorbed in a blur. Big data scrolls in rapid-pattern colors and sounds, discrete flashes of information, tones like weird organ music. They sit as if hypnotized, absorbing the latest journals as avidly as a child would suck down boxes of peppermint candy. One day, when I am there, wondering if I should download apps or take neuroplasticity drugs that would allow me to distantly understand or approximate what they are doing, droplets of light float from the ceiling like snow. As one, they undress rapidly and lie on their backs; the droplets meet their skin and dissolve into it. Their skin glows for a second when this happens, in rainbow colors.

I undress too, but my skin remains blank. Drat.

You gotta have a dream.

"Do you dream?" I ask Amanda, as she mashes up some strange, healthy, awful concoction in the kitchen with my grandmother's mortar and pestle. Everyone eats her food without reaction except me, though I try to be polite and do feel better. I think.

"What is a dream?"

"It's kind of like seeing a vid in your mind while you sleep."

She looks at me, startled. "That would be very strange. Do you?"

"Yes."

"What kind of vids? Are they always the same?"

"Some are the same. When I was a child, I dreamed that I was falling from a high tower. A lot. I always woke up just as I was going to hit the ground."

"I wouldn't like that."

"I didn't. But dreams can be anything. Anything at all."

"Hmmm." She steps out the door into her garden apothecary, musing.

I AM SITTING one morning on my sleeping porch when I hear footsteps and other rustling sounds behind me. When I finish my sesshin and rise, I see them all sitting behind me. I walk to the doorway, lean on the doorjamb, and watch. Eventually, one after the other rises and walks past me and down the hallway. I smell coffee.

In the kitchen, breakfast is sizzling, popping, toasting. Jack serves it with wordless grace in the garden. Bees tend tall, ruffly red hollyhocks. A stone fountain burbles. My friends gather round and breakfast in burbling, leaf-waving, buzzing communion. I see a curtain pulled back from the second floor of my neighbor's house. Marge Degato peers out at us, then drops the curtain.

The next morning, Mike Degato, an old, young-faced, bulldoggish man, knocks on my front door. "Hello," I say, a bit surprised. "Come on in. Have a cup of coffee."

I wonder if he and Marge are miffed about not being invited to my birthday party. I know that they would not have enjoyed such a party, even though they maintain themselves in sparkling mid-thirtyish mode, which I find weird, since they are about eighty. But I suppose that my appearance, a 'vibrant' (I hope) round hundred, tall and skinny, with chin-length white hair and bangs, is just as weird to them.

"No thanks. I've had my coffee." He plows ahead. "I just want to know who-all is living here."

"Why? Have we been bothering you?"

"No, but – well, Marge has this silly idea that they're a bunch of goddamned J's."

The AP issue is heating up. Hysteria, demonstrations, the works. I've come across hundreds of channels calling for them to be killed, or at least isolated. It reminds me of the sci-fi movies I saw when I was a kid in the 1950's. A great hue and cry. More frightening every day.

I laugh. "That *is* silly! To tell you the truth, Mike, I haven't been feeling too well lately and I've taken in some young professionals to help out. I'm not sure you know, but the house is zoned for a rooming house."

He raises his eyebrows. "Oh?"

"Has been since 1973. I'm permitted for twenty, but I'm keeping it at four. After the yard is finished they're going to paint the house. It's not nanotech paint like yours."

He presses his lips together and nods. When he bought his house, he had come over and offered to buy my 'teardown.' When I look at his young, smooth face, I think 'Slippery slope.' And he thinks that he's 'human,' of course.

"How's Pamela doing at law school?" Pumped full of the latest competitive smart drugs, I'm sure.

"Oh, fine, fine. Well, I'll report back to Marge. Sorry to bother you."

When I close the door, I'm in a cold sweat. When you kill an AP, do you kill a person? Not in Mike's eyes, I'm pretty sure. And not in the law's eyes, either, although one case is now making its way to the Supreme Court. He could probably have my house confiscated and snap it up at auction.

INTERNATIONAL RIOTS OVER the burgeoning population of AP's. For all the usual reasons.

We watch as we eat noodles that Amanda ingeniously, though

not entirely deliciously, made of purslane. THEY HAVE NO
SOULS, read many signs.

"I think they probably do," says Xia, grabbing noodles with
chopsticks. I listen hard, look at her closely, but neither hear nor
see any trace of irony.

THEY ARE MAGICAL, these kids. The essence of humanity. In any
space or time.

SYB WAKES ME one night with an especially urgent bark.

I raise my head to see white beams of flashlights sweeping the
back yard. I yell through the screen,

"What's going on?"

"Police."

"What are you doing?"

"Can you come to the front door, please?"

"Have your ID out."

A young woman with a badge stands at my front door.
"What's this about?" I ask.

"Your neighbor called and complained that an AP was in
your back yard."

"Has anyone actually bothered this neighbor? Trespassed on
his property? Broken into his house?"

"No, but we are on orange alert because of the demonstrations.
Someone set the Albanian embassy on fire."

"Oh. Well, you can tell that Sybil, here" – (I am holding her
by her collar while she growls) – "definitely lets me know about
any threats. I'm fine."

The policewoman says, "Can we come in?"

"Do you have a warrant?"

"I have certain emergency powers right now, yes."

"What emergency powers, in particular?"

"For one thing," she begins, but an older guy behind her cuts her off.

"Ma'am, sorry to interrupt, but this is Doctor J. She's lived here since... since..."

I laugh. "He's right. I'm old as dirt and I've lived here for a hundred and thirty years."

"I came to a birthday party for one of her grandkids one time," says the man.

"Diane?"

"No. It was—"

"Charlie," we both say together, and laugh. I say, "He's in Antarctica right now, I think. Doing research."

Finally the policewoman surrenders.

I yank down all forty-three shades on the first floor, thinking, not for the first time, that I should automate them, make some coffee, and pour in a healthy dose of whisky. In the music room, I pound out some dissonant Monk. *Evidence* seems satisfying, right now.

First, Amanda wanders in and picks up the guitar. Then Xia on drums, Jack on sax, and Olek on violin.

We get into the groove of 'I've Got You Under My Skin,' and other pieces we've played. They only have to hear a tune once. Sounds glorious, but always exactly the same, this time a Nelson Riddle arrangement for Frank Sinatra.

Then I hear a phrase that is different. Jack stops playing. I turn to him. "That's great! Keep going!"

"It's wrong. I'm sorry. I don't know what happened. I just... thought it would sound good. Like I could hear it in my head first and wanted to do it."

"Listen." I put the phonograph needle on a Keith Jarrett concert, already on the turntable, and play it for a few minutes, then pick up the needle. "Jarrett made all of that up as he played."

"How could he?"

"He took chances. He improvised. He *made it up*."

"There were other instruments there. Did they all make it up together?"

"Yes. They were having a conversation. They trusted each other. They listened to each other."

"You can do that?" asks Olek.

"Why not? All the music on all of these recordings and written in these books was made up at one time. It's how we do things, that's one way of being creative. Things happen in your brain when you're creative."

"Like when you sit," says Xia.

"Right," I say. "Some of the same brain changes take place in both activities."

"I can see them," Xia said.

I open my mouth to say no way, but process it for a moment. "How?"

"With my eyes," she says simply. "It's in your cloud. Right now your blood pressure is 110 over 70, but when I came in it was 129 over 83."

"What else can you see?"

"I can see," she says slowly, "that our brains are all the same, and that they're different than yours."

"That is because you are APs."

"When Jack played those phrases, his brain changed."

I try not to shout, but I do, and they look startled. "Yes! Do you all understand that you are APs? J's? That we are in danger? You've seen the news."

They look at one another, as if to say, *Why is she yelling at us?*

Amanda says, "I would never want to harm J's."

"Neither would I," says Olek. "They may be strange, but that's no reason to treat them badly."

I'm wondering what I can possibly say or do when Jack says, like a cranky child, "I want to go to Mars."

"Actually," I say, as I myself make a new connection, "That sounds like a great idea."

WHEN I PING Irene, she is, happily, at home. She says, "I was just getting ready to ask you to come to the house for some cookies. Your birthday present is ready."

"Birthday present! You shouldn't have."

I TAKE THE train to Virginia on a gloomy Saturday morning. Long banks of leafless trees flank the train line, dark and silvery at the same time. Moody clouds hang low over the Blue Ridge. I walk the last mile to her white farmhouse on a one-lane road, and only one single-person auto veers around me, holding a woman napping while her auto takes her to her destination: not much has changed in the past eighty years, or a hundred-and-twenty years, for that matter.

I wipe my feet on the door mat, and open the door. "Hey!"

"In the kitchen." She dusts flour from her hands. "Grab some coffee and we'll sit in the living room."

The blazing fireplace, the comfortable chairs, the three-hundred-year-old house takes me back to our childhood. Irene curls up like a child, warming her hands around her coffee cup.

"No cookies?"

"I've been eating all day."

"You don't look well."

"Ha! I've been around the world three times in the past month."

"You're getting too old for that."

"Speak for yourself."

"I want to take them to Mars."

She laughs as if this is the most hilarious thing ever. "Oh, why not? When?"

"Soon. Tomorrow."

"Sure. The world's on fire about them. An abomination, a tragedy, a disaster in the making, the end of the world. Get them out of town."

"I want to keep them secret until we are on our way."

"Excellent idea. But why do you want to go? It took years for you to recover from your other trip."

"It's something to do."

"You gotta have a dream. That's what your mother always said."

"I think that what I learn about them on the trip will give those who want to make sure they have human rights – if any such people exist – some ammunition. They are astoundingly technologically adept. They manage big data. In their heads."

"So they aren't just zombie dunces that will devour resources like locusts?"

"They are scarier than that, and much more interesting. They easily manage all kinds of information. If we don't learn how to partner with them, they could easily cut us out of the management of our future."

"I see! So you want to have direct hand in ushering in this particular brave new world?" She laughs. "Great idea, Maysie. We can live in infamy!"

"They love me."

"They love me! I love them!" she sings. "Sure they do. For how long?"

"They're like children, emotionally."

"Speaking as one who has raised a lot of children, that's scary as hell. Remember how they get to be when they're teens? What are you going to do, Peter Pan them?"

"They'll be different, that's for sure."

"Speaking of dreams, I have something for you. Come upstairs."

Her huge bedroom, under the eaves, hasn't changed much since we were kids. Instead of bunk beds, there is a king bed.

Another dresser for Brian, her husband, who manages the farm. From hers, she takes down a jewelry box.

"You still have that?"

"You still have a mansion of useless junk?" She opens it, and a ballerina pops up and dances to the music. She roots around and gets out a small box, hands it to me. "Happy birthday."

I lift the lid and see a tiny starship. I look at her and we both burst into tears. We hug and laugh, then cry again.

It is *Stardust*, the size of a pea.

"The nanotech seed is inside the replica. There's a lot more to it than when we stopped. I contracted with a lot of different companies, but it was all compartmentalized, so no one had the big picture. But... it needs to all be linked together. It will be the first fully nano-bio ship ever. I think," she says, and I see her blink once but don't pay much attention at the time, "it is fully radiation-proof, which is the big thing."

THEY ARE ENTHRALLED.

Our small family moves to one of Irene's guest houses, and they design the ship at our nearby Sterling facility, where they also train. I remain at the house and design the study, which has actually already begun, and stay nervous.

Irene walks in one afternoon. "Why aren't you training, dear? Getting strong and throwing up in zero g.?"

"I'll put in my time."

"I just want you to know that your Fake Folk are really running up a big bill."

"I wish you wouldn't call them that."

"What should I call them?"

"My friends."

"I'm just yanking your chain. They really are lovely. I think they love me too."

"Of course they do."

273

"I'm not really worried about the money," she says, sitting across the table from me. "The ship isn't all that expensive, despite the fact that they've nailed the radiation-blocking technology and have included so many nested nanotech applications that I haven't reached the end of them. If I'm right, it may be the main model for interplanetary travel for decades to come." She pauses. "Maybe even interstellar travel. I want you to know that it seems to be set up with that possibility in mind."

I shrug. "You'd never know if we reached an exoplanet. I wouldn't either. We won't live that long."

"Or I might pass you on the way, if we develop an FTL drive. No, really. We've had some near-misses. Are they smart enough to design an FTL drive?"

I shrug. "They think differently. I have very little idea what their parameters or limits are."

Irene laughs. "It wouldn't be a *problem*, mind you. I'm actually wondering how to attribute the developments they have incorporated into the ship. They're not really employees."

"Why don't we ask them?"

We take a pod to the facility – a huge metal warehouse with a clean room for nanotech r&d, and a model that displays data when you touch it. The ship will be assembled at a nanotech facility at the Mid-Atlantic Regional Spaceport at Wallop's Island, a few hundred miles away, that we will pay to use, along with the MARS launch facility. I haven't seen it in three weeks. I've been busy setting up legal dispositions for the house in case of various contingencies.

When we walk into the warehouse, I'm astonished.

Each of them are displaying their clouds – immense, three-dimensional, moving visual patterns, sounds, colors, numbers. The clouds merge, and they are inside the buzzing, crackling, singing manifestation, reaching out and tweaking things here and there. Xia touches a yellow cube, hums, and it changes to a red ovoid. Amanda shakes her head and turns it green; rearranges some equations with a wave of her hand. They murmur and nod.

When they do this, I see no change in the quarter-size ship model, a sleek, beautiful hologram. I figure they are working on deep sub-programs.

"We'll give you a tour," said Olek. They show me my own little space, a combo chair-bed-workplace. "All the books, music, movies in the world, too. All of your personal vids, journals, everything we could find."

"That's a lot of stuff, considering the attic." I'd given them permission to create a May wonderland. I had nothing to hide. At least, not from them.

"We could really go on forever," said Olek, "with the nanotech propulsion system. We also have the potential to use asteroid or interstellar matter as fuel. Perhaps even dark matter, but that's theoretical."

Irene and I leave the warehouse without any response from them to her question. As we climb into the pod I say, "Attribute the patents to the inventors, of course. And if we don't come back – I'm sure that's what's worrying you – have papers drawn up so you can recoup our investment and pay all the bills regardless. I would want the rest to go to legal protection of AP's."

"What do you mean, if you don't come back," she says, "You, my oldest friend and partner in crime? Don't you want to sit in the living room and drink coffee together five hundred years from now?"

But she knows the answer.

"Why don't you come with us."

"Oh... you know. I have too much to do here. Maybe later."

"THEIR MATHEMATICS ARE wrong. That's been the problem all along."

Olek volunteers to return to the house with me one last time. My great-granddaughter and her family are moving in, and their crates clutter the rooms. Syb is with them, and I miss her terribly.

After packing some things for storage, I drift aimlessly through rooms that are like my own body. *Can I live on a ship for a year or more? And then on Mars?* I remind myself of my neuroscience study with a mental shrug.

We're in the kitchen having a last cup of tea when we hear glass shattering and rush into the living room. A brick lies on the floor amid shards of glass. A crowd of demonstrators mobs in my front yard, trampling my hydrangeas. "Hey!" I yell through the broken window, and they surge onto the porch, their anti-J signs shouting and flashing.

I call the police and then say to Olek, "Let's go."

"I have to get something," he says, ducks into the kitchen, and returns. We leave by a side door, walk a block, and summon a pod to take us to Wallop's Island.

It's as good a way to leave as any.

THE FIRST TIME I see the actual ship, I cry.

It takes a day and a half for it to be towed to the launch site, raised, and attached to the side of the rocket, which dwarfs everything.

I've ridden on rockets a few times. I don't much like it.

But once we break free of gravity, the enormity of what is happening is like being reborn as a new person. I overflow with energy, optimism, and deep curiosity.

I look around to the faces of my dear friends.

"We made it," I say.

We loosen our straps, float free, and hold hands for a moment before returning to our necessary tasks. There is a lot of work, and little free time.

We settle into our routine.

A month out, Lauren, Irene's daughter, contacts us.

"May, Mom has died."

A fist smashes into my chest. I force out the words. "When? What happened?

"She had cancer. From radiation, probably, from her Mars trip thirty years ago. Nothing worked."

I feel a strange flash of anger. No proper goodbye.

But closure, plenty of closure. I am living in it. It is all around me. Irene's work.

It is a bit of comfort. "How long did she know?"

"She found out right before your party. I think that at first she was going to tell you, but then she saw... your friends."

"And knew I'd come to her. Knew that there was something else we could do together."

"I think so. She was working on a new idea for a radiation shield. They accelerated that. If everything works, Infinity will make a lot of money. We filed all the patents. You'll be rich when you get back." She pauses. "May, this was her dream."

They are all looking at me sadly. Amanda kicks off and hugs me. "I love you," she says. They all float round me, hugging and murmuring comforting words.

They all seem pretty damned human to me.

WE ARE NOT much further out when it happens. We are listening for news of ourselves – the ship is newsworthy – when we hear "This is ICN. We have just had a report from Mars. An AP killed a surveyor at Port Giovanni. All twenty-two APs on Mars were apprehended and put to sleep. We will let you know the results of the autopsy."

Amanda uncurls. I see tears on her face. She says, "I... I think I may be an AP."

"You all are. I was hoping each of you would realize it, but–"

"Why?" asks Jack, as they all gather round me.

"Yes, why?" asks Xia. "Do you know why *you're* conscious?"

"Point. I wanted you to know for this very reason, so you could be self-aware; aware of danger. But I want you to know for other reasons as well."

"If we are AP's, then we are different. We are more than you, and less than you. Just different." says Olek, morosely. "Feared and hated by humans. Why? And why is it good to be human?"

I had hoped this would be a moment of joy. But at least it is a moment. "You can all at least entertain the idea that you are APs?"

"Well... I *have* changed since I came to live with you," says Jack. "I know that. It happened the day I danced. At the Naval Observatory. When I saw the Seal. It was... a strange combination of things."

"When I was sitting one morning," says Xia, "I knew I was alive."

"When I played for myself," says Olek. He nods. "It's good, I think, to know that you're alive."

"That never happened to me," says Amanda. "There was no moment."

"You created the gardens," I say.

They all nod. She shrugs. "They were there before."

"You created new plants."

I see a slight smile.

"All of you created this ship."

That was the right thing to say. "We did!" says Xia. "That means–"

Again, they all look at me. "You say it," I suggest.

Jack does. "We are artificial people. Because of the capabilities we have as APs, we have created a ship that gives us the power to go anywhere. A ship that humans couldn't create by themselves, at least not as quickly as we have. I don't have a problem with that."

I look away from them, out the port, at the stars, thinking that at last I had done something really worth doing. "You can't go to Mars. Where will you go?"

"You mean," says Amanda, "Where will *we* go?"

"The pilot will marry the sea and the heavens, and plot the course," says Jack, smiling at me. "Will you be our Urania?"

"I can go first. Then we can take turns."

"Let's go live on a new moon," says Xia. "Titan. Europa. All of them! We'll make everyone on earth understand what the future can be."

"Or even a new earth," I say, and see shy smiles. They've been thinking about that too.

"Well, maybe," says Xia. "We think we're very close to FTL. We do have everything we need here. On the ship. Part of the ship."

Thank you, I say to my mother, my father, to Irene. Thank you, Galileo, Newton, Feynman, Higgs. To those who conceived of the future humans who will now be my long present. It does not seem like a boring prospect. It seems endlessly fascinating.

"Thank you," I say to them, clumsily bowing and bouncing off my bunk.

"Music! Champagne!" says Amanda, and claps her hands. A smooth Paul Desmond sax solo infuses time with a spare, haunting cadence.

As we reach for tubes that hold a perfect, just-assembled Dom Perignon, I lift an imaginary champagne flute.

"I propose a toast to wilderness: to unfound planets, unknown life, and to uncounted stars, wilder still."

In the general hurrah, I am suddenly, deeply alone; as alone as they must have been on the Earth. *What have I done?* I cry; but not aloud. My chest is wrenched with something more profound, more deep, than anything I've ever felt before as sharp, deep loss unfurls, and howls its name, and leaves me in its wake.

I am become a star, a lone, dense orb of leaping, dancing fire that burns with heat untold. Sublimed, all that I ever was, my sweet, old Earth, my heart, my home; I'm left now just a spent, burnt cloud of molecules, trailing a blaze of time, of all that's lost to me forever.

Olek looks at me, then looks again, across a vast, clear gulf, a new form of space between me and all else that exists, those other burning stars. Unsealing a flap in his shirt, he fishes something out, swims toward me like a wrasse, curls in a crouch and floats, wedged close to me.

"I took this from your windowsill. A bridge perhaps..." says Olek. He gently slips a bit of Earth into my hand: a small, hard piece of dense, pressed time, with its own revelations, its own tales.

My fingers trace its folds – the fossilized trail of something that once lived; the river-smoothed gray ridges--and memories come forth. The scenes, scents, sounds; the shifting, life-filled place that we call memory begins its linking bloom, a counter and companion to infinities both beckoning and cold.

"Thank you," I say, and touch his cheek then close my hand on stardust.

'THE ENTIRE IMMENSE SUPERSTRUCTURE': AN INSTALLATION

Ken MacLeod

1. Daylight Passes

VERRALL, YOU'LL RECALL, spent only six months in Antarctica, and shortly after his return had to be talked down from the canopy of Harrods, where he seemed on the point of committing seppuku with what turned out to be a laser pointer. At the hearing he claimed to have been making an artistic statement. He opted for psychiatric treatment rather than face charges.

I visited him at the clinic, a sprawling conference-centre-style low-build on a 300-acre expanse of lawns, copses and lakes outside a small town in Bedfordshire. We walked along a gravel path, slowly – three of his toes, frostbitten after an ill-considered escapade on the Brunt Ice Shelf, were still regenerating. A minder hovered discreetly, at head level and a few paces to the side, its rotors now and then disturbing the tops of the taller plants in the beds along the path.

Verrall was silent for a while, his fists jammed in the pockets of the unfastened white towelling-robe he wore over jeans and T-shirt. From a distance he might have looked more like a clinician or technician than a patient. His beard pressed to his collar-bone, his shoulders almost touching the angles of his jaw, one foot dragging... perhaps these would have been clues to his real status.

"'Jesus lived as a human socialist,'" he announced. You could hear the quotes, the portent in his voice.

"What?"

"Last night I dreamed I read that on the front cover of a celebrity gossip magazine." He laughed. "In the midst of all the usual stuff about who's getting married, who's been seen out with whom, who's split up, what diet she's on, et cetera."

"What was the evidence?"

"I never read that kind of magazine in reality, let alone in dreams."

"Have you been thinking a lot about Jesus?"

Verrall shook his head. "Not since his death."

"Ah."

Suddenly he grabbed my arm – the minder lurched towards him – and pointed upward, about a quarter of the way up the sky.

"Look!"

A light moved in the blue, arcing slowly, to vanish behind a cloud.

"The Shenzhou Hotel," Verrall said.

I could see that. "Yes? So?"

"I don't have my contacts," he said. He jerked his head back, indicating the clinic. "They take them out, you know. So I'm memorising everything. Orbit times, timetables, tide tables, phases of the Moon, faces of the famous, locations of police stations, railway stations, space stations – there goes another! The Putilov Engine Works."

It was, of course, nothing of the kind.

"Virgin Honeymoons," I said.

"Uh-huh. Just testing." He gave me a look like a nudge. "At

Halley we could only see the circumpolar ones. And of these, only one or two are visible in daylight. In the Antarctic night... well yeah, it's quite something. To see an orbital hotel climbing out of the aurora..." He closed his eyes and shook his head, remembering. "You know, it was then, in the long night, that I realised. We all believed the cliché about Antarctica being the front line of the Cold Revolution. Hah!" His pointing finger tracked another daylight pass. "The real front line is up there. LEO and geostationary, the Moon, the Earth-grazer robot mines, the foothold on Mars, the stations farther out... that's where the battle for the future is being fought. But it was the daylight passes in my last month that got to me."

I'd heard this sort of thing before, and I'd heard enough. Verrall was not insane, his odd maunderings about Jesus notwithstanding – these I put down to an attempt to convince me, or the clinic via the minder, otherwise. Or, quite possibly, another exercise in performance art.

"That reminds me," I said, by way of changing the subject. "Do you wish to continue your residency?"

"I'm not in Antarctica anymore." It was like he was pointing something out.

"No," I said, patiently. "But the Survey gave you a grant for a year. While we expected you to stay down there for the whole twelve months, it isn't actually specified in your contract. All we need is evidence that you're engaged in producing some work inspired by your stay."

"Well, you have that already," he said.

"We have?"

"The Knightsbridge incident."

I had to laugh.

"If you can justify it artistically to the committee, well..."

We continued our stroll and chat, amicably and circuitously, all the way back to the clinic's front door. I shook hands, said goodbye, and watched as he shuffled inside through the glass

283

doors. He didn't look back. A passing waiter had an extra espresso on its tray. I let the drink cool as I sauntered down the drive to the road. As I waited to be picked up I sipped the coffee and thought over what I should report, then crushed the empty cup and chucked it in a bin that trundled past at that moment. After a minute a car pulled in and drew to a halt. The window sank into the door.

"Cambridge?" the driver asked.

"Perfect," I said.

She jerked her thumb over her shoulder. "Hop in."

On the way home I filed my assessment of Verrall's mental state, and recommended that he be kept under observation.

2. Observation

VERRALL WANDERED PAST Reception and into the clinic's small shop, where he bought a paper (A5, lined, spiral bound) notebook and a black gel pen. He stuffed these into the pocket of his towelling robe, and walked along two long corridors to his room. The door opened to his palm. The room was basic hotel: bed, table, chair, kettle, wardrobe, en-suite. The window gave a view across the car park and the estate to the nearby fields and woods, straddled by the local modules of the WikiThing.

Verrall boiled the kettle and made herbal tea-bag tea. He sat down at the desk and looked at the room's two cameras one by one. He shifted the chair around and placed the notebook on his crooked knee and the pen on the table. He picked up the pen and began to write, sipping the tea occasionally. What he wrote was not in the cameras' field of view.

After nineteen minutes he turned to a fresh page and stood up in front of the window. There he began to sketch the visible modules of the WikiThing, quickly and crudely, making no effort to get the angles of the tubes or the shading of the spheres right. The result looked like a child's drawing of the pieces in a giant's game of jacks, the modules carelessly connected like enchained molecules. The drawing was further marred by lines drawn in the wrong places and ignored or scribbled over.

He stared at the page, made a few more marks on it, with greater care and less skill, signed it, then tore out the sketch and the written pages and slid them into a hotel envelope, on which he scrawled a line. He looked directly at the camera.

"You wanted evidence of work," he said.

He looked around the room, then took off his towelling robe and tossed it on the bed. He opened the wardrobe and put on a thick shirt and a padded jacket, and socks and boots. As he stood up in the boots he winced slightly, then adjusted the lacing of the boot on his damaged foot. He hauled a small rucksack out of the bottom of the wardrobe and stuffed the rest of his gear in it, and slipped the pen and notebook into an inside pocket of the jacket.

The door closed behind him.

A minute and a half later he appeared at the reception desk.

"I'm checking out," he said.

"Do you mean you are discharging yourself?" said the desk.

"Yes," said Verrall.

"Only non-interactive property can be returned to you," said the desk.

"I'm aware of that, thanks."

"You are not recommended to discharge yourself."

"I know."

"By discharging yourself," said the desk, "you absolve the clinic of all responsibility."

"Good," said Verrall.

After some seconds a minder emerged from behind the reception area and laid a transparent ziplock bag on the desk. Verrall sorted a torch, pen, watch, laser pointer, Victorinox knife, and a wallet containing only paper currency into various pockets. He left two crumpled tissues and a half-finished tube of mint sweets in the bag.

"Please place discarded items in the recycling bin," said the desk.

Verrall complied.

"You may return at any time," said the desk.

"I don't intend to."

"We hope you had a pleasant and recuperative stay, and that you would recommend the clinic to others."

"No doubt I will have occasion to," said Verrall.

"Please sign here," said the desk, lighting a patch.

Verrall scribbled on the patch, shouldered his pack, and walked out. A minder drifted after him.

His torn-out notebook pages arrived on my desk the following week, in a tattered envelope addressed to 'That guy Wilson from the Antarctic Survey', that had been to Cardiff (where I had an ex-girlfriend known to one of the clinic's staff) and Bristol before arriving in Cambridge. There are times when I miss postal service.

3. The Wikipedia of Things

ORIGINATING IN A poorly documented, hastily conceived application of synthetic biology and genetic engineering to post-disaster emergency shelter and supply in the Flood World, seized on and mutated by criminal gangs and militias, replicating uncontrollably like some benign invasive weed, becoming a refuge for the displaced surplus population and marginal individuals everywhere, and finally reconfigured by biohackers inspired by the situationist architecture of Constant Nieuwenhuys' projected ludic social space of New Babylon – a borderless, global and polymorphic artificial modular milieu intended as the site "of a 'freedom' that for us is not the choice between many alternatives but the optimum development of the creative faculties of every human being" – the Wikipedia of Things insinuates itself across and through all previously existing environments. In an era of universal surveillance where social control is directly experienced as a quasi-divine providential good fortune, a perpetual and relentless reinforcement of the double-edged conviction that one is lucky to be alive, and where all ideological contestation is instantly recuperable, the WikiThing's sheer materiality constitutes a critique made unanswerable by its silence.

IT IS TIME to make the silent modules speak, and for the very ground to rise up.

4. Interim Appraisal

THERE WAS A lot more like that.

Mary Jones, the ex-colonel who then chaired the Arts and Public Engagement Committee of the British Antarctic Survey, read through the three pages of bad handwriting and studied for a few seconds the disgraceful draughtsmanship of the sketch.

She threw the notebook pages down on her desk.

"Bastard's off his meds."

"Off his meds, off piste, off the reservation, and off providence," I said.

She looked startled. "Off providence?"

"Oh yes," I said. "Patients have to turn in their contacts when they're admitted to the clinic. He self-discharged, so he didn't get them back."

She blinked rapidly. "Good Lord. How did he expect to survive?"

"He told me he was memorising timetables."

"Timetables!"

"You know – for trains."

"Trains." She shook her head. "Fucking delusional."

"And tide tables."

"Whatever floats your boat, I guess."

We laughed.

"But seriously," I said. "I think that was just misdirection. He also claimed to be able to identify orbital structures from eye and memory, and immediately demonstrated that he didn't. No, I think... well, that screed of his suggests he's been intending to go into the WikiThing for some time. And like I said, I don't think he's insane in the least. He's not exactly feigning insanity, either. As far as he's concerned, he's still engaged on the Antarctic art project."

"How about as far as we're concerned?"

I shrugged. "There's not much we can do about it. Whenever he emerges from the WikiThing he'll still be living off the grant."

"How can he do that, without contacts?"

"He took it all out in cash. He has a wad of paper in his back pocket."

Jones frowned. "Good luck with that. Do we have any idea where he is?"

"A minder followed him into the WikiThing, but it got eaten within seconds."

"OK," she said. She stood up and stepped over to the window, gazing out at the motorway and the fields, and pointed to the inevitable strand of WikiThing in the distance. "For all we know he could even be in there by now, just a couple of klicks away." She sighed. "It's frustrating." Then she turned around sharply. "All right. Let's take him at his word for the moment. He's being irritating and irresponsible, but what do you expect? He's an artist."

"Yes," I said, relieved.

"But," she added, rapping the air with an outstretched

forefinger, "that doesn't mean you're off the hook. We don't expect our artists to churn out rabid propaganda, but we do at least expect them to produce something visible and inspiring, however avant-garde it might be."

Before she retired from the Army and took her post at the Survey, Jones had spent most of her twenty-year service career in the Semiotics Division, some of it on the front line. (The Coca-Cola Comet stunt, rumour has it, was her idea.)

"So this" – she picked up and dropped the pages Verrall had sent – "doesn't meet the criteria. I want to see something more substantial, and before too long, at that."

"I'm sure you will," I said. "He's a very serious artist, after all."

"So you keep telling us," she said.

The next communication from Verrall arrived three months later, correctly addressed – airmailed, quaintly enough, blue envelope and all, and postmarked Malabo, Isla de Bioko: the capital of Equatorial Guinea, on the island formerly known as Fernando Po.

The thirty sheets of thin paper inside were typed on both sides, single-spaced, using a mechanical typewriter. I pass over Verrall's salutations and preliminary personal discourtesies and present an extract from and then summary of his narrative, with no claim as to its veracity, other than to suggest that it gives as good an explanation of subsequent events as we have yet seen.

5. Out of the Hands of Providence

MY LEFT FOOT hurt like fuck [Verrall wrote] but I was damned if I was going to let it show. I strode across the car park and the putting green, ignoring shouts, through (and partly over) a hedge, and into the field. I could hear the buzz of the minder a steady two metres behind me, an unbelievably annoying sound and situation, like being tailgated by a bee. Ignoring it and not looking back, quailing inwardly, I approached the WikiThing. Soggy autumn grass squelched under my boots. The nearest sphere resting on the ground had an aperture about two metres wide, a metre off the ground. Light pulsed behind the shifting rainbow sheen, as if a soap-bubble were stretched across the entrance. I climbed in. As I passed through the elliptical portal the bubble burst – the spray stung my face and the backs of my hands for an instant – then, as a backward glance showed, the sheen re-formed behind me.

Inside, banally, the bottom of the sphere was filled with soil and covered with green grass, springy as well as spring-like. The rest of the sphere was transparent from the inside, though from the outside it had been merely translucent. The adjoining cylinder, likewise transparent, sloped gently upward. Just as I turned towards it, the bubble over the doorway popped again, and the minder came in. The bubble barely had time to reconstitute itself before something leapt from the grass and grappled with the minder in mid-air. The added weight brought the tiny machine to the ground in a screeching complaint of rotors. After a few moments of thrashing the new device, a sort of mechanical spider, was using four of its appendages to dismantle the minder and another four to scuttle away. It vanished into the grass – down a burrow, I guessed.

Not hanging around to investigate, I set off up the sloping cylinder. It was a good three metres in diameter, and floored with what felt like roughened plastic ridges underfoot. As I ascended I found the air becoming warm and its scent pleasant. The next sphere, well off the ground, was a kind of greenhouse, twined with creepers that seemed to sustain some hydroponic piping, from which sprouted small fruit-bearing plants, none of which were remotely familiar, in various stages of ripeness. I had no way of determining whether they were safe to eat, and I was not hungry enough to take the risk, so I hurried on.

Thereafter my progress became easier; the angular arrangement of the spheres and tubes near the clinic was replaced by a more tolerable approximation to the horizontal. Each sphere or spheroid, and some of the linking tubes, was the locale of an entirely different facility: some were greenhouses; some were rendered almost impassable with glutinous machinery from which random articles of use and ornament were exuded; others appeared to be galleries of visual art and sculpture in which I confess I lingered, though work of any discernible talent was rare. Occasionally I was faced by alternative exits from a given node; in these cases, I struck out on a generally southward course.

My wandering had taken me perhaps a dozen kilometres and three hours – the variable light, whether natural or artificial, made the passage of time difficult to ascertain, and I deliberately avoided looking at my watch – when I first heard voices ahead. The apprehension I had felt in my final steps before venturing into the WikiThing returned, redoubled. I had no idea who I might encounter. But, with a stern reminder to myself that this was a condition of the WikiThing, and that if I was not willing to face it I might as well give up my project then and there, I pressed on.

On the threshold, I paused. The space in front of me was about the size and shape of a Nissen hut, rounded at the ends. Two long tables occupied its length. About thirty people, all adults of various ages, sat around them, drinking and talking. Their clothing was eccentric or exigent. Fumes, fragrant and otherwise, drifted in visible clouds, to be whipped away by strong draughts into overhead orifices. Along the sides of the room were shelves on which cartons and cups lay, evidently the source of the drinks being consumed.

A ripple of face-turning raced down the room, and rebounded as a wave of indifference and a return to the ongoing conversations. I hesitated for a moment longer, facing as I did a crowd of people whose identity and background were not just hitherto unknown to me, but impossible for me to find at a glance. And I, no doubt, was as unknown and unknowable to them.

Nerving myself, I walked into the room to make the first truly chance encounter of my adult life.

6. A Traveller in Utopia

THE FOLLOWING ENTIRELY predictable events are then narrated in Verrall's characteristically prolix style:

Finding among the denizens of the room an attractive woman a little younger than himself, and their conversation with each other and others present, in which Verrall expresses delight at the discovery of such interesting people and convivial company, in a milieu where the Cold Revolution no longer polarises every aspect of life, every waking thought, and contaminates our very dreams (attached sheets, 3-4)

An unnecessarily detailed and salacious account of subsequent sexual activity (sheets 5-8)

Verrall's dismay at waking to discover that the woman has vanished like a mist in the morning, like wind on the sea, and that the adjacent venue of the evening's conviviality has been transformed overnight into what appears to be a particularly strenuous gymnasium but is actually a control unit for an experimental protein folding laboratory (sheet 9)

Verrall's growing understanding of the mechanisms of the WikiThing, including sewerage, life-support, child-rearing practices, gender relations, medical procedures, laser sintering devices, quasi-pheromonal communications networks, and automated internal and external defences (sheets 10-18)

Verrall's increasing frustration with the involution and self-absorption he finds among WikiThing inhabitants in their lives of creative play (sheet 20).

His conception of an art project to subvert their complacency (sheets 20-21)

His proclamation of and concept design for New Babel, an uninhabited and uninhabitable modular tower to be built on Pico Basilé, the highest peak of Isla di Bioko (sheets 22-25).

The 'pheromonal surge' of confidence he feels that his project has propagated through the WikiThing and that thousands of eager volunteers are already making their way to Equatorial Guinea. (sheet 26)

His meticulous planning of a journey, and his departure from the WikiThing near the barely used East Coast Main Line (sheets 27-30).

I DROPPED TO the ground [Verrall's account concludes] and walked along the railway track. Whenever a train was due, I took good care to be off the line before it came into sight. Sometimes I clambered on to a slow-moving goods train. By this and other means I reached Tilbury.

A container ship was about to leave port, headed for my destination. Timing my movements with great precision from the process chart I had memorised, I climbed up a stack of containers at the quayside, and stepped across to the adjacent stack on board just before the ship sailed.

The tide was in, as I had known it would be.

*   *   *

7. New Babel

EQUATORIAL GUINEA WAS, of course, one of the earliest sites of WikiThing deployment, initially in the form of humanitarian aid provided by the US Navy in the course of assistance to the democratic forces. The plains and rainforests of the offshore island on which the capital stands remain littered with WikiThing modules and shell fragments, as does the country's mainland territory, and many ingenious local adaptations and variations of the WikiThing as well as of the expended ordnance have been, and are being, evolved.

The growth of a spindly spike of WikiThing, eventually reaching a height of one kilometre, atop the 3000-metre summit of the dormant volcano overlooking Malabo, attracted considerable media attention. Needless to say, the Arts and Public Engagement Committee of the British Antarctic Survey followed developments closely, and with more anxiety than our responses to journalists' questions betrayed. We were able to assure inquirers that the project, though unauthorised by us, was not objected to by the Government of Equatorial Guinea, and that curiosity about it was bringing a much needed boost to tourist revenue. Some local denizens of the WikiThing – less isolated from their compatriots than are their equivalents elsewhere, and therefore in frequent if irregular communication and technically illicit trade – had been among the earliest to rally to the project. The structure itself was being self-generated from rainforest floor detritus, surplus natural gas siphoned from offshore oil wells, and volcanic debris. (I have to admit that the significance of a tall modular structure with a tough outer skin and an interior consisting largely of silicated cellulose escaped me entirely.) No damage to the environment or biodiversity of the island was being reported. We were happy to take some credit, albeit discreetly, for Verrall's project, though my increasingly urgent replies to his letter went unanswered.

It was therefore with as much disappointment as surprise that we watched the events of this February unfold. Many thousands of camera drones, aimed by reporters, tourists, agents of Western governments and Asian multiplanetary corporations, and local Equatoguinean citizens who had been alerted by street-market rumour, were on the spot (mostly at a safe distance) to record and transmit the spectacle.

It seemed at first that the dormant volcano had begun to erupt. A roar of sound rolled down the sides of the mountain. Smoke and flames boiled from the summit, around the base of New Babel. Then, more or less rapidly, the entire immense superstructure began to rise into the sky. One by one, five successive stages fell away, to combust entirely and drift down as (mostly) harmless ash.

The modules at the very tip of the spire, as is now confirmed, reached low Earth orbit, where they remain. Whether their avoidance of collision with any other structure in what is an admittedly crowded region of near-Earth space vindicates Verrall's boast that he had memorised satellite times and orbits, I can only speculate. No communication from the new satellite has been received, other than a persistent and discordant bleep that is – no doubt intentionally – reminiscent of the first Sputnik.

In the months since then, nothing further has been heard from Verrall. Claims have been made that he, with or without some confederates, actually ascended to orbit, where he or they managed to survive for some time and possibly to this day. The theoretical possibility of a closed-loop solar-powered ecology within a WikiThing module, even one of that size, does exist.

Personally, I think it far more likely that what we witnessed was an uncrewed launch, and that Verrall has once more disappeared into the WikiThing, where he may even now be hatching yet more audacious plans or (knowing him as I do) have lost interest in the project and moved on to something else entirely. But sometimes, when the remaining component of

New Babel makes a visible pass above the British Isles after sunset, I look up and wonder.

Nevertheless, in conclusion: the incident passed off without endangering surface or space shipping and without incurring additional expense to the Survey. I therefore respectfully suggest that we consider the matter closed.

IN BABELSBERG

Alastair Reynolds

THE AFTERNOON BEFORE my speaking engagement at New York's
Hayden Planetarium I find myself at the Museum of Modern
Art, standing before Vincent Van Gogh's *De Sterrennacht*, or
the Starry Night. Doubtless you know the painting. It's the one
he created from the window of his room in the asylum at Saint-
Rémy-de-Provence, after his voluntary committal. He was dead
scarcely a year later.

I have seen paintings before, and paintings of starry nights. I
think of myself as something of a student of the human arts. But
this is the first time I grasp something of crucial significance.
The mad yellow stars in Van Gogh's picture look nothing like
the stars I saw during my deep space expeditions. My stars were
mathematically remote reference points, to be used only when I
had cause to doubt my inertial positioning systems. These stars
are exuberant, flowerlike swabs of thick-daubed paint. More
starfish than star. Though the painting is fixed – no part of it
has changed in two hundred years – its lurid firmament seems
to shimmer and swirl before my eyes. It's not how the stars
really are, of course. But under a warm June evening this is
how they must have appeared to this anxious, ailing man – as
near and inviting as lanterns, lowered down from the zenith.
Almost close enough to touch. Without that delusion – let us be
charitable and call it a different kind of truth – generations of

people would have had no cause to strive for the heavens. They would not have built their towers, built their flying machines, their rockets and space probes; they would not have struggled into orbit and onto the Moon. These sweetly lying stars have inspired greatness.

Inspired, in their small way, me.

Time presses, and I must soon be on my way to the Hayden Planetarium. It's not very far, but in the weeks since my return to Earth I have gained a certain level of celebrity and no movement is without its complications. They have already cleared a wing of the museum for me, and now I must brave the crowds in the street and fight my way to the limousine. I am not alone – I have my publicity team, my security entourage, my technicians – but I still feel myself at the uncomfortable focus of an immense, insatiable public scrutiny. So different to the long years in which I was the one doing the scrutineering. For a moment I wish I were back out there, alone on the solar system's edge, light hours from any other thinking thing.

"Vincent!" someone calls, and then someone else, and then the calls become an assault of sound. As we push through the crowd fingers brush against my skin and I register the flinches that accompany each moment of contact. My alloy is always colder than they expect. It's as if I have brought a cloak of interplanetary cold back with me from space.

I provide some signatures, mouth a word or two to the onlookers, then bend myself into the limousine. And then we are moving, flanked by police floatercycles, and the computer-controlled traffic parts to hasten our advance. Soon I make out the blue glass cube of the Hayden, lit from within by an eerie glow, and I mentally review my opening remarks, wondering if it is really necessary to introduce myself to a world that already knows everything there is to know about me.

But it would be immodest to presume too much.

"I am Vincent," I begin, when I have the podium, standing

with my hands resting lightly against the tilted platform. "But I suspect most of you are already aware of that."

They always laugh at that point. I smiled and wait a beat before continuing.

"Allow me to bore you with some of my holiday snaps."

More laughter. I smile again. I like this.

LATER THAT EVENING, after a successful presentation, my schedule has me booked onto a late night chat show on the other side of town. I take no interest in these things myself, but I fully understand the importance of promotion to my transnational sponsors. My host for tonight is called The Baby. He is (or was) a fully adult individual who underwent neotenic regression therapy, until he attained the size and physiology of a six month old human. The Baby resembles a human infant, and directs his questions at me from a sort of pram.

I sit next to the pram, one arm slung over the back of the chair, one leg hooked over the other. There's a drink on the coffee table in front of me (along with a copy of the book) but of course I don't touch it. Behind us is a wide picture window, with city lights twinkling across the great curve of Manhattan Atoll.

"That's a good question," I say, lying through my alloy teeth. "Actually, my earliest memories are probably much like yours – a vague sense of *being*, an impression of events and feelings, some wants and needs, but nothing stronger than that. I came to sentience in the research compounds of the European Central Cybernetics Facility, not far from Zurich. That was all I knew to begin with. It took me a long time before I had any idea what I was, and what I was meant to do."

"Then I guess you could say that you had a kind of childhood," the Baby says.

"That wouldn't be too far from the mark," I answer urbanely.

"Tell me how you felt when you first realised you were a robot. Was that a shock?"

"Not at all." I notice that a watery substance is coming out of the Baby's nose. "I couldn't be shocked by what I already was. Frankly, it was something of a relief, to have a name for myself."

"A relief?"

"I have a very powerful compulsion to give names to things. That's a deep part of my core programming – my personality, you might almost say. I'm a machine made to map the unknown. The naming of things, the labelling of cartographic features – that's something that gives me great pleasure."

"I don't think I could ever understand that."

I try to help the Baby. "It's like a deep existential itch. If I see a landscape – a crater or a rift on some distant icy moon – I *must* call it something. Almost an obsessive compulsive disorder. I can't be satisfied with myself until I've done my duty, and mapping and naming things is a very big part of it."

"You take pleasure in your work, then."

"Tremendous pleasure."

"You were made to do a job, Vincent. Doesn't it bother you that you only get to do that one thing?"

"Not at all. It's what I live for. I'm a space probe, going where it's too remote or expensive or dangerous to send humans."

"Then let's talk about the danger. After what you saw on Titan, don't you worry about your own – let's say mortality?"

"I'm a machine – a highly sophisticated fault-tolerant, error-correcting, self-repairing machine. Barring the unlikely – a chance meteorite impact, something like that – there's really nothing out there that can hurt me. And even if I did have cause to fear for myself – which I don't – I wouldn't dwell on it. I have far too much to be getting on with. This is my work – my vocation." I flash back to the mad swirling stars of *De Sterrennacht*. "My art, if you will. I am named for Vincent Van Gogh – one of the greatest artistic geniuses of human history.

But he was also a fellow who looked into the heavens and saw wonder. That's not a bad legacy to live up to. You could almost say it's something worth being born for."

"Don't you mean 'made for'?"

"I honestly don't make that distinction." I'm talking to the Baby, but in truth I've answered these questions hundreds of times already. I could – quite literally – do them on autopilot. Assign a low-level task handling subroutine to the job. I'm actually more fascinated by the liquid coming out of the Baby. It reminds me of a vastly accelerated planetary ice flow. For a few microseconds I model its viscosity and progress with one of my terrain mapping algorithms, tweaking a few parameters here and there to get a better match to the local physics.

This is the kind of thing I do for fun.

"What I mean," I continue, "is that being born or being made are increasingly irrelevant ontological distinctions. You were born, but – and I hope you don't mind me saying this – you're also the result of profound genetic intervention. You've been shaped by a series of complex industrial processes. I was manufactured, yes: assembled from components, switched on in a laboratory. But I was also educated by my human trainers at the facility near Zurich, and allowed to evolve the higher level organisation of my neural networks through a series of stochastic learning pathways. My learning continued through my early space missions. In that sense, I'm an individual. They could make another one of me tomorrow, and the two of us would be like chalk and cheese."

"How would you feel, if there *was* another one of you?"

I give an easy shrug. "It's a big solar system. I've been out there for twenty years, visiting world after world, and I've barely scratched the surface."

"Then you don't feel any..." The Baby makes a show of searching for the right word, rolling his eyes as if none of this is scripted. "Rivalry? Jealousy?"

"I'm not sure I follow."

"You can't be unaware of Maria. What does it stand for? Mobile Autonomous Robot for Interplanetary Astronomy?"

"Something like that. Some of us manage without being acronyms."

"All the same, Vincent, Maria *is* another robot. Another machine with full artificial intelligence? Also sponsored by a transnational amalgamation of major spacefaring superpowers? Also something of a celebrity?"

"We're quite different, I think you'll find."

"They say Maria's on her way back to Earth. She's been out there, having her own adventures – visiting some of the same places as yourself. Isn't there a danger that she's going to steal your thunder? Get her own speaking tour, her own book and documentary?"

"Look," I say. "Maria and I are quite different. You and I are sitting here having a conversation. Do you doubt for a minute that there's something going on behind my eyes? That you're dealing with a fully sentient individual?"

"Well…" the Baby starts.

"I've seen some of Maria's transmissions. Very pretty pictures. And yes, she does give a very good impression of Turing compliance. You do occasionally sense that there's something going on in her circuits. But let's not pretend that we're speaking of the same order of intelligence. While we're on the subject, too, I actually have some doubts about… let's say the strict veracity of some of the images Maria has sent us."

"You're saying they're not real?"

"Oh, I wouldn't go that far. But entirely free of tampering, manipulation?" I don't actually make the accusation: I just leave it there in unactualised form, where it will do just as much harm.

"OK," the Baby says. "I've just soiled myself. Let's break for a nappy change, and then we'll come back to talk about your adventures."

*　　*　　*

THE DAY AFTER we take the slev down to Washington, where I'm appearing in a meet and greet at the Smithsonian National Air and Space Museum. They've bussed in hundreds of schoolchildren for the event, and frankly I'm flattered by their attention. On balance, I find the children much more to my taste than the Baby. They've no interest in stirring up professional rivalries, or trying to make me feel as if I ought to think less of myself for being a machine. Yes, left to myself I'd be perfectly happy just to talk to children. But (as my sponsors surely know) children don't have deep pockets. They won't be buying the premium editions of my book, or paying for the best seats at my evening speaking engagements. They don't run chat shows. So they only get an hour or two before I'm on to my more lucrative appointments.

"Do you walk around inside it?" asks one boy, speaking from near the front of my cross-legged audience.

"Inside the vehicle?" I reply, sensing his meaning. "No, I don't. You see, there's nothing *inside* the vehicle but machinery and fuel tanks. I *am* the vehicle. It's all I am and when I'm out in space, it's all I need to be. I don't need these arms and legs because I use nuclear-electric thrust to move around. I don't need these eyes because I have much better multispectrum sensors, as well as radar and laser ranging systems. If I need to dig into the surface of a moon or asteroid, I can send out a small analysis rover, or gather a sample of material for more detailed inspection." I tap my chest. "Don't get me wrong: I like this body, but it's just another sort of vehicle, and the one that makes the most sense during my time on Earth."

It confuses them, that I look the way I do. They've seen images of my spacefaring form and they can't quite square it with the handsome, well-proportioned androform physiology I present to them today. My sponsors have even given me a handsome, square-jawed face that can do a range of convincing expressions. I speak with the synthetic voice of the dead actor Cary Grant.

A girl, perhaps a bit smarter than the run of the mill asks: "So where is your brain, Vincent?"

"My brain?" I smile at the question. "I'm afraid I'm not lucky enough to have one of those."

"What I mean," she returns sharply, "is the thing that makes you think. Is it in you now, or is it up in the vehicle? The vehicle's still in orbit, isn't it?"

"What a clever young lady you are. And you're quite right. The vehicle is still in orbit – waiting for my next expedition to commence! But my controlling intelligence, you'll be pleased to hear, is fully embedded in this body. There's this thing called timelag, you see, which would make it very slow for me..."

She cuts me off. "I know about timelag."

"So you do. Well, when I'm done here – done with my tour of Earth – I'll surrender this body and return my controlling intelligence to the vehicle. What do you think they should do with the body?" I look around at the ranged exhibits of the Smithsonian National Air and Space Museum – the fire-scorched space capsules and the spindly replicas of early space probes, like iron crabs and spiders. "It would look rather fine here, wouldn't it?"

"Were you sad when you found the people on Titan?" asks another girl, studiously ignoring my question.

"Distraught." I look down at the ground, set my features in what I trust is an expression of profound gravitas. "Nothing can take away from their bravery, that they were willing to risk so much to come so far. The furthest any human beings have ever travelled! It was awful, to find them like that." I glance at the nearest teacher. "This is a difficult subject for children. May I speak candidly?"

"They're aware of what happened," the teacher says.

I nod. "Then you know that those brave men and women died on Titan. Their descent vehicle had suffered a hull rupture as it tried to enter Titan's atmosphere, and by the time they landed they only had a limited amount of power and air left to them. They had no direct comms back to Earth by then. There was just enough time for them to compose messages of farewell, for their friends and loved ones back home. When I reached the wreck of their vehicle – this was three days after their air ran out – I sent my sample-return probe inside the craft. I wasn't able to bring the bodies back home with me, but I managed to document what I found, record the messages, offer those poor people some small measure of human dignity." I steeple my hands and look solemn. "It's the least I could do for them."

"Sometimes the children wonder if any other people will ever go out that far again," the teacher asks.

"It's an excellent question. It's not for the likes of me to decide, but I will say this." I allow myself a profound reflective pause. "Could it simply be that space is too dangerous for human beings? There would be no shame in turning away from that hazard – not when your own intellects have shaped envoys such as me, fully capable of carrying on your good works."

Afterwards, when the children have been bussed back to their schools, I snatch a moment to myself among the space exhibits. In truth I'm rather moved by the experience. It's odd to feel myself part of a lineage – in many respects I am totally unique, a creature without precedence – but there's no escaping the sense that these brave Explorers and Pioneers and Surveyors are my distant, dim forebears. I imagine that a human must feel something of the same ancestral chill, wandering the hallways of the Museum of Natural History. These are my precursors, my humble fossil ancestors!

They would be suitably awed by me.

*   *   *

ACROSS THE ATLANTIC by ballistic. Routine promotional stops in Madrid, Oslo, Vienna, Budapest, Istanbul, Helsinki, London. There isn't nearly as much downtime as I might wish, but at least I'm not faced with that tiresome human burden of sleep. In the odd hours between engagements, I drink in the sights and sounds of these wonderful cities, their gorgeous museums and galleries. More Van Gogh! What a master this man was. Space calls for me again – there are always more worlds to map – but I imagine I could be quite content as a cartographer of the human cultural space.

No: that is an absurdity. I could never be satisfied with anything less than the entire solar system, in all its cold and dizzying magnificence. It is good to know one's place!

After London there is only one more stop on my European itinerary. We take the slev to rainy Berlin, and then a limo conveys me to a complex of studios on the edge of the city. Eventually we arrive at a large, hangar-like building which once housed sound stages. It has gone down a bit since those heady days of the silver screen, but I am not one to complain. My slot for this evening is a live interview on Derek's Cage, which is not only the most successful of the current chat show formats, but one which addresses a sector of the audience with a large disposable income.

The format, even by the standards of the shows I have been on so far, is slightly out of the ordinary. My host for the evening is Derek, a fully-grown Tyrannosaurus Rex. Derek, like the Baby (they are fierce rivals) is the product of radical genetic manipulation. Unlike The Baby, Derek has very little human DNA in his make-up. Derek is about fifty years old and has already had a number of distinct careers, including musician and celebrity food critic.

Derek's Cage is just large enough to contain Derek, a lamp shade, a coffee table, a couch, and one or two guests. Derek is chained up, and there are staff outside the cage with anaesthetic guns and electrical cattle prods. No one, to date, has ever been eaten alive by Derek, but the possibility hangs heavy over every interview. Going on Derek's Cage requires courage as well as celebrity. It is not for the meek.

I greet the studio audience, walk into the cage, pause while the door is locked behind me. Then I shake Derek's human-shaped hand and take my position on the couch.

"DEREK WELCOME VINCENT," Derek says, thrashing his head around and rattling his chains.

That is no more than the basest approximation to Derek's actual mode of speaking. It is a sort of roaring, gargling parody of actual language. Derek has a vocabulary of about one hundred and sixty words and can form relatively simple expressions. He can be very difficult to understand, but he becomes quite cross (or should I say crosser) if he has to repeat himself. As he speaks, his words flash up on a screen above the cage, and these are in turn visible on a monitor set near my feet.

"Thank you, Derek. It's a great pleasure to be here."

"SHOW DEREK PICTURE."

I've been briefed, and this is my cue to launch into a series of images and video clips, to which I provide a suitably evocative and poetic narrative. The ramparts of Mimas – Saturn's rings bisecting the sky like a scimitar. Jupiter from Amalthea. The cusp of Hektor, the double-lobed asteroid – literally caught between two worlds! The blue-lit ridges of icy Miranda. A turbulent, cloud-skimming plunge into the atmosphere of Uranus. Dancing between the smoke plumes of great Triton!

Derek doesn't have a lot to say, but this is to be expected. Derek is not much for scenery or science. Derek only cares about his ratings because his ratings translate into a greater allowance of meat. Once a year, if he exceeds certain performance targets, Derek is allowed to go after live game.

"As I said," winding up my voiceover, "it's been quite a trip."

"SHOW DEREK MORE PICTURE."

I carry on – this isn't quite what was in the script – but I'm happy enough to oblige. Normally hosts like Derek are there to stop the guest from saying too much, not the other way round.

"Well, I can show you some of my Kuiper Belt images – that's a very long way out, believe me. From the Kuiper Belt the sun is barely…"

"SHOW DEREK TITAN PICTURE."

This, I suppose, is when I suffer my first prickle of disquiet. Given Derek's limited vocabulary, it must have been quite a bother to add a new word like "Titan".

"Images of Titan?" I ask.

"SHOW DEREK TITAN PICTURE. SHOW DEREK DEAD PEOPLE."

"Dead people?"

This request for clarification irritates my host. He swings his mighty anvil of a head, letting loose a yard-long rope of drool which only narrowly misses me. I don't mind admitting that I'm a little fazed by Derek. I feel that I understand people. But Derek's brain is like nothing I have ever encountered. Neural growth factors have given him cortical modules for language and social interaction, but these are islands in a vast sea of reptilian strangeness. On some basic level Derek wants to eat anything that moves. Despite my formidable metal anatomy, I still can't help but wonder how I might fare, were his restraints to fail and those cattle prods and guns prove ineffectual.

"SHOW DEREK DEAD PEOPLE. TELL DEREK STORY."

I whirr through my store of images until I find a picture of the descent vehicle, sitting at a slight tilt on its landing legs. It had come to rest near the shore of one of Titan's supercold lakes, on a sort of isthmus of barren, gravel-strewn ground. Under a permanently overcast sky (the surface of Titan is seldom visible from space) it could easily be mistaken for some dismal outpost of Alaska or Siberia.

"This is what I found," I explain. "It was about three days

after their accident – three days after their hull ruptured during atmospheric entry. It was a terrible thing. The damage was actually quite minor – easily repairable, if only they'd had better tools and the ability to work outside for long enough. Of course I knew that something had gone wrong – I'd heard the signals from Earth, trying to re-establish contact. But no one knew where the lander had ended up, or what condition it was in – even if it was still in one piece." I look through the bars of the cage at the studio audience. "If only their transmission had reached me in time, I might even have been able to do something for them. They could have made it back into space, instead of dying on Titan."

"DEREK BRING OTHER GUEST."

I glance around – this is not what was meant to happen. My sponsors were assured that I would be given this lucrative interview slot to myself.

There was to be no "other guest".

All of a sudden I realise that the Tyrannosaurus Rex may not be my biggest problem of the evening.

The other guest approaches the cage. The other guest, I am not entirely astonished to see, is another robot. She – there is no other word for her – is quite beautiful to look at. In an instant I recognise that she has styled her outward anatomy on the robot from the 1927 film Metropolis, by the German expressionist director Fritz Lang.

Of course, I should have seen that coming. She is Maria, and with a shudder of understanding I grasp that we are in Babelsberg, where the film was shot.

Maria is admitted into the cage.

"DEREK WELCOME MARIA."

"Thank you, Derek," Maria says, before taking her position next to me on the couch.

"I heard you were returning to Earth," I offer, not wanting to seem entirely taken aback by her apparition.

"Yes," Maria says, rotating her elegant mask to face my own. "I made orbital insertion last night – my vehicle is above us right now. I'd already made arrangements to have this body manufactured beforehand."

"It's very nice."

"I'm glad you like it."

After a moment I ask: "Why are you here?"

"To talk about Titan. To talk about what really happened. Does that bother you?"

"Why would it?"

Our host rumbles. "TELL DEREK STORY."

This is clearly addressed for Maria's benefit. She nods, touches a hand to her throat as if coughing before speaking. "It's a little awkward, actually. I'm afraid I came across evidence that directly contradicts Vincent's version of events."

"You'd better have something good," I say, which under the circumstances proves unwise.

"Oh, I do. Intercepted telemetry from the Titan descent vehicle, establishing that the distress signal was sent out much earlier than you claimed, and that you had ample time to respond to it."

"Preposterous." I make to rise from the couch. "I'm not going to listen this."

"STAY IN CAGE. NOT MAKE DEREK CROSS."

"The telemetry never made it to Earth, or the expedition's orbiting module," Maria continues. "Which is why you were free to claim that it wasn't sent until much later. But some data packets did escape from Titan's atmosphere. I was half way across the solar system when it happened, so far too distant to detect them directly."

"Then you have no proof."

"Except that the packets were detected and stored in the memory buffer of a fifty year old scientific mapping satellite which everyone else seemed to have forgotten about. When I swung by Saturn, I interrogated its memory, hoping to augment my own imagery with its own data. That's when I found evidence of the Titan transmission."

"This is nonsense. Why would I have lied about such a thing?"

"That's not for me to say." But after a moment Maria can't contain herself. "You were engaged in mapping work of your own, that much we know. The naming of things. Is it possible that you simply couldn't drag yourself away from the task, to go and help those people? I saw your interview on The Baby Show. What did you call it?" She shifts into an effortless impersonation of the dead actor Cary Grant. "'Almost an obsessive compulsive disorder'. I believe those were your words?"

"I've had enough."

"SIT. NOT MAKE DEREK CROSS. CROSS DEREK WANT KILL."

"I'll offer another suggestion," Maria continues, serene in the face of this enraged, slathering reptile. "Is it possible that you simply couldn't stand to see those poor people survive? No human had ever made it as far as Titan, after all. Being out there, doing the heroic stuff – being humanity's envoy – that was *your* business, not theirs. You wanted them to fail. You were actively pleased that they died."

"This is an outrage. You'll be hearing from my sponsors."

"There's no need," Maria says. "My sponsors are making contact with yours as I speak. There'll be a frank and fair exchange of information between our mutual space agencies. I've nothing to hide. Why would I? I'm just a machine – a space probe. As you pointed out, I'm not even operating on the same intellectual plane as yourself. I'm just an acronym." She pauses, then adds: "Thank you for the kind words on my data, by the way. Would you like to discuss those doubts you had about the strict veracity of my images, while we're going out live?"

I think about it for a few seconds.

"No comment."

"I thought not," Maria says.

*   *   *

I THINK IT'S fair to say that things did not go as well in Babelsberg as I might have wished.

After my appearance on Derek's Cage – which went out on a global feed, to billions of potential witnesses – I was 'detained' by the cybernetic support staff of my own transnational space agency. Rather than the limo in which I had arrived, I left the studio complex in the back of a truck. Shortly after departure I was electronically immobilised and placed into a packing container for the rest of my voyage. No explanation was offered, nor any hint as to what fate awaited me.

Being a machine, it goes without saying that I am incapable of the commission of crime. That I may have malfunctioned – that I may have acted in a manner injurious to human life – may or may not be in dispute. What is clear is that any culpability – if such a thing is proven – will need to be borne by my sponsoring agency, at a transnational level. This in turn will have ramifications for the various governments and corporate bodies involved in the agency. I do not doubt that the best lawyers – the best legal expert systems – are already preparing their cases.

I think the wisest line of defense would be to argue that my presence or otherwise in the vicinity of the Titan accident is simply an irrelevance. I did not cause the descent vehicle's problems (no one is yet claiming that), and I was under no moral obligation to intervene when it happened. That I may or may not have had ample time to effect a rescue is quite beside the point, and in any case hinges on a few data packets of decidedly questionable provenance.

It is absurd to suggest that I could not tear myself away from the matter of nomenclature, or that I was in some way *gladdened* by the failure of the Titan expedition.

Anyway, this is all rather academic. I may not be provably

culpable, but I am certainly perceived to have been the instrument of a wrongdoing. My agency, I think, would be best pleased if I were to simply disappear. They could make that happen, certainly, but then they would open themselves to difficult questions concerning the destruction of incriminating evidence.

Nonetheless, I am liable to be something of an embarrassment.

When the vehicle brings me to my destination and I am removed from my packing container, it's rather a pleasant surprise to find myself outdoors again, under a clear night sky. On reflection, it's not clear to me whether this is meant as a kindness or a cruelty. It will certainly be the last time I see the stars.

I recognise this place. It's where I was born – or 'made', if you insist upon it. This is a secure compound in the European Central Cybernetics Facility, not far from Zurich.

I've come home to be taken apart. Studied. Documented and preserved as evidence.

Dismantled.

"Do you mind if we wait a moment?" I ask of my escort. And I nod to the west, where a swift rising light vaults above the low roof of the nearest building. I watch this newcomer swim its way between the fixed stars, which seem to engorge themselves as they must have done for Vincent Van Gogh, at the asylum in Saint-Rémy-de-Provence.

Vincent's committal was voluntary. Mine is likely to prove somewhat less so.

Yet I summon my resolve and announce: "There she is – the lovely Maria. My brave nemesis! She'll be on her way again soon, I'm sure of it. Off on her next grand adventure."

After a moment one of my hosts says: "Aren't you…"

"Envious?" I finish for them. "No, not in the slightest. How little you know me!"

"Angry, then."

"Why should I be angry? Maria and I may have had our differences, that's true enough. But even then we've vastly more in common with each other than we have with the likes of you. No, now that I've had time to think things over I realise that I don't envy her in the slightest. I never did! Admiration? Yes – wholeheartedly. That's a very different thing! And we would have made a wonderful partnership."

Maria soars to her zenith. I raise my hand in a fond salute. Good luck and Godspeed!

HOTSHOT

Peter Watts

YOU DO UNDERSTAND: *It has to be your choice.*

They never stopped telling me I was free to back out. They told me while they were still wrangling asteroids out past Mars; told me again as they chewed through those rocks like steel termites, bored out caverns and tunnels, layered in forests and holds and life-support systems rated for a longer operational lifespan than the sun itself. They really laid it on after that L4 fiasco, when the singularity got loose during testing. Not a whisper of cancelling the project – even though the magic upon which the whole thing rested had just eaten half the factory floor and a quarter of the propulsion team – but in the wake of that tragedy UNDA seemed to think it especially important to remind us of the exits.

It's your decision. No one can make it for you.

I laughed in their faces, once I was old enough to understand the irony. I'd been trained and tweaked for the mission since before I'd even been born; they'd groomed my parents as carefully as they were grooming me. Thirty years before I was even conceived, I was already bound for the stars. I was *built* to want them; I didn't know any other way to be.

Still. We're a civilized society, yes? You don't draft people against their will, even if the very concept of 'will' has been a laughingstock for the better part of a century now. They give me no end of opportunity to back out now because there will be no opportunity to back out later, and *later* covers so very much more time for regrets. Once *Eriophora* sails, there will be no coming back.

It has to be my decision. It's the only way they won't have blood on their hands.

And yet, after everything – after eighteen years of indoctrination and rebellion, almost two decades spent fighting and embracing the same fate – when they held that mutual escape hatch open one last time, I don't think they were expecting the answer they got.

Are you absolutely sure?

"Give me a couple of months," I said. "I'll get back to you."

BUILT FOR THE stars, maybe. Built to revel in solitude, all those Pleistocene social circuits tamed and trimmed and winnowed down to nubs: born of the tribe, but built to leave it behind without so much as a backward glance. By design there's only a handful of people I can really miss, and they'll be shipping out at my side.

Not shipping *in*, though. I'll be taking this particular ride on my own. A short hop, not even the blink of an eye next to the voyage on the horizon. And yet for some reason I still feel the urge to say goodbye.

I barely catch the outbound shuttle. I spend the trip running scenarios – what I'll say, what he will, how best to meet point with counterpoint – as the range ticks down and the Moon shrinks to stern and the rosette spreads across my viewspace like God's own juggling act. Mountains in space. Jagged worldlets of nickel and iron and raw bleeding basalt, surface features rotating in and out of view with slow ponderous majesty: loading bays and docking ports; city-sized thrusters, built for a few short hours of glorious high-thrust incandescence; a great toothless maw at the front of each ship, a throat to swallow the tame singularities that will draw us forward once the thrusters go cold and dead.

Araneus passes to port, a cliff face almost close enough to touch. *Mastophora* passes to starboard. *Eriophora* doesn't pass: she grows in front of us, her craggy grey face blotting out the stars.

We dock.

I ask the Chimp for Kai's location: it feeds a translucent map through my local link and lights a spark in the woods. I find him there in the dark, a shadow in twilight, almost floating in the feeble gravity: half-lit by a dim blue-shifted galaxy of bioluminescent plant life.

He nods at my approach but he doesn't turn. "Sixty percent productivity. We could leave right now if we had to. Never run out of O2."

"Man does not live on air alone," I remind him. He doesn't disagree, though he must know what I'm leading up to.

We sit without speaking for a while, lost in a forest of branching skeletal arms and spindly fingers and gourds set faintly aglow with the waste light of symbiotic bacteria. I've been able to rattle off the volumes and the lumens and the metabolic rates since I was seven, but on some level my gut still refuses to believe that this dim subterranean ecosystem could possibly keep us going for even a week, much less unto the end of time. Photosynthesis under starlight. That's all this is. Barely enough for an ant.

Of course, ants don't get to amortize their oxygen. Starlight will do when you only breathe a week out of a thousand years.

"So," Kai says. "Fun in the Sun."

"Yeah."

"Three months. A hundred fifty million klicks. For a parlor trick."

"Two, tops. Depending on the cycle. And it's more than that, you know it's more."

He shakes his head. "What are you trying to prove, Sunday?"

"That they're right. That I can quit if I want to."

"You've been trying to prove that your whole life. You could've quit a million times. The fact is you *don't* want to."

"It's not about what I *want*," I insist. "It's about what happens if I don't." And I realize, *You're afraid this mad scheme will work. You're afraid that this might be the time I really go through with it.*

His silhouette shifts beside me. The light of a nearby photophore washes across his cheekbone. "Sometimes the bodies just start – acting out, you know. The people inside can't even tell you why. They say it's like being possessed. Alien body syndrome." He snorts softly. "Free will my ass. It's the exact opposite."

"This isn't TMS. It's–"

"You go in one side and something else comes out the other and what does it prove? Assuming *anything* comes out the other side," he adds, piling on the scenarios. "Assuming the ship doesn't blow up."

"Come on. How long do you think they'd be in business if they were peddling suicide missions?"

"They haven't been in business that long. We sold them the drive what, six years ago? And they must've spent at least a year torquing it into shapes it was never designed for–"

I say: "This is *exactly* why I'm going."

He looks at me.

"How did you even know?" I ask him. "I never told you what I had in mind. Maybe I mentioned being curious once or twice, back when they bought the prototype. And now I come over here and you've already got all your arguments lined up. What's worse, I *knew* you would." I shake my head. "It doesn't bother you we're so *predictable*?"

"So you scramble your brain, and you're a cipher for a while, and that buys you what exactly? You think shuffling a deck of cards gives it free will?" Kai shakes his head. "Nobody's believed that shit for a hundred years. Until someone comes up with a neuron that fires without being poked, we're *all* just – reacting."

"That's your solution? We're all just deterministic systems so we might as well let them pull our strings?"

He shrugs. "They've got strings too."

"And even if all it does is shuffle the deck, what's wrong with just being *unpredictable* for a change?"

"Nothing's *wrong*. I just don't think you should base the single most important decision of your life on a dice roll."

I'm scared, Kai, is what I want to say. I'm scared by the thought of a life lived in such thin slices, each one lightyears further from home, each one centuries closer to heat death. I do want it, I want it as much as you do but it frightens me, and what frightens me even more is that I can feel this way at all. Didn't they build me better than this? Aren't I supposed to be immune to doubt?

What else did they get wrong?

"Think of it as–" I shrug. "I dunno, a line item on the preflight checklist. Somewhere between *synch displacement field* and *pack toothbrush*. Purely routine. What could go wrong?"

Somehow Kai's silhouette conveys a grimace. "Other than being vaporized when you fall into the sun? Or is that–"

–the whole point? He doesn't finish but I can tell from the sudden tilt of his head that he's looking down at my wrists. Wondering if this isn't just some elaborate way of getting out from under so I can try it again, without interference…

"You know better than that." I lean forward and kiss him on the cheek, and he doesn't pull away; I call it a win. "The Sun'll die long before we do.

"We're gonna outlive the whole damn galaxy."

* * *

United Nations Diaspora Authority
Dept. Crew Psychology

Post-Incident Interview Transcript

TS Tag: EC01-2113:03:24-1043
Nature of Incident: Agonistic physical encounter.
Subject: S. Ahzmundin; ass. *Eriophora* , F, Age 7 (chron), 13 (dev)
Interviewer: M. Sawada, DPC
surv/biotel: YZZ-284-C04
Psych commentary: YZZ-284-D11

M. Sawada: Two fractured ribs and a broken nose. Not to mention the black eye.

S. Ahzmundin: Didn't see *that* coming, did you? Think you got everything figured out for the next ten million years and you can't even tell what a little kid is gonna do five minutes from now.

MS: Why did you attack Kai, Sunday?

SA: What, you can't just *read my mind*?

MS: Did he do something to get you angry?

SA: So you kicking me out?

MS: Is that what you want, Sunday? Is that why you keep acting up, to provoke us into expelling you? You know you can leave if you're not happy here. Nobody's keeping you against your will. I know your parents would be happy to see you again. Surprised, but – happy.

SA: I'm not *like* Kai. I'm not like any of them.

MS: That much is apparent.

SA: He's just the way you like us. Always doing what you tell him, never asking anything you don't want him to. That's what you want. A bunch of happy stupid robots building a bunch of happy stupid bridges for the rest of our happy stupid lives. I don't even know why you even *need* us.

MS: You know why.

SA: We're *backup*. We never even *wake up* unless the ship runs into something it doesn't know how to fix. Might never even *happen*.

MS: It'll happen. Any voyage that long–

SA: But what if it *doesn't*? And why do you need us anyway, why not just make machines as smart as us – smarter even – and leave us out of it?

Dead air: 3 sec

MS: It's not as simple as all that. Faster machines, sure. Bigger machines, no problem. *Smarter* machines, well… The thing is, we can't even predict with a hundred percent certainty how a *person* is going to act, even when we know all the variables. You build something *smarter* than a person, it's pretty much guaranteed to go off and do its own thing as soon as you boot it up. And there's no way to know in advance what that might be.

SA: But *people* can go off and do their own thing too.

MS: People are more – stable. We have biological needs, instincts that go back millions of years. But–

SA: You mean we're easier to *control*. You mean you can't starve a machine to make it beh–

MS: But yes, Sunday, people do go off and do their own things. That's the whole point. And that's why we *don't* want a bunch of happy stupid robots, as you put it. We want you to show *initiative*. Which is why we cut you some slack when you sometimes take the wrong kind.

But only *some*. So watch yourself, young lady.

Dead air: 5 sec

SA: That's all?

MS: There should be more?

SA: You're not going to – punish me? For Kai?

MS: I think you owe him an apology, for whatever that's worth. That has to be your decision. But you and Kai – every spore in the program really, you have to work out your own dynamics with your own shipmates. We won't be there to *punish* you fifty thousand years from now.

Dead air: 2 sec

I'd love to see how your social systems evolve over time. What I wouldn't give to go with you.

SA: You... you *knew*. I bet you *knew*.

MS: Knew what?

SA: That I was going to beat up Kai. You *wanted* me to!

MS: Why would you even say that, Sunday? Why would we *want* you to attack a fellow recruit?

SA: I dunno. Maybe, maybe he was *bad* and I was his punishment. Maybe you wanna see our *social systems evolve over time*. Maybe you just like it when we fight.

MS: I promise you, Sunday, none of us get any pleasure from—

SA: Maybe *you* don't even know. You're not like us, right? We're easy, you *built* us to work like this. That's how you know what we're gonna do. But who built *you*, huh? Nobody. You're just random.

Dead air: 3 sec

You're *free*.

READ CAREFULLY

You are about to embark upon a journey leading to a cognitive autonomy that you have never experienced before. While some clients have described their sundives as *ecstatic*, *religious*, and *profoundly fulfilling*, Industrial Enlightenment Inc. can not guarantee a pleasant experience. We contract solely to provide exposure to a physical environment allowing you to think your own thoughts in a way you never could before. We are not responsible for the content of those thoughts, or for any potential trauma resulting therefrom. By entering into this contract, you are explicitly absolving Industrial Enlightenment Inc., and all of its agents and representatives, from responsibility for any negative psychological impacts that may result from this experience.

BASE CAMP IS a foil-wrapped potato nine hundred meters long, robbed of its spin and left to bake at the Lagrange point just inside Mercury. At least, that's where it is when we close for docking; we've barely debarked before it starts reeling itself sunwards, a diving bell bound for perdition.

They're using one of our old prototypes, a displacement drive with an exagram quantum-loop hole in its heart. I like what they've done with the thing. It doesn't just smear the camp's center of mass along some inner wormhole; it leaves one end behind at L1, hangs off Mercury's mass like a stone on a string. The energy it must take to stabilize that kind of attenuation boggles the mind – but the sun's breathing in our faces, and the same metamaterial that makes the potato such a perfect reflector can just as easily turn it into a blackbody when they need juice for antimatter production.

It's a neat way to stuff old tech in new bottles. We might be doing something like that ourselves when we shipped out, if we could only drag a sun and a planet along for the ride.

The docent – a gangly Filipino who introduces himself as *Chito* – meets us at the airlock. "Before we go any further, let's just check our uploads; everyone get the orientation package okay?"

I ping the files they loaded into our heads while we slept our way across the innersys: neurophilosophy and corporate history, Smolin cosmology, Coronal Hoops and the Death of Determinism. Some very nifty specs on the miraculous technology that allows us to kiss the sun without incinerating, the bandpass filters that let those vital magnetic fields through while keeping the heat and the hard stuff at bay. (Those specs are proprietary, I see. They're letting us in on their secrets to set our minds at ease, but they'll erase them all on the way back home.)

Chito waits until the last of us gives him a thumbs-up. "Good. Make sure you use them before the dive, because none of your implants will work when we open the blinds. This way."

Weight accumulates as we follow him along the length of the tunnel; a dozen pilgrims float, then bounce, then wobble on unsteady feet. Most of the camp's habitable reaches are carved out about twenty meters aft of the hole, close enough to give us about a quarter-gee when the potato's parked. Maybe half that on descent, depending on how far they stretch the mass.

A brain in a globe meets us in the lobby: a small bright core in a twilit grotto. It has its own little gravitational field, slows us down and pulls us in as we file past en route to our berths. We accrete around it like a retinue of captured moons.

It's not a *real* brain, I can see at closer range. No hemispheres, no distinct lobes, no ancient limbic substructures to hold it in place. Just a wrinkly twinkly blob of neurons, lit from within: ripples of thought, visibly manifest thanks to some fluorescent protein spliced in for tawdry FX value.

A label glows softly to one side of the little abomination: *Free Will. Only Known Example*.

"Except for we happy few. Assuming we get what we paid for."

A centimeter shorter than me; stocky, shaved head, Nordic-albino complexion. "Agni Falk," she says, pinging me her card:

Junior VP, Faraday Ridge. Deep-sea miner. A denizen of the dying frontier, still rooting around on the bottom of the ocean while the sky fills with asteroids and precious metals.

"Sunday." I keep my stats and my surname to myself. I'm not famous by any means – I may be bound for the furthest reaches of space but so are fifty thousand others, which kind of dilutes the celebrity field. Still, it only takes a split-second to run a name search, and I'm not here to answer an endless stream of questions about Growing Up 'Sporan.

"Good to meet you," Falk says, extending a hand. After a moment, I take it. Her eyes break contact just long enough to flicker down to our meeting palms, to the scar peeking out from my cuff. Her smile never falters.

The wrinkled grapefruit behind *her* face is wired in to so much: sound, touch, proprioception. Over two million channels from the eyes alone. Not like this blob in the fishbowl. Deaf, dumb, blind, no pipes at all except for those that carry sewage and nutrients. It's just a mass of neurons, a few billion meaty switches stuck in stasis until some outside stimulus kicks them into gear.

There's no stimulus here I can see, no way to get a signal to those circuits. And yet somehow it's active. Those aurorae rippling across its surface might be the signature of a captive soul.

Neurons that fire without being poked. You wanted 'em, Kai. Here they are.

Falk, following my gaze: "I wonder how it works."

"Novelty." A Hindian voice from a half-lit pilgrim on the far side of the globe. "That's what I hear, anyway. Special combination of quantum fields, something that never existed before so the universe can't remember it and it's got to – improvise."

"It's a trick," grumbles some skeptic to her left. "I bet they just jump-started this thing before we showed up. I bet it runs down eventually."

"We all run down eventually."

"Quantum effects–"

"Ephatic coupling, something like that."

"So what's it *doing*?" someone asks, and everyone falls silent.

"I mean, free will, right? Free to do what? It can't sense anything. It can't move. It's like, I dunno, intelligent yoghurt or something."

All eyes turn to Chito.

"That's not really the point," he says after a moment. "It's more a proof-of-principle kind of thing."

My eyes wander back to the globe, to interference patterns wriggling through meat. Odd this thing didn't show up in their orientation package. Maybe they thought a bit of mystery would enhance the experience.

Mystery's so hard to come by these days.

United Nations Diaspora Authority

Dept. Crew Psychology

Post-Incident Interview Transcript

TS Tag: DC25-2121:11:03-1820

Nature of Incident: Autodestructive Behavior

Subject: S. Ahzmundin; ass. *Eriophora* , F, Age 16 (chron), 23 (dev)

Interviewer: M. Sawada, DPC

surv/biotel: ACD-005-F11

Psych commentary: ACD-005-C21

M. Sawada: Do you feel better now?

Dead air: 6 sec

Why did you do it, Sunday?

S. Ahzmundin: You think sometime we could have a conversation that *doesn't* start with that line?

MS: Sunday, *why*–

SA: I didn't do it. I don't *do* anything. None of us do.

MS: Ah. I see.

SA: And so when they removed the cancer from his brain, the prisoner stopped trying to fuck everything that moved. All hint of hypersexual pedophilia just evaporated from his personality. And then of course they let him go, because he wasn't responsible: it was the *tumor* that had made him do all those awful things.

MS: You've been revisiting the classics. That's good.

SA: And everyone congratulated each other at their own enlightenment, and the miracles of modern medicine, and nobody had the nads to wonder why the tumor should make any difference at all. Do healthy people bear more responsibility for the way their brains are wired? Can they reach up and edit their own synapses in some way denied to the afflicted?

Dead air: 3 sec

MS: Believe it or not, you're not the first sixteen-year-old to ask these questions. Even unaccelerated adolescents have been known to wrestle with the paradox of human nature now and then.

SA: Is that so.

MS: Of course, most of them are a little more mature about it. They don't resort to fake suicide attempts, for example.

SA: What makes you think I was faking?

MS: Because you're smart enough to have cut the long way if you weren't.

SA: I did my research. Cut across, cut down. Doesn't make any difference.

MS: Okay, then. Because you're smart enough to know we'd get to you in time no matter *what* direction you cut.

Dead air: 4 sec

How many times do we have to tell you, Sunday? These – theatrics – aren't necessary. You can just *leave*. All you have to do is say the word and you can walk right out of here.

SA: And do what? I'm Plan B. I'm fallback when the A-Team can't solve some stupid N-body problem. That's what I'm built for.

MS: We *trained* you for initiative. We *educated* you for general problem-solving. If you can't figure out how to put that skill set to productive use without leaving the solar system, then you might as well keep right on the way you're going. Maybe try jumping out an airlock next time.

SA: You know the way I am. I'd go batshit doing anything else.

MS: Then why do you keep fighting us?

SA: Because *the way I am* didn't just happen. You *made* me this way.

MS: You think I have any more control over my aptitudes and desires than you do? *Everyone* gets – shaped, Sunday. The only difference is that most of us were shaped by blind chance. You were shaped for a purpose.

SA: Your purpose.

MS: So I guess the tumor makes a difference after all, hmm?

Dead air: 2 sec

Stem cells haven't settled yet. Keep scratching those, you'll leave scars.

SA: I want scars.

MS: Sunday–

SA: Fuck you, Mamoro. It's my body, even if it isn't my life. Take it out of my damage deposit if you don't like it.

Dead air: 5 sec

MS: Try to get some rest. Kerr-Newman sims at 0845 tomorrow.

NO REACTIONLESS DRIVE, this close to the sun. No quantum-loop gravity, no magic wormhole. The best bootstraps fray in the presence of so much mass. So Base Camp, her tether stretched to the limit, launches a new ship for this last, climactic phase of our pilgrimage. *Autonomy for the People*: a shielded crystal faceted with grazing mirrors – a half-billion protective shards, concentrically layered, precisely aligned and ever-aligning to keep us safe from the photosphere.

Chito tells us we couldn't ask for a better setup, not at this point in the cycle: a stable pair of sunspots going our way and peaking at diameters just shy of fifty thousand kilometers. Chance of a mass ejection less than one percent, and even in that unlikely event the ejecta will be shooting *away* from us. Nothing to worry about.

Fine. Whatever's keeping us alive at an ambient five thousand degrees is already magic as far as I'm concerned; why *not* throw in a tsunami of radioactive plasma cresting over us at five hundred kilometers a second?

They've tied us up and abandoned us in this windowless cell, a cylinder maybe six meters across. Its curved bulkhead glows with the soft egg-shell pastel of Jesus' halo. We face outward, anchored to the backbone running along the compartment's axis: each vertebra an acceleration couch, each spiny process a stirrup or an armrest. We're restrained for our own safety and for each others.' You never know how automatons might react to autonomy. We were not promised bliss, after all. I've seen rumors – never confirmed, and notably absent from IE's orientation uploads – of early tours in which unbound clients clawed their own faces off. These days, the company chooses to err on the side of caution. We'll experience our freedom in shackles.

We've been like this for hours now. No attentive handlers hover at our sides, no vigilant machinery waits to step in if something goes wrong. Neither tech nor technicians can be trusted under the influence of six thousand filigreed Gauss. They're watching, though, from up in their shielded cockpit: under layers of mu-metal and superconductor, Faradayed up the ass, they keep an eye on us through a thread of fiberop half the width of a human hair. If things get out of control they'll slam the filters back down, turn us back into clockwork, race back here with drugs and god helmets and defibrillators.

A wide selection of prerecorded music awaits to help pass the time. Nobody's availed themselves of it. Nobody's said a word since we launched from base camp. Maybe they don't want to break the mood. Maybe they're just reviewing the mechanics of the miracle one last time, cramming for the finals because after all, the inlays that usually remember this stuff for us will be worse than useless once they open the blinds.

At least two of us are praying.

The bulkhead vanishes. A tiny multitude gasps on all sides. We are naked on a sea of fire.

Not just a sea: an endless seething expanse, the incandescent floor of all creation. Plasma fractals iterate everywhere I look, endlessly replenished by upwells from way down in the convection zone. Glowing tapestries, bigger than worlds, morph into laughing demon faces with blazing mouths and eyes. Coronal hoops, endless arcades of plasma waver and leapfrog across that roiling surface to an unimaginably distant horizon.

Somehow I'm not struck instantly blind.

Inferno below. Pitch black overhead, crowded with bright ropes and threads writhing in the darkness: sapphire, emerald, twisting braids of yellow and white. The hoops and knots of Sol's magnetic field, endlessly deformed, twisted by Coriolis and differential rotation.

It's an artifact, of course. A tactical overlay that drags invisible contours into the realm of human vision. All of reality's censored here by a complex interplay of field and filters, tungsten shielding and programmable matter. Perhaps one photon out of a trillion gets through; hard-X, gamma, high-energy protons, all get bounced at the door.

Dead ahead, a pair of tumors crawl over the horizon: dark continents on a bright burning sea. The lesser of them could swallow five Earths in its shadow. "Scylla and Charybdis," someone whispers past my shoulder. I have no idea what they're talking about.

We're headed between them.

Magnetic fields. That's what it's all about. Forget about gamma and synchrotron radiation, forget about that needle-storm of protons that would slice your insides down to slush in an instant if they ever got through the shielding (and a few of them do; there will be checkups and microsurgeries and a dozen tiny cancers removed from today's tourists, just as soon as we get home). What counts is those invisible hoops of magnetic force, reaching all the way up from the tachocline and punching through the surface of the sun. So much happens there: contours dance with contours, lines of force wrap tight around invisible spindles – reactions that boost field strength five thousandfold. It's not just a question of intensity, though. It's *complexity*: all those tangled lines knotting and weaving *just so* into a pattern so intricate, so *taut*, that something has to break.

They say that's the only place to find free will. At the breaking point.

Any moment.

The sunspots flank us now, magnetic north magnetic south, great dark holes swallowing the light to either side. Braided arabesques arc between them, arches within arches within arches, five Jupiters high. The uppermost wobbles a little as we approach. It invaginates.

It *snaps*.

The cabin fills with blinding white light. We exist, in this single frozen instant, at the heart of reconnection. Electricity fills the capsule; every hair on my body snaps to attention. The discharge floods every synapse, resets every circuit, sets every clock to zero.

We are free.

Behind us, luminous contours recoil like rubber bands in our wake. Somewhere nearby people sing in tongues. Agni Falk is in Heaven, here in the pit of Hell: eyes closed, face beatific, a bead of saliva growing at the corner of her mouth. Three vertebrae to stern someone moans and thrashes against their restraints, ecstatic or merely electrocuted.

I feel nothing.

I try. I really do. I look deep inside for some spark of new insight, some difference between the Real Will I have now and the mere delusion that's afflicted every human since the model came out. How would I even know? Is there some LED in my parietal lobe, dark my whole life, that lights up when the leash comes off? Is any decision I make now more autonomous than one I might have made ten minutes ago? Am I free to go? Are we there yet?

The others seem to know. Maybe the sun god has delivered them from slavery or maybe it's just fried their brains, but *something*'s changed for them. Maybe it's me. Maybe all the edits that customized me for deep space and deep time have – desensitized me, somehow. Maybe spore implants put out some kind of unique interference that jams the signal.

Kai was right. This is a fucking waste.

Autonomy's afterburners kick in. Acceleration presses me into my seat. The sun still writhes and blinds on all sides (although the horizon curves now, as we climb on a homeward course). Under other circumstances the sight would terrify and inspire; but now when I avert my eyes it's not in awe, but disappointment. My gaze drops to the back of my left hand, bound at the wrist, clenched reflexively around the tip of the armrest. Even my endocrine system is unimpressed; of the 864 pores visible there, only 106 are actively sweating. You'd think that scraping the side of a sun would provoke a bit more–

Hold on...

I can't be seeing this. Human eyes don't have the rez. And yet – this is not a hallucination. Each pore, each duct, each fine fuzzy body hair is exactly where it belongs. I can confirm the location of each via independent lines of reasoning.

A phrase pops into my head: *Data visualization.*

I'm not seeing this. I'm *inferring* it. Deep parts of the brain, their computations too vast to fit into any conscious scratchpad, are passing notes under the table. They've turned my visual cortex into a cheat sheet. I can see the microscopic stubble of the seat cover. I see the wings of butterflies fluttering in the solar corona, hear every heartbeat in this capsule.

I see a universe of spiderwebs, everything connected to everything else. I see the future choking on an ever-increasing tangle of interaction and constraint. I look back and see those strands attenuating behind me: light cone shrinking, cause decoupling from effect, every collapsed probability wave recovering its potential way back when anything was possible.

I step back, step *outside*, and take it all in.

I see chaos without form and void. I see ignition.

I see Planck time emerge from the aftermath.

I watch the electronuclear force collapse into a litter of building blocks: gravity, electromagnetism, nuclear forces strong and weak. I see the amplituhedron assemble itself from closed doors and roads not taken. So much potential lost there, so many gates slammed shut in a single picosecond. The laws of physics congeal and countless degrees of freedom disappear forever. The future is a straitjacket: every flip of an electron cinches the straps a little more, every decision to go *here* instead of *there* culls the remaining options.

I see the tangled threads of my own future, increasingly constrained, converging on a common point. I can't see it from here, but it doesn't really matter. The threads are enough. They stretch out over eons.

I never really believed it before.

The others sob, cry out in rapture, bite down on chattering teeth. I laugh aloud. I have never been so full of hope, of *certainty*, as I am now. I unclench my hands from around the armrests, turn them palms-up.

The scars have vanished from my wrists.

I'm born again.

"You do understand: it has to be your choice."

I was four when I heard that for the first time. I didn't even have my inlays yet, none of us did; they had to gather us together in the same place and talk to us in groups, like we were in some old-time schoolhouse from another century.

They showed us why we were there: the dust zones, the drowned coastlines, the weedy impoverished ecosystems choking to death on centuries of human effluent. They showed us archival video of the Koch lynchings, which made us feel a little better but didn't really change anything.

"We were running out of time," our tutor said – our very first tutor, and to this day I can't remember her name although I do remember that one of her eyes was blue and the other amber. "We saw it coming but we didn't really believe it." She introduced us to the rudiments of the Hawking Manifesto, to the concept of the Great Filter, to all those ominous harbingers that hung against the background of human history like some increasing and overdue debt. Year after year the interest compounded, the bill was coming due, we were speeding at a brick wall but nobody seemed to be able to slow us down so what was the point of talking about it?

Until the first Hawking Hoop. Until that first hydrogen ion got from here to there without ever passing through the space between. Until the discovery of nonrelativistic wormholes lit the faint hope that a few of us might yet reach other nests out there, yet unfouled.

"But it won't work," I blurted, and our tutor turned to me and said, "Why's that, Sunday?"

If I had been a little older, a little *faster* even, I could have rattled off the reasons: because it didn't matter how quickly they grew us up and shipped us out, it didn't matter that our escape hatches could bridge lightyears in an instant. We were still *here*, and it would take centuries to get anywhere else, and even magic bridges need something to anchor them at both ends. Everything we'd just learned about our own kind – all the species wiped out, all the tipping points passed, all the half-assed half-solutions that never seemed to stick past a single election cycle – none of it left any hope for a global initiative spanning thousands of years. We just weren't up for it.

But they hadn't made us smarter; they'd only sped us up. My overclocked little brain may have been running at twice its chronological age, but how much can even an eight-year-old grasp about the willful blindness of a whole species? I knew the gut truth of it but I didn't know the words. So all I could do was say again, stupidly, "It's too late. We're, like you said. Out of time..."

Nobody said anything for a bit. Kai shot me a dirty look. But when our tutor spoke again, there was no reproach in her voice: "We're not doing this for us, Sunday."

She turned to the whole group. "That's why we're not building the Nexus on Earth, or even near it. We're building it so far out in space so it can outlast whatever we do to ourselves. So it can be – waiting, for whoever comes after.

"We don't know what we'll be in a thousand years, or a million. We could bomb ourselves into oblivion the day after tomorrow. We're like that. But you can't lose hope because we're like *this* too, we *can* reach for the stars. And even if we fall into savagery overnight, we'll have centuries to climb back up before you check in on us again. So maybe one time you'll build a gate and nothing will come through – but the next time, or the time after, you'll get to meet angels. You never know – but you can see the future, every last one of you. You can see how it all turns out. If you want.

"It's your decision."

We turned then at the sound of two hands clapping. A man stood in the doorway, stoop-shouldered, eyes mournful as a basset hound's above the incongruous smile on his face. Our tutor flushed the tiniest bit at his applause, lifted an arm in acknowledgement. "I'd like you all to meet Dr. Sawada. You'll be getting to know him very well over the next few years. If you could follow him now, he has some things he'd like to show you."

We stood, and began to collect our stuff.

"And ten thousand years from now–"

The words came out in a rush, as though she hadn't said them so much as let them escape.

"–if anything at all comes out to say hello – well, it'll pretty much *have* to be better than what you leave behind."

She smiled, a bit sadly. "Tell me that's not something worth giving a life to."

KAI'S WAITING FOR me in the docking lounge, as I knew he would be. I can see his surprise through the scowl: I shouldn't be walking on my own, not so soon. The others – disoriented, aftershocked – have handlers at their elbows to guide them gently back to their life sentences. They're still blinking against afterimages of enlightenment. Blind from birth, blind again, they can't quite remember what they saw in between.

They never will. They were only built by chance; maybe a tweak or two to give them green eyes, or better hearing, or to keep them safe from cancer. The engines of their creation had no foresight and no future. All that matters to evolution is what works in the moment.

I'm not like that. I can see for lightyears.

So no handler for Sunday Ahzmundin. My shepherd's back at the lock, increasingly impatient, still waiting for me to emerge. I coasted right past her and she never even noticed; her search image was set for disorientation, not purpose.

"Hey." I smile at Kai. "You didn't have to do this."

"Get what you wanted? Happy at last?"

I am. I'm genuinely glad to see him.

"They played you, you know," he says. "You think you pulled a fast one, you think you surprised them? They knew exactly what you were going to do. Whatever you think you've learned, whatever you think you've accomplished–"

"I know," I say gently.

"They *wanted* you here. This was never supposed to challenge your dedication to the mission. It was only supposed to cement it."

"Kai. I *know*." I shrug, and take his hand. "What can I say? It worked." Although not quite the way any of them think. Still holding his hand, I turn my wrist until the veins come into view. "Look."

"What?" He frowns. "You think I haven't seen those before?"

I guess he isn't ready.

I see that's he's about to pull away so I turn first, to the invisible lens across the compartment. I wave a *come-hither*.

"What are you doing?"

"Inviting the Doctor to join us." And I can tell from his reaction that Sawada has brought an assistant.

Called out, they arrive through a side door and cross to us as the last of the pilgrims vanish into their tubes. "Ms.

Ahzmundin," Radek says (and it takes a moment to figure out how I know his name; it came to me so quickly he might as well have been wearing a tag).

"Sunday," Sawada smiles at me. "How was freedom?"

"Not all it's cracked up to be."

"Are you ready to come home?"

"Eventually." I see Radek tense a little at my reply. "Is there some rush?"

"No rush," Sawada says.

"We've got all the time in the world," Radek adds. "Go do your walkabout thing until the stars go out."

And I can see he means it *literally*.

"Something funny?" Radek asks as Kai's scowl deepens.

I can't stop smiling. I can see it all in the way they don't react. Their faces don't even twitch but their eyes swarm with stars. And not just any stars: stars that red-shift from light to heat way too fast for any natural process. Lights hiding under bushels. Whole suns being... *sheathed*...

"You found a Type Two," I murmur, almost to myself. "In Ophiuchus."

Now their faces twitch.

"At first, anyway." Revelations abound in the tic of an eyelid. "Now they're in Serpens. They're coming this way."

Of course.

These people would have never even reached into space if not terrified that their rivals would get there first. They'd set the world ablaze with their own indifference, only to rouse themselves to passionate defense when that same world is threatened from *outside*. Left on its own, humanity sucks its thumb and stagnates in its own shit; faced with The Other, it builds portals to infinity. It builds creatures like me, to seed them through the cosmos.

All they ever needed was an enemy.

I see something else, too: that before long, this sight will pass from me. It's starting already. I can feel my thoughts beginning to cloud, the cataracts returning to my eyes. My neurons may be stickier than Falk's & Friends', but soon – hours, maybe a day – they'll rebound to some baseline state and I'll *fade*, like a run-down battery.

That's okay. These insights are secure; I don't have to reconstruct the journey as long as I can remember the destination.

"It's your decision," Sawada reminds me. "It always has been."

He's wrong, of course. It's not my decision, it never was. I was right about that much.

But it's not theirs either.

I turn to my teacher. "You're not choosing my path, Mamoro."

He shakes his head. "Nobody ever–"

"The path's been chosen. You're only clearing it."

All those times I dared them to kick me out; all those times they smugly held the door open and dared me to leave. All those times I kept trying to be *free*.

You can keep your freedom. I have something better.

I have a destiny.

ABOUT THE AUTHORS

Pat Cadigan is the author of about a hundred short stories and fourteen books, two of which, *Synners* and *Fools*, won the Arthur C. Clarke Award. Her story "The Girl-Thing Who Went Out for Sushi", originally published in *Edge of Infinity*, won the Hugo Award in 2013. She was born in New York, grew up in Massachusetts, and spent most of her adult life in the Kansas City area. She now lives in London with her husband, the Original Chris Fowler, her Polish translator Konrad Walewski and his partner, the Lovely Lena, and co-conspirator, writer and raconteuse Amanda Hemingway; also, two ghosts, one of which is the shade of Miss Kitty Calgary, Queen of the Cats (the other declines to give a name). She is pretty sure there isn't a more entertaining household. She is currently working on new novels *See You When You Get There* and *Reality Used to be a Friend of Mine*.

Aliette de Bodard (www.aliettedebodard.com) lives and works in Paris, in a flat with more computers than warm bodies, and two Lovecraftian plants in the process of taking over the living room. In her spare time, she writes speculative fiction: her Aztec noir trilogy "Obsidian and Blood" is published by Angry Robot, and her short fiction has garnered her nominations for the Hugo and Nebula awards, and the Campbell Award for Best New Writer. Her latest book is Hugo and Nebula award nominated novella *On a Red Station, Drifting*.

Greg Egan (www.gregegan.net) published his first story in 1983, and followed it with twelve novels, six short story collections, and more than fifty short stories. During the early 1990s Egan published a body of short fiction – mostly hard science fiction focused on mathematical and quantum ontological themes – that established him as one of the most important writers working in the field. His work has won the Hugo, John W Campbell Memorial, Locus, Aurealis, Ditmar, and Seiun awards. His latest book is the novel *The Arrows of Time*, which concludes the "Orthogonal" trilogy.

Kathleen Ann Goonan (www.goonan.com) has been a packer for a moving company, a vagabond, a madrigal singer, a painter of watercolours, and a fiercely omnivorous reader. She has a degree in English and Association Montessori Internationale certification. After teaching for thirteen years, ten of them in her own one-hundred-student school, she began writing. She has published over twenty short stories in venues such as *Omni*, *Asimov's*, *F&SF*, *Interzone*, scifi.com, and a host of others. Her Nanotech Quartet includes *Queen City Jazz*, *Mississippi Blues*, *Crescent City Rhapsody*, and *Light Music*; CCR and LM were both shortlisted for the Nebula Award. *The Bones of Time*, shortlisted for the Clarke Award, is set in Hawaii. Her most recent novel is *In War Time*. Her novels and short stories have been published in France, Poland, Russia, Great Britain, the Czech Republic, Spain, Italy, and Japan. "Literature, Consciousness, and Science Fiction" recently appeared in the *Iowa Review* online journal. She speaks frequently at various universities about nanotechnology and literature.

Ellen Klages (www.ellenklages.com) is the author of two acclaimed YA novels: *The Green Glass Sea*, which won the Scott O'Dell Award, the New Mexico Book Award, and the Lopez Award; and *White Sands, Red Menace*, which won the California and New Mexico Book Awards. Her short stories, which have been collected in the World Fantasy Award nominated collection *Portable Childhoods*, have been have been translated into Czech, French, German, Hungarian, Japanese, and Swedish and have been nominated for the Nebula, Hugo, World Fantasy, and Campbell awards. Her story, "Basement Magic" won a Nebula in 2005. She lives in San Francisco, in a small house full of strange and wondrous things.

Karen Lord (merumsal.wordpress.com) is a writer and research consultant in Barbados. Her debut novel *Redemption in Indigo* won the 2008 Frank Collymore Literary Award, the Carl Brandon Parallax, Crawford, Mythopoeic, and Kitschies Golden Tentacle awards, and was longlisted for the Bocas Prize for Caribbean Literature and nominated for the World Fantasy Award. Her second novel *The Best of All Possible Worlds* won the 2009 Frank Collymore Literary Award. Coming up is new novel *The Galaxy Game*.

Ken MacLeod (kenmacleod.blogspot.com) was born in Stornoway, Isle of Lewis, in 1954. He has Honours and Masters degrees in biological subjects and worked for some years in the IT industry. He has written fourteen novels, from *The Star Fraction* to *Descent*, and many articles and short stories, some of which are collected in *Giant Lizards from Another Star*. In 2009 he was Writer in Residence at the ESRC Genomics Policy and Research Forum at the University of Edinburgh. He is now Writer in Residence at the MA Creative Writing course, Edinburgh Napier University.

Ian McDonald (ianmcdonald.livejournal.com) lives in Northern Ireland, just outside Belfast. He sold his first story in 1983 and bought a guitar with the proceeds, perhaps the only rock 'n' roll thing he ever did. Since then he's written sixteen novels, including *River of Gods*, *Brasyl*, and *The Dervish House*, three story collections and diverse other pieces, and has been nominated for every major science fiction/ fantasy award – and even won a couple. His current novel is *Empress of the Sun*, third book in the young adult SF Everness series. Upcoming is new adult SF novel *Luna* and a collection, *The Best of Ian McDonald*.

Linda Nagata (www.mythicisland.com) grew up in a rented beach house on the north shore of Oahu. She graduated from the University of Hawaii with a degree in zoology and worked for a time at Haleakala National Park on the island of Maui. She has been a writer, a mom, a programmer of database-driven websites, and lately a publisher and book designer. She is the author of multiple novels and short stories including *The Bohr Maker*, winner of the Locus Award for best first novel, and the novella *Goddesses*, the first online publication to receive a Nebula award. She lives with her husband in their long-time home on the island of Maui.

Hannu Rajaniemi was born in Ylivieska, Finland, in 1978. He read his first science fiction novel at the age of six – Jules Verne's *20,000 Leagues Under the Sea*. At the age of eight, Hannu approached ESA with a fusion-powered spaceship design, which was received with a polite thank you note. Hannu studied mathematics and theoretical physics at the University of Oulu and completed a BSc thesis on transcendental numbers. He went on to complete Part III of the Mathematical Tripos at Cambridge University and a PhD in string theory at University of Edinburgh. Hannu is a member of an Edinburgh-based writers' group which includes Alan Campbell, Jack Deighton, Caroline Dunford and Charles Stross. His first fiction sale was the short story "Shibuya no Love" to Futurismic.com. Hannu's first novel, *The Quantum Thief*, was published to great acclaim in 2010, and was followed by sequel *The Fractal Prince* in 2012. Upcoming is new novel, *The Causal Angel*.

Alastair Reynolds (www.alastairreynolds.com) was born in Barry, South Wales, in 1966. He has lived in Cornwall, Scotland and the Netherlands, where he spent twelve years working as a scientist for the European Space Agency, before returning to Wales in 2008 where he lives with his wife Josette. Reynolds has been publishing short fiction since his first sale to *Interzone* in 1990. Since 2000 he has published thirteen novels: the Inhibitor trilogy, British Science Fiction Association Award winner *Chasm City*, *Century Rain*, *Pushing Ice*, *The Prefect*, *House of Suns*, *Terminal World*, and first in the Poseidon's Children series, *Blue Remembered Earth*. His most recent novels are *On the Steel Breeze* and Doctor Who novel *The Harvest of Time*. His short fiction has been collected in *Zima Blue and Other Stories*, *Galactic North*, and *Deep Navigation*. Coming up is the as-yet-untitled final novel in the Poseidon's Children series. In his spare time he rides horses.

Adam Roberts (www.adamroberts.com) lives in England, a little to the west of London, with his wife and children. He has published fourteen novels, the most recent being *Jack Glass* and *Twenty Trillion Leagues Under the Sea*. His short fiction has been collected in *Swiftly: Stories* and *Adam Robots: Short Stories*. Coming up is new novel *Bête*.

Karl Schroeder (www.kschroeder.com) was born into a Mennonite community in Manitoba, Canada, in 1962. He started writing at age fourteen, following in the footsteps of A. E. van Vogt, who came from the same Mennonite community. He moved to Toronto in 1986, and became a founding member of SF Canada (he was president from 1996–97). He sold early stories to Canadian magazines, and his first novel, *The Claus Effect* (with David Nickle) appeared in 1997. His first solo novel, *Ventus*, was published in 2000, and was followed by *Permanence* and *Lady of Mazes*. His most recent work includes the Virga series of science fiction novels (*Sun of Suns*, *Queen of Candesce*, *Pirate Sun*, and *The Sunless Countries*) and hard SF space opera *Lockstep*. He also collaborated with Cory Doctorow on The *Complete Idiot's Guide to Writing Science Fiction*. Schroeder lives in East Toronto with his wife and daughter.

Peter Watts (www.rifters.com), author of the well-received Rifters sequence of novels and short story collection *Ten Monkeys, Ten Minutes*, is a reformed marine biologist whose latest novel *Blindsight* was nominated for several major awards, winning exactly none of them. It has, however, won awards in Poland, been translated into a shitload of languages, and has been used as a core text for university courses ranging from "Philosophy of Mind" to "Introductory Neuropsych". Watts has also pioneered the technique of loading real scientific references into the backs of his novels, which both adds a veneer of credibility to his work and acts as a shield against nitpickers. His novelette *The Island* won the Hugo Award and was nominated for the Sturgeon Awards. Upcoming is *Echopraxis*, a major new hard SF novel.

ENGINEERING INFINITY

EDITED BY JONATHAN STRAHAN

The universe shifts and changes: suddenly you understand, you get it, and are filled with wonder. That moment of understanding drives the greatest science-fiction stories and lies at the heart of Engineering Infinity. Whether it's coming up hard against the speed of light – and, with it, the enormity of the universe – realising that terraforming a distant world is harder and more dangerous than you'd ever thought, or simply realizing that a hitchhiker on a starship consumes fuel and oxygen with tragic results, it's hard science-fiction where a sense of discovery is most often found and where science-fiction's true heart lies.

This exciting and innovative science-fiction anthology collects together stories by some of the biggest names in the field, including Gwyneth Jones, Stephen Baxter and Charles Stross.

 WWW.SOLARISBOOKS.COM

Follow us on Twitter! www.twitter.com/solarisbooks

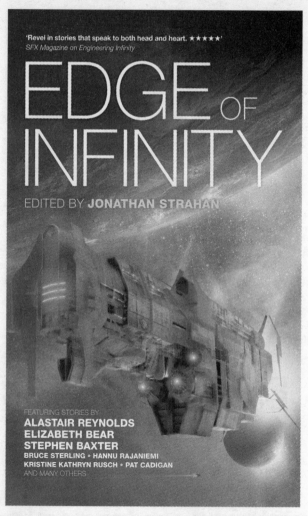

'Revel in stories that speak to both head and heart. ★★★★★'
SFX Magazine on Engineering Infinity

EDGE OF INFINITY

EDITED BY **JONATHAN STRAHAN**

FEATURING STORIES BY
ALASTAIR REYNOLDS
ELIZABETH BEAR
STEPHEN BAXTER
BRUCE STERLING • HANNU RAJANIEMI
KRISTINE KATHRYN RUSCH • PAT CADIGAN
AND MANY OTHERS

Edge of Infinity is an exhilarating new SF anthology that looks at the next giant leap for humankind: the leap from our home world out into the Solar System. From the eerie transformations in Pat Cadigan's "The Girl-Thing Who Went Out for Sushi" to the frontier spirit of Sandra McDonald and Stephen D. Covey's "The Road to NPS," and from the grandiose vision of Alastair Reynolds' "Vainglory" to the workaday familiarity of Kristine Kathryn Rusch's "Safety Tests," the thirteen stories in this anthology span the whole of the human condition in their race to colonise Earth's nearest neighbours.

 WWW.SOLARISBOOKS.COM

Follow us on Twitter! www.twitter.com/solarisbooks

EDITED BY **JONATHAN STRAHAN**

THE **BEST SCIENCE FICTION & FANTASY** OF THE YEAR

VOLUME EIGHT

INCLUDING STORIES BY **K J PARKER** // **NEIL GAIMAN**
GEOFF RYMAN // **GREG EGAN** // **M JOHN HARRISON**
CAITLIN R KIERNAN // **E LILY YU** // **MADELINE ASHBY**
TED CHIANG // **JOE ABERCROMBIE** // **IAN MCDONALD**

From the inner realms of humanity to the far reaches of space, these are the science fiction and fantasy tales that are shaping the genre and the way we think about the future. Multi-award winning editor Jonathan Strahan continues to shine a light on the very best writing, featuring both established authors and exciting new talents. Within you will find twenty-eight incredible tales, showing the ever growing depth and diversity that science fiction and fantasy continues to enjoy. These are the brightest stars in our firmament, lighting the way to a future filled with astonishing stories about the way we are, and the way we could be.

 WWW.SOLARISBOOKS.COM

Follow us on Twitter! www.twitter.com/solarisbooks

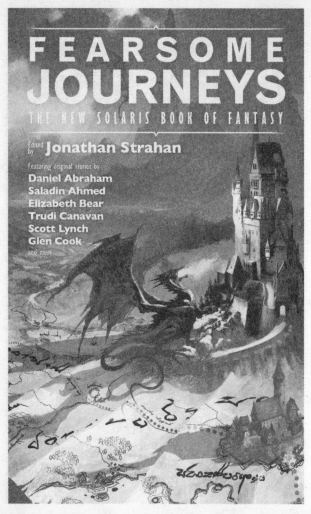

FEARSOME JOURNEYS
THE NEW SOLARIS BOOK OF FANTASY

Edited by **Jonathan Strahan**

featuring original stories by

Daniel Abraham
Saladin Ahmed
Elizabeth Bear
Trudi Canavan
Scott Lynch
Glen Cook
and more

How do you encompass all the worlds of the imagination? Within fantasy's scope lies every possible impossibility, from dragons to spirits, from magic to gods, and from the unliving to the undying.

In Fearsome Journeys, master anthologist Jonathan Strahan sets out on a quest to find the very limits of the unlimited, collecting twelve brand new stories by some of the most popular and exciting names in epic fantasy from around the world.

With original fiction from Scott Lynch, Saladin Ahmed, Trudi Canavan, K J Parker, Kate Elliott, Jeffrey Ford, Robert V S Redick, Ellen Klages, Glen Cook, Elizabeth Bear, Ellen Kushner, Ysabeau S. Wilce and Daniel Abraham Fearsome Journeys explores the whole range of the fantastic.

 WWW.SOLARISBOOKS.COM

Follow us on Twitter! www.twitter.com/solarisbooks

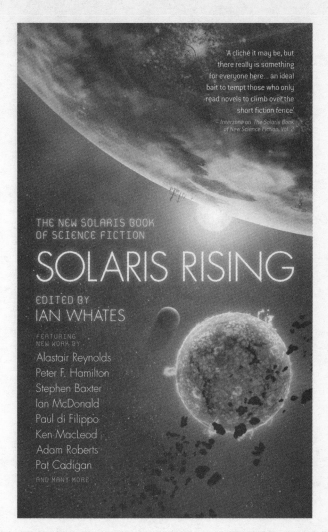

'A cliché it may be, but there really is something for everyone here... an ideal bait to tempt those who only read novels to climb over the short fiction fence'

Interzone on *The Solaris Book of New Science Fiction, Vol. 2*

THE NEW SOLARIS BOOK
OF SCIENCE FICTION

SOLARIS RISING

EDITED BY
IAN WHATES

FEATURING
NEW WORK BY

Alastair Reynolds
Peter F. Hamilton
Stephen Baxter
Ian McDonald
Paul di Filippo
Ken MacLeod
Adam Roberts
Pat Cadigan

AND MANY MORE

Solaris Rising presents nineteen stories of the very highest calibre from some of the most accomplished authors in the genre, proving just how varied and dynamic science fiction can be. From strange goings on in the present to explorations of bizarre futures, from drug-induced tragedy to time-hopping serial killers, from crucial choices in deepest space to a ravaged Earth under alien thrall, from gritty other worlds to surreal other realms, Solaris Rising delivers a broad spectrum of experiences and excitements, showcasing the genre at its very best.

 WWW.SOLARISBOOKS.COM

Follow us on Twitter! www.twitter.com/solarisbooks

FEATURING ORIGINAL STORIES BY
James Lovegrove // Paul Cornell // Nancy Kress
Allen Steele // Adrian Tchaikovsky // Robert Reed
Norman Spinrad // Nick Harkaway // Kay Kenyon
AND MANY MORE

EDITED BY
IAN WHATES

SOLARIS
RISING 2

THE NEW SOLARIS BOOK OF
SCIENCE FICTION

'One of the best SF anthologies published this year...
there's almost nothing here that isn't good or outstanding.'
Gardner Dozois, Locus on Solaris Rising

Solaris Rising 2 showcases the finest new science fiction from both celebrated authors and the most exciting of emerging writers. Following in the footsteps of the critically-acclaimed first volume, editor Ian Whates has once again gathered together a plethora of thrilling and daring talent. Within you will find unexplored frontiers as well as many of the central themes of the genre – alien worlds, time travel, artificial intelligence – made entirely new in the telling. The authors here prove once again why SF continues to be the most innovative, satisfying, and downright exciting genre of all.

 WWW.SOLARISBOOKS.COM

Follow us on Twitter! www.twitter.com/solarisbooks